A KISS TO REMEMBER

Surrounded by a jungle of tall grass and wrapped in an Indian's arms, Liana felt very small, but not weak. "No," she said once again, this time more forcefully. "I must go."

"Kiss me," he said, "or I'll tell everyone what you said about Boston Harbor."

"Why would you wish to make trouble for me?" Liana asked without thinking, but as she watched the cocky grin spread across his lips, she knew. "You despise me, don't you? You want to harm me as badly as you want to harm my father and . . ."

Christian had heard enough silliness. He silenced her ramblings with what had become his favorite method. He slipped his hand around her neck to hold her still and kissed her with brutal abandon. He felt her squirm and her fists strike his chest, but he did not relent. "Why don't you scream for your father?" he murmured into her hair. "Do you want to visit England even less than you want to kiss me?"

"Beast!"

"You can do better than that, dear."

"My father would rather see me dead than married to you," Liana said. "Now let me go before you get us into more trouble than the whole Barclay clan can handle."

But rather than release her, Christian pulled her closer. When she tried to yank herself free, he held her so tightly that she couldn't move. She struggled, but even as she did so, she felt desire overcoming her anger.

"How," she asked, trying to resist him, "how could a man who moves with the force of a hurricane have been named Christian?"

For answer, he kissed her. . . .

BOOK YOUR PLACE ON OUR WEBSITE AND MAKE THE READING CONNECTION!

We've created a customized website just for our very special readers, where you can get the inside scoop on everything that's going on with Zebra, Pinnacle and Kensington books.

When you come online, you'll have the exciting opportunity to:

- View covers of upcoming books
- Read sample chapters
- Learn about our future publishing schedule (listed by publication month *and author*)
- Find out when your favorite authors will be visiting a city near you
- Search for and order backlist books from our online catalog
- Check out author bios and background information
- Send e-mail to your favorite authors
- Meet the Kensington staff online
- Join us in weekly chats with authors, readers and other guests
- Get writing guidelines
- AND MUCH MORE!

**Visit our website at
http://www.zebrabooks.com**

FORBIDDEN LEGACY

Phoebe Conn

Zebra Books
Kensington Publishing Corp.

http://www.zebrabooks.com

ZEBRA BOOKS are published by

Kensington Publishing Corp.
850 Third Avenue
New York, NY 10022

First Printing: July, 1998
10 9 8 7 6 5 4 3 2 1

Printed in the United States of America

One

Stalking the slender redhead, the young Indian brave crept along the bank of the James River with a fluid stealth. Clad in fringed buckskins and moccasins, his thick ebony hair tied at his nape, he looked as savage as any of his Seneca kin. His skin was a golden bronze, his eyes as black and bright as obsidian, his features gently handsome.

Each time his pretty prey paused to look out at the river, he melted into the high marsh grass, a tawny shadow fading into the gently waving greens and golds. When she moved on, he followed, his footsteps silent on the mud. He pursued her until she crossed the invisible boundary onto his family's land.

She was trespassing now, and well within his rights, his hands twitched with eagerness to take her captive. He waited one more step, two, three, then had to hastily withdraw as she again paused in her wanderings. The sweeping river's lazy roll to the sea hissed in his ears, urging him on. But he held his breath, forcing himself to watch, and wait, until at last she moved on down the path.

Seizing what could be his last opportunity before she turned back for home, he lunged with a terrifying speed, grabbed her around the waist, and lifted her clear off her feet. He clamped a hand over her mouth before she could scream for help, and carried her into the thick grass. It closed around them like a living door, welcoming them into its cool depths.

The girl beat on his arms and kicked, but the brave was far too tough a young man to be bothered by her ineffectual blows. She tried to bite his hand, but he dug his fingers into her cheeks to force her mouth open. The grass ripped her cap from her head and tore at her billowing skirt as he pushed on; he did not stop until he burst through to the edge of the barren field where his cousin, Beau Barclay, stood waiting.

Christian released his disheveled prisoner then, but grabbing for her hand, pulled her back against his side before she could get away. "I think I've won the bet, cousin. Her red hair proves she's one of Ian Scott's brats."

Incensed by his manhandling, Liana Scott continued to try and break free, but Christian just caught her other hand and twisted them both behind her back. "Bastard!" she fumed. "I want no part in your games. You've won no bets with me."

Just turned eighteen, Beau was a year and a half younger than Christian. Both young men were tall and muscular, but Beau was fair-haired and blue-eyed, and no one would have guessed they were related had they not known Beau's father and Christian's mother were siblings. A studious lad, Beau was enrolled at the College of William and Mary. Christian was equally bright, but he was wild clear through and preferred the skills his father had taught him to any vain attempts by his numerous tutors.

"Aye, you've won," Beau agreed reluctantly. "The question now is, what are you going to do with her?"

Christian jerked Liana around to face him. Her green eyes were full of angry tears and her fair skin flushed with terror, but she was still undeniably a rare beauty. He stared at her for several seconds, letting the insolence of his gaze fill her mind with all manner of despicable torments before he replied. "I'm going to send her home with a message for our father. Will you deliver it for me, sister dear?"

"I am no sister of yours, you heathen wretch!"

" 'Heathen wretch'?" Christian repeated with a rich, rolling laugh. His voice was deep, with the same dark edge as his manner. "I'm neither heathen nor wretched, dear little sister. Nor am I a bastard since your father was married to my mother."

"Lying snake!" Liana screamed. "He was not!"

Beau reached out to touch her arm. She was wearing a peach-colored muslin gown and in the struggle with Christian, the neckline had slipped off her shoulder, revealing a luscious expanse of creamy skin. He doubted she had ever noticed him, but he had been acutely aware of her for several years. Such an unlikely infatuation was a secret he had never shared with anyone, least of all Christian, who would have taunted him cruelly had he known.

"He's telling the truth," Beau swore. "They were wed."

Astonished by the audacity of the young men's claim, Liana spit on Beau's boots. "Dissembling swine!" she shouted. "All the Barclays are strangers to the truth!"

"Really?" Beau looked surprised and immediately consulted Christian. "I've never heard that. Have you?"

Before Christian could respond, Liana added another insult. "That's because no decent soul will speak with any of you!"

Amused by her spirited defiance, Beau placed his hands over his heart and attempted to look stricken to the core. "Please, dear cousin, you wound me deeply."

"Scatterbrained twit! I'm no more your cousin than I am this crazed savage's sister!"

Beau winked at Christian. Now that Chris had provided an opportunity to meet Liana, he was intent upon making the most of it. "I'm beginning to like this girl. Do you think her father will allow me to call on her?"

"Don't waste your breath," Liana screamed. "Better

save it for your prayers because you're going to need them once my father hears about this outrage!"

Having heard enough of her venomous epithets, Christian took both of Liana's wrists in one hand and used the other to grab hold of her long, flowing hair. It wasn't coarse like his, but as fine as silk as he wound it around his fingers. "I believe she's begging us to kiss her, Beau. If we don't, she'll have no real reason to complain."

"I'd sooner kiss a cottonmouth moccasin than either of you weasels!"

Definitely eager to kiss her, Beau nevertheless laughed at her disgust. "While I'm not unpopular, there are young women who would swoon at the mere chance to kiss Christian. I'd take it, if I were you."

"Kiss the skunk yourself!"

"She does have admirable spirit," Christian noted with a sly grin. "But what sister of mine wouldn't?"

"Lunatic! I'm not your sister!"

At the best of times, Christian had limited patience, and this game had begun with a serious intent he now took pains to disclose. He shook Liana to silence her, then yanked her so close he could feel the gentle stream of her breath against his cheek. "Your father was my mother's husband and when she died trying to give me life, he cut open her belly to save me. That makes him as much my father as the Indian who calls me son. And you, sister dear, are going to tell him you know his secret and that it can no longer be kept. Tell him you know all about me, and that he ought not deny the truth of my birth."

As Liana stared up at him in shocked silence, Christian lowered his mouth to hers and kissed her with a long, slow, demanding passion that left her so dazed he had to hold her up when he drew away. "I'll wait for you here tomorrow afternoon, and if you don't come to me, I'll find you again, and again," he added in a threatening whisper.

As soon as he had released her, Liana wiped her mouth

on the back of her hand. "I'd sooner go looking for the devil himself!" she shouted, and with a final angry glance toward Beau, she darted into the tall grass and ran back toward the river.

Beau gave a low whistle. "I was only teasing when I dared you to catch one of the Scott kids. Why in God's name did you choose her?"

Disregarding Beau's complaint, Christian started for home along the path at the edge of the field. In early spring, the tobacco plants were still in seed beds sprouting under sheets of muslin, and wouldn't be transplanted to the fields for another couple of months. He looked out over the land that would one day belong to him and Beau and felt a depth of pride nothing could tarnish.

"Because I despise Ian Scott," he turned to explain, "and because I could."

Beau nodded, for Christian possessed daring in abundance, if not, as he saw it, the wisdom to know when to use it. "Well, you may heartily dislike him, but it sure didn't look as though you despised his daughter."

Christian laughed at that, but refused to admit Beau had guessed the truth. He had seen Liana in town and admired not only her beauty, but the pride with which she carried herself. That she was Ian's daughter made her completely unavailable, and therefore doubly appealing. "She's nothing special," he lied, "but even if she were, I got the impression she wasn't in the least bit fond of me."

Beau quickened his step to keep up with him. "Just because she referred to you as a 'heathen wretch,' 'lying snake,' 'crazed savage,' and a 'lunatic?' "

Christian combed the tangled fringe on his sleeves. "Don't forget 'bastard,' Beau. That's everyone's favorite name for me."

That was precisely why Beau had omitted it from the list. "Well, at least she didn't call you a 'scatterbrained twit.' "

"Have you met her before?"

"No—what makes you ask?"

Christian turned and gave him a playful jab to the shoulder. "She described you so well." He took off at a run then and Beau sprinted after him. They were closer than brothers, but Christian was older, faster, stronger, and Beau couldn't overtake him before they reached the yard of the magnificent brick mansion where they had been raised. Then there were too many watchful eyes, and they had to end their race and enter the house together.

Once Liana reached the river's edge, she had to stop to catch her breath, but it took far longer to stop trembling. She stumbled along until she came to a weathered bench where she could rest without being observed from her house. She was infuriated still, but so curious about Christian's preposterous tale she was far more eager to prove it a lie than to tattle on him.

She knew her family's history well and could not believe her mother was her father's second wife when such a fact had never been mentioned in all her seventeen years. Her father was a kind and generous man, a former British officer who had married into a wealthy Williamsburg family and had assumed control of their plantation when his in-laws had died. He was a member of the House of Burgesses, and respected by everyone.

He had brought Liana and her two brothers up to believe their closest neighbors, the Barclays, were a dissolute lot to be ignored and avoided. Liana wiped her eyes on her sleeve and tried to remember all the bits and pieces of gossip she had ever heard about the Barclays. She knew Christian's father was a Seneca Indian called Hunter. She had occasionally caught a glimpse of the savage in town, but from what she had heard, he was wed to a Barclay. Liana had seen the woman even less often than Hunter, and believed she was something of a recluse, but what woman wouldn't be with such a husband?

Then there was Byron Barclay, who ran the Barclay plantation with hired field hands rather than slaves as most Virginians did. He had wed an Acadian widow soon after Braddock's defeat at the outbreak of the French and Indian War, and no one had ever forgiven him for that. Liana knew who the Barclays were, and recognized their children, because except for Publick Times in April and October when the legislature met and the courts were in session, Williamsburg was a small community, and she knew almost everyone.

She wiped her mouth again and winced, for Christian's brutal kiss had bruised her lips and left them tender. "Bastard," she cursed again. She had been only seven or eight years old when she had first seen him in town. He had been clad in golden-brown buckskins like his father, and she had been so fascinated by them both she had stared at them quite rudely.

Her mother had pulled her into the doorway of an adjacent shop and cautioned her never to glance their way again, but she had not explained why. Liana had assumed it was merely because they were Indian, which to a child was wonderfully strange, but now she wondered if the reason had not been far more personal. Whatever the basis for her mother's admonishment, she had disobeyed her on numerous occasions because she had continued to look for Christian whenever she was in town. He rarely attended church, so she saw him only a few times a year, but had remembered him vividly.

He was handsome, in a darkly menacing way, unlike any of her suitors. He was never at any of the elegant parties she attended with her parents, and seldom glimpsed at church. "Church!" she cried. If her father had ever been married to a Barclay, then surely there would be a record at the Bruton Parish Church, and wouldn't this supposedly

deceased woman be buried in the cemetery? she wondered. Hearing her brother, Morgan, shout her name, she
was so startled she leaped to her feet; then, praying the
afternoon's ordeal had left her unchanged, she started toward him.

"Yes, what is it?" she called.

Like his older sister, Morgan also had deep red hair and
sparkling green eyes. Only thirteen months younger, at
sixteen he had already equaled his father's height, but still
possessed a childlike love of fun. As he approached, he
called out, "What's happened to your cap? Mother won't
be pleased if you get all freckled."

Only then did Liana remember losing the pretty, lace-
edged cap in the marsh grass. She reached up, confirming
its loss. "It blew off into the river," she replied, "but just
a minute ago, so I'm sure the sun's done me no harm.
Now what is it you want?"

"Mother was about to send out a search party, so I told
her I'd find you. Had you forgotten we're having dinner
guests? She's counting on you to arrange the flowers."

"Guests?" For a moment, Liana couldn't recall an en-
gagement for the evening, then finally remembered several of her father's friends were coming for dinner. She
lifted her skirt and hurried her pace. "Thank you for coming for me, Morgan. I'd forgotten all about tonight." With
good reason! she thought to herself.

"Sean O'Keefe would be heartbroken should he learn
you didn't have the date circled with a heart in your diary.
He's so smitten it's pathetic."

Because they were so close in age, Liana and Morgan
had long been confidants and she accepted his opinion
as the truth. "He's an attractive man, but too old for me."

"He's not a day over thirty."

"Well, yes, that may be true, but still—"

" 'But, still—' " Morgan mimicked. "Most men don't
marry until that age, Liana. Don't you expect to marry a

man who's old enough to have established himself in the world so he can take care of you? An army officer was good enough for Mother. It ought to be good enough for you."

Immune to her brother's teasing, Liana couldn't shake thoughts of Christian and was barely listening. Christian had closed his eyes as he had bent down to kiss her and his lashes had been so long and thick they had made shadows on his cheeks. She had watched him grow up, if only in a few brief sightings a year, but she was ashamed to realize he fascinated her now every bit as much as he had when they were children. It was true there was a strange wildness about him, but it was almost magical in nature.

"Liana, don't you like Sean at all?"

"Hmm? Of course I like him, but that's just not enough."

"What more is there?"

"Love, of course. I won't wed a man I don't love."

Morgan rolled his eyes. "Sean's not the first man who's tried to win your heart and failed. We ought to put up mock tombstones in the yard to commemorate all your conquests."

"Don't be absurd." They were approaching the house now, and Liana reached out to catch his arm and drew him to a halt. "Have you ever heard anyone mention that Father might have been married before he wed Mother?"

"What?" Morgan frowned, then shook his head. "What makes you ask such a ridiculous question?"

While Liana shared a great deal with her brother, she wasn't willing to share her encounter with Christian and Beau. He would be as infuriated as she was, and probably go after them. After feeling Christian's strength firsthand, she could not allow Morgan to take the risk of fighting him.

"Let's just say it was a bit of gossip I overheard."

Morgan wiped his forehead on his sleeve, but his frown

remained. "Tell Father, and he'll stop the rumor at its source."

Liana licked her swollen lips and wondered if such a direct confrontation would be wise. Then again, when she considered the intensity of Christian's demand, anything less appeared equally unwise. She glanced back over her shoulder. The Barclays' impressive home wasn't visible from the yard of her own, but she had seen it from the road. Remembering it now, she could so easily imagine Christian standing on the balcony, gazing her way. It gave her chills. She rubbed her arms briskly to dispel them.

"All right, I'll try and find time tonight. Don't you say anything to him, please."

"I won't, but why would he keep a first marriage secret?"

At the mention of secrets, Liana could only shrug, for until that very afternoon, she had never had a scandalous secret of her own.

To long-time residents of Williamsburg, Ian Scott's home was still known by the name of his wife's family, and called the Frederick plantation. To Sean O'Keefe, James Murray, and Thomas Lane, all British officers newly arrived in Virginia, it was Ian Scott's place. Son of a prominent London barrister, Ian had never been poor, but his marriage to Robin Frederick had made him a member of the colonial gentry. He had resigned his commission in the Coldstream Guards at the close of the French and Indian War, but had remained a staunch friend of the British officers who served in Virginia and frequently welcomed them to his home.

Ian was well aware of the attraction many of his young British friends felt for his daughter, and hoped she might eventually find one to her liking. A series of what he regarded as shortsighted, if not downright stupid, attempts by Parliament to tax the colonies to pay for the lengthy war with the French had created a mood of discontent in America that made Ian fear for the future of the colonies. To have Liana married to a proper Englishman, rather than some fractious colonial lad, was, therefore, tremendously appealing.

The dining room of the Scotts' beautifully detailed Georgian home was a yellow as pretty as sunshine. By candlelight, the walls took on an elegant golden glow that flattered everyone, but most especially Liana, who was dressed in a silk gown in a lush copper shade. She was seated between Morgan and her other brother, Cameron, who, at thirteen, always pestered their guests with endless questions. It was his ambition to follow his father's example and enter the military; no detail of the military life was too small to escape his interest.

Sean O'Keefe was seated directly opposite Liana and found her such an enchanting sight, he had to constantly remind himself to eat his dinner. He was convinced that Virginian honey-cured ham was the best in the world, but even that failed to distract him. Liana glanced his way only occasionally, but each time she did, he smiled and nodded, as pleased by a brief gaze as he would have been by a kind word. Hoping to impress her, he hinted at a coming announcement.

"An advantage of being in the military is that we're often privy to information before the general public." Seeing he had everyone's attention, and most especially Liana's, he continued. "Last December's regrettable incident in Boston Harbor won't go unpunished much longer."

"The tea party!" Cameron interjected with a wide grin. Then, realizing a British officer would not regard the event in such playful terms, he quickly looked down at his plate.

"Ah, well, yes, the tea party, if you wish," Sean agreed. "Anyway, Parliament has decided upon a just punishment for the people of Boston, and it should serve as a warning to all those who dispute Parliament's right to levy taxes."

Alarmed, Ian sat forward. "If you have privileged information, Captain O'Keefe, you ought not to share it at the dinner table."

Embarrassed that his effort to impress Liana had met with a justifiable rebuke, Sean nodded and fell silent. Thomas Lane poked him in the ribs and James Murray shot him a piercing glance. Surrounded by disapproval, he was surprised when Liana's expression remained one of rapt interest.

"Do you think King George might ever deign to visit the colonies?" she asked.

Hoping to redeem himself, Sean supplied an immediate answer. "He is the King of England, Miss Scott, and that's where he stays."

"And you believe that's also where he belongs?" Liana pressed.

"Well, yes, of course."

Anticipating his sister's next comment, Morgan began to chuckle to himself. His mother looked only mildly interested, and his father raised his hand as though he meant to interrupt, but he did not. Cameron's eager gaze swept the three red-coated guests.

"I've heard, although certainly not in this house, that there are a great many Americans who firmly believe we have little need of an English king, or a Parliament which includes none of our representatives."

Finally prodded into speaking, Ian's tone was emphatic. "That is more than enough, young lady. Politics is not a suitable topic for ladies at any time, and I'll not have the king's authority questioned at my table."

"I'm merely making the point that it is indeed a pity that neither the king nor his ministers feels the need to visit the land they claim to know how best to govern."

"The British Empire is vast," Ian insisted, "and the American colonies are only one part. Now enough of such a distressing subject. The centerpiece you arranged is especially lovely this evening. I hope that means we'll have an abundance of flowers this spring."

Keenly aware that her father's shift in subject was meant to silence any further talk of anything meaningful, Liana thanked him for the compliment, but failed to enter into the conversation when it strayed to subjects no more exciting than the weather or who owned the fastest horse. After dinner, she remained with her mother while her younger brothers accompanied their father and his British guests into his study.

"My darling, I do wish you'd watch your comments more closely," Robin advised. "We're all aware of the complaints against the Crown, but discussing them openly with British officers is not only unladylike, but foolish in the extreme."

"Do you really believe Sean might accuse me of sedition?"

"No, certainly not. He's too much in love with you for that, but you mustn't put him or his friends in the unenviable position of having a reason to do so. No matter what occurs in Boston, and Sean's comment made me very curious, your father will remain loyal to the Crown."

"And what about you, Mother dear?"

Robin was a petite woman, who at thirty-eight, still had a trim figure and glossy, dark-brown hair. Her three redhaired children were still something of a shock each time she looked at them. They were so clearly Ian's offspring that she saw nothing of herself in any of them. Soft-spoken and shy, she admired her courageous daughter enormously. "Your father knows what is best in such matters."

"But he wasn't born here, and we were."

"True," Robin admitted with a soft sigh. "I wish you had been old enough when we visited London to have memories of the trip. It's such a splendid city. When we first married, I thought your father might wish to return home permanently, but it was my sister and her husband who took up residence there."

Her mother and Aunt Sarah had kept up a lively correspondence over the years, and Liana felt as though she knew her and her English cousins even if she could not recall visiting them. It wasn't her aunt who interested her now, though, but her mother's mention of marriage. "Was there a particular reason you believed Father would wish to return home?"

Robin was working on a piece of embroidery, and waited until she had rethreaded her needle before she replied. "He was born in London, sweetheart, and I thought he might miss the excitement of the city."

"But he didn't?"

"No, he was more than content here."

Liana went to the settee and sat down beside her mother. Dissimilar not only in coloring but also in temperament, they had never been as close as some mothers and daughters. Still, Liana hesitated to upset her needlessly. "How long had you known Father before you married him?"

Puzzled by the question, Robin looked away for a moment. "Let's see now. I suppose we'd been acquainted a couple of years or more before we became serious about each other."

Liana was attempting to find the most tactful way to inquire as to whether her father might have been wed previously when he entered the parlor followed by their guests and her brothers. The opportunity lost, she rose—and struggled to hide her frustration. The young men were all in high spirits, but seeming preoccupied, her father contributed little to the conversation in the next hour. When the young officers at last excused themselves, she walked with Sean to the door.

"I hope we'll be able to spend more time together at the Tuttles' party tomorrow night," he confided softly. "I do so enjoy dancing with you."

Sean was an attractive man with thick brown hair and hazel eyes but there was something about his smile that had always struck Liana as being a bit too predatory. It wasn't a smirk, but more of a triumphant grin, and she really saw no cause for such elation. "You dance very well," she answered. "I shall look forward to having you as a partner."

Sean glanced around and finding his host and hostess talking with James and Thomas, he reached for Liana's hand and drew it to his lips. When she pulled away, he released her instantly. "I'm sorry. I didn't mean to be too forward."

Liana wasn't offended, nor had she been touched by the sweetness of his impulsive gesture. She simply did not care enough about Sean to appreciate either his devotion or painful uncertainty. "Good night, Captain"

Disappointed to see none of his own enthusiasm reflected in Liana's eyes, Sean bade her good night and left with his friends. Morgan and Cameron raced up the stairs, while their mother followed at a sedate pace. Ian started back toward his study, and having kept Christian's accusations to herself as long as she possibly could, Liana followed him.

"I wonder if I might have a word with you, Father."

Ian sank into the chair behind his desk and poured himself another brandy from the crystal decanter he never allowed to slip past half full. "Another time, baby. I'm too tired tonight."

Liana came forward anyway. "This won't take a moment. I heard a disturbing bit of gossip, and I need your opinion."

Slumped back in his chair, Ian looked far from eager to hear it. "I thought you knew better than to give credence to innuendo."

Liana leaned against the edge of his desk and smoothed her fingers over the finely polished wood. "Of course I do, but this was something about you."

"Me?" Ian took a swallow of brandy and let it slide slowly

down his throat. "I lead the most placid of lives. How could anyone possibly gossip about me?"

The study was lit only by the lamp on the desk, and surrounded by shadows, Liana felt that she was treading on dangerous ground despite her father's reassurance. She found it impossible to look at him as she asked her question. "Is it true that Mother is your second wife?"

Not having expected such a shattering probe into his past, Ian left his chair with astonishing haste. He circled his desk and, grabbing Liana by the shoulders, shook her as angrily as Christian had. "Tell me who put such a damning thought into your head! Tell me this instant!"

"It is true then?"

"Tell me his name," Ian demanded even more harshly.

Already sore from Christian's mauling, Liana tried not to let the pain he was causing her show. She had never seen her father so angry, and yet, she saw something more: fear, and that troubled her all the more. For reasons she could not begin to justify or explain, she felt compelled to protect Christian as she replied, "I was walking down by the river and met Christian Barclay. He called me his sister."

Ian released his only daughter with a strangled cry and turned his back on her. "He's been raised on lies. You two have no common blood and I forbid you ever to speak to him again. Now go to bed and stop pestering me with his spiteful tales."

Liana observed him silently until, growing impatient, he turned back toward her. His expression was contorted into a vicious mask of rage, and still she stood her ground. "If I know the truth, Father, I can defend you against insults. Won't you please tell me your side?"

"There is no truth to his story, only the vilest of lies." Shoving her aside, he strode from the room and into the night.

Liana was tempted to have a swig of brandy herself, but

instead she snuffed the lamp and went upstairs to her room. She had been raised in what she had always regarded as the happiest of families. That her father could harbor a secret that tormented him still after what had to have been at least twenty years was completely unnerving. Who was lying now, she wondered. The father she adored—or a handsome savage?

Determined to find out, she would go into town as she often did on a Saturday morning, but tomorrow she would stop by the church and cemetery before she began her shopping. She had that right, she was certain, for her father's past was also her own. If Christian Barclay could call himself her brother, for whatever misguided reason, then she was determined to discover why.

Two

Colonial Williamsburg had its beginnings in the modest settlement of Middle Plantation. The College of William and Mary was founded there in 1695, and when in 1698 fire destroyed the Burgesses' meeting house in Jamestown for the fourth time, the small town became the new capital of the Virginia Colony. Renamed to honor King William III, expansion of the city was then carefully planned by the Royal Governor, Francis Nicholson.

Located on a rise well-drained by small creeks and bordered by the James and York Rivers, Williamsburg was a most agreeable spot. The college was at the west end of the town's narrow road. Nicholson broadened the rutted lane into an impressive boulevard one hundred feet wide and named it for His Highness William Duke of Gloucester. At the east end of the wide avenue, he designated land for the construction of the Capitol. A spacious market square with sites for a courthouse, powder magazine, and guard house was established midway between. In his city plans, Nicholson also drew in a Governor's Palace on the north side of town.

Running parallel above and below Duke of Gloucester Street were Nicholson and Francis Streets. Along streets bisecting the main thoroughfare, half-acre lots provided enough space for each new resident to construct a home and have a garden. Merchants opened shops to serve the

growing community, and supported by the additional pa-
tronage of the wealthy plantation owners in the surrounding countryside, the town prospered. A hub not only of
commerce but also of religion, politics, and entertainment,
it was a fitting capital for the hardy and ambitious colonists
who had made Virginia their home.

After Liana left her brothers to visit with their friends
who lived in town, she made no pretense of shopping but
instead went straight to the Bruton Parish Church. The
elderly groundskeeper was pulling weeds at the cemetery
gate, and she approached him with a cheerful wave.
"Good morning, Henry. Would you please be so kind as
to direct me to the Barclay family plot?"

Rising slowly, Henry squinted into the sun and recognized Liana from her stunning red hair. "Aye, Miss Scott,
it's down the path and to your right. Do you see the rise?
That's where you'll find them."

"Thank you." Liana followed the path with a most unladylike haste and swiftly arrived at the location Henry had
indicated. The Barclays had been one of the original families of Middle Plantation, and there were worn headstones
bearing the Barclay name dating back to the 1690's. She
passed those with no more than a brief glance, but slowed
to a stop when she came to the more recent markers. Almost afraid to read the inscriptions, she forced herself to
study the first.

It was the tombstone of a young woman who had died
at eighteen. Liana whispered her name: Melissa Barclay
Scott. Before she could blink away a rush of angry tears,
a shadow passed over the marble marker and she knew
before she turned to face him just who it would be.

Christian nodded slightly. "Yesterday you called me a
'lying snake', among other despicable names, for speaking
the truth about my mother. Now you should know who
the real liar is."

Unable to meet his taunting gaze, Liana looked away.

Henry had interrupted his work to observe them, but was too far away to overhear their conversation. Still, having worked in the cemetery for so many years, he would know the names of each person buried there, and she had the most uncomfortable feeling that he knew exactly what was being said. Taking that supposition one step further, she realized all of her parents' friends must know her father had once been married to a Barclay, and she could not understand why the truth had been kept from her and her brothers.

Christian was again clad in buckskins, but he did not seem nearly so threatening as he had out in the fields. He was every bit as handsome, however, which was something Liana would rather not have noticed. "I owe you an apology. To have insulted you so rudely was unforgivable, but you should never have approached me as you did."

A slow smile played across Christian's lips. "I will forgive your rudeness if you will forgive mine."

Uncertain which of them had made the greatest error, Liana was relieved. "Thank you. That's very gracious of you. I really don't understand any of this." She turned back toward Melissa's tombstone. "How long were your mother and my father married?"

"They eloped in April, 1754, and my grandparents insisted they remarry in church in May. They had been together seven months when she died on my birthday that November. From what I've been told, your father adored my mother. He refused to see me, though. First because he blamed me for the death of the woman he loved, and later, when he discovered I was not his, he despised me for being Indian. I can only imagine what he then thought of my mother. He had been welcomed into the Barclay family as a son, but he never set foot in our house again."

Intrigued by his shocking tale, Liana gestured toward a nearby bench. "Please come and sit with me awhile."

Christian followed her and waited until she had taken

a seat before taking his place beside her. She was dressed in pale green, and the color flattered her even more than the peach gown she had been wearing the previous afternoon. "If you would like proof, we can go into the church and I'll show you the book where they signed their names after their wedding."

The hostility of her father's reaction to her questions had already convinced Liana of their truth. That Melissa's tombstone bore the Scott name was all the additional documentation she required. "No, I believe you." Anxious for this perplexing meeting to go well, she clasped her hands in her lap. "What did you hope to accomplish by telling me about my father and your mother? What is it you really want, Christian?"

The innocence of her gaze prompted Christian to temper his response. "I wanted you to know the truth. What other reason could there be?"

Sitting so close, Liana found it difficult not to watch his lips as he spoke. With the memory of his bruising kiss still fresh in both her mind and body, that was most disconcerting. "For what purpose? Did you believe my father would wish to share such a painful part of his life with his children? Or were you merely attempting to make trouble for us all?"

Christian slid his finger down the flushed curve of her cheek and watched her shiver with what he hoped was pleasure rather than dread. "I was conceived in sin and born of death. What could anyone possibly expect of me but endless trouble?"

Liana turned toward his subtle caress, frightened, thrilled, and more confused than ever. "Brother trouble," she whispered, and his lips silenced whatever else she might have wished to say. She felt the softness of his buckskins beneath her palms, but while she had raised her hands to his chest, she could not summon the strength to push him away. His kiss was soft and gently stirring rather than demanding; lost in the blissful moment, Liana couldn't think at all. She could only feel, and to the depths of her soul Christian's affection felt right. All too soon, he drew away.

Christian slid off the bench and knelt in front of Liana. He placed his hands on her knees, and pressed his chest against her legs. Trapping her on the bench, he had her full attention. "Melissa Barclay lacked the courage to admit she loved an Indian brave, so she wed your father. He was safe, respectable, devoted," he said, pronouncing each word with an insulting sneer. "Don't make the same mistake."

With a fluid ease he stretched to his full height and walked away before Liana could catch her breath, but she knew something extraordinary had just taken place. "A kiss and a warning," she sighed, uncertain what to make of Christian's astonishing advice. She closed her eyes, searching her memories for glimpses of him. She had known the very first time she had seen him that he deserved to be remembered, but had he also been watching her over the years?

She had to remain seated in the cemetery until she had regained her composure before she dared venture into the shops, but when at last she felt strong enough to go, she paused to say a prayer at Melissa's grave. Christian's kiss had taught her as no words ever could just what torments the young woman must have endured. Had Melissa survived her son's birth, she would have been branded with names too vile for Liana to repeat even to herself. Feeling a poignant kinship to the long-dead young woman, there was a tear in her eye as she turned away.

Rejoining her brothers an hour later for the ride home, Liana gave a slight shake of her head to warn Morgan not to question her within Cameron's hearing. Unfortunately,

Cameron saw Morgan nod and was positive they were plotting against him. "All right, I saw that. I'm not just some little kid who can't understand what's going on anymore so you two might as well explain now because I won't shut up even after we get home."

"He is thirteen," Morgan agreed.

Cameron was growing so rapidly his clothes had to be altered nearly every week, but Liana really didn't think he was mature enough to discuss his father's failings. Morgan stood up for him, though, and after several minutes of coaxing, she revealed the secret she had not really wanted to keep. Again shielding Christian, she mentioned only that she had found Melissa's tombstone.

"After church tomorrow," she suggested, "go on out to the cemetery. Follow the path on the right to the crest. You'll find her buried there."

Morgan had expected his sister's investigations to disprove the rumor she had shared yesterday, and he was as shocked and dismayed as Cameron. "I've never heard Father say one nice thing about the Barclays," he complained. "How can he possibly have been married to one?"

"His distaste for them appears to have come after his bride's death," Liana proposed. "My questions upset him so badly last night, I don't believe we ought to refer to Melissa Barclay in his presence. Let's just pretend we don't know any more than we ever did."

Cameron leaned out past Morgan to study his sister's expression. "That would be like trying to pour an egg back into its shell, Liana. We can't pretend not to know. Besides, the real question is, why has Father pretended all these years that Mother was his only wife? What if Melissa weren't the only other one? Maybe he had half a dozen wives before he married Mother and we have brothers and sisters all over the place."

Liana assured him that could not be true. "He must

have been heartbroken when Melissa died, and we ought to respect his silence in the matter.''

"When did she die?" Morgan asked.

"November, 1754."

"And when was it that he married Mother? December of what year?"

"It was in 1755," Liana answered.

"Well, I suppose that is a year of mourning, but he could not have been all that heartbroken if he married Mother just a year later."

Sorry that she had ever confided in Morgan, Liana made another attempt to distract his attention from the past. "He and Mother are happy together. It's not surprising he wouldn't want to dwell on a tragedy in his past, and I don't want either of you to pester him for the details."

Morgan frowned unhappily. "Sorry, Liana, but I can't help but wonder what else he might be hiding. My God, do you suppose the whole town knows he was married to a Barclay?"

"Probably."

"That's why he's always made them sound so awful, isn't it?" Cameron asked. "So we'd not be friends with any of them and learn the truth."

"He's always insisted we tell *him* the truth," Morgan reminded them. "He's never been able to tolerate a lie, but he's been telling us one all these years."

Mortified by the conclusion Morgan had drawn, Liana reached out to touch his sleeve. "Please, don't either of you say anything to anyone about this or it will be sure to get right back to Father," Liana warned. "Think of Mother's feelings, too. Growing up on neighboring plantations, she and Melissa might have been good friends."

"And Father obviously liked Melissa better." Morgan gave a low whistle. "I wish you hadn't found out about this, Liana. It makes me feel sort of sick."

"Try and forget it," she advised. "That's what I'm going

to do." But as they rode by the Barclay plantation, she was as eager as her brothers for a glimpse of the stately brick mansion. Their home was of a similar Georgian design with a columned façade and gambrel roof, but somehow, the Barclay residence looked almost appealing, rather than forbidding as it once had.

"We must try and understand Father's reluctance to discuss his past, and forgive him for it," Liana stressed, but even as she spoke, she wondered what it was that had driven Christian to apprise her of a twenty-year-old scandal. He wanted something. She was sure of it, and from the desire that flavored his kisses, she was afraid it was her.

Liana had just completed dressing that evening when her father knocked on her door. Surprised to see him, she stood back to allow him to enter. "I'm sorry about last night," she murmured softly. "I shouldn't have pried into your past."

Liana was dressed in a sumptuous gown of gold silk and with her hair styled atop her head in a crown of curls, Ian thought she looked as beautiful as a princess. "You're more lovely every day, Liana, and infinitely wiser than I am. I came to beg your forgiveness, you see. I was harsh when I should have been honest, but I've been so content with your mother, I'd thought I had buried the past. When you threw it into my lap last night, I reacted very badly and I apologize. I'll admit to being married to Melissa Barclay, but I don't want to talk about the details, now or ever. I can only hope that you'll respect my wishes."

Because she already knew far more than he realized, Liana found it difficult to reply. Instead, she kissed his cheek, picked up her fan, and linked her arm through his as they walked down the stairs to leave for the Tuttles' party. Morgan and Cameron were standing in the hallway. They were as handsomely dressed as their father in blue silk coats over lighter blue waistcoats and knee britches, but Liana saw the confusion in their eyes and understood its cause.

She held her breath, praying their father would note nothing amiss, and she was enormously relieved when he did not. As soon as Robin joined them, they went out to the carriage and, once on their way, discussed the coming party. While her brothers teased her about Sean O'Keefe she was so grateful they had not chosen a more distressing topic, that she did not really mind.

"He is such a nice young man," Robin enthused as she smoothed out the folds of her plum-colored gown. "He has a calm and steady gaze. I admire that in a man."

Liana had to agree with her mother's assessment, for Sean had impressed her as a calmly capable sort. She supposed that characteristic would serve him well in battle, but it certainly did not make him an exciting companion. Opening the gold fan that matched her polonaise, she stirred the night air into a cooling breeze—but it failed to soothe her troubled emotions.

She had never seen Christian at a party, but she had the strangest sensation, a premonition perhaps, that he would be there. It was enough to make her plead to return home, but convincing herself she was allowing her imagination to make more of their last conversation than she should, she rode on without making such a ridiculous demand.

The Tuttle plantation bordered the Scotts' on the southeast, and they were among the first to arrive. Liana and Amanda Tuttle were good friends, but she was not even tempted to confide that she had met Christian, or what she had learned about her father. Instead, she assumed what she hoped would be her former carefree attitude and did her best to enjoy the party. Rather than inquire as to the guest list, she simply kept an eye on the door, until the parlor had become too crowded to see the late arrivals.

The furniture had been removed to make room for

dancing, and once there were enough present to begin, the string quartet played a minuet. Sean O'Keefe was at Liana's elbow in an instant, and with Thomas Lane eager to dance with Amanda, Liana convinced herself it had only been a guilty conscience which had made her imagine Christian would be present. She smiled as she took Sean's hand, but while his fingers were warm, she felt none of the thrill Christian's slightest touch aroused.

"You look so very beautiful tonight," Sean whispered as they moved close to bow.

"Thank you, Captain." He looked splendid in his uniform, and when the music brought them together again, she told him so. He looked so pleased, Liana felt sad that she could not offer equally enthusiastic compliments on other aspects of his personality. She danced the next tune with Thomas Lane, and the following number with James Murray. Then, apparently jealous of the British officers, young men she had known all her life crowded around, vying to be her next partner. Liana loved to dance. She was not only graceful, but accomplished and knew the steps of not merely the most popular dances, but all the ones they would do that evening.

While she had convinced herself it was silly, whenever there was an opportunity to peruse the crowd, she did so. Wigs were worn by only a few men now, and most of those were of her parents' generation, so there were plenty of dark-haired young men in the room. From the back, Liana didn't recognize Amanda's partner, but this was a dance in which the women progressed and as he reached out to take her hand, she was astonished to find the elegantly dressed man was Christian. She stopped so suddenly, the woman dancing behind her bumped into her back.

"I'm so sorry," Liana hastily apologized, and badly embarrassed, she moved closer to Christian.

Christian regarded her with a wicked grin. He was dressed in a gray satin coat with a ruffled shirt, white waist-

coat, and knee breeches. Like those of most of the male
guests, the buttons on his coat and buckles on his shoes
were silver. He appeared to be as comfortable in the well-
tailored clothes as he had been in buckskins, but there
was more than a mere trace of insolence in his manner.

"You look more surprised than delighted to see me tonight, Miss Scott," he confided with a sly wink.

Uncertain how to reply to such an impertinent greeting,
Liana pretended a rapt interest in the intricate steps of
the dance, but the energy flowing through his hand into
hers created a tingle she could not ignore. The musicians
slowed the tune through a difficult passage, but he kept
to the dance's rhythm without losing the beat. His hold
on her hand was a bit too tight, however, and whenever
the steps called for them to circle each other, he wrapped
himself around her with unseemly vigor.

"You dance almost too well, Mr.—" Liana hesitated, un-
sure of what to call him.

Christian leaned forward to whisper in her ear, his
breath hot against her cheek. "I'm Christian Scott Hunter,
but you may call me whatever you wish, sister dear."

Liana sent an anxious glance toward the nearest couple, but they were laughing together and hadn't overheard Christian's remark. "Please, you mustn't call me
that."

Christian's response was a flash of sparkling white teeth
in a rakish grin. Dressed in gray-and-white, his hair an inky
black, his bronze skin provided his only touch of color; he
was a far more impressive figure than any of the other
brightly attired gentlemen. He was relaxed, obviously comfortable at the crowded party, but the playful glint never
left his gaze.

Before Liana had satisfactorily settled the question of
how he was to address her, she had to move on to the next
partner. After the shock of finding Christian there, to have
Beau Barclay take her hand wasn't at all disturbing. She

managed a polite smile, but made no attempt to engage him in conversation and when the dance finally drew to an end, she excused herself and slipped outside to catch her breath.

"I hope you don't mind that I've followed you," Sean said as he approached her.

Distracted, Liana would have preferred her own company to his, but she was too well-bred to speak such thoughts aloud. "It's rather cool," she cautioned instead. "We shouldn't stay outside long."

"No, it wouldn't be wise," Sean agreed. "What do you know about the last of your partners?"

Liana stared at him, certain he knew everything there was to know and was only testing her. Horribly uncomfortable, she shrugged. "Beau is one of the Barclays. While our plantations are close, our families aren't."

Sean leaned forward slightly and lowered his voice. "It will do you no credit to accept his attentions. His family is among the most vocal when it comes to protesting the king and Parliament's lawful actions. Perhaps after Boston Harbor is closed, they will reassess their views."

Shocked by his offhand disclosure, Liana's eyes widened in surprise. "Is that what you meant to tell us last night, that Boston Harbor is to be closed?"

Sean rested his finger lightly on her lips. "Hush. It must remain a secret for another few days, but yes, it will happen and that's only the first of the punishments the king will mete out to the obstinate people of Massachusetts. I trust the good citizens of Virginia know better than to provoke his wrath."

"My father was right. You ought not to be sharing privileged information as party banter."

Liana attempted to move past Sean to return to the party, but he blocked her way. "I'm not merely making amusing conversation, Liana. I'm trying to warn you that these are difficult times, and you must choose your friends wisely."

"I always have," Liana informed him coldly.

Sean's gaze did not soften. "Should there be a rebellion, women will be hanged for treason as swiftly as men."

"If you are attempting to disgust me, you have succeeded, Captain. Now please stand aside and allow me to pass."

Certain his warning would soon prove valuable, Sean responded with a graceful bow and stepped out of her way. He did not question Ian Scott's loyalty, but the continual lack of encouragement he received from Liana, coupled with her tendency to ask provocative questions, had made him suspect her sympathies did not match her father's. Determined to correct the unfortunate error in her thinking before she could do herself, or the Crown, harm, he returned to the party eager to dance with her again.

A tall, slender brunette, Amanda Tuttle was a delightfully uninhibited young woman. A few months younger than Liana, she was equally popular. Inviting Liana upstairs to her bedroom to rest a moment before supper was served, she immediately turned their conversation to her favorite subject: men.

"Sean O'Keefe is quite handsome, but you don't really like him much, do you?"

Shivering with the memory of his beastly threat, Liana confirmed her friend's suspicions. "He is used to ordering his troops about, and I don't appreciate it when he treats me in the same fashion."

Amanda leaned close to her mirror and pinched her cheeks to bring out more color. "This was the first time my parents have ever invited any of the Barclays to a party, but after having danced with Beau and Christian, I'm going to insist they're included in the future. Christian is no more than a handsome savage, of course, but apparently Beau won't accept invitations that don't include him. I suppose that's admirable loyalty since they're merely cousins. I find Beau incredibly appealing. What do you think of him?"

Liana was surprised by how badly it hurt to hear Christian dismissed as though he were of no consequence when she considered him every bit as bright and attractive as Beau. "Christian is the better dancer," she finally replied.

"Do you really think so? I favored Beau. He has the lighter touch."

"Yes, that's certainly true. I think we better get back to the party, don't you?" Fluffing out her ruffled and tiered skirt, Liana walked toward the door, but waited there for Amanda.

"We're seventeen," Amanda reminded her. "It's time we began encouraging serious suitors. Maybe you're not interested in Beau Barclay, but I certainly am. He's handsome, and rich. What more could a woman want in a husband?"

Amanda's brown eyes were alight with mischief, but Liana did not share her mood. She did not know which had been more unsettling, Christian's taunts or Sean's threats, but she would have preferred to have done without either. "I simply don't feel any need for a husband as yet," she exclaimed, "but I am hungry. Let's go have some supper."

Amanda reached out to hold the door closed. "Not just yet. First I want your promise that if you're out riding and see Beau Barclay, you'll send him on down here to call on me."

"In the unlikely event that our paths cross, I will definitely send him this way."

"Good." Amanda yanked open the door and practically skipped down the stairs. Liana followed with a slow, measured step, and for the first time in her life, felt older than her seventeen years.

* * *

When Christian and Beau returned home, they found their younger brothers and sisters waiting up for them. At sixteen, Beau's sister, Dominique, was thoroughly peeved that she had not been allowed to attend the Tuttles' party with them. Thirteen-year-old Belle thought it was hilarious that Dominique had been kept home, and their younger brother, Jean, at ten, did not care one whit about the party but had stayed up with the others anyway.

Although she was eighteen, Christian's sister, Johanna, was so painfully shy she had not even wanted to attend. She'd relaxed with her family, but did want to hear all the details now. His brother, Falcon, was Dominique's age and would never have exchanged his buckskins for the fine clothes parties required. He was not particularly interested in how the evening had gone, but he was a curious lad who had not wanted to go to bed and miss hearing about what had happened.

"Who had the prettiest gown?" Dominique asked. She was as blond as her French mother, and possessed of a rare yet innocent beauty.

Beau kicked off his shoes and stretched out on the settee. "All the gowns looked like the same satin, silk, and lace as yours to me. Amanda was dressed in pink. That's all I remember."

"Is she very pretty?" Johanna asked.

"She's not nearly as pretty as you," Beau exclaimed. It pained him that Johanna had no male callers, but with so many attractive young women in Williamsburg, a girl who was half Seneca apparently could not compete.

"He's right," Christian assured her. He leaned back against the mantel and crossed his arms over his chest. "Amanda is a mite too tall. She's real skinny, and her hair curls in a wild tangle. She seems popular, though, so some men obviously like her."

Dominique plucked a peppermint out of the candy dish

and popped it in her mouth. "If Amanda doesn't suit your tastes, was there a woman who does?"

Christian saw the same question reflected in Beau's eyes, but chose not to reveal the truth. "I'm waiting for you to grow up—you know that."

"You've kept me waiting too long as it is," Dominique complained. "I'm looking for a beau who isn't just all talk like you are."

Falcon had been pacing the parlor, but having heard enough, started for the door. "You better be careful what you demand from a man," he called over his shoulder, "or you might find yourself with a brat before you have a husband."

"Falcon!" Dominique leaped from her chair and chased her cousin up the stairs, but he made it up to the room he shared with Jean on the third floor and locked the door before she could catch him.

Laughing at their antics, Beau swung his legs off the settee, stood and stretched. "I'll bet the rest of you can't get upstairs and into bed before I count to ten. One, two—" Before he reached three, Belle and Jean were racing up the stairs. Johanna rose, but looked to be in no hurry.

"What did you really think of the party?" she asked.

Christian shrugged. "I overheard all manner of interesting things, but with so many Tories present, none was spoken very loud."

While Beau knew Christian was keenly interested in politics, he doubted his cousin had paid attention to anyone other than Liana Scott. "It was a nice party," he began, "but I can't imagine why the Tuttles asked us, unless they are leaning away from their Tory friends."

"Or attempting to walk right down the middle," Christian proposed, "but they will have to take sides eventually."

"You two may enjoy plotting rebellion, but I surely don't. I'm glad you enjoyed the party, though. Good night."

"Good night, Johanna," both young men called.

Beau bent down to pick up his shoes. "You've not mentioned Liana. I couldn't tell if she was pleased to see you there tonight or not. She barely smiled at me."

Christian slapped his cousin on the shoulder as he walked by him toward the door. "She was definitely pleased to see me. She was just too stubborn to admit it."

"Be careful with her," Beau cautioned as he followed Christian up the stairs, but he knew he was wasting his breath even as he spoke. Christian did not even know the meaning of the word "caution," but he certainly hoped Liana did.

Three

The scene after the party was not nearly so tranquil at the Scott residence as it had been at the Barclays'. An intensely private man, Ian had been unwilling to voice his objections when he had seen Liana dancing with Christian, but he had seethed in miserable silence until they had returned home. He then sent his sons up to bed, kissed his wife good night, and marched Liana into his study. The walls were a deep emerald green, and lit by the single lamp on the desk, the room was as dark and forbidding as his mood.

"We stood in this very room last night," Ian reminded his only daughter, "and I forbade you ever to speak with Christian again. Did you honestly believe you could openly defy my wishes at the Tuttles' tonight without drawing my notice, or my wrath?"

Liana licked her lips nervously. In her opinion, what her father had observed was an inconsequential exchange compared to what had transpired between Christian and her that morning in the cemetery. She had definitely defied his wishes then, and she was embarrassed now to realize how quickly his stern command had slipped her mind.

"I did not even realize he was there until a change in partners brought us together. I was shocked," Liana readily admitted, "but didn't realize I ought to excuse myself immediately. To do so would have been awfully rude."

Ian stared down at his daughter. The green of her eyes so closely matched his own that in many ways, looking at her and his sons was like gazing into a mirror. While his hair was graying, it had once been as glorious a red as hers and she reminded him all too much of himself. Love had once made a fool of him, and he did not want to see her suffer the same tragic fate.

"It may have been rude, but it would have been prudent. It is not on a mere whim that I've ordered you to avoid him. He told you about Melissa and me for one purpose only, and that was to do us a grave injury. He's as dangerous a man as his father.

"I watched him tonight. He looked as comfortable in fine clothes as his cousin, but underneath he's his father's son and whatever dwells in his black Indian heart is twisted and evil. I wish to God I'd let him die with his mother. Had I but known what he was, I would have."

Her father's anger was so deep that not even his hushed tone could disguise his rage. Frightened, Liana backed away. "I don't want any part of your feud with the Barclays," she insisted. "If, as you claim, Christian has some evil intent, then the more I avoid him, the more aggressively he will pursue me. I would prefer merely to remain indifferent. That would be the very last thing he wants, and he'll soon grow bored with me."

"If he were any other young man I would agree, but he is an Indian! Don't you understand what that means? He isn't like us. He doesn't think logically or rationally. He seeks only to take what he wants. His father wanted Melissa. I won't allow you to be Christian's prey. Now either you give me your solemn vow that you will never speak to him again, or your mother and I will make immediate arrangements to send you to your Aunt Sarah's in England. The choice is yours. Which is it to be?"

As the eldest, Liana had led rather than followed her brothers while growing up. She had shared the same tutors, played the same games; as a result, she had a far more independent nature than most young women her age. "If he's the rogue you claim him to be, he'd follow me, wouldn't he?"

"Liana!"

Ian looked ready to spit fire, but Liana remained composed. "I would enjoy a trip to England, but certainly not being banished. I can think for myself and I'm in no danger of being seduced by anyone. It might interest you to know that Sean O'Keefe told me Boston Harbor is to be closed, and he thought he could curry my favor by threatening me with dire consequences if I were disloyal to the Crown."

As distracted by that news as Liana had hoped he would be, Ian gaped in horror. "The harbor is to be closed? When?"

"He didn't say, but soon, I think. Sean also hinted that other punitive action would follow. I can't believe all the citizens of Massachusetts are openly defying the king, but apparently they are all to be punished."

"My God." Forgetting Christian for the moment, Ian slumped back against his desk. "Boston is a major port. Closing it is unthinkable."

"Apparently the matter has already been decided. That's what Sean meant to tell us at dinner Friday night. Obviously he did not foresee how badly you would take the news."

Ian shook his head. "It's our duty to obey the king, but when his actions have grown increasingly foolish, or in this case, disastrous, it is exceedingly difficult to be loyal."

That was easily the most inflammatory statement Ian Scott had ever made, and while Liana agreed, she was shocked to hear him say it nevertheless. "Perhaps we ought to wait for the public announcement. Maybe Sean misunderstood."

"I only wish I had that hope. No, closing Boston Harbor will be a catastrophe, no matter what the terms." Ian walked around his desk, slid into his chair, and reached for the decanter of brandy. "Go on to bed."

Liana hesitated, but not wanting to reopen their argument about Christian, she wished him a good night and left before he recalled why he had invited her into his study in the first place.

Sunday afternoon, Johanna was drawing water from the well when she saw a stranger coming up the path. He was thin and walking with a slow, rolling gait as though he had covered a great many miles. Men frequently came by the plantation looking for work, but her Uncle Byron wasn't hiring anyone now. Feeling sorry for him, Johanna waited by the well, knowing she could at least offer a refreshing drink and a meal.

The young man removed his dusty cocked hat as he approached. He had dark brown hair, brown eyes, and one of the most charming smiles Johanna had ever seen, but his clothes were worn and patched. He was carrying a heavy pack slung over his shoulder, and dropped it when he reached her.

"Good afternoon," he greeted her. "Is this the Barclays' place?"

Up close, the young man looked even more worn out than he had on the path. Feeling very sorry for him, Johanna extended a tin cup. "Yes, it is. Would you like a drink?"

"Thank you, I sure would." He drank three cupfuls before wiping his mouth on his sleeve and handing her back the cup. "I heard the Barclays hire workers rather than own slaves. Is that true?"

"Yes. It looks as though you've come a long way." Johanna had been working in the garden and was dressed in a simple bodice and skirt of homespun fabric. It did not even occurred to her that the stranger had mistaken her for a servant, but she would not have corrected his misconception even if it had.

"Too long," he replied. "I'm David Slauson."

"How do you do, David? I'm Johanna Hunter."

"I know it's Sunday, but is the overseer around?"

Before Johanna could reply, David began to sway slightly. "Mr. Slauson, are you all right?" Seeing that he most assuredly was not, she rushed to his side and guided him over to the bench surrounding the well. "Here, sit down a minute and rest."

"Thank you." Badly embarrassed, David caught her hand as she pulled away. "Please don't tell anyone I nearly fainted. I'll never get a job here if they think I'm not strong enough to work."

Johanna patted his hand. "It's a long walk from town. Anyone would be tired, and I'll bet you haven't eaten today, either."

David hung his head. "I think I had something to eat yesterday."

Most of the young men who came there seeking work were loud country boys who were strong and willing, if not long on manners, but David Slauson impressed Johanna as being from a far more genteel background. "You just sit right here and rest. I'll bring you something to eat from the kitchen."

While that was a tempting offer, David made his feelings known. "I'm no beggar."

"I know you're not." Johanna hurried to the kitchen where the cook, Rosemary McBride, was still cleaning up after dinner. "Do you have something we can serve a weary traveler?"

The Barclays never turned a man away without a meal,

and Rosemary quickly dished up a plate of veal and bacon, then added green beans, a thick slice of cornbread, and poured a tankard of cider. "Here you are, Miss Johanna. There's more if he's still hungry."

"Thank you, Rosemary." Johanna often ran errands between the main house and the outbuildings and on any day could just as easily be found in the kitchen or laundry as the parlor. She told herself she was merely doing a good deed, but she felt an unaccustomed longing to tend to David Slauson, and the thought that he would soon be gone pained her.

He had dozed off so she had to give his shoulder a shake to wake him when she returned with the ample meal. "Here you are. Just let me know if you'd like more, and I'll fetch it."

Tears welled up in David's eyes as he looked up at her. "But this is too much," he protested weakly.

Touched by his reluctance to admit to being hungry, Johanna sat down by his side. "All right then, eat only what you want and I'll throw the rest to the hogs. You needn't worry anything will be wasted."

Taking the pewter mug and plate, David's hands shook so badly he could scarcely grip his fork. He forced himself to take small bites and chew thoroughly, but had Johanna left him on his own, he would have gulped down every bite and crumb in less than a minute. "This is all so good," he murmured.

"The cook will appreciate your compliments."

David found it easy to smile at the sympathetic young woman. She had beautiful skin with a slight copper blush he assumed was due to exposure to the sun. Her dark eyes were framed with a long sweep of black lashes, but what he could see of her hair from the curls peeking out from beneath her frilly cap was a sunstreaked dark brown. "You're awfully pretty," he said with a smile.

Unused to men's attentions, Johanna merely shrugged

nonchalantly. "You must still be rather dizzy. Wait until you've finished eating to decide how I look."

Surprised that she did not seem to realize how lovely she was, David paused to pursue the matter. "Don't be coy. You must have a great many gentleman friends who say the same thing."

Perplexed that he would think so, Johanna wasn't sure how to reply. "No, that's not true."

Feeling better with each mouthful, David couldn't help but tease her. "No, what? You've no gentleman friends, or they don't flatter you as they should?"

There was now more color in his cheeks, and believing a young man as handsome as he would expect her to know how to carry on such a flirtatious conversation, Johanna thought she better leave before he discovered otherwise. "You came here looking for work," she reminded him as she stood. "Finish your dinner, and I'll see what I can do."

"No, wait. Can't you stay with me a while longer? It's been a long time since I talked with such a pretty girl."

Johanna shook her head, and rounding the corner of the house, entered through the back door. She found her uncle working in his study and rapped lightly at the partially open door. "Uncle Byron? May I come in, please?"

Byron Barclay looked up from his ledger. "Of course, Johanna. What do you need?"

"There's a young man here looking for work."

In his mid-forties, Byron was still fit and trim, but he rose from his desk with a weary stretch. "I'll send him on his way. Did you give him something to eat?"

"Yes, but—" Uncertain how to phrase her request, Johanna blocked his way to delay him a moment. "He's not like the others. Isn't there something he could do for us?"

Byron rested his hands lightly on her shoulders. She and Beau were the same age, and he loved her as much as his daughters. "Johanna, you know you're my favorite niece. If you want me to hire the man, just say so."

Johanna raised her hand to muffle her giggles. "I'm your only niece, Uncle Byron."

"So? You're still my favorite. I'll tell you what—I'll talk with him a minute, and if he impresses me, as he's obviously impressed you, I'll give him a job. Is that fair?"

Johanna was enormously relieved and her face lit up with a delighted smile. "Oh, yes, thank you."

"Don't thank me yet. Just wait right here so he's not too distracted to answer my questions. What's his name?"

"David Slauson. He's sitting out by the well."

"David Slauson," Byron repeated. "That has a nice sound." He gave her a quick kiss on the cheek and then, welcoming a break from his work, went outside to conduct the interview. David got to his feet as he approached. Noting he was a handsome young man, Byron knew immediately why Johanna liked him. He made an extra effort to greet him warmly.

"Good afternoon, Mr. Slauson. I'm Byron Barclay. My niece tells me you're looking for work. What experience have you had?"

"Your niece?" David looked up at the magnificent house and feared he had made a terrible blunder. "I didn't realize Johanna, Miss Hunter, was your niece. She was so nice to me. I hope I didn't insult her."

He looked so sincerely pained by that possibility, Byron agreed with Johanna's assessment: David Slauson had little in common with their typical fieldhand. "Your experience, rather than my niece, is the issue under discussion, Mr. Slauson."

David turned his hat in his hands. "I studied for the ministry at Harvard, but the truth is, I just didn't have the calling. I've tutored some, clerked in shops, been a proofreader for a printer, but I'm tired of cities and thought if I worked on a plantation for a while, I could learn enough about farming to manage a small place of my own one day."

Byron wasn't encouraged by what seemed to be David's own admission that he tended not to have much in the way of perseverance. "Just what is it about cities that offends you?"

"Well, I don't know that I'd say I was offended exactly, but I've been in both Boston and Philadelphia and they were crowded and dirty. The people weren't unkind, but they weren't friendly, either. My parents are dead. I've no family. I want someplace to call my own and I just couldn't find it in a city."

"So you came to Virginia."

"Yes, sir. I did. I'm not lazy. Here, I've brought letters of recommendation with me. They'll tell you I'm a good worker."

Byron waited while David searched through his pack for the letters. When the young man finally located them, he handed them over with obvious pride. Byron read through them and found the printer's letter especially complimentary, but the others also praised the young man's industry. He returned them to their stained envelopes and gave them back to David.

"Let me see your hands."

"Yes, sir." David had washed up in a creek and was relieved his hands were clean but that wasn't what Byron was looking for.

"Your hands confirm your story, Mr. Slauson. They don't look as though you've ever done any hard labor."

"No, sir, I haven't, but that doesn't mean I can't."

Byron stepped back and eyed David slowly from head to toe. It wasn't merely David's strength and endurance that concerned him, however, but Johanna's welfare. Hunter had taken Falcon out to gather branches for arrows, so he could not ask his opinion. Alanna was as dear a soul as her daughter Johanna and would never have turned David away, but Byron considered it seriously now. "How old are you?" he asked suddenly.

"I'm twenty-six, sir."

"All right, let's understand each other, Mr. Slauson. I believe a man ought to have purpose, a sense of direction, but it sounds to me as though you're simply adrift on the sea of life. Now, I'm willing to give you a chance, and if the work proves too hard for you just come and tell me and I'll have my driver take you into town to look for work elsewhere. Don't think you have to sneak off in the middle of the night."

"No, sir, Mr. Barclay. I wouldn't do that."

"Good. Now, in addition to Johanna, I have two daughters so we have beautiful young women aplenty here. You are to treat them with respect, or the fact that you might be an excellent worker won't matter. If I hear so much as a whisper of complaint from any of the women here, you'll be fired immediately, but being out of work will be the least of your problems. Understood?"

The light in Byron's blue eyes was as cold as steel, and David had no difficulty comprehending the nature of his threat. "Yes, sir, but you needn't have any worries. I know how to treat a lady."

"Good—now come with me and I'll show you your quarters, but I can't guarantee you'll like any of the other field hands. Farming is all they know, and they're liable to make your life miserable just for sport."

David responded with a weary sigh. "I know their kind."

He did not seem discouraged, though, and admiring his courage, Byron walked him down to the line of cabins where their field hands lived, introduced him to the boisterous lads, wished him luck, and left him on his own. When he returned to his study, he found Johanna's gaze much too anxious for mere concern over a weary traveler's plight and hoped he had made the right decision.

"David's a nice young man, Johanna, and I hired him, but I doubt he'll stay long so don't allow yourself to become attached to him. He's well educated, and meant for better things than working here. I realize that's why you liked him, but it's why he won't stay here long as well."

"He was just so forlorn," Johanna replied.

"You have your mother's sensitive soul, child, and that's a blessing for us all, but don't risk your heart on David Slauson." He kissed her forehead, and knowing she would not heed a word of his advice, he let her go with a silent prayer he would not soon come to regret hiring a handsome stranger.

Too restless to remain indoors on a sunlit Sunday afternoon, Liana went out for a walk along the river. She was sorry to have lost one of her favorite caps, and when she found herself near the spot where Christian had grabbed her, she followed the trail through the bent and tangled grass. Sighting a bit of white just ahead, she forged on, pushing against the tall marsh grass with broad strokes to clear her way.

When at last she reached the cap, she was disappointed to find the lace trim had been ripped away along one whole side, but she was a talented seamstress and could repair it. She folded the cap and slid it into her pocket. Relieved to think she had recovered the only evidence linking her to Christian, she turned back toward the river only to find him blocking her way. Shocked to have come across him so unexpectedly, she swiftly realized the frequency with which they met could not possibly be due to coincidence.

"You've been following me, haven't you?"

Christian was as amused by her question as he was by the astonished arch of her well-shaped brows. "I wondered how long it would take you to realize that. When I was five, my father taught me to track deer through the forest. Tracking someone as colorful as you is no challenge at all."

"And you are **obviously** a man who relishes a challenge, aren't you?"

"Obviously." **What** Christian would have liked to have relished was her, **but** he remained where he stood. "At the party last night, **one** of the British officers followed you like a shadow. **Are you** fond of him?"

Without conscious thought, Liana made a face. "His manners aren't **nearly as** elegant as his looks," she replied. "He actually **believed** threatening to have me hanged for treason would impress me favorably."

As appalled as she had been, Christian inched forward. "Your family is known for its loyalty to King George. Why would the captain suspect you of treason?"

"It's merely the way he thinks. He's been trained for war, and when people hear Boston Harbor has been closed, he may very well have the opportunity to fight in one."

Christian was adept at hiding his emotions and did not let his amazement at her shocking announcement show. "When is this to happen?"

"Soon, but please, you mustn't quote me. Wait, and I'm sure you can read about it in the *Virginia Gazette.*"

Christian had hoped only for another entertaining interlude with Liana, but the fact that she was privy to such a damning secret was an unexpected bonus. "I am serious now, Liana, so tell me the absolute truth. Where do your sympathies lie, with the Crown, or with those who have no use for a tyrant and long to see the colonies free?"

Clad in golden buckskins that blended well with the marsh grass, Christian embodied the freedom Liana knew many colonists craved. The wording of his question made it plain where he stood, but while she was flattered he would ask for her opinion in such a vital matter, she doubted the wisdom of revealing it. "My father speaks for our family," she replied instead.

"He welcomes the closing of Boston Harbor then?"

"No, certainly not. He regards it as a disastrous error on the king's part."

"As well he should," Christian agreed. "I'm pleased to learn his loyalty to King George hasn't entirely clouded his judgment. You ought to cultivate the captain's affections, Liana. He might confide all manner of useful information and you can rest assured I will put it to good use."

"Are you suggesting that I spy for you?"

Christian took another step, closing the distance between them. "No, of course not. Spying would be treason. I'm merely asking you to encourage the captain to confide in you. If you then choose to confide in me, it's the captain who'll be at fault for being indiscreet, not you."

Perhaps it was her initial dismay at encountering him, but Liana knew she ought to go home immediately. Not only was he an unsettling individual, but the subject of their conversation was making her far too uncomfortable. "I've been forbidden to speak with you, threatened with banishment to England, and with good reason, it seems. If you're recruiting spies, then you're obviously plotting rebellion and you ought to be worried about what I will tell Captain O'Keefe, not about what I might pass on to you from him."

Before Christian could respond, they heard Ian calling Liana's name. He was down by the river, but should he follow her footprints into the grass, he would be upon them in an instant. "Get down," Christian whispered, and reaching for Liana's hands, he pulled her down beside him and turned so that the gold of his buckskins would hide her rose-colored gown. "Hush." He laid his fingertips on her lips, but very lightly, and caressed her cheek before again taking her hand.

Her heart pounding a furious rhythm, Liana held her breath. Ian Scott was not given to idle threats, and should he find her with Christian she knew her trunk would be packed before nightfall. She closed her eyes and strained

to listen, but her father's next call was faint. He was moving
further away. Still, she did not trust herself to breathe
deeply until he could no longer be heard.

"I must go," she insisted.

"Not yet." Holding her in a confining embrace, Christian kissed Liana with a magical sweetness that left her
clinging to him when he at last released her. He gazed
into her eyes and smiled at the confusion he saw reflected
in their emerald depths. "You must kiss me this time," he
urged.

Surrounded by a jungle of tall grass and wrapped in an
Indian's arms, Liana felt very small, but not at all weak.
"No," she argued. "I must go."

"Kiss me, or I'll tell everyone what you said about Boston
Harbor."

"Why would you wish to make trouble for me?" Liana
asked without thinking, but as she watched the cocky grin
spread across his lips, she knew. "You despise me, don't
you? You want to harm me as badly as you want to harm
my father, and—"

Christian had heard enough silliness and silenced her
ramblings with what had become his favorite method. He
slipped his hand around her neck to hold her still and
kissed her with the same brutal abandon he had shown
the first time he had marked her with his mouth. He felt
her squirm and her fists strike his chest, but that was such
a slight annoyance he did not relent until he was thoroughly satisfied. He grabbed her shoulders as he drew away
slightly.

"Why don't you scream for your father? Do you want to
visit England even less than you want to kiss me?"

"Beast!"

"I know you can do better than that, sister dear."

"I am not your sister!" Liana insisted in a frantic hiss.

Christian watched the tears welling up in her eyes and
felt only pride. "Would you rather call me husband?"

In an afternoon rife with danger, Liana could not even imagine what had possessed him to ask such an outrageous question. She swept the delicious bronze of his skin with an anxious glance before daring to meet his heated gaze. It would have been so easy to become lost in him, but she refused to give him that satisfaction and pushed against his broad chest.

"My father would rather see me dead than married to you. Now let me go before you get us into more trouble than the whole Barclay clan can handle."

Rather than release her, Christian yanked her close. "It's not your father I'm asking. It's you."

Frightened, Liana struggled to break free. She promised herself that she would not leave her house for a week, but first she had to get there. Desperate, she bent down and bit his hand hard enough to draw blood.

With an angry shove, he pushed her down into the grass. "I'm going to make you very sorry for that, sister, but it will have to wait until the next time we meet."

Holding his aching hand against his chest, he stepped over her and strode off toward the fields but Liana was too shaken to move for several minutes. "How could a man who moves with the force of a hurricane have been named Christian?" she wondered aloud. She felt as though she had survived a terrible storm and rose shakily to her feet. She would not have to be forbidden to see Christian when he made each of their meetings much worse punishment than her father could devise.

Trying to recapture the composure that continually eluded her in Christian's presence, Liana made her way back to the river, but as she stepped out of the thick stand of marsh grass, she saw her father again coming up the path. She swallowed hard, and wondered if London weren't especially nice in the spring.

"Liana, where in God's name have you been?" Ian shouted.

With a sudden inspiration, Liana pulled the cap from her pocket. "This blew away the other day as I was walking here, and because it's one of my favorites I went searching for it. Found it, too."

"Proper young ladies do not wade through the marsh grass, Liana. I swear, there are times when I doubt you will ever grow up. Now, hurry along. Captain O'Keefe has come to call and it was most embarrassing when you were nowhere to be found."

"I'm sorry, Father." Liana moved ahead of him and hoped she could control the tremor in her hands before she reached the house. "Did you mention what I'd told you about Boston Harbor?"

"No, I most certainly did not and if Sean is so stupid as to reveal other equally inappropriate information, please keep it to yourself. I want no part in whatever intrigues he may enjoy."

As they neared the house, Liana had the disturbing sensation that they were being watched. She dared not look around and make her father suspicious, but she could feel a creepy tingling down her spine and knew Christian might have started out in the direction of his home, but he could have doubled back. The dogwoods were beginning to blossom, surrounding the house with idyllic beauty, but Liana failed to appreciate it. Instead, she saw only a convenient screen for a wily Indian brave. Determined to discourage him, she greeted Sean with a delighted smile.

"Captain, how good of you to call," she said loud enough for her voice to carry to the flowering trees. As usual, in his bright red coat, white breeches, and black boots, Sean looked absolutely magnificent. "We had such a wonderful time last night, didn't we?" She took his arm as they entered the house and braced herself for what she feared would be another distressing conversation, but after what she had endured with Christian, boredom was most welcome. It wasn't until she was safe inside that she dared

glance out a window. Certain she had seen a flash of buckskin, she wondered just how close Christian would dare to
come.

His father may have taught him to track deer, but he
had proven himself adept with human prey, too. She shiv-
ered as she imagined how he might wish to repay her for
biting him. She swung back toward Sean, but could not
find any comfort in using him for refuge. They walked
into the parlor and sat down together, but having one too
many secrets of her own, she made no effort to encourage
him to disclose anything more.

She simply wasn't cut out to be a spy, but when Sean
began to brag about how quickly the people of Boston
would be subdued, and order restored to Massachusetts,
she wondered if it weren't already too late to make such
a cautious choice. She had grown up considering herself
to be as English as her father, but sitting there with Sean,
she felt wholly American. Jarred to her very soul by that
realization, she wondered what would become of her and
her beloved Virginia when King George discovered just
how deep the seeds of rebellion had already been sown.

Four

Monday morning, Liana awakened with a slow stretch. A lingering trace of an amusing dream brought a lazy smile to her lips. Her room had a splendid view of the James River on the east, but the rose-tinted walls didn't take on the sun's golden glow until late afternoon. The bedroom's seductive blush was a feminine delight, but lacking the encouraging brightness that invaded her brother's rooms at dawn, Liana often found it difficult to begin a new day.

She rolled onto her back and pushed up her nightgown's lace-trimmed sleeves. Completely relaxed, she tried to recall if she had anything of any particular importance to accomplish that day. Finished with her formal education, she now took on only the studies which truly interested her. She loved to read, and had several books which she had left at midpoint calling for her attention. There were also tunes she ought to practice on the harpsichord, but nothing else came to mind.

Her mother was always busy working on a piece of embroidery, but Liana usually found that once they began a conversation, her project would lay idle in her lap. It wasn't that she couldn't manage two tasks at one time, but simply that once she began pursuing a diverting topic, she needed her hands to gesture. She used them now to cover a wide yawn, and fully awake, sat up. She shook her hair from her eyes, and noticing an intriguing bit of color on her snowy white spread, she leaned over to pick it up.

The instant her fingers brushed the soft buckskin pouch, she knew who had left it. Overcome with fright and shame, she clutched it to her breast and hurriedly left her bed. A quick search of the room reassured her she was alone, but her heart was still pounding wildly as she sat back down on the edge of her four-poster.

The fringed pouch was of a size a man might hang from his belt. The front was adorned with intricate beadwork while the back had been left plain. Liana knew only one man who wore buckskins, and the fact that Christian had had the audacity to sneak into her bedroom to leave such a distinctive token absolutely terrified her.

She had told him she had been threatened with a prompt voyage to England for merely speaking with him. Had he hoped her mother would come into her room to wake her that morning, find the pouch before she had a chance to hide it, and immediately send her away? What if she had bitten him? She certainly didn't deserve to be banished from her home and she could not think of anything else he could have hoped to accomplish by leaving such an incriminating item on her bed.

She drew in a ragged breath and fought to think clearly rather than sink further into panic. Because she had found the pouch, she had the option of disposing of it or handing it over to her parents herself as proof of Christian's unwanted attentions. However, thoughtful consideration convinced her that confiding in her parents would only compound her problems.

She never locked her door, never even thought of it because she lived in a household where each individual's privacy was respected. No one entered another's room without knocking politely and waiting for a response. The Barclays obviously didn't adhere to any such thoughtful conventions.

She could not help but wonder how long Christian had stood by her bed. Had he dared remain only a few minutes, or had he tarried there, silently observing her? That he had simply entered her bedroom was a chilling thought. That he might have stayed as long as he pleased was completely unnerving.

Liana fingered the pouch nervously, finally noticing it contained something; almost afraid, she raised the beaded flap. Nestled inside was a tightly folded piece of paper. Too curious not to read the message, she removed it and smoothed out the creases. Christian had never been at a loss for words with her, but he had wasted none here.

He had written her name, asked her to meet him at the river at four that afternoon, and added his signature. The brief letter was penned in bold strokes, the handwriting as masculine as she would have expected. The ink was thick and black, the paper an expensive cream-colored vellum, but it was a command rather than an invitation.

"Insufferable peacock!" she exclaimed. She wasn't his woman to order this way and that. Determined to prove it, she swore she would be anywhere that afternoon other than the bank of the James River. Infuriated with Christian now, she left her bed for the second time, yanked open the dresser drawer where she kept her lingerie, and buried the handsome pouch in a back corner. Slamming the drawer shut gave her such an incredible burst of satisfaction that she instantly resolved to do far more damage than a single bite should he dare to come near her again.

The spring weather was glorious, and Liana spent the morning helping her mother in their flower garden. After the midday meal, she couldn't summon the necessary attention to practice her music or read classical literature, so she chose to complete her perusal of a beautifully illustrated book on butterflies. Her mind proved as erratic as the insect's flight; concentration was impossible. Curled up on the window seat in the sitting room, her attention was so frequently drawn to the river that she silently cursed the young man she had met there.

Liana's restlessness did not go unnoticed. Robin was content to do needlework by the hour, but sensed the afternoon was becoming uncomfortably long for her daughter. Neither of them napped unless there was a party in the evening, and that night they would remain at home.

"Why don't you go out for a walk, dear?" Robin suggested. "I've had quite enough fresh air for the day, but you needn't stay in to keep me company. While I usually envy you your energy, it's most distracting when you're unable to sit still."

Reluctantly, Liana closed her book. All day she had struggled unsuccessfully to suppress thoughts of Christian, and now with four o'clock drawing near, she feared the only way to banish the scoundrel from her life was to confront him. Gathering her courage, she rose and set her book aside.

"Yes, I think I will go out for a while, but I won't be long."

"I hope you weren't waiting for a young man to call, as I'd so hate to see you disappointed."

Certain she had more than enough trouble with an ardent captain she couldn't seem to discourage and an Indian brave who continually exceeded the limits of good manners, Liana laughed softly. "I'd not expected anyone to come by this afternoon. Amanda's actively seeking a husband, but I'm not."

Robin knotted her thread and snipped it. "Indifference is a surprisingly effective aphrodisiac, my darling. Men love to do the pursuing, you see, and the less interested you seem, the harder they will strive to impress you."

Puzzled by her mother's advice, Liana approached her.

"What do you suggest I do then, chase them away with abundant charm?"

Robin paused to smile at her lovely daughter before re-threading her needle. "Be yourself and follow your heart. When you meet the right young man, you'll know how to behave."

Having learned the details of her father's first marriage, Liana didn't torture her mother with questions about it, but she couldn't help but be curious as to when her mother had fallen in love. She hoped it had been after her father had lost Melissa, rather than before. Resting her hand on the back of the settee, she leaned down to kiss her mother's cheek, and with renewed resolve left the house to tell Christian precisely what she thought of him for sneaking into her bedroom like a thief.

Hidden in the tall grass, Christian watched Liana rush toward him along the path, but the ferocity of her expression warned him her mood was anything but good. No coward, he stepped out to meet her with a courtly bow. "Good afternoon, Miss Scott. I hope you've had a pleasant day."

Even knowing Christian would be there, Liana was still startled by his remarkably handsome appearance. In buckskins or fine silks, he was easily the most attractive man she had ever met. Distracted, she had to remind herself that by his unprincipled actions, he had proved his heart was every bit as black as her father claimed. "We mustn't risk being seen talking out here in the open," she replied crossly.

Christian gestured broadly to hold back the marsh grass, and nodded for her to precede him on the trail they were rapidly creating with their frequent secret meetings. He followed her to the trampled spot where they had hidden from her father the previous afternoon. When she turned to face him, the fury in her gaze was still burning brightly.

"You're not pleased I came to your room," he stated before she could accuse him of trespassing.

"Wouldn't you be equally outraged had I invaded the privacy of your bedroom?"

Unable to hide his delight at that possibility, Christian responded with a ready grin. "Only if you hadn't awakened me."

"Is there no end to your conceit?" Disgusted by his mocking gaze, Liana continued in the same fiery tone. "Had my father found you sneaking through our home, he would have shot you dead."

Christian shook his head, and the afternoon sun lent his ebony hair a burnished glow. "There's no danger of him ever hearing me. If you like, I'll call on you every night just to prove it."

Liana rested her hands on her hips. "Don't you dare. You may find torturing my family amusing, but it's a dangerous sport even if you won't admit it. You appear to be passably intelligent. Surely you can find more appropriate diversions."

She was dressed in a pale lavender gown trimmed in purple ribbon, but her deceptively sweet appearance didn't match her speech. Christian attempted to focus his attention on her eyes rather than the lush fullness of her bosom. "Only 'passably intelligent?' " he asked.

Liana looked away, suddenly realized she was trapped by the surrounding grass, and with a furious step pressed on until she reached the open expanse of tobacco fields. She then had to yank her cap back into place, but she didn't miss a beat of her argument. "You think so highly of yourself you certainly don't need any compliments from me," she declared.

Christian spoke with deliberate calm. "Perhaps not, but I would like to hear them all the same."

"Then you ought to try behaving like a gentleman for a change."

Christian moved closer. "Why? Do you kiss your fine captain the way you kiss me?"

"I told you he threatened me, so he's no gentleman either, and you're the one who's kissed me," Liana cried, "not the other way around!"

Christian's glance strayed to her heaving bosom, and he decided taunting her provided enormous rewards. "I've decided to forgive you for biting me," he announced suddenly. "You shouldn't have done it, but you did me no real harm."

"How generous of you," Liana scoffed. "But I'll make no bargains with you this time, and I won't forgive you for spying on me, or breaking into my home."

Thoroughly enjoying himself, Christian's stance was relaxed. "The door was unlocked, so I can't be accused of breaking in."

Liana shook her finger at him. "You can be accused of more misdeeds than I have time to list, Mr. Hunter. The only reason I came here today was to demand that you stay away from my family and me. Don't come any closer to our home than this, or you'll put yourself in grave danger."

Christian cocked a brow. "You told your father I was in your room?"

Exasperated with him for being obtuse, Liana continued in a scolding tone. "No, of course not, or you'd most likely be in bed with several broken bones."

Christian feigned immense distress. "That's no way for a man to treat his firstborn son."

"You are no more my father's son than you are my brother! This conversation has become too tiresome to continue. I'm going home." Intending to go around him, Liana took a step toward the tall grass, but Christian reached out to stop her.

"Wait, we haven't discussed why I asked you to meet me."

"You didn't ask. You sent a command."

"Still, you came." Christian took great pride in the fact that she had obeyed. "I agree that visiting your room is too dangerous for us both. We need to decide upon a better method to signal each other when we wish to meet. I thought we could tie a ribbon to the marsh grass at the beginning of our trail whenever one of us wants to speak to the other. Then we would know to come here that afternoon."

Astonished, Liana's mouth fell agape, and Christian playfully snapped his fingers beneath her chin to close it. "How can you possibly imagine that I'd want to summon you? The idea is absolutely preposterous, and I refuse to even consider it."

"You came to meet me today," Christian pointed out slyly.

"Only to tell you to stay away, which was obviously a mistake."

"Was it?" They were standing very close, and when Liana shifted her gaze from his eyes to his lips, he needed no further invitation. He caught himself before he took it too far, but it had not been easy when her lips were so soft, her taste luscious, and the subtle fragrance of her perfume enchanting. He could have kissed her for hours, and still not had enough, but he would never have admitted his growing weakness for her and forced himself to concentrate on the matter at hand.

"I want you to leave pastel ribbons," he explained. "Tie them loosely so anyone who sees one will think it's slipped from your hair and caught on the grass. I'll leave only black ribbons. Should we miss each other somehow, keep coming here each afternoon at four until we meet."

His voice was softly reassuring, his plan clearly thought out before he had shared it with her, and despite her best effort to spit on his moccasins and flee, Liana found herself replying with a distracted nod. God help her, had she lost her senses completely? She had been forbidden to see him, and she understood why, but as maddening as he was, she could not seem to stay away.

"Do you have any questions?" he asked.

His arms were looped around her waist, and yet she didn't feel confined. "Only one. Why were you named Christian?"

He laughed, and fearful they would be discovered, Liana covered his mouth with her hand. He caught it, and placed a kiss in her palm. "My stepmother lost her whole family in an Indian massacre in Maine. She had been sent to a neighboring farm on an errand and came home to find her parents, two little sisters, and a baby brother dead. The little boy's name was Christian, and because he had only a few weeks of life, she gave me his name so that he might live again."

Liana had not known what she had expected, but his story was so very sad she was deeply touched. "I don't understand how your stepmother could have wed an Indian," she replied in a choked whisper.

Christian sighed softly, as though he feared she might never understand. "She loved my father, and unlike Melissa, she saw him as a man rather than a savage and did not blame him for other Indians' evil deeds."

He inclined his head, and anticipating his next kiss, Liana relaxed against him. She had accused him yesterday of despising her, but if this was the way hatred tasted, then it was glorious. He broke away all too soon, and taking her hand, led the way through the marsh grass to the river.

"Tie a ribbon right here whenever you need me, and I'll come," he promised.

Liana watched in mystified silence as he disappeared into the grass, his buckskins visible only for an instant, and then lost among the shadows. She turned toward the river, and forced herself not to cry out that she needed him now. A painful knot filled her throat and she blinked away the tears she dared not shed.

Torn between her parents' wise counsel and the dangerous longings of her heart, it was impossible for Liana not to think of Melissa Barclay. She knew Melissa must have made a series of desperately wrong choices, or she would not have wed one man and died giving birth to another's child. Liana swore she would not repeat the same tragic error.

Just because Sean O'Keefe's kiss didn't thrill her clear to her soul as Christian's did, didn't mean that there wasn't another man, and a proper gentleman, who wouldn't prove to be equally enticing. "I'll keep telling myself that," Liana murmured as she started toward home. "There's another man who'll be both dashing and suitable. I'll just wait for him to find me, and then everything will be as wonderful as it should be."

She repeated that fervent desire all the way home, but by the time she arrived, Christian's haunting kiss hadn't even begun to fade from her mind.

That night, Christian sat slouched in a wing chair opposite his Uncle Byron's desk, his left leg carelessly hooked over the arm. When there were women present, he had been well-trained to assume more appropriate postures, but alone in the study, the men of the family could behave as they wished. Beau was pacing up and down beside him, and Hunter was at the window peering out at the night. The Indian glanced over his shoulder, caught Christian's eye, and shook his head.

Seated behind his desk, Byron was sipping his second glass of brandy, but its intoxicating warmth had done little to mellow his mood. "The harbor's to be closed June first. We're outraged here in Virginia. Think how badly the people of Boston must be reacting."

"We've all been betrayed," Beau exclaimed. "Either we're Englishmen or we're not. From the despicable way King George is treating us, it's clear he holds little regard for us as subjects."

"I don't need a king to tell me who I am," Hunter swore softly.

"Neither do I," Byron agreed, "and I'm tired of the increasingly ludicrous decisions being foisted on us by a Parliament which demands our loyalty but repays us with a contemptuous disregard for our rights."

Beau slapped a tattered pamphlet on his father's desk. "Samuel Adams will write a whole new round of protests over this."

"Words," Hunter sneered, "aren't deeds."

Christian was in full agreement with the seething discontent rife in the colonies, but he tended toward his father's detached cynicism rather than his cousin and uncle's vocal dissent. He was not merely waiting for the inevitable revolution to begin, he was eagerly anticipating it. "I think we ought to give Sam Adams some help."

"Don't you think Patrick Henry's speeches do that?" Byron asked.

"Yes," Christian conceded, "but he only has a forum when the House of Burgesses is in session. We could distribute propaganda of our own whenever the need arose."

"Surely it has now," Beau declared.

Hunter turned to face his companions. "This is your uncle's house, Christian. Every action brings a consequence, and you must not leave him open to retaliation if you are the one urging Virginians to defy the king."

Suddenly feeling at a disadvantage, Christian left his chair. His father's equal in height, he faced him squarely. "When have you ever been cautious?"

Hunter's dark eyes narrowed slightly, and for a brief instant, he looked as though he might give his son the cuffing he deserved, but instead he moved toward the door.

"I can't deny the truth of your words," he replied. "If I had ever been cautious, you'd not be alive. Don't repeat my mistakes."

Christian waited until his father had closed the door to speak. "You've been open in your disgust with the king's actions for so long, uncle, I didn't think my suggestion would offend you."

Byron gestured toward the crystal brandy decanter, but Christian shook his head. "I'm not offended—far from it—but Hunter's right. There will be enormous sympathy for Boston's plight, and if it's carefully managed, the benefits could be great for all the colonies. There's also a tremendous risk involved. There are many residents of Williamsburg who are loyal to King George. At the slightest provocation, they'd accuse me of sedition, and applaud if I were sent to England for trial."

Christian hadn't even admitted he had spoken privately with Liana Scott, so he could scarcely convey her warning that the British were already suspicious of their family. "It's true we might have been more discreet in the past, but if the pamphlets aren't signed, it will be impossible to attribute them to us. We're not alone here in our opposition to Parliament's endless attempts to extort money from us without giving us any say in the matter."

Byron glanced from his blond son's fiercely determined frown to his dark-eyed nephew's sly smile and nodded. "All right, work up a sample pamphlet. Then if I believe your ideas are worth sharing, we'll weigh the risk of publishing it. I just hired a new man, David Slauson, who's worked for a printer. I'll speak with him about the feasibility of owning and operating our own small printing press."

"Can he be trusted?" Beau asked.

"He's almost painfully sincere, and he's very taken with Johanna, so I'm inclined to trust him."

"Johanna's too good for the hired hands," Christian complained. "I think I'd better speak with the man."

Beau raised his hand. "That's your father's right, Chris, not yours, so talk with David if you like, but don't intimidate him. I've already warned Johanna, not to take any interest in him because I doubt he'll be with us long, but while he is here, we might as well use what skills he has. Now that's enough for tonight. I miss my wife, and don't want to take any further risk of her forgetting me."

"As if Aunt Arielle ever could." Christian stepped back to allow his uncle to pass, but he intended to remain in the study with Beau.

Byron paused at the door. "I wish both of you would encourage your friends to take an interest in Johanna. She's lovely, and while she is shy, she would still enjoy entertaining callers."

As soon as his uncle left, Christian returned to his chair and again struck a casual pose. "What shall we do first, cousin, plot rebellion or search for suitors for my sister? Either task will surely provide a challenge."

Beau slipped into his father's chair behind the desk and reached for pen and paper. Embarrassed, he did not know quite how to respond to his father's suggestion. "He's right. Johanna is lovely."

"Yes, she is, but she's also half Indian, which not many people outside our family see as an advantage." Perplexed, Christian frowned darkly. "Neither Falcon nor I cares what others think, but Johanna is a delicate creature who deserves someone who'd adore her. Unfortunately, I can't think of a single candidate among the loud lot we call friends, can you?"

On a sudden impulse, Beau spoke up. "I'd marry her myself if she'd have me."

While it was true first cousins sometimes married, Christian was shocked by Beau's announcement. "Do you love her?"

Flustered, Beau shrugged. "Well, of course, I love her."

"Yes, I know, but as a cousin. Marriage requires another kind of love."

Mystified, Beau leaned forward. "Are there different kinds?"

They had grown up in the same household, but there were times, like now, when the sixteen months separating them seemed more like a decade. Christian sighed wearily. "The love between cousins is a warm, natural bond, but a marriage without passion would be very dull indeed."

Liana Scott came instantly to Beau's mind, and he nodded with an understanding tinged with sorrow. She certainly inspired the most passionate of thoughts, but she had treated him so coolly at Amanda Tuttle's party he knew she had absolutely no interest in him. It was probably a good thing, too, considering what their families thought of each other.

"For a start, let's insist that Johanna comes with us to parties from now on," Beau suggested. "I doubt many men even know she exists, and once they meet her, they'll surely be interested. After all, she is a Barclay, and that counts for a great deal in Williamsburg. Now give me some help here on this pamphlet. How shall we begin?"

"How about a drawing of a swine wearing a crown?"

"Be serious, Chris!"

"I am being serious." Christian settled deeper into the comfortable chair. "The king's a greedy swine who's using the colonies as a trough. I say it's time we kicked him out."

Beau stared at him a long moment. "I was hoping for a more compelling argument, not merely insults."

"What do you want to do, describe the king's actions as merely misguided or shortsighted rather than the arrogant blunderings of a tyrant?"

Beau tapped the end of the pen on the desk. "Perhaps we ought to prepare two versions. I'll take a calm, reasoned approach, and yours can be as inflammatory as you wish.

We'll let my father be the editor—and he can decide which is the best. After all, he may not approve of either and insist upon writing his own."

"Not after reading my suggestions, he won't," Christian boasted proudly. He rose and stretched. "I'm going out for a walk."

"Well, I intend to stay here and work. Shall we give ourselves until the end of the week to compose our samples?"

"Take as long as you like—mine will be ready tomorrow." Actually looking forward to venting his hatred for the king, Christian left the house whistling. His first stop was the cabins where the field hands worked. Most were seated around a fire, trading insults and boasts in much the same fashion he and his cousin had been. It wasn't difficult to spot David Slauson, as his was the only face Christian didn't immediately recognize.

David was seated slightly apart from the others, attempting to read by the light of a battered lantern. From what Christian could overhear without intruding, David was taking considerable teasing from the men, who probably couldn't read had they wanted to. He was ignoring their taunts and turning the pages with a steady hand. Clearly more suited to being a printer's assistant than raising tobacco, Christian didn't stop to question him. He took it as a good omen that a man who knew something about printing had arrived just when they had a need for him.

Completely at home in the night, Christian angled down toward the river, and not really caring where he walked, he was startled to look up and find Liana's house in the distance. He hadn't meant to visit her again so soon, but his feet had taken him there anyway. He laughed to himself and squatted down to watch a while.

He caught the faint strains of a melody from a harpsichord and wondered if Liana were the one playing. He could easily imagine her slender fingers moving over the keys and he longed to feel the warmth of her palms against his chest. He wondered when the next formal party was, and whether he might possibly be invited. A devilish plan brought a smile to his lips and he turned for home, knowing his sudden concern for his sister would be believed. But while he hoped Johanna would enjoy the parties they encouraged her to attend, if Liana were present, he knew he most certainly would.

Five

Christian followed his mother and aunt out into the herb garden after breakfast Tuesday morning. He had described Alanna to Liana as his stepmother, but because she was the only mother he had ever known, he never thought of her as such. "Mother," he called softly, "I need to speak with you about Johanna. This also concerns Dominique, Aunt Arielle," he added.

Intent upon gathering herbs for the remedies Arielle prescribed for the household, Alanna was carrying a basket and shears. Enormously proud of her eldest son, she regarded him with a delighted smile. A slender beauty in her late thirties, her golden blond hair was tucked neatly under her cap and her green eyes sparkled with curiosity. "I sincerely hope you're not having such a serious disagreement with your sister and cousin that it requires our mediation," she replied.

Equally curious, Arielle moved close. An Acadian who had been wed to Byron Barclay for nearly nineteen years, she had learned English as a child in addition to her native French. In her early forties, her hair was as blond as her lively daughter's, and her figure equally alluring. Her eyes were blue and glowed with intelligence and wit. "Please, Christian, don't tease us. Whatever the problem, your mother and I will endeavor to solve it."

Now that he had their attention, Christian took care to

state his case clearly. Johanna was too sweet a young woman to have ever caused either of her brothers a moment's trouble, but his cousin, Dominique, was a vixen who had always delighted in pestering her siblings and cousins. The two young women were such opposites in temperament it was difficult for him to include them in a single thought, but he gave it his best effort.

"Johanna complained of being too shy to attend the Tuttles' party with Beau and me, while Dominique wasn't allowed to go because she's just sixteen. With Dominique along for support, I believe Johanna would have had as good a time as everyone else. There will be a great many more parties this spring and summer. I'd like you to encourage Johanna to attend, Mother, and will you permit Dominique to go with us, Aunt Arielle?"

Disappointed in his choice of topic, Alanna's shoulders sagged slightly and she gripped the basket handle more tightly. "Until Melissa forced me, I didn't attend parties myself when I was young. I would hate to make Johanna go where she doesn't feel comfortable. It would be torture for her, Chris."

"But if she never meets anyone, how is she to find a husband?"

Alanna exchanged a startled glance with Arielle before responding. "I had no idea you were so concerned about your sister's future. Have you spoken to your father about this?"

"No, it was something Uncle Byron said which got me thinking. Johanna may prefer solitude, but perhaps we're making a mistake in indulging her. Our home is as safe as a cocoon, but if she never leaves to experience what little taste of the world Williamsburg society offers, she could easily suffocate in the very security she craves. Years from now, I don't want her to hate us for sheltering her if it costs her the chance to be loved and marry."

"Such a serious topic deserves our complete attention,"

Arielle suggested. "Come, let's sit down while we talk." She gestured toward the adjacent bench where she often sat to sort herbs into the small bunches she dried for her cures. When Alanna and Christian were seated beside her, she summed up the problem succinctly. "Johanna is much too reserved to encourage a young man's attentions while my darling, Dominique, was born flirting. Each needs to learn from the other ways to enhance her chances of being accepted by the fine families here."

"That's certainly true," Alanna agreed, "but I never expected to marry and have children." She reached out to take Christian's hand. "Until you were born and needed so much more than an aunt." She hesitated, then broke into a beguiling smile. "It was your father who changed my mind about marriage, and we've been blessed in so many ways. Your mother was the expert on romance, and I wish she were here to advise us. Frankly, I've always believed love can't be forced. It comes on its own terms, and I've just assumed Johanna would fall in love one day."

"With whom?" Christian didn't wait for a reply. "A British soldier the king might quarter here to suppress the rebellion his every oppressive action incites?"

Frightened by such a dire prediction, Alanna tightened her grip on his hand. "Do you honestly believe it will come to that?"

Unmoved by her anxious expression, Christian spoke what he saw as the truth. "I certainly hope so. The colonies have outgrown any need for a king, but he's unlikely to let us go without a fight. I think we ought to find husbands for Johanna and Dominique now, before the current unrest explodes into war and no personal plans of any kind can be made."

"Oh, dear." Alanna looked ready to cry. "Well, the threat of war between England and France didn't keep you and Byron apart, Arielle, but what do you believe is best for our daughters?"

Arielle looked past Alanna to Christian. He was a very confident young man, and she found it easy to confide in him. Her voice was softly accented with French, and she had never felt welcome in Williamsburg. "Perhaps our worries are premature. We did not expect the Tuttles' invitation. What if there aren't any others?"

"I've already thought of that," Christian assured her. "Beau and I will start spending more time in town strengthening what friendships we have, and on Sundays, we'll make a point of being more sociable after church. We'll receive invitations aplenty if we make it known we'd welcome them, and then we'll host parties of our own."

Alanna sat back against the bench. "Dominique is such a charming girl—she's sure to draw attention from men. Johanna is not only shy, though, she's also half Seneca. I couldn't bear it if we insisted she attend a party and she were insulted or ignored."

"She won't be," Christian announced firmly. "Beau will be her escort and I'll be Dominique's, so neither will ever be without a partner. I wouldn't suggest this if I didn't believe the need was urgent. We're content here with each other and have such little need for anyone else that we've neglected to cultivate as many friends as we should have. With the present discontent, we dare not give anyone a reason to denounce us."

Having survived the heartless expulsion from Acadia, Arielle had even more contempt for King George III than the rest of the Barclays. "I know firsthand how little the king's word means," she declared. "Byron has made no secret of his disgust with Parliament, and if the situation worsens, we'll provide a convenient target for the Loyalists' retaliation. I think we better make plans to start entertaining at once."

Alanna let out an anguished moan. "Our family celebrations overwhelm me. I'm not certain I can be a charming hostess to people I barely know."

"We'll all help you," Christian insisted. "Is it agreed then? Johanna and Dominique will accompany Beau and me whenever there's a party?"

Alanna gestured helplessly. "They'll need new party clothes."

Arielle stood and picked up the basket. "Let's hurry and gather the herbs—then we can take the girls into town to the dressmaker's. I'm so glad you thought of this, Christian. Not being a native of Williamsburg, I fear I've not given nearly enough thought to our daughters' acceptance here."

Christian had to hide his smile as he left his mother and aunt, but he was inordinately pleased they had accepted his suggestion for introducing Johanna and Dominique to eligible young men. It not only provided him with a much-needed excuse to see more of Liana Scott, there was also an excellent chance the two young women would meet the men they would marry. He just hoped they had sense enough to select men whose political views matched their family's rather than Loyalists he might later have to fight.

After dinner Friday evening, Byron again met with Hunter, Beau, and Christian in his study. He read through Beau's sample pamphlet first and found it to be a scholarly summation of the grievances long circulating in the colonies. Beau had described how widespread protest had resulted in the oppressive Stamp Act of 1765 being overturned. He had then discussed the Townshend Acts of 1767, which had imposed import duties, and how after violent opposition all provisions had been repealed in 1770 with the single exception of the duty on tea. He proclaimed the Boston Tea Party an act of heroism and urged continued defiance of Parliament's edicts in support of the good citizens of Massachusetts.

"This is very good, Beau," Byron complimented sincerely. "You've an accurate presentation of facts as well as a strong argument for continued protests. Now show me what you've done, Christian."

Christian handed over his work and Byron could not help but laugh at the cleverly drawn cartoon showing a grossly swollen crowned boar rooting through a trough in the shape of the thirteen colonies. He laughed so hard, tears came to his eyes. He needed a moment to compose himself before he read the accompanying text, but he then found Christian's pamphlet not the gentlemanly tract Beau had produced, but inflammatory throughout.

"Avaricious swine, penurious pig, insatiable hog," Byron read and pounded on his desktop, he was so amused. "I had no idea you had such a gift for words, Christian. This is a masterpiece and your cartoon is superb."

Christian glanced over at Beau, who looked anything but pleased. "Are you saying I've won the contest, uncle?"

Byron leaned back in his chair. "I didn't know you two were having one, but yes, yours is the better of the two for what we had in mind. Not that yours isn't well done, Beau. It is, but we've no idea how long we might be able to distribute our views, and if it's only once, then we ought to do our damnedest to do the most damage. Ridicule is a powerful weapon, and Lord knows, King George III deserves every bit we can heap on him."

"I didn't realize abusive humor was what was required," Beau complained.

Hunter moved to the desk and picked up his son's work. He read through it quickly and while he didn't break into laughter as Byron had, his smile was unusually wide. "This ought to outrage the Loyalists, but how can you be certain they won't trace it to us?"

Christian had a ready answer. "Beau and I have been into town twice this week. We just listened, and didn't contribute to any of the discussions on the closing of Boston Harbor. We hope to attend more parties like the Tuttles', and we intend to take Johanna and Dominique with us. They ought to have suitors, and it will provide us with the opportunity to assess our neighbors' opinions toward the king.

"I hope we'll soon be able to host a party here. While I don't believe it's necessary to hide our true feelings behind a neutral façade, we can easily appear to be so interested in our own welfare, no one will suspect us of blanketing the town with pamphlets hostile to the king."

"I don't want Johanna involved in your schemes," Hunter instantly decreed.

"Fine, then you find her a husband. Do you want a Seneca brave rather than a white man?"

Hunter responded with a low, derisive snort. "She would be even more out of place among the Seneca than you would."

"There's a party at the Langs' Saturday night, and Mother has already seen to it that Johanna will have a new dress. Are you going to tell her she can't go?" Christian asked.

"Your mother approves of this?"

"Yes, and so does Aunt Arielle. Mother didn't speak to you about it?"

"She will tonight."

"I knew about the party," Byron interjected, "and gave Dominique my permission. Our daughters are of an age to accept callers, Hunter. Even if we would like to keep them here with us forever, they'll want their own families soon."

Hunter nodded, but still appeared distressed. "What about the man who worked for the printer? Have you spoken to him?"

"Not yet, but I asked him to come around tonight. I'll see if he's at the back door."

"If you can do without me, I'd like to go," Hunter said.

"Of course," Byron replied. "I'll let you know what we decide."

Hunter and Byron left the room together, leaving Christian and his cousin to wait alone. "Let's not argue over the pamphlet's content," Christian offered. "Let's just agree to subvert the king's authority at our every opportunity."

Beau nodded grudgingly, but he was still disappointed his father hadn't praised his version as much as Christian's fiery rhetoric. "How are we going to distribute the pamphlets?"

"I'm the better rider, so I'll do it. Besides, if I'm caught, no one will particularly care. You, on the other hand, are the scion of the Barclay family, and need to maintain a more law-abiding image."

Beau was astonished by Christian's low opinion of himself. "You can't doubt that we'd defend you."

"No, of course not, but far more is expected of you than me and we both know it."

Before Beau could argue, his father returned with David Slauson. The unassuming young man was so puzzled by Christian's choice of buckskins that he didn't realize he was Johanna's brother when they were introduced. While offered a chair, he declined and remained standing, his hat clutched tightly in his hands.

Byron returned to his seat behind the desk and briefly explained their needs. "You've worked for a printer, Mr. Slauson. There's some material I'd like to publish. If I provide the funds, could you purchase the necessary equipment—discreetly, of course—and operate a small press here on our plantation?"

David had expected a discussion of his work, and while he had done his best, he had feared a reprimand. To be asked about operating a printing press completely flustered him. "I proofread copy," he explained, "so errors could be corrected before documents received their final printing. I wasn't a printer's devil or apprentice, Mr. Barclay."

"But you did work in the printshop?"

"Well, yes, but I took orders and balanced the accounts. I didn't operate the press."

"But you must have observed its operation from time to time?"

David could not even imagine why he was being quizzed so intensely. "That's true, I did, but there's still a difference between watching a task and knowing how to do it expertly."

Byron sent questioning glances to his son and nephew. Both young men shook their heads in disappointment, but Byron wasn't ready to give up on his plan. "I have a schooner, Mr. Slauson. If I put you on it and sent you down to Charleston, could you make the required purchases for me?"

Overwhelmed by the proposed errand, David looked down at the scuffed toes of his boots. "A press isn't that easy to come by, Mr. Barclay. Most come from Europe. Then there's the type, ink, and paper. It may sound simple to you, but it's really an enormous project."

"Then you better leave in the morning," Byron directed. "I'll see you have a crew."

"You'd trust me to do this, sir? I mean no disrespect, but you barely know me."

Byron cocked his head slightly as he looked David up and down. "If I didn't believe I could trust you, I wouldn't have hired you in the first place. If you must, work a few days in a printshop to make certain you're familiar with the process, and then purchase what you can from their older equipment. I don't need anything elaborate, as we'll just be printing an article or two every now and then. Say you've been hired by an eccentric inventor, or scientist, or make up whatever story you like. I'll give you cash so you'll not have to give any names, and even if someone insists, don't give them mine. Do I make myself understood, Mr. Slauson?"

David was positive he had said he had no idea how to run a printing press, but Byron Barclay had just ordered him to purchase one. He wasn't sure he liked being given so much responsibility, but he had gotten only a fleeting glimpse of Johanna since he had been hired and thought perhaps this special assignment might bring him up to the house more often. Thinking of her, he nodded.

"Yes, sir, I'll do my best for you."

"I knew you would. Be at the dock at dawn and I'll have the money for you. Return as promptly as you possibly can as this matter is urgent."

"Yes, sir. I will."

Christian waited until David had left the study to offer a comment. "I assume you'll send another man you're positive you can trust along with him?"

"Yes, several," Byron replied. "I'd send you two but I don't want anyone to be able to identify you later as the men who purchased printing equipment. This whole operation must be conducted with the utmost secrecy. There was a printer, John Zenger was his name, who edited the *New York Weekly Journal* back in 1753. He published articles criticizing the colonial governor and was arrested for it.

"At his trial, his attorney argued that while what Zenger had done was against the law, he had merely printed the truth. The jury liked that argument and acquitted him. Now as I see it, all we intend to do is print the truth about King George III, but with feelings so mixed here, I'd rather not have to rely on getting a jury who agreed with our version of the truth. You two are clever enough not to brag to your friends about this, aren't you?"

"Most definitely," Beau assured him. "In fact, I doubt we should say anything to the rest of the family. Not that they would ever betray us, but to prevent them from being accused of complicity."

Byron picked up Christian's pamphlet. "Have you shown this to anyone else?"

"No, sir, I've not. My father hadn't seen it until tonight."

Byron slipped it and Beau's sample into his desk drawer and locked it. "Then it's agreed—only the three of us, Hunter, and David Slauson will be told what we're doing. After we publish the first pamphlet, we may be questioned by the authorities because we've been vocal in our complaints over the years, but let's pretend to be flattered and admit nothing."

Christian liked that idea. "I'll make a woodblock of the cartoon, but I'll make certain no one else sees me doing the carving."

Byron rose and ushered his young co-conspirators to the door. "Let's join the ladies, and make them think we've nothing on our minds but the Langs' party."

With Liana already filling a great deal of his mind, Christian found it easy to agree.

Theodore Lang raised tobacco, as did his neighbors. He was a portly gentleman with little to recommend him in the way of looks, but he had such an engaging wit that he and his wife, Lenore, a woman many years his junior, were enormously popular. They had three sons and four daughters, all of whom had inherited their attractive mother's appearance rather than their homely father's charm.

Beau and Christian knew the two eldest Lang sons well enough to win an invitation to the party, but neither wanted his sister to marry into the family. As they rode to the Langs' in their carriage, they used the time to enumerate every stupid thing any of the Lang boys had ever done. Despite the fact that Christian had been involved in many of the incidents, he recounted them as though he had merely been a witness.

"I understand," Dominique said. "The Langs have

wealth, but little in the way of character. You needn't worry that Johanna and I will elope with any of them tonight."

"Elope?" Johanna gasped. "My only worry is that I'll get so confused I won't be able to remember the steps of the dances and everyone will laugh at me."

"No one is going to laugh at my sister," Christian assured her with a confidence the shy girl sorely lacked. When they reached the Langs', he and Beau exchanged a knowing glance over their sisters' heads, and proudly escorted them into the brightly lit home. They had timed their arrival perfectly, and joining the rest of the guests, drew the most attention.

"My God," Morgan Scott leaned down to whisper in his sister's ear. "Who is that?"

Not knowing what to expect, Liana turned to find Christian entering the room with a blonde of such radiant beauty every eye in the room was firmly fixed on her. Stunned to think Christian might kiss this comely blonde with the very same ardor he showed her, Liana's heart fell clear to her satin slippers. She noted the young woman's stylish rose-colored gown and coquettish smile and did not care who she was. The fact that she was with Christian was enough to make Liana despise her. Feeling sick clear through, she hid her anguish behind her fan.

"I've no idea. Why don't you introduce yourself?"

"Come with me," Morgan urged.

"Father doesn't want us to have anything to do with the Barclays," Liana reminded him, "so I'd rather not speak with Christian Hunter for any reason."

She noted Beau's arrival with an attractive brunette, and too distraught to care where he and his cousin had found such lovely young women, she crossed the crowded room to where Amanda Tuttle was standing. Amanda had yet to notice Beau, and quickly began a running commentary on the gowns the other female guests were wearing.

Liana's gown of pale green silk was exquisite, but she

barely listened to Amanda. She had not gone down to the river once since last speaking with Christian for fear she would find a black ribbon and then be faced with the agonizing choice of whether or not to meet him. Now she doubted he had even thought of her if he had such a lovely houseguest. Jealousy was something new to her, and she did not like the wretched uncertainty one bit.

"Oh look, there's Beau," Amanda declared with a delighted squeal. "Who do you suppose that is with him?"

Liana didn't care in the slightest, but turned as though she shared Amanda's keen interest. "I'm sorry, but I don't recognize her."

"Neither do I," Amanda confided. "There's something familiar about her, though." Her eyes narrowed momentarily, and then she relaxed and reached out to touch Liana's arm. "Doesn't Christian have a sister?"

"I've really no idea."

"I do believe I see a resemblance. Did the Barclays really think they could dress a squaw in a fine gown and pass her off as a lady?"

Torn as she was by her feelings for Christian, Liana still did not approve of Amanda's remarks. "If that is Christian's sister, then she is as much white as Indian and I don't believe she can accurately be referred to as a squaw."

Startled, Amanda regarded her friend more closely. "Why are you being so sensitive? She's not related to you."

The conversation had taken such an embarrassing turn, Liana was actually relieved when Sean O'Keefe and James Murray joined them. "Good evening," she greeted them warmly.

"I wasn't certain anyone would be pleased to see us tonight," Sean replied.

"Are you referring to the nonsense about Massachusetts?" Amanda asked. When the officers nodded, she tapped Sean on the chest with her fan. "Liana's father is as loyal to the Crown as mine, so you'll always be welcome in our homes."

Sean's eyes had not left Liana's face. "That's good to hear, Miss Tuttle, but not everyone shares your views."

"Well, those who don't are of little consequence, sir."

"Do you agree, Miss Scott?" Sean asked.

Liana recognized his challenge but she was in no mood to discuss politics, and bit her tongue rather than denounce what she thought could be accurately described as the king's abuses. "This is a splendid party—let's just enjoy it without regard for the endless disputes between the colonies and the king."

Sean responded with a wide grin. "What these colonies need is more beautiful women with your sense, Miss Scott. I do hope you'll allow me the first dance, as well as the last."

"If not several in between?" Liana teased, but her whole body felt as though it had turned to lead, and she doubted she could summon the energy to take a single step, let alone an entire dance. When the music began, she took Sean's hand, but all she really wanted to do was excuse herself and return home where she wouldn't be tortured at every turn by a glimpse of Christian Hunter and his pretty blonde. It wasn't until the third dance that a change in partner brought her into Christian's arms; more hurt than she would ever admit, she quickly looked away.

"I've waited all week for your signal," he whispered as they moved close to bow.

"You'll wait longer still," Liana replied.

"Then I shall have to summon you," Christian teased.

Liana risked glancing up at him, and regretted it instantly. He was again clad in gray satin and remarkably handsome. "I shouldn't think you'd have the time," she remarked as she looked away.

"I shall always have time for you," Christian promised. He sounded sincere, but Liana knew he couldn't possibly be telling the truth. "Isn't it a strain to keep so many women entertained?"

Christian tightened his hold on her hand and this time when the dance brought them together, he pulled her shockingly close. "There's no one else," he swore.

Tears stung Liana's eyes as she replied with a caustic hiss. "Save the flattering lies for your blonde."

Christian started to laugh, then realized Liana was truly provoked. It was time to change partners again, but rather than leave her infuriated, he slipped his arm around her waist; instead of passing her on to the next man, he spun her right out the open doorway onto the terrace. He didn't release her even then, but taking her hands, drew her near.

"The blonde is my cousin, Dominique. Did you truly believe I brought her here tonight just to make you jealous?"

"Let me go!"

"Look at me, Liana!"

It was dark out on the terrace, but the music and laughter from inside echoed all around them. Positive she had revealed far too much, Liana felt thoroughly humiliated and raised her eyes slowly to his. "I'm sorry," she apologized quickly. "I have no right to comment on whom you wish to escort to parties."

"You have every right," Christian argued, "but no reason to complain."

When he kissed her this time, Liana trembled slightly, then responded with grateful abandon. All too soon she realized they were standing a few feet from a roomful of people who would never understand nor forgive her for succumbing to Christian's bold advances. Their imagined condemnations drowned out the soft, sweet voice of her heart, and wrenching free, she dashed back into the party.

Her exit with Christian had not changed the even numbers required for the dance, but she could not rejoin it without forcing another young woman out. Hoping no one had noted their departure, she hurried upstairs to the front bedroom, where she planned to sit in a darkened corner until she had composed herself. Near tears for caring as much as she did about Christian, she heard the music end, then the applause before the musicians began their next tune. It was one of her favorite dances, but she couldn't bring herself to go back to the party and sat that one out, as well as the next. When a young woman came to the doorway, she turned away rather than greet her.

"Excuse me," Johanna called, "is it all right if I rest here a moment?"

"Yes, of course," Liana answered.

"You don't appear to be enjoying the party any more than I am," Johanna surmised softly. She moved to the mirror above the dresser and pushed a stray lock of hair back into place. "My hair is straighter than straw," she complained, "and just refuses to curl." When Liana made no comment, Johanna moved away from the mirror. "Forgive me, I didn't mean to bother you."

Only dimly aware of what the young woman had said, Liana finally glanced her way and recognized the brunette who had come to the party with Beau Barclay. "I'm sorry, I didn't mean to be unfriendly. I'm Liana Scott."

Johanna sighed sadly. "Then I must surely have disturbed you. I'm Johanna Hunter and for reasons no one has ever explained to me, our families do not get along."

Intrigued by the soft-spoken young woman, Liana leaned forward and smiled. "Let's not be bound by ancient feuds. Are you related to Christian Hunter?"

"I'm his sister. Do you know him?"

Liana's chest still hurt with what was becoming an all-too-familiar ache. "Yes, we've met." She rose and spent a moment straightening out her voluminous skirt. "It's nice to meet you, Johanna. I hope you'll come to more parties now that you've tried one."

Johanna followed Liana to the door. "One may be all I can stand, but thank you, anyway."

Now that they were out in the lighted hallway, Liana had no trouble recognizing Johanna as Christian's sister. Her features were far more delicate, but she had the same dark eyes and long, thick lashes. Squaw indeed, she thought to herself, and took an almost malicious delight in introducing Johanna to Amanda, who, after her initial shock, treated the pretty brunette as a friend.

Beau had seen Christian sweep Liana Scott out to the terrace. Nearly beside himself with rage, it was all he could do to wait until the music stopped to confront him. Then, trapped between Dominique and two of the Lang brothers who were determined to impress her, he could not leave. He did not care that Liana had remained outside with his cousin only a few minutes. He had seen her pained expression when she had reentered the ballroom and feared she had again been abused. When he at last caught up with Christian, he was barely able to hold his temper.

"How dare you take further liberties with Miss Scott?" he cried. "Wasn't dragging her through the marsh grass humiliation enough?"

Christian turned around and this time drew Beau out onto the terrace. "This is neither the time nor the place for an argument on any subject," he insisted. "Now who's with Dominique and Johanna?"

"Dominique is surrounded by the Langs, and Johanna's gone upstairs to fix her hair, but they aren't the issue here. Miss Scott is, and I don't want her troubled any further."

Surprised he had not realized Beau was fond of Liana before now, Christian tried not to laugh. "Believe me, cousin, she welcomes my kind of trouble."

Beau pulled back his arm and would have punched Christian right in the face had Christian's reaction not been much more swift. He raised his arm to block Beau's blow, and then moved toward the door. "I'll fight you when we get home, but not here. Have some consideration for our sisters' feelings, even if you have none for mine."

As he stepped back into the ballroom, Christian saw Liana talking with Johanna and for a terrible instant he feared his sister might reveal things he did not want Liana to know. Then he realized she would never speak ill of him just for spite. Relaxing slightly, he longed to join them; then, seeing Ian Scott moving their way, he dared not. He went to rescue Dominique from the Lang brothers instead, but with an awareness that was nearly pain, he didn't lose sight of Liana for the entire evening.

Six

Ian separated Liana from her friends without pausing for introductions. He simply nodded to acknowledge the brunette he failed to recognize and then wrapped his hand around his daughter's upper arm and led her aside. "The Barclays are here again and if you can't give me your word you'll avoid them, we'll say our good-byes now."

Had he confronted Liana as she had fled the terrace, she would have burst into tears, but she was now sufficiently composed to respond calmly. "I'll do my very best." That was not the truth, but she spoke the words so easily even she did not recognize the lie.

"Good. Have you seen your brothers?"

"Not since the dancing began." Liana hoped Morgan had sense enough not to let their father catch him with Dominique. Parties used to be such enjoyable affairs, but nothing had been the same since the afternoon Christian had briefly taken her captive and claimed they were kin. Now parties were filled with such tortuous intrigues she almost wished her father would take her home.

The next set of dances was about to begin, and when her father left to search for her brothers she rejoined Amanda and Johanna to await a partner. James Murray quickly sought her out and while she did not know him nearly as well as she knew Sean, she smiled as though she were truly delighted. She could sense Christian, though, his presence still as strong as when she had been in his embrace.

He remained on the far side of the room; the music did not bring them together, but it was his touch she felt in every other man's hand. She caught a glimpse of him late in the evening, and noticed how his stance accented the gentle curve of his spine where it met his hips. Overwhelmed by the memory of his kiss, she had to look away but saw little else before it was time to go.

As they waited for their carriage after the party, Christian was relieved everything had gone well. Johanna leaned against him as she suppressed a yawn, and looked pleasantly tired rather than disappointed. Dominique had made more conquests than he could count, and even now was waving happily to a crowd of young men who wore such shamelessly adoring expressions he was thoroughly sickened. As their carriage pulled to the front of the line, he took her hand to tear her away from her admirers. Moving between them and Dominique, he said good night in such an emphatic tone they finally grasped the sad fact that the evening was over.

Beau climbed into the carriage after Johanna and Dominique, and once Christian was seated, he signaled the driver to take them home. He was then the one who couldn't resist a final glance toward the Langs' home, but Liana wasn't among those still waiting for a carriage. He sat back and pretended a rapt interest as Dominique asked Johanna which of her many dance partners she had liked best.

"They were all nice," Johanna insisted.

Exasperated with her taciturn cousin, Dominique tapped her hand with her fan. "Yes, of course, they couldn't have behaved otherwise, but some were poised and others clumsy and slow. I can't believe you couldn't tell the difference."

Johanna looked to her elder brother for advice. "Did you find a difference in grace among your partners?"

Amused by her innocence, Christian smiled. "Most definitely."

"Really?" Johanna appeared intrigued. "Whom did you most enjoy?"

Christian caught Beau's eye, and knew his cousin was waiting for the one name he dared not speak. "Other than you and Dominique?"

Knowing he was teasing her, Johanna giggled and hid behind her fan. "I know you too well, Christian. You liked them all."

The gentle teasing continued until they arrived home, where this time they found not their younger brothers and sisters waiting up, but their parents. "Are we expected to give some sort of a report?" Christian asked.

Hunter was leaning against the mantel, his wife seated close by. Beau left Arielle on the settee and came forward. "Not a detailed report, merely a brief summation of how you enjoyed the party."

"It was wonderful!" Dominique enthused. "I met so many nice young men, and each asked if he might come to call."

"And you told them all yes, didn't you?" Arielle asked.

"Well, I couldn't be rude, Mother. What would you have had me say?"

"Let's discuss this while you prepare for bed." Arielle rose, and with a fond smile for her husband, she ushered her spirited daughter from the parlor.

"Dominique has a marvelous time wherever she goes, but what did you think of the evening, Johanna?" Byron inquired. "Were you equally entertained?"

Johanna toyed with her fan. Dominique had attempted to teach her how to use the delicate device to flirt shamelessly, but she had taken her practice no further than her bedroom mirror. "Yes, Uncle Byron. It was a wonderful party with beautiful music and delicious food. I didn't step on too many men's feet during the dancing, and I met several young women who were kind enough to be friendly. But I do believe they were more interested in Christian and Beau than me."

"That's not true," Christian rushed to deny. "I'm sure they truly liked you."

While very pleased that her daughter had had a good time, Alanna was still concerned. "Were there any young men who asked if they might call on you?"

Johanna blushed deeply. "Yes, but they were army officers and I did not think they'd be welcome here."

Suddenly realizing they had made an error in leaving Johanna out of their plans, Byron hid his alarm. "I hope you didn't tell them so, Johanna."

Johanna's dark eyes widened in dismay. "Oh, no, of course not. That would have been unforgivably rude. I was merely so vague in my response I thoroughly confused them."

"Good. The latest British moves against Massachusetts have heightened emotions considerably, and I don't want you drawn into political arguments when you should be enjoying an evening of dancing."

"I wouldn't even try to discuss politics as forcefully as you do, uncle," Johanna assured him, then covered another yawn. "May I please be excused? I'm not used to staying up this late."

"Of course, my darling." Alanna left her chair, slipped her arm around her daughter's waist, and whispered a delicious secret that made the quiet girl laugh. The men waited in companionable silence until the two women were safely upstairs before they discussed the evening any further.

Christian peeled off his gray satin jacket as he spoke. "I

heard rumblings all evening, but it's impossible to say whether those who believe as we do were in the majority. I'm afraid there were as many excuses for Parliament's latest excesses as condemnations, and everyone is looking over his shoulder to see who's listening before he speaks."

Beau nodded. "I had the very same impression. Some voices fell silent when I approached, so I took them for staunch Loyalists, but the undercurrent of dissension continued throughout the party."

"But you said nothing either in support of the king or against him?" Byron probed.

"No, sir, I commented on nothing more significant than the choice of wine."

"I did the same," Christian volunteered. "Tensions are palpable, but I believe the majority of people are deeply perplexed and don't know which side to support. The Loyalists are stubbornly set in their ways and will justify the king's actions all the way to their graves, but those opposed are not nearly as vocal about it."

"Then our pamphlets will serve a two-fold purpose: to condemn the king, and inspire dissent," Byron suggested with clear relish. "I'm proud of you both—now let's get to bed. We could all do with a good night's sleep."

Christian and Beau appeared to agree, but remained in the parlor after their fathers had gone upstairs. "I don't want to fight you, but I will," Christian then uttered in a challenging tone. "You know as well as I do that I can't present myself at the Scott residence and be welcomed as a caller. If I'm to speak with Liana at all, it will have to be a hurried exchange whenever we're at the same party. She doesn't need you to defend her, either. She's fully capable of looking after her own best interests."

"It's Ian you're really after, isn't it?" Beau responded accusingly.

Christian refused to dignify that question with a response. He simply stared at his cousin in the same silent manner his father used to intimidate those who opposed him. At the Langs' party, he had behaved in a manner which allowed him to blend easily into the white man's world. Now, hearing what he considered a ridiculous argument, he retreated behind the cool strength he had inherited from Hunter.

Beau recognized Christian's intractable expression all too well, but he refused to back down. "A gentleman treats all women well, not merely those in his family. Don't use Liana as a target for your hatred. No woman deserves that."

Beau was so incorrect in his allegations, Christian just shook his head sadly. "You don't know what you're talking about, cousin. In fact, I think you're manufacturing an argument where none exists simply as an excuse to fight me. Isn't your real complaint about your father choosing my pamphlet over yours?"

Beau scoffed at that. "No, of course not. How dare you accuse me of being so petty!"

"How dare *you* accuse me of tormenting Liana to get even with her father for abandoning me! Now I'm going to bed. Good night." Christian did not let down his guard as he turned away. Fully expecting Beau to come after him, he remained alert, but Beau did not even follow him up the stairs, let alone try and strike him a blow. Relieved, Christian entered his room and cast off his clothes. Nude, he walked to the window and wished he could see Liana's home but the rolling land hid the estate as surely as the marsh grass hid his trail.

He ran his hand down the flatness of his belly and wished it were Liana's fingertips. She may have run from him tonight, but soon he hoped she would be unable to stay away.

Hunter paced the bedroom he shared with Alanna as he waited for her to tell their daughter good night. When she at last came through the door, he rushed toward her. "What did she say? Did she really enjoy herself tonight, or were the other guests rude to her?"

Alanna gave him a reassuring kiss before she replied. "She's bashful rather than flirtatious like Dominique, but danced just as often, and found the courage to be friendly with the girls her age. I want a man as fine as you for her, though, and she didn't mention meeting anyone special tonight."

"There are no other men as fine as me," Hunter teased.

"Perhaps not, but surely there will be one who is close enough to please her."

"Do I still please you?"

Hunter's deep voice had taken on a seductive edge, and Alanna slipped her hands beneath his buckskin shirt to caress his bare skin. He had always had a magical appeal, and just touching him brought a delicious thrill. "More than I can say," she whispered.

"Then show me." Hunter lifted her off her feet as he kissed her with a savage passion that twenty years of kisses hadn't quenched. He had given up the life of the Seneca for her, and yet he had lost nothing in the exchange. He wanted the same blissful love for his daughter and sons, but in his heart, he did not really believe such a miracle was possible.

Among the last of the guests to leave the Langs', Ian found his family strangely quiet on the ride home. He held Robin's hand, and wished aloud the evening could have been purely social. "I strongly believe political arguments belong in the taverns, and I hope none of you were bothered by anything you might have heard tonight."

Morgan had spent every moment he could with Dominique, but he knew precisely to what his father was referring. "There seem to be many people who don't agree with the closing of Boston Harbor, nor with the other sanctions imposed on Massachusetts."

"We're not among them," Ian stated firmly, as usual speaking for the whole family.

Cameron was sleepy and content to stare out the carriage window, but Morgan pursued the matter. "You're an Englishman through and through, so things always look different to you, but when was the last time those born here in the colonies applauded one of Parliament's acts?"

Ian leaned back against the seat and exhaled slowly. "It's late, and I'm far too tired to discuss serious issues coherently. Let's talk about this tomorrow, or the next day, son."

"Can we discuss it honestly?" Morgan inquired.

"Of course we can," Ian exclaimed. "What other way is there?"

Morgan nudged Liana with his elbow, and she knew he was referring to the first wife their father had never deigned to acknowledge. Having learned about Melissa and Christian, they all viewed their father differently now. Perhaps quizzing him on his political views was preferable to confronting him about his past, but Liana was uneasy all the same. She rubbed her temples and after an exhausting evening looked forward to bed, but when she awoke the next morning, none of her problems had disappeared during the night.

Sean O'Keefe came to call on Liana Sunday afternoon. Still stinging from the pointed remarks sent his way during the Langs' party as a visible representative of King George III, he swiftly began to criticize the political scene in the colonies as anything but calm. She listened politely as he repeated the same standard answers as her father: Parliament knew what was best for the colonies, and any opposition to their policies was not only foolish, but sedition.

Too nervous to remain in the parlor, Liana invited Sean to stroll in their garden, and without realizing it, soon led him down to the river. She asked the most insightful questions possible, but none of his answers satisfied her. "The harbor's to be closed, the Massachusetts charter revoked, town meetings forbidden without the governor's approval, troops quartered in colonial homes, and soldiers accused of capital crimes are to be sent to England for trial, where they are sure to have a sympathetic jury. Doesn't that seem rather harsh retaliation against an entire colony when a few private citizens were responsible for dumping a load of tea overboard?"

Mistakenly believing he was making good progress in his efforts to impress Liana, Sean chose to regard her obvious bias as amusing. "You mustn't trivialize the incident. A refusal to pay import duties is a serious crime, and the colony was dealt with accordingly. Listen to your father, Liana. He's very wise and understands far more than you."

Sean took her arm to guide her around a muddy spot in the path. "I've heard Lord Dunsmore, Virginia's governor, has a list of families whose loyalty to the Crown is suspect. While your father's name certainly isn't on it, I would hate to see yours. Rather than question Parliament's authority, why don't you use that keen wit of yours to gather information? I understand the Barclays have long been critical of the Crown. As your closest neighbors, it shouldn't be difficult for you to gain their confidence and provide evidence against them."

Liana halted abruptly and turned toward him. Sean was an attractive man, and wore his superbly tailored uniform proudly, but he had threatened her with hanging once, and his suggestion she turn spy was equally repugnant. She was as revolted as when Christian had suggested she cultivate Sean's attentions for the information she could then pass along from him.

"The Barclays and Scotts haven't spoken in years, so what you ask is impossible even if I were inclined to spy, which I'm not." She continued on the way, her glance focused on the churning waters of the river rather than her companion. "I don't believe we ought to discuss politics any further. The subject has simply become too dangerous."

"I'd not have joined the army if I didn't enjoy danger," Sean replied, "but I'll discuss anything you wish."

For a moment, Liana was at a loss to find any subject she cared to discuss with him; then she spied a black ribbon snagged in the grass up ahead, and instantly took Sean's arm to turn him back toward home. "I've suddenly become so thirsty I doubt I'll be able to do more than croak. Please, tell me something of your home in England. Your fondest memory, perhaps?"

Sean frowned slightly, then nodded. "That would be of Christmas, when the whole family was together."

Liana found it much easier to listen to Sean reminisce than to abide his defense of the decrees which were fast becoming known in the colonies as the Intolerable Acts. He had a surprising charm when describing his family, but she was enormously relieved when he bid her good-bye. It was after four, and fearing she had already missed Christian, she raced back along the riverbank. He was there. He plucked the telltale ribbon from the grass and then led her into their secret preserve.

"Haven't you grown weary of that captain yet?" he asked when they reached the first small clearing.

Alarmed that he had again been spying on her, Liana opened her mouth to complain, but knowing how little her earlier protests had meant, realized it would be a stupid waste of breath. "Dreadfully, but that can't be why you left a ribbon." Now that she was there, Liana was startled to realize she had not once questioned the wisdom of coming. Christian was dressed in his buckskins, and it was difficult to recall this was the same young man who had looked so splendid in satin and silk last night. "Please, say whatever it is you wish to, and I'll be on my way."

"Beau fears I'm abusing you." Christian moved closer than he had any right to stand. "Do you feel abused?"

Liana looked up, drinking in the sight of him and not knowing how to reply. "Not in any conventional sense," she finally managed to murmur.

Christian brushed her cheek with his fingertips. "Then how?"

What he did was invade her senses to create a sad, sweet longing she did not know how to describe, but she felt more alive with him, and more lonely without him, than she had ever thought possible. She released a sibilant sigh. Her mother had been confident she would recognize the right man when she met him, but Liana doubted she would ever meet another as appealing as Christian. In so many ways he was the right man, but he was also completely wrong.

He had asked if she possessed more courage than Melissa, and she feared that like his mother, she was already lost. Tears welled up in her eyes and she turned away to hide them. "Captain O'Keefe says Dunsmore has a list of families known to be disloyal to the Crown. The Barclays are on it."

Not surprised, Christian slipped his arms around her waist and pulled her back against him. She was wearing the pretty peach-colored gown she had been wearing the day he'd crept up behind her and plucked her off her feet. Recalling how much fun that had been, he leaned down to rub his cheek against hers. "When I asked you to pass on information from the captain, you refused. Why have you changed your mind?"

Liana placed her hands over his. His fingers were long and slim, his skin a rich golden brown that invited her touch, and his warmth radiated clear through her. "Each of you has asked me to spy on the other and the answer's no. I can't share my father's loyalty when Parliament continually spits on us, but it doesn't naturally follow that I can support rebellion, either."

"Why not?" Christian breathed against her ear. He closed his eyes and savored her perfume.

"I've read too much history to see any glory in war."

History was one of the few subjects Christian did read and he gave her a loving squeeze. "I appreciate your warning, and we'll be careful to keep our views to ourselves." He turned her around slowly and caught her lips in a gentle kiss as soon as she was again facing him. "I think you're a born rebel, though," he added with a smile, but he wasn't convinced he could trust her.

His eyes were so dark Liana felt herself slipping into an abyss of desire. Like molten chocolate, his glance was both hot and sweet. Chocolate was her favorite candy, and just looking at him kindled a delicious craving. The smile that tugged at the corner of his mouth convinced her he would like to satisfy cravings of a far more exotic sort, and she pushed against his chest to put more distance between them.

"This is lunacy," she remarked flippantly. "We're not children playing secret games. We're adults, and—"

Christian yanked her back into his arms and silenced her protest with a lingering kiss. When he at last drew away, he demanded the truth. "It's not a war that frightens you. It's that something might happen to me. Why can't you admit that you care for me when it's plain in your every kiss that you do?"

Liana had been raised to believe it was a man's place to court a woman, not the other way around. Mortified that he saw what was in her heart, and fiercely determined not to admit it, she twisted out of his grasp. "It's absolutely impossible to have any kind of an intelligent conversation with you so I won't even try. Good day, Mr. Hunter, and good-bye."

Christian laughed at her bright blush, which assured him as vividly as her delectable kiss that she adored him. He pulled the black ribbon from his pocket and drew it through his fingers. Liana Scott had touched something inside him he had not even known existed, and he was positive he warmed the very same place in her.

He was also exquisitely aware of where their shockingly inappropriate romance was leading. Ian Scott had refused to acknowledge his existence as a child, but he could not deny him as a man, and most especially not when he was determined to have his only daughter. Christian wrapped the ribbon around his knuckles and slid it back into his pocket. He would wait a while before sending another summons, and maybe then Liana would miss him enough to admit how much she cared.

Despite a heavy burden of misgivings, David Slauson returned from Charleston with the printing equipment. "The press is old and the type worn, but I believe they will do for the small amount of work you described. I bought ink and paper, too, at what I think you will agree was a fair price."

Byron had seen the schooner *Southern Breeze* tie up at the dock and had met David while he was still on board. He was pleased with the earnest young man's purchases and handed him a generous bonus from the expense money he had not spent. "Let's wait until after dark and then move the press to one of the tobacco sheds. It will be safe there until the harvest in the fall and you'll have plenty of room to work. As soon as you have everything set up, I'll give you the first of the articles I'd like printed."

"I'm sure I can operate the press, Mr. Barclay. I just hope I can produce work of a high enough quality to please you."

"We're not publishing Shakespeare's sonnets," Byron advised, "so the only requirement is that your work be legible. You can promise that, can't you?"

"I certainly hope so, sir."

"Good. Meet me here tonight at eight and we'll move everything to the shed."

David promised he would be there, and deeply curious as to what Byron wished to print, he hoped the afternoon would pass quickly. On his way to his quarters, he stopped by the well for a drink. It was as close as he dared go to the house without an invitation. As always, he tarried, hoping Johanna might appear. Drinking slowly, he tried to look lost in thought, not lazy.

He was about to move on when Johanna came around the corner of the house, singing happily to herself. She was dressed in a simple muslin gown and carrying several sprigs of peppermint. Once again, she looked like a servant who'd been sent to the garden, but this time he knew better. When she looked up and saw him watching her, she appeared to be badly embarrassed, but he thought her shyness charming.

"You have a lovely voice," he called to her.

Johanna hadn't even caught a glimpse of David in the last week, but had been afraid to ask her uncle if he had gone. Glad he hadn't left, she pretended a sudden need for a drink of water. As she sipped it, she inquired as to how he was getting along.

"Pretty well, thank you. Your uncle runs this plantation with a firm but compassionate hand and I enjoy working for him. Thank you again for helping me get a job here. How have you been?"

Johanna replaced the tin cup on its hook and leaned back against the well. She sifted the peppermint through her fingers as she considered how best to reply. Attending the Langs' party had been the most exciting thing that had happened to her in a great while, but she thought it would be cruel to tell him about it when he had not been invited. She had enjoyed having several pretty new gowns, but that was too frivolous a thing to report.

"I've been very well, thank you, but then my Aunt Arielle

is what the Acadians call a *sage femme*, and she keeps us all
well with her herbs and potions."

"Your uncle has a French wife?"

Johanna nodded. "We have a most interesting mixture
of people here."

"You certainly do." David had been shocked the first
time he had seen Hunter, but wasn't sure what the man
did there. "The Indian frightens me, though. I've only
seen him a time or two, and while he appears to be thoroughly civilized, I can't help but pray that he'll stay that
way."

Taken aback by that offhand remark about her father,
Johanna didn't know how to reply. "What have you heard
about him?" she asked apprehensively.

"Nothing, actually," David explained. "If your uncle
trusts him, I'm sure he's all right. At least I hope he is."

"Are you afraid of being murdered in your bed?"

David laughed rather than admit he most certainly was.
"Not if you aren't."

Johanna did not consider her father a fit target for humor
and straightened up abruptly. "Good day, Mr. Slauson."

Even before she had turned away, David knew he had
said something to offend her and he was dreadfully sorry.
"Wait!" He hurriedly caught up with her. "It isn't my place
to say who your uncle employs, and Lord knows I'm grateful he hired me. Please don't tell him I mentioned the
Indian. I don't dare risk offending him."

David looked sincerely pained by that possibility, and
Johanna was quick to reassure him. "Believe me, Mr.
Slauson, the fact that my father terrifies you is something
I plan to keep to myself."

"Your father!" David gasped. "You can't possibly mean
the Indian is your father."

Johanna reached up to remove her cap, and with a single tug released a profusion of long, straight hair which
tumbled down over her shoulders and fell clear past her

waist. Near her face, the sun had lightened the color, but falling free, it was a rich, glossy sable. "There, do I look more like a savage now?" She watched the light of horrified recognition fill David's eyes and wondered why she had ever found him appealing. She entered the house before he had recovered enough to speak, but she doubted he could have said anything she wished to hear.

Seven

David Slauson reached the schooner first that evening and anxiously paced the deck, silently berating himself for insulting Johanna. She had been so kind to him, and the fact that he had repaid her with thoughtless remarks pained him greatly. He had no money to buy her a gift which might soften her mood, and he feared he would never be able to make an eloquent enough apology.

When he heard men approaching, he expected Byron and perhaps a few of the brawnier field hands. He was aghast to see the Indian and the buckskin-clad young man he had met earlier, along with Beau, walking up the path with his employer. He wiped his hands on his pants and, certain Johanna must have reported his derogatory remarks, waited for what he feared would be a hideous beating. To his amazement, Byron's only interest was in moving the press and supplies; the Indian gave him little more than a passing glance.

They were merely waiting until he had set up the press, David decided. Once he had explained how to run it, he was sure all four men would gang up on him. His hands were shaking so hard, he could barely support his end of the press as they carried it down the gangplank.

"Let's stop a minute," Christian called out at the bottom, and the others came to a halt. Over six feet in height, the press was an awkward burden, and they all welcomed a rest. "If this is too heavy for you, just say so," he whispered to David.

"No, I'm fine," David mumbled, still quaking. At the other end of the press, Beau had a lantern to light their way up the path. David was grateful his face was in shadow as he was sure he looked no braver than he felt.

"Let's go," Christian called, and the procession continued down the path toward the tobacco drying sheds. Fortunately, they were not far from the dock and Byron chose the closest one to hide the press. The men maneuvered it into a convenient corner and set it down. Wrapped in a tarpaulin, they did not have a good look at the wooden contraption until Christian helped David remove the protective covering and Beau raised the lantern.

"Well, that certainly looks like a press," Byron exclaimed. He reached out to give it a shake and was relieved when it didn't wobble. "Let's go back for the type and the rest of the gear."

David held his breath, but no one uttered a cross word as they made their way back to the schooner. "I may have bought more ink and paper than necessary, but I got it at such a good price, I thought it was the prudent thing to do."

"It certainly was," Byron assured him.

"Let's leave the cases wrapped," David proposed. "Otherwise, we might lose some of the type carrying them to the shed."

Working independently now, the men made a second trip to the shed and stacked the paper and ink beside the press. David looked around for a table on which to place the cases of type, but there wasn't one and he had to set them on the ground. He straightened up and struggled to find the courage to face whatever abuse might now be heaped on him.

"You've had a long day, Mr. Slauson," Byron said. "Let's meet back here in the morning."

"I think it would be best if Slauson and I worked alone," Christian offered. "That way, if someone hands you a pamphlet, it will be the first time you see it and you won't have to worry about fooling anyone with your response."

"None of us will betray you," Beau argued.

"I know that," Christian assured him. "But should you have to account for your time tomorrow, you'll have an alibi."

David listened to the Barclays' discussion with growing alarm. "Just what is it you wish me to print?" he asked when they fell quiet. "You mentioned articles, but not that they were to be printed in secret."

Byron nodded. "Please forgive me if I've put you in an awkward position, Mr. Slauson. I plan to print a pamphlet denouncing Parliament's heinous actions against Massachusetts. If your politics, or your conscience, prevent you from working on such a project, then I'll excuse you as soon as you teach my son and nephew how to operate the press. You may be assured that we'll never tell anyone you were in any way involved if you have even the slightest trepidation."

Still afraid they were going to hold him accountable for insulting Johanna, David finally found the courage to glance toward Hunter, but the Indian was standing in a relaxed pose, regarding him with no more than casual interest. There wasn't anything in the least bit threatening in his manner, but he was the only Indian brave David had even seen this close and he quickly clasped his hands behind his back so no one would notice how badly he was shaking. Thinking the young man beside him must be his son and Johanna's brother, he managed a hesitant smile.

"I've met a great many men in my travels," he finally revealed, "who have no more need of a king than I do. I'll be proud to help you print those sentiments in any way you choose."

Byron reached out to shake David's hand. "Good. I'll

tell the other men you're doing household repairs so your presence will be accounted for the next few days. How long do you think it will take you to print two hundred pamphlets?"

"I'll need to set the type and I'm uncertain how long that will take. Then, because I'm new at it, I can't make an accurate estimate of how long I'll need for the printing. A couple of days at the very least."

"Fine. Recover everything, and you and Christian can begin work in the morning."

While the others left, Christian remained behind with David. He helped him drape the tarpaulin over the press and then picked up the lantern Beau had thoughtfully left behind. "Are you always this nervous? Or is the possibility of going to prison for sedition what's troubling you?"

Even dressed in buckskins, Christian did not look wholly Indian, which was why David hadn't been terrified of him at their first meeting. Now, knowing he was Johanna's brother, he feared anything he might say would be repeated. "I'm just not all that confident about running the press. It's a simple procedure, but still, there are tricks to every trade and I'm afraid I don't know them."

Christian clapped him on the back. "Running the press is the least dangerous part of this project, Slauson, so you needn't agonize so. Besides, I think teaching me how to operate it will strengthen your skills sufficiently to allow us to get the work done without too much trouble. I've a woodblock cartoon I want to do first, and that will give us a chance to practice using the ink and press before we move on to setting type."

As they walked back toward the house, David found himself caught up in Christian's enthusiasm, but when he angled off toward the cabin where he lived, all his doubts came tumbling back. Apparently Johanna really did intend to keep his comments about her father to herself, but the fact that she had heard them had done more than enough damage.

While Christian and David worked with the press the next morning, Amanda Tuttle came by Liana's house to invite her to go riding. It was a pastime Liana had long enjoyed, but that day her mind wandered so frequently she had a difficult time following her friend's conversation. As always, Amanda wanted to talk about men, but this time she had a new tack.

"You were right to scold me for calling Johanna Hunter a squaw. She was really very nice. Would you mind if I began including her on our rides, or when we go into town together? After all, she lives right on the way, and it wouldn't be any bother to stop for her."

At Johanna's name, Liana had instantly focused on Amanda's next words, but her heart fell when she heard them. "You needn't worry that our relationship will suffer if you befriend her," she replied, "but my father has forbidden me to have anything to do with the Barclays, so I'm afraid I'll have to ask you to see her on your own."

Greatly intrigued, Amanda pulled her gray gelding to a halt. Fashionably attired in a deep green habit and matching hat, she looked every inch a fine lady. Liana was clad in a russet outfit that blended perfectly with her sorrel mare's glossy hide and her own red hair. The colorful pheasant feathers on her hat were from a bird her father had shot in the fall.

"Well, I know the Barclays' politics aren't ideal, but surely your father can't mind if you spend time with Johanna. After all, she's far too shy to try and influence us."

Liana wanted to continue their ride, but Amanda was blocking the way and she did not want to send her mare wading through the tall grass at the side of the road to go around her. "I agree with you that his edict is unnecessary in Johanna's case, but he is my father, and I ought to obey his wishes. Besides, if it's Beau who interests you, shouldn't you try to become better acquainted with his sister, Dominique, rather than his cousin?"

Amanda rolled her eyes. "It's plain she doesn't need more friends. I swear Beau and Christian were the only young men at the Langs' party who weren't so absolutely fascinated by Dominique that they behaved as though she were the only girl there. Why, even your brother Morgan trailed after her like a bloodhound tracking a deer. It was positively embarrassing to watch so many men make fools of themselves over her. Just think how poor Johanna must have felt growing up in her shadow."

"I believe Johanna is the eldest, so that analogy doesn't apply."

Exasperated, Amanda tossed her curls. "Must you be so logical? Whatever their ages, it's plain no one sees Johanna with Dominique around. Besides, cultivating Dominique's friendship would be far too obvious. I don't want Beau to think I'm chasing him."

"Certainly not." Liana gestured with her riding crop, and Amanda turned her horse back to the trail.

"How would your father ever find out if you came with me to see Johanna? He's so used to our going places together, he'd never suspect anything different."

"Please don't encourage me to disobey my father, Amanda. Just respect my decision and let it go."

"You're ruining a perfectly good plan." Amanda's lips puffed out in a stubborn pout. "Sean O'Keefe is so madly in love with you, you needn't do anything more than smile to lure him, but I need more help with Beau."

"You're pretty and charming," Liana argued. "I'm sure he's noticed you. It would be unkind to befriend Johanna for any reason other than a sincere interest in her, and that wouldn't please any of the Barclays."

"What makes you an expert on the Barclays if you're not allowed to speak with them?"

Fearing she had let slip information she had no wish to reveal, Liana drew in a sharp breath, but a quick analysis of her last remark convinced her she hadn't. "That's just common sense, Amanda. From what I know, the Barclays are somewhat reclusive. Whatever occurred between them and my father happened a long time ago and I've no wish to dredge up ancient arguments. Please, let's talk about something else."

"You're being awfully mysterious today, Liana. Are you sure you aren't interested in Beau yourself?"

Highly amused because Amanda's guess was so far from the truth, Liana's sparkling laugh was a musical trill but the brief burst of mirth didn't reach her eyes. She had grown up confiding in her best friend, but now she had to keep her innermost thoughts strictly to herself. That she wasn't being honest with anyone pained her; eager to change the subject, she asked what Amanda planned to wear to the next party, and then failed to listen to a word she said.

There was a hawk circling overhead, and Liana envied the ease with which he dipped and soared on the morning breeze. She and Amanda had ridden along the road into town so often she could have slept the whole way and not become lost. As they approached the entrance to the Barclay plantation, she strove to remain relaxed, holding her mare's reins in a gentle clasp. But the whole time she was hoping Christian might have chosen precisely the moment they rode by to start on his own way into town.

She amended the daydream to include Beau so Amanda would be too distracted to notice what transpired between Christian and her, but neither young man appeared. The cottonwoods were blooming, and they passed vivid patches of blue lobelia and lacy fountains of wisteria along the trail. Virginia contained such splendid natural beauty, Liana thought it truly a pity King George III could not be bothered to come for a visit.

"Do you agree with your father's political views?" Liana asked suddenly.

Shocked by such an unexpected question, Amanda needed a moment to reply. "Virginia is a British colony, and none of us can deny our English roots, so why people wish to defy Parliament is beyond me. After all, we are a part of England and ought to be no less loyal than the rest of the king's subjects."

"So you're comfortable siding with the Loyalists?"

"Well, of course, aren't you?"

Riding in splendid isolation, Liana longed to be able to speak the truth about something—and did. "No. If we're truly a part of Great Britain, then why have we no representatives in Parliament?"

"Don't be silly," Amanda scolded. "America is a colony, and none of the colonies have members in Parliament."

"Why not if we are English, too?"

"Because we don't, that's why." Amanda raised her chin. "Do you ask Sean O'Keefe that kind of question?"

"Yes, upon occasion I have."

"Isn't he appalled?"

Liana looked at Amanda and saw her clearly for the pampered girl she was. She loved pretty clothes, elegant parties, and delicious gossip, but she had never had an original thought in all the years Liana had known her. There had been a time when the companionship Amanda offered had been enough, but now Liana needed someone far wiser in whom to confide. Sadly, she did not have such a person among her circle of friends.

"Yes, I suppose he is, but I do believe he regards the attempt to align my views with his a welcome challenge."

Liana had heard Loyalists compared to small children still clinging to their mother's skirts. Having a king was a comfort, for it was the way things had always been, and change, even a beneficial one, was terrifying to a child. Liana raised her eyes to the hawk and recognized his freedom for the blessing it was. She enjoyed that very same freedom, but for now, it was only in her thoughts.

Bare chested, Christian stood back to watch David operate the press. "I certainly hope that the fact that the box where you place the form, or for now the woodblock, is called a coffin, isn't a bad omen."

David shot him a worried glance. "Let's pray it isn't." He patted ink over the surface of the woodblock with the ink pad, a leather ball attached to a handle. "There, I think that's enough. If the impression isn't as dark as you'd like, I'll use more ink on the second try."

Hinged to the coffin was the tympan. The lower part held the paper, and the upper section, the frisket, folded down over it to keep the paper in place. David carefully positioned a damp piece of paper in the tympan, folded the frisket, and then slid the coffin along the rails until it was directly beneath the platen, a thick slab of hardwood. He slipped a bar into the screw to lower the platen onto the coffin and tightened it until he felt certain the ink had been firmly pressed into the paper.

When he released the pressure on the screw, Christian rolled the coffin back along the rails, folded back the frisket and tympan, and peeled away the proof of his cartoon. He held it up and laughed at the bloated swine he had carved with such delighted vigor. "What do you think? Is it clear enough the hog's made a trough of the colonies?"

David came around the press to examine the proof, and while Christian's artwork had the bold simplicity of all woodblocks, the message was unmistakable. "It's very good. I wasn't even sure we could do your cartoon on the press, but it works. Now all we have to do is print two hundred more, fold the paper, and print your text on the inside."

"I'll run the press," Christian told him. "You set the type." He had brought along his sample pamphlet and held it out to David. "If, after reading this, you think of any more ways to describe the king, make a note of them. I'm going to compare him to a bullfrog next and call him a tyrannical toad."

As David had brought only one leather apron, he quickly removed it and handed it to Christian. "You'll need this to keep the ink off your buckskins. Now let me see what you've written." His fingers stained with ink, he took the pamphlet by the corner. Reading it filled him with a potent mixture of amusement and dread. "You've not only a flair for words, but the courage to use them in ways few men would dare. Do you honestly believe we can get away with this?"

Christian tied the apron around his waist and reached for another piece of paper. "That will be part of the fun, Slauson. Now let's see if I can print two hundred cartoons before you can set the type."

David envied Christian his lean, muscular body, and doubted he could win any contest between them involving speed or strength. "The goal is to set the type accurately, Mr. Hunter. We'd gain nothing if I were to set it quickly— with so many errors it would all have to be redone."

"Call me Christian. We needn't have a race if you don't wish to, but the sooner we get this done, the less likely we are to be discovered." He shoved the coffin along the rails, twisted the screw to lower the platen, and made a second print of his cartoon. "I can't imagine spending every day doing such a repetitive task, but this won't be so bad every once in awhile."

David bent down to unwrap the cases holding the type. The letters were arranged not alphabetically, but for the compositor's convenience. The top section held the capital letters, the bottom the small. Unfamiliar with the organization of the cases, he had to search for each letter he slipped into the frame called a composing stick. "I'm afraid I have no tolerance for monotony, either. That's why I've not found any work I want to pursue as a career."

"Just stay with us. No one has ever died of boredom here."

While David appreciated that invitation, he was doing so poorly with Johanna, he doubted he would have any reason to remain there for long. When he had the first line of type set into words, he separated them with brass slivers and went on to the second. "I'll be able to work faster when I learn the location of the letters. For now, I'm afraid I'm dreadfully slow."

"You spend far too much time apologizing, Slauson. Save your breath and just work."

"Yes, sir."

Christian laughed at David's continued diffidence and reached for another sheet of paper. He had to scatter the cartoons around on the floor to dry, and was swiftly surrounded by his work. By the time he reached twenty-five, the first was dry. He had seldom done anything which had given him such a heady sense of accomplishment; he gave the press an affectionate slap before reaching for the next piece of paper. By noon, he had his two hundred cartoons.

"Do you think I ought to make extra copies in case we ruin a few when we add the text?"

"It sounds like a good idea. Go ahead." David paused to transfer the type from the composing stick to the metal pan known as the galley. He had completed half the page, and hurried to get the rest done. He dropped a letter into the dirt and took care to clean it off before sliding it into the composing stick. Compositors usually worked standing at a table which held the cases at eye level but he was positive it was his inexperience rather than the location of the cases which was causing his problem.

"If we do this again, give me the text to set while you carve the cartoon. Then I'll have it ready to print when you're finished."

Christian liked the earnest young man, and agreed. "I'll do that, but first I want to see the reaction to our first edition."

"What sort of reaction do you expect?"

"The Loyalists will be outraged, puff themselves up like pigeons, and squawk about the vile disrespect to the king. Those who are not enamored of the Crown will share our sense of humor and have a laugh at the king's expense. The good citizens who are too timid to take sides will look around to make certain no one is watching, and then I hope they'll have the courage to laugh, too. Their initial laughter should inspire reflection, and they should begin to question Parliament's actions, find them oppressively absurd, and move closer to our side."

David glanced over his shoulder. "Won't everyone be curious as to the author's identity?"

"Most definitely, but because I'm half Indian, most people assume I neither read nor write, so I won't be on anyone's list."

Christian had tossed out that opinion without any hint of shame, and David longed to question him about his sister. Unfortunately, he could not think how to begin. "I thought you merely preferred buckskins. It didn't occur to me that you might be Indian until I saw you with your father."

"I favor my mother, and my sister favors hers. Our little brother, Falcon, is most like our father. He's the truly wild one. He's just too young for it to show."

"How can he be any wilder than this?" David gestured toward the cartoons scattered about.

"As my father would say, these are merely words, not deeds."

"I don't believe I've heard him speak."

"He's as fluent as you and me, Slauson. If you greet him, he won't respond in grunts."

"Oh, no, I didn't think that. I hope I haven't insulted you, too."

Christian laid the last of the extra copies aside and walked around the press to face David. "If you've insulted anyone, I'm unaware of it. You needn't worry about the hands. Most aren't clever enough to understand they've been insulted even when they have."

David knew he had said too much, and fumbling with another letter, dropped it into the dirt. "I'm sorry. Perhaps I'm trying too hard to hurry."

Christian wiped his hands on his apron. "What you need is a rest and something to eat. I'll go up to the kitchen and see what Polly has ready."

David cleaned off the errant letter and slipped it into the composing stick before sitting back to rest. Christian was such a personable young man; he had enjoyed working with him so much that the morning had passed quickly. He debated asking his advice on how best to apologize to Johanna, and then feared he would be imposing on a friendship that was probably dreadfully one-sided. He stood up, brushed off the seat of his pants, and after gathering up the dry cartoons, began to fold the paper to get it ready to print the text.

This was easily the most dangerous thing he had ever done, and almost giddy with the risk, he tried to emulate Christian's swaggering courage. Rich men all walked with a confidence he had never felt, but Christian's gait held a faint trace of his father's soft step as well. "What a curious family," he exclaimed to himself, but he dared not dream he could ever be a real part of it.

That night, Byron went into town with Beau and Christian. They played billiards in the Raleigh Tavern, and to make sure their presence would be remembered, bought several rounds of the popular inn's arrack punch for the other patrons. Distilled from the fermented mash of malted rice and mixed with molasses, the potent brew quickly instilled a boisterous good cheer. Christian had only a sip, but pretending to have had far more, got so surly and loud his uncle soon sent Beau off to escort him home, but neither young man went there.

"I still think it's a bad idea for you to be involved in this," Christian argued as they mounted their horses.

"One rider can't possibly distribute all the pamphlets in a single night," Beau reminded him. "You've no choice about accepting my help. Now I'll handle the town, and you cover as many as you can of the outlying plantations."

"Stay away from the guard house," Christian warned. "In fact, don't even go down Duke of Gloucester Street."

"It's a long street." Beau urged his horse close to Christian's as they pretended to head for home. "I want to cover at least part of it, but don't worry, I won't slap a pamphlet into a British soldier's hand."

"Don't put one in anyone's hand." Christian was dressed in a loose-fitting white shirt and black pants so if he was seen, he would be mistaken for a hundred other men. "Leave them rolled under door handles on the shops and slipped into the fences at houses. Then get home as quickly as you can."

"I'll be back well before you," Beau boasted. When they came to the corner, he turned south on Blair Street, heading for St. Francis.

Filled with a keen sense of exhilaration, Christian put his fears for Beau aside and urged his horse to a gallop. He had an enormous amount of ground to cover, but a great many of the large plantations were owned by Loyalists and he wanted to make certain each and every one awoke to find a pamphlet on his doorstep. Nearly flying along the road, he dropped off half a dozen before reaching Ian Scott's place.

It was now past midnight, and boldly riding up to the darkened house, he sent a pamphlet sailing onto the porch. Then, with a silent salute, he sped off. It was so easy to imagine Ian's face turning purple with rage, he couldn't help but wish he could be there to see it. As for Liana, he hoped she would admire the author, even if she did not know his name, and marvel at his daring.

Unable to sleep despite the long outing with Amanda, Liana heard a rider approaching the house with a haste that had to signal a dire emergency. Leaving her room carrying a candle, she waited on the landing, then realized that apparently no one else was awake to admit the late caller. She hurried down the stairs, opened the door and peeked out, but the rider had changed directions and the sound of his horse's hoofbeats was growing faint.

Thinking the incident very odd, she was about to close the front door when she spied a piece of folded paper lying on the porch. Surprised anyone would wish to deliver a message with such shocking haste and not wait for a reply, she stepped out to retrieve it. When she turned it over and saw the crowned boar, she gasped; then, thinking the cartoon wonderfully clever, she began to giggle.

Still standing barefoot on the porch, she opened the pamphlet and read what proved to be a most imaginative description of King George's contemptuous mistreatment of the colonies as a whole, and Massachusetts in particular. She paused more than once to look back at the cover, and thought the artist had done a superb job of illustrating the penurious pig the author had criticized in such entertaining fashion. She was reading the pamphlet for a third time when her father found her out on the porch.

"I thought I heard someone," he said. He had taken

the time to cover his nightshirt with a robe and pull on his boots. He looked past her and, seeing no one, noticed the pamphlet in her hands. "What have you got there?"

Liana immediately wiped the smile from her face. "Someone's idea of humor." Sorry she had not been quick enough to hide it, she placed it in his hands.

Ian's eyes widened as he recognized the distinctive outline of the hog's trough. "My God," he moaned. "What nonsense is this?" He read only the first couple of sentences and began to shake with rage. He had brought a candle with him, too, and touching the corner of the pamphlet to the flame, he lit it and threw it off the porch to burn in the grass.

"Did you see who left that vile piece of trash?"

Frightened by the intensity of his anger, Liana took a step back. "No. I heard a horse, and thought someone must have come with an important message. The pamphlet was all I found."

Ian glared off into the night. "I should go after the bastard. Whoever he is, he deserves to be drawn and quartered for slandering the king with such vicious lies."

Liana knew better than to point out that while the author of the pamphlet had definitely given his views a stinging slant, he had not distorted the facts. There were plenty of people who believed Parliament was levying unfair taxes on the colonies, and that the sanctions against Massachusetts were much too severe. The pamphlet had certainly been an audacious indictment of the king, but she doubted it could truly be dismissed as vicious lies.

She covered a yawn and made a remark she hoped her father would construe as agreement with his bias. "It's not worth losing more sleep over. I'm going back to bed."

As she passed by him, Ian caught her arm. "I don't want to find you out here in your nightgown ever again. If you should hear another rider at this late hour, wait for me to respond."

"Yes, sir." Liana went on back in the house. As she climbed the stairs she wondered how other families would react to the pamphlet, which was clearly meant to encourage dissent and condemn complacent obedience to a king who, in her opinion, wanted only their taxes and nothing whatsoever to do with them.

The spring nights were cool. Snuffing the candle, she got back into bed and pulled the covers up to her chin. The pamphlet would spark all kinds of debate and that would definitely make the next party all the more entertaining. The identity of the author would provide hours of discussion before anyone got around to analyzing the inflammatory text. She wondered what Christian would say, and hoped she would soon have an opportunity to ask him.

Eight

Amanda Tuttle's father found the Barclays' pamphlet next to his place at the dining room table. He began to swear as soon as he saw the cartoon, and by the time he had read the text he was in no mood to eat breakfast. "Where did you get this?" he bellowed, and with frantic apologies, the housekeeper explained it had been found early that morning on the front porch. Incensed by the sentiments expressed in the pamphlet, Joshua crumpled it into a tight ball and tossed it into the unlit fireplace, but not ten minutes later, Amanda fished it out.

The same scene was repeated throughout Williamsburg as its residents awoke and found the emotionally charged leaflet. Some regarded it as hilarious; others, like Ian Scott and Joshua Tuttle, called for the immediate arrest of the author. By ten a.m., even the most timid of souls had read it and formed an opinion. Whether or not they shared that opinion was another thing, but there was little talk of anything else in the shops and out on the plantations.

Thinking she had something remarkable to share, Amanda hastened to show Liana the pamphlet and was disappointed to learn she had read it during the night. "I'm not surprised your father burned it. Mine intended to do the same, but I stole it before he lit the fire."

Stretched across her bed, Liana found Amanda's keen interest in the anonymous pamphlet surprising. "Only yesterday you were quick to defend the king. Has reading this simple essay made you reassess your views?"

"Certainly not," Amanda exclaimed. She had heated an iron and done her best to press the wrinkles from the sensational leaflet, but only because it was sure to cause a furor. "I think it's utter nonsense, but the real question is, who wrote it?"

"Does it really matter?" Liana argued. "It expresses in plain terms what a great many people believe."

Dressed in a profusion of pink ruffles, Amanda's gestures were accented with soft silk flutterings. "Of course it matters who wrote this. He has to be found and silenced. This sort of vicious libel can't be allowed to continue."

Reaching for the leaflet, Liana traced the swine's truculent expression with her fingertip. Rendered in bold strokes, the cartoon boar made as lasting an impression as the incendiary text. "The author might be caught, but I doubt his opinions will be silenced. The king and Parliament have no one to blame but themselves for stirring dissent. It's a natural result of their policies."

Amanda snatched the pamphlet from Liana. "I wonder about you," she scolded. "Keep making comments like that, and you'll surely lose Sean O'Keefe."

Liana leaned back against the pillows propped against the headboard and searched her mind for any comment that wouldn't reveal just how little such a possibility pained her. "It's important for a man and woman to have compatible views. If Sean and I don't, then our friendship won't progress any further, nor should it."

"Do you honestly believe your father would allow someone who wasn't loyal to the king to court you?"

Liana shrugged. "Probably not, but my problems are insignificant compared to those that inspired this author to take up his pen. We've been sheltered too long, Amanda. It's time we both realized the opinions we hear in our homes aren't necessarily the only ones in Virginia."

Amanda made a face. "I'm well aware the malcontents have been grumbling for years, but that doesn't mean we have to be influenced by them."

Liana sat up, slid off her bed, and smoothed out the skirt of her pale yellow gown. "Let's go outside. It's too pretty a day to waste indoors."

As soon as she moved off the bed, Amanda slipped the leaflet into her pocket. "What do your brothers think of the pamphlet?"

"They had no chance to see it. Would you like to show them your copy?"

Amanda frowned as she considered the idea. "No, I better not. Confiding in you is one thing, but I don't want to be accused of spreading such evil lies."

Knowing how easily Amanda twisted the facts to suit her father's opinions, Liana changed the subject to the coming party at the Withrows'. Another wealthy family who revered the king, they would provide amusements aplenty, but not a sentence of substantive dialog the whole evening. The fact that until recently she had been content with such vacuous companions filled her with shame, but she could not think of a way, short of pretending to be deathly ill, to avoid them.

Eager to discover what Liana had thought of his pamphlet, Christian tied a black ribbon to the marsh grass before noon. He then had to endure an uncomfortable wait until four, hoping all the while she had seen his signal and would respond. Not wishing to waste his time if she failed to come, he searched along the riverbank for a frog, and having found a splendid specimen, knelt down to observe him as the inspiration for another cartoon.

Anxious to discuss the leaflet, Liana had walked down to the river after Amanda had gone home, hoping she would find a ribbon and carrying one of her own to leave as a summons if she didn't. When she saw the black streamer, she reacted with delighted surprise, then made a point of hiding her excitement when she returned at four. She found Christian fascinated with a frog hopping along in the mud rather than hidden in the grass, and worried aloud that he had grown careless.

"I'll not be able to come here again if someone sees you. Or is that what you want? Are you hoping I'll be sent to England and you'll be rid of me?"

Christian rose, and again took care to pluck his ribbon from the grass before he pushed the rushes aside to reveal their trail. He nodded for her to precede him. "If you truly believe I'd deliberately try and harm you, then why have you come?"

Liana dared not reveal he was fast becoming the only person with whom she cared to talk. Instead, she laughed at his question. "The way we met proves you love danger, so don't deny that the prospect of humiliating me hasn't crossed your mind."

"I swear to you, it hasn't!"

He looked so painfully sincere that Liana regretted ever mentioning her suspicions. "Then please don't lounge around at the river's edge while you're waiting for me. It looks as though you're blatantly courting disaster, even if it isn't your intention."

Christian gave a mock bow. "Forgive me. I'll wait here for you from now on."

His smile, while warm, wasn't as rakish as usual, nor was his glance as bright. He looked tired, and rather than scold him for that presumptuous comment, Liana held her tongue. "Someone left a leaflet at our house last night. Did the Barclays get one, too?"

"What sort of leaflet?"

"You'd know what I mean if you had seen it. There was a swine wearing a crown on the cover."

"Oh, yes, we got one. Had a good laugh out of it, too.

I don't imagine your folks thought it was funny though, did they?"

Liana looked around, wishing there was somewhere to sit. Responding to her unspoken request, Christian pulled his knife, cut a hefty clump of marsh grass, and folded it into a cushion. He waited until she had settled herself upon it, and then knelt by her side. Their eyes were level now, and sheltered by the tall grass, their conversation instantly took on a more intimate tone. Embarrassed, she looked away.

Christian stroked her cheek to coax her to face him. "Tell me what they said," he invited softly.

Liana found it easier to focus on the fringe at his shoulder than on his eyes as she described the scene when her father had found her reading the pamphlet. "Amanda said her father was outraged, too, so I'm afraid the authorities will conduct a relentless search until they find the author. I hope he has the sense to leave Williamsburg before he's caught."

"Why? Would it pain you if he were?"

Liana hesitated a long moment. "Let's just say I understand his complaints."

"And share them?"

Liana felt as though the comfortable world she had known had begun to tilt, and with each new day she was in greater danger of slipping right off the edge. It was a frightening sensation, and she didn't know how to hold on. "You *are* trying to get me banished to England, aren't you?"

Christian shook his head. "Never. Why are you so afraid to speak your own views rather than parrot your father's?"

"I don't believe 'fear' is the right word."

"Liana, answer me!"

"You needn't shout." Huddled close to him in the grass, Liana felt a kind of security that was completely unlike her family's comfortable bonds. Without conscious thought, she reached out to comb the fringe on Christian's sleeve. The long strands were soft and spilled through her fingers like water.

"My brothers and I are so close in age we were educated together so at an early age I was encouraged to think, to analyze issues carefully and to come to my own conclusions. Most young women aren't permitted that type of freedom, but it can be a curse as well as a blessing. At the end of the war with the French, there were those, like Benjamin Franklin, who said the colonies would be so grateful to England for the victory, we'd become even more loyal.

"There were French statesmen who predicted just the opposite, however, and believed that without a common enemy to bind us, the colonies would soon seek their independence from Great Britain. What I see happening is just that: a natural progression in the colonies from dependence upon England to a desire for a sovereign nation of our own. It can't come without bloodshed, though, for old loyalties are hard to break. My father was born in England, and although he's been here more than twenty years, he's still an Englishman at heart and always will be. I love him dearly, but I know I'll never be able to convince him that what's best for the colonies isn't necessarily what's best for England, or him."

Liana's sparkling green eyes were flecked with gold, her long lashes dark like her brows. Her flawless skin was the pale perfection of buttermilk. As Christian listened to her calmly voiced opinions, he was struck not merely by her beauty but by her seriousness as well. She was nothing like Dominique, who shamelessly flattered every man she met, nor did she resemble his sister, who was a solitary creature more at home in the garden than with men. Liana reminded him most of his Aunt Arielle, who was both bright and stubborn and still occasionally cursed his Uncle Byron in blistering French.

"I had expected only a word or two, not a summary of the situation from a historical perspective," he replied with an engaging chuckle, "but I agree with you. Like children who grow up and must go out on their own, the colonies have outgrown their need for a distant king who rules like a tyrannical toad. I don't wish to make things difficult for you at home. It is enough that you value freedom. You needn't convince your father we're right."

"We?" Liana repeated incredulously. She really didn't see how that pronoun applied to the two of them, and yet when Christian leaned forward to capture her lips in a fervent kiss, she felt how right it was. She slid her hand across his shoulder and around his neck to hold him, but he made no move to pull away. Instead he kissed her a second time, and a third. Eager, demanding, he enfolded her in a confining embrace and she leaned into him, drinking in his warmth and savoring the taste of him.

When he rested his forehead against hers for a moment to allow them both to catch their breath, she pulled away the thong that bound his thick, black hair at his nape; it spilled down his back in wild disarray. He flashed the rakish grin she had missed earlier, and with a careful tug, removed her cap and then the combs that tamed her long, red tresses. He brought a handful of her soft, glossy hair to his face and inhaled the sweet scent of her perfume.

The afternoon light was filtered through the marsh grass, sprinkling their faces with starry patterns. When they kissed again, all sense of separateness ceased. They were joined not just for the sweet intensity of the moment, but on a deeper level than either had dreamed possible. Liana slipped her hands under Christian's shirt to caress his back and sighed slowly as her fingertips slid down his spine.

Inspired by her seductive touch, Christian yanked off his shirt and pressed Liana's face against his bare shoulder. He wound his fingers in her hair and nibbled her earlobe. Pulling her across his lap, he tickled her throat with the tip of his tongue, then spread a trail of tender kisses along the gentle swell of her breasts rising above her bodice. The snug fit of her gown prevented him from moving lower, but it was all he could do not to rip away the clothes that hid what he knew had to be the most luscious of feminine bodies.

Her hands were in his hair, pressing his face close, and overcome with longing, he leaned back to search her face for the truth he tasted in her kiss. He didn't want to frighten her, only to win the words she had stubbornly refused to speak. "If I were to go to your father and ask for you, what would you say?"

Shocked that he would even suggest such a suicidal course, Liana pressed her fingertips to his lips. "No, you mustn't even consider speaking with him. He'd be furious you would even dare to ask. He'd throw you out and send me to England within the hour." Tears welled up in her eyes. "I can't bear to think I might never see you again."

"And I can't bear to leave you here," Christian responded angrily. "What would you have me do?"

Flustered, Liana tried to rise, but Christian pushed her back down into the grass. "Please. What you ask is impossible. Let me go," she begged.

Christian released his hold and raised his hands. "I won't keep you here against your will, but meeting in secret and exchanging stolen kisses isn't nearly enough for me. Is it for you?" He held his breath, praying again that she would speak of love.

Liana shook her head slowly, fumbled around for the combs he had tossed aside, used them to secure her hair, and replaced her cap. "No," she finally assured him. "Nothing's been the same since I met you, and I need more time to decide what to do."

"What *can* you do?" Christian challenged.

Liana stared into his dark brown eyes and knew choosing him meant turning her back not only on the family she loved, but all her friends as well. It was an agonizing dilemma, and yet, she could see no other way. She brought his hand to her lips and kissed his knuckles. "You've come to mean so much to me, but please, don't ask for more than I can willingly give."

"I want your heart and soul," Christian whispered against her lips.

"You have them." Liana kissed him one last time, her passion a match for his, before she pulled away and with a choked sob, left him alone in the small clearing.

Her perfume clung to his skin, and Christian moaned with desire as he watched the tears she'd shed at their parting trickle down his chest. He caught a salty droplet and brought it to his lips. Cursing his own folly, he knew he had gotten exactly what he deserved for going after Ian Scott's daughter, but it did not change his determination to have her.

Liana attended the Withrows' party that weekend, but none of the Barclays were there. At first relieved she would not have to avoid Christian, she soon began to miss him and looked for him vainly all evening. Sean O'Keefe and his friends were treated with respect here, but continually questioned as to whether or not the author of what had quickly become known as the swine pamphlet had been found.

Sharing a cup of punch with Liana, Sean vented his frustration. "The leaflet had to have been printed elsewhere, because the type doesn't match that used by the local printer."

"How clever of you to investigate such a detail. Do you suppose the pamphlet could have come from Boston?"

"It's possible, but someone distributed it here. Probably several people, in fact. There's no way of knowing how far the treasonous conspiracy might extend until we apprehend one of the members."

"You've no clues?"

Sean scanned Liana's expression but found only innocent curiosity rather than any hint of deception. "Not a one, but if the swine pamphlet is followed by another, it will double our chances of catching the culprits."

Liana waited for him to explain how, but Sean changed the subject and she was left wondering. He was a proficient dancer, but he lacked Christian's grace, and no matter how hard she tried, she couldn't find more than an occasional smile for him. He appeared to be content with that for the evening, but she returned home feeling sad and lonely.

The next week, news reached Virginia of Parliament's passage of the Quebec Act, and Morgan pressed his father for details at the dinner table. "How can Parliament permit the continued usage of French civil law, or recognize the Roman Catholic Church? The French lost the war, and they don't deserve any such special considerations."

Feeling forced to defend Parliament, Ian reluctantly laid his knife and fork aside and wiped his mouth on his napkin. "It's merely a gesture, Morgan, meant to quell dissent among the French colonists in Quebec. You needn't concern yourself because it has nothing to do with us."

"Perhaps not," Liana agreed, "but extending the boundaries of the Province of Quebec to the Ohio River down into land previously claimed by Massachusetts, Connecticut, and Virginia certainly does. How are we to expand if the way is blocked in the West?"

Ian sent Robin a pleading glance, but the dear woman just shook her head and he had to continue with only her moral support. "Parliament has to consider not merely our interests, but Canada's as well."

"You fought in a war with France over control of the

Ohio Valley," Liana reminded him. "A lot of good men must have died to win territory Parliament has just given right back to the French."

"The people of Quebec are English now," Ian exclaimed.

"Of course they are," Morgan commented sarcastically. "But they speak French, have French civil law, and worship in Catholic churches. They're very strange Englishmen, if you ask me."

"Well, no one has asked you," Ian replied. "Now let's discuss a less stressful topic." He waited, but while Robin continued to eat her dinner, his children stared at him with disbelieving eyes. "All right, the Quebec Act is a blow," he finally admitted, "and I'm not pleased with it either."

Enormously relieved to have finally won the truth from their father, Morgan gave a delighted whoop. "I'll bet there will be another pamphlet," he announced. He had seen a copy of the first at the home of a friend, and was still dismayed that his father had burned theirs without letting them all read it.

"I absolutely refuse to discuss libelous trash at this table," Ian proclaimed, and he stubbornly directed the conversation to the studies he hoped his sons would undertake in the fall.

While appearing to listen attentively, Liana was actually wondering about the author of the infamous pamphlet. She thought Morgan was right, for if the Quebec Act did not inspire sufficient anger to prompt a second issue, then nothing would. They couldn't be the only ones to have considered the prospect either, and she feared Sean O'Keefe might already have soldiers stationed behind trees waiting for the midnight messenger to reappear. That thought was troubling, but she had no idea whom to warn.

* * *

Three nights later, Liana was awakened after midnight by the sound of a rider drawing near. Although consumed with curiosity as to his identity, she went no farther than the top of the stairs, where she waited for her father to appear. When he had not left the room he shared with her mother after five minutes, she assumed they must be sleeping far more soundly than she had been and had not heard the horseman. Still, she had been warned not to go out at night, and did not want to disobey him.

Knowing she could never wait until morning to read the next pamphlet, she tiptoed down the hall to Morgan's room. She tapped lightly, and when there was no response, knocked more insistently. Her brother responded with a muffled protest, but a moment later came to the door.

"I think another pamphlet's been left on the porch. Father forbade me to go out and look for it. Will you please—"

Before she could complete her question, Morgan pushed by her and flew down the stairs. Then, catching himself before he made too great a commotion, he opened the front door slowly. Moonlight flooded the foyer as he darted out, then quickly returned, waving a leaflet.

Liana's hands shook with excitement, making her candle difficult to hold, but she touched her lips with her other hand, warning him to be silent. When he rejoined her at the top of the stairs, they went into his room to read the pamphlet. Morgan carried it over to his desk and lit the lamp from Liana's candle.

Unlike the first issue, this leaflet had no satirical cartoon on the front. Instead, there was a map of the Ohio Valley with the outline of the Province of Quebec dripping down over it like blood. On the inside, there was a list of the men from Williamsburg who had lost their lives in the French and Indian War, followed by the single question: Did our heros die in vain?

Liana took a deep breath. "Sean thought the first pamphlet was printed elsewhere and merely distributed here, but clearly the author knows Williamsburg too well to be a stranger."

The light from the lamp cast Morgan's features in high relief; his expression reflected none of his amusement upon seeing the cartoon of the crowned swine. "I was expecting another joke at the king's expense, but this is every bit as serious as it should be. We've been betrayed, Liana. Not merely these men listed here, but all of us."

Awakened by their voices, Cameron pushed the door open and peered in. "What's going on?"

Morgan motioned for him to come in. "We've received another pamphlet. What do you think of it?"

Cameron held it close to the lamp. Instantly recognizing the cover for the bitter indictment it was, he did not need to read all the names inside. "Should we wake Father?" he asked. "He ought to see this."

"Yes, he should," Liana agreed, "but tomorrow will be soon enough. Come on, let's go back to bed."

"After seeing this, how can you just go back to sleep?" Morgan asked in an anxious whisper.

"I don't know that I can, but I'm going to try." She paused for a last look at the pamphlet, and something about the boldness of the cover caught her eye. The map of the Ohio Valley was rendered in the same strongly masculine style as the grossly insulting swine, so it had obviously been done by the same artist. It was a block print, not a drawing, but still, the style was hauntingly familiar and she grew perplexed.

"Do either of you have friends who draw?" she asked.

Prompted to reexamine the cover art, both young men looked past the design to the technique. "Not this well," Morgan replied, and Cameron had no such talented friends, either. "Do you?" they asked.

"No, but this reminds me of something I've seen, I just can't remember what."

"A sign in town perhaps?" Cameron suggested.

Liana shook her head. "I really can't recall. I'll see you in the morning. Shall we wait until after breakfast to show the pamphlet to Father?"

"I'd like to wake him now," Morgan admitted, "but I suppose we should allow him to wake on his own and have breakfast before we confront him again. I don't see how he can be insulted, though, when he isn't pleased with the Quebec Act, either."

Leaving her brothers to discuss how best to approach their father in the morning, Liana returned to her room. As expected, sleep didn't come easily, and just as she was about to drift off, she remembered Christian's note. A flash of firm, black strokes streaked across her mind. Horrified by the possibility that he might be the artist, she left her bed and carried her candle over to her dresser.

The beaded pouch lay hidden right where she had left it. Opening it with trembling fingers, she removed the tightly folded note. Looking past the words, she studied the slant of the downward strokes. Bold slashes of ink, they were as distinctive as the signature and even without comparing the note side by side with the block print, Liana was convinced she had discovered the identity of the artist.

She refolded the note and again hid it within the pouch at the back of her lingerie drawer. She knew she would never be able to sleep now, and lay across her bed waiting for dawn, when she intended to leave a ribbon for Christian. She had sworn she would never have a need to summon him, but she had one now and prayed he would respond as promptly as she always had.

Christian had gone down to the river to leave a ribbon for Liana and was stunned to find a pale pink streamer already in place. Elated, he returned at four and waited as he had promised in the small clearing hidden among the marsh grass. When he heard a soft rustling as she made her way toward him, he tried to contain his joy but his smile still grew too wide. As soon as she reached him, he pulled her into a warm embrace.

"I'm glad you called for a change," he confessed before kissing her soundly.

Christian had always given affectionate farewells, but Liana was nonetheless shocked by the enthusiasm of his greeting. "Wait," she responded when she caught her breath. "I've an important question I must ask."

Not nearly satisfied with a single kiss, Christian nonetheless tried to be patient and slackened his hold on her. "Go right ahead, and I'll try and find the correct reply."

"Another pamphlet was delivered last night." Christian nodded, but she rushed on before he could speak. "Something about the way the map on the cover was drawn got me thinking. I saved the note you sent me, and the boldness of the strokes is exactly the same. Are you the artist? Are the Barclays distributing them?"

"That's two questions."

"Christian, answer me!"

Casting off all hint of humor, Christian stared down at her. Her cheeks were flushed, her eyes glowing with the intensity of her suspicions, but she was the daughter of a staunch Loyalist, and he dared not trust her with the truth. There weren't that many people outside his family who had ever seen his handwriting, let alone saved a sample, so there was little chance anyone else would recognize any illustrations as his. Unless, of course, he admitted he was the artist and she reported it to the authorities.

"I'm flattered you saved my note," he confided honestly, "but I doubt there's anything particularly remarkable about my writing. I thought this latest leaflet was positively inspired, as it focused on the true cost in blood of the Quebec Act. My Uncle Elliott was killed by the Abenaki just prior to the hostilities leading to General Braddock's defeat, and his name's in the pamphlet. Both my father

and my Uncle Byron fought with Braddock, and in the
French and Indian War.

"Your father fought in that war as well. Isn't your family
as outraged as mine that Parliament has given away territory clearly owned by Virginia? What does your father say?"

Christian hadn't answered her question, and Liana
wasn't so distracted by his not to notice how evasive he
had been. "Yes, we feel every bit as betrayed as everyone
else must. My father read the pamphlet after breakfast,
went into his study, and hasn't come out since. He's fond
of brandy, but I've never seen him begin drinking so early
in the day. He's supported the king when the issues were
abstract, like taxes, but this is the first to really involve him
directly and it's hurt him badly."

"Good, then perhaps he'll finally see the laws Parliament has continually foisted upon us for what they really
are."

His buckskins provided a soft cushion for her cheek,
and Liana relaxed against him. "I'm frightened."

He hugged her more tightly. "Why?"

"My father isn't a man who makes compromises easily."

Christian couldn't help but laugh at that, and Liana
quickly backed out of his arms. He caught her hand, but
she remained aloof, her chin tilted at a belligerent angle.
"I'm not laughing at you," he assured her, "but Ian Scott
refused to make the compromise that would have allowed
him to accept the child of the wife he adored. Instead, he
denied I ever existed. Now he's being forced to accept the
truth about Parliament, and if he takes that equally hard,
all I can say is that he deserves to."

Liana yanked her hand from his. "I didn't come here
to argue about my father."

"He's also mine," Christian reminded her.

"Will you please stop saying that? You're plainly Hunter's
son, not my father's."

Christian nodded. "I'm also my mother's son, and she was Mrs. Ian Scott."

"Where is this leading?" Liana threw right back at him. "All I want to know is if you are behind the pamphlets and it's plain you've no intention of revealing it if you are. Dredging up your old argument with my father has absolutely nothing to do with it." Then, with the same sudden clarity with which she had recognized his hand in the map, she saw something far more damning.

"Wait a minute, I'll take that back. If you are publishing the pamphlets, and I think there's a very good chance you are, then it isn't to impress others with your political views, is it? Your only goal is to humiliate my father. Well, Parliament has succeeded in doing that on its own."

Liana backed away from the handsome brave. "How could I have been so blind? You are evil, Christian, and even if you leave all the black ribbons in the world, I'll never meet you here again."

"Liana!" Christian reached for her, but she twisted free and plunged into the grass, forging her own tortured trail to the river. She was too angry to listen, and in his heart, he knew she was very close to the truth. He sincerely agreed with those wanting independence for the colonies, but the fact that Ian Scott was on the other side gave the Loyalists a face he already despised. But that hatred did not extend to Ian's lovely daughter.

Nine

Desperate to avoid another disastrous scene with David Slauson, Johanna peeked out the window to make certain he wasn't in the yard before she left the house to run errands. She hated having to be so wary. It was annoying to have to stop to be sure the way was clear before she went out to the kitchen or laundry. It was also a continual reminder of what a tremendous disappointment the handsome young man had been.

Even worse, thoughts of him always triggered the fear that every young man she met would be equally appalled when he learned she was part Seneca. She had spent her whole life sheltered in the bosom of a loving family, but now the outside world was beginning to intrude and she didn't like it one bit. She and her mother were close, but Johanna couldn't express her growing discomfort without hurting her feelings and she would never do that.

Her Aunt Arielle was knowledgeable about so many things, but being French, was an outsider, too. Dominique was so full of life she would never be able to understand how isolated Johanna felt. Recalling the young women she had met at the Langs' party, Johanna wished she could talk with Liana Scott, who had impressed her the most, but there was no way the two of them could ever be friends.

Preoccupied, she wandered down to the dock, sat down on the edge, and dangled her feet off the end as she had as a child. There were a great many advantages to remaining a child, but at eighteen, she knew she could no longer delay growing up. Sunshine sparkled on the water, but failed to lift her dismal mood.

"Whatever are you doing out here?" Belle called as she walked out on the dock. Johanna's thirteen-year-old cousin had always preferred fishing to playing with dolls, and Falcon was her usual companion. "It's too late to fish, and where is your pole?"

Johanna raised her hand to shade her eyes as she looked up at Belle. As pretty as Dominique, Belle was always into one kind of mischief or another. That afternoon she was barefooted, and the hem of her striped blue dress was damp. "Just look at you," Johanna exclaimed. "You'll have to bathe before supper."

Unconcerned, Belle just shrugged and sat down cross-legged beside Johanna. "You ought to come fishing some morning. The best time is just before dawn when the mist is still floating above the river. The fish just leap onto your hook then."

It was plain Belle considered that her favorite time of the day, but Johanna wasn't convinced she was right. "Somehow I just never got interested in fishing the way you and my brothers did."

"Fishing isn't much of a challenge. All it takes is patience, and you've got plenty of that."

"Thank you, Belle. Maybe I will come out with you someday soon."

Having convinced Johanna of the benefits of fishing, Belle dropped the subject. She bent her leg, looped her arms over it, and rested her cheek against her knee, "This is a good place to think, isn't it?"

Johanna tried not to laugh, but it was impossible to get much thinking done with such inquisitive company. "Yes, I'm sorry I haven't come out here more often."

"I don't blame you for preferring the garden to the

house. Dominique's got another caller. Can't remember this one's name, but he looks as befuddled as all the rest."

Johanna thought "dazzled" was a more apt description, but didn't correct her young cousin. "In a couple of years, you'll have your share of callers, too."

Belle made a face. The bridge of her nose was sprinkled with freckles, and her blond curls were barely tamed by her cap. "Not if I can help it. Most of the men who come to see Dominique are witless fools—I sure don't need such useless company."

"Dominique's very beautiful. It's no wonder her callers get flustered. I hope you'll understand that when young men flock to visit you and be as considerate as Dominique."

Belle looked aghast. "I'm not going to pamper fools. But what about you—where are your callers?"

With the tactless grace of a child, Belle had asked the question Johanna could no longer suppress. "When I went to the Langs' party, there were a couple of army officers who asked if they might call but I told them I'd rather they didn't. I knew the king's soldiers wouldn't be welcome here, and I really didn't like them all that well anyway."

"There are plenty of other men in Williamsburg."

Johanna gazed out over the water. "Yes, but they want pretty blondes like you and Dominique."

"Do you really think so?"

"Yes, I'm afraid that's true." Tears welled up in Johanna's eyes, but she quickly turned away to hide them.

"Well, I don't," Belle declared. "You're every bit as pretty as we are, and there are plenty of men who like brunettes." The dock creaked under the weight of a man's step and Belle turned to find David Slauson watching them. "You're the new man, aren't you?" she greeted him.

David could not recall ever seeing a prettier child, and answered without thinking. "Yes, I am. I hope you two are being careful there. I wouldn't want you to fall off the dock and drown."

Belle laughed and got to her feet. "We know how to swim. No sane person lives on the river without learning how, and there's nothing wrong with our minds, is there, Johanna?"

"Not a thing," Johanna replied, but she remained seated and continued to gaze out at the James River. She wanted to reach out and grab Belle's ankle to keep her there, but the youngster moved away too quickly. She left the docks and with a graceful, dancing skip started back toward the house, forcing Johanna to face David alone. When he knelt by her side, she shook her head.

"We've absolutely nothing to say to each other, Mr. Slauson. Please go."

"I won't bother you long," he promised. "I just wanted to tell you again how sorry I am for making such a careless remark about the Indian I'd seen here when I didn't know he was your father. I grew up in Boston where we didn't see one Indian a year, and while I know that's no excuse, I was frightened of them. I've done some work with your father since we last talked and he seems like a fine man. Being new here, I hadn't had a chance to meet him, and—"

"Mr. Slauson, please. Don't embarrass us any further. Just go."

Frustrated that her tone hadn't softened, David reluctantly rose to his feet. "I truly am sorry."

"Yes, I'm sure you are."

David hesitated to leave, but when Johanna continued to refuse to glance his way, he grew too discouraged to stay and left the dock with a slow, shuffling step. He went over to the tobacco shed where the press was hidden and made certain everything was stored out of sight. It was too late in the day to begin work on something new, so he stood in the doorway, watching the river and gathering the courage to move on.

When he saw Christian later, he couldn't hide his sorrow. "I've enjoyed working for you," he explained, "I really have, but I think my coming here was a mistake and I ought to leave."

Caught by surprise, Christian immediately began to argue. "Look, I need you to operate the press. I know you don't fit in with the other field hands, and I'll ask my uncle to assign you more work that doesn't involve them. Will that make you happy?"

David slid his hands into his hip pockets and dug his toe into the dirt. "I appreciate what you're offering, but I've made such a mess of things that I have to go."

"What mess? What are you talking about?"

David was reluctant to discuss such a personal issue, especially since it involved Christian's sister. "There was someone I'd hoped to impress, and instead, I just insulted her. If I stay, I'll make us both even more miserable."

Christian had no idea to whom he was referring, but his scowl was convincing, and he refused to let David go without learning more. "Tell me who you're talking about, and I'll do my best to help you apologize."

"I've already tried, and she just told me to go away."

"So you're giving up?"

Thinking Christian remarkably dense, David gazed toward the heavens. "What else can I do? I've never had much luck with women."

Christian reached out and gave David's shoulder a hearty shove. "To hear you tell it, you've never had much luck with anything and it's no wonder if you quit so easily."

Startled, David caught himself. "You don't know anything about me."

"I know enough. Now you may think because I belong to a wealthy family everything comes easily, but you're wrong. There's a young woman I'm trying to impress, too, but her father despises me, and right now, she's not fond of me, either. In similar circumstances you'd probably give up, but I never will. I intend to have that girl, and nothing her father says or does will stop me. Now, show some courage for a change. Tell me your young woman's name and I'll help you make up with her."

"I'd know you'd try, but—"

Christian stepped close and spoke in a threatening whisper. "Give me her name or I'll beat it out of you."

David couldn't blame him for becoming frustrated, but it was still very difficult for him to speak the name. "It's Johanna," he finally confessed. "I met her the first day I came here. She's the one who got me this job."

Christian had never dreamed David was talking about his sister. Dumbfounded, he stared at him a moment too long, and then caught himself. "Johanna is the sweetest girl in the world. How could you possibly have insulted her?"

"I'd really rather not say."

Christian turned away. "Then I'll have to ask her."

"No! Wait." Fear was making David's mouth too dry to speak, and he was worried that no matter what he said, Christian would be as deeply insulted as Johanna had been. He wanted to walk away, but Christian had demanded that he show more courage, and he did not want to be thought of as a coward. Choosing his words with care, he disclosed how he had mentioned his surprise at finding an Indian brave there.

Christian didn't need to hear any more. "I understand. When he was young, my father worked on a trading post up on the Hudson River and he used to fight for money. Whenever some new traders would come wandering into the post, the men who knew my father would suggest a fight. Because no one expected much of an Indian, there would always be a lot of money wagered against him, but he never lost, not even once. You fell right into the same trap. They just saw an Indian brave, and made up their minds what that meant.

"It's no wonder Johanna won't speak to you, but the real question is, how much do you care?"

"Enough to leave," David explained with a helpless shrug.

"That's the wrong answer." Christian rested his hands on David's shoulders. "Now I promised to help you and I will, but you have to care enough not to quit, no matter how difficult it is to win her forgiveness. If you can't give me your word on it, then there's no reason to bother helping you because you will have proved you're not man enough for her."

Feeling utterly defeated, David couldn't meet Christian's gaze. "I've nothing to offer her."

Christian dug his fingers into David's shoulders and grinned as he winced. "The story of how Hunter came to be my father is too long to tell, but if an Indian brave can become part of the Barclays, there's nothing to keep a white man of good character out. Now go on and have supper with the rest of the hands, and we'll start working on Johanna tomorrow."

When Christian dropped his hands, David's first impulse was to run, but he stood his ground. "I really didn't expect you to help me. I don't understand why you are."

David Slauson was six feet tall, bright, handsome, and the most insecure individual Christian had ever met. He was also the only man who had ever expressed an interest in Johanna, but Christian wasn't about to reveal that. "I love my sister, and I'd like to see her happy. If you have any chance at all of giving her a happy life, then I want to see you have it." He walked off while David was still wondering about his motives, but before going to bed, he stopped by Johanna's room.

Already dressed in a snowy white nightgown, she was brushing out her hair, but stopped while she waited for Christian to confide the reason for his visit. As soon as he mentioned David Slauson, she gestured emphatically with her brush. "Oh, no, I don't even want to hear it."

Refusing to leave, Christian leaned back against her

door. "Well, you are going to hear it anyway. David's such a shy soul. He reminds me a lot of you. He's absolutely mortified to have insulted you, and I think you ought to forgive him. After all, he wasn't saying anything that most people don't think when they see an Indian. Father's used to it, and he's proud of being Seneca. So am I."

Johanna sat down on the edge of her bed. Her bedroom was painted the same shade of pale blue that she frequently wore, and by lamplight, it was a decidedly melancholy hue. "I wish I could say I'm proud, too, but I'm just confused. I've never felt as though I'm part Seneca and part white. I'm just me."

"Whatever you are, it's plain David Slauson is smitten. He's so discouraged he wants to leave. If you don't care anything about him, I'll tell him to go."

Johanna left the bed and came toward him. "Oh, no, you mustn't do that. He came such a long way looking for work and it would be exceedingly foolish of him to leave just because he doesn't get along with me."

Christian responded with a sly chuckle. "Why is it so difficult for a woman to admit she likes a man?"

"Aren't men supposed to speak of their feelings first? At least, I think that's the way it's supposed to happen. Why don't you ask Dominique? She's the expert on men. I don't know anything at all."

"You know a great deal," Christian argued, "and you're the one who ought to have the houseful of callers."

Johanna raised her chin proudly. "We both know that won't ever happen." Feeling very much alone, she thought of David and how tired and sad he had looked when she had first seen him trudging up the road. Dominique's callers all rode fine horses, but David didn't even own an old mule. "I don't mean to be cruel to David," she admitted with a sigh. "After all, he only said what a lot of people must think. Still—"

"Even with your hair down, you don't look Indian,"

Christian murmured softly. "You look like Mother so it's no wonder David thought he could confide his fears in you. You needn't forgive him if you don't want to, though. He's nice enough, but there will be other men."

That optimistic prediction pierced Johanna's heart. "I wish I believed that."

"There will be!"

At that, what came instantly to Johanna's mind were handsome, black-eyed Seneca braves and she knew she would feel no more comfortable with them than she did with British officers. She had felt at home with David, though, for a while at least, and that had meant a great deal to her, perhaps too much. She had not even realized how pathetically lonely she was until he arrived, and it was plain he was lonely, too.

"Convince David to stay, and I'll forgive him," she finally promised.

"I'll do my best, but don't wait too long. He's already in grave danger of dying from a broken heart."

"I thought that only happened in novels and poems."

"No, I'm sure he's in mortal peril. Ask him to tell you something about himself. Maybe he's an orphan who's never known love."

"Are you deliberately trying to make me feel guilty?"

Christian broke into an easy grin as he opened her door. "No, not at all. Let me know what happens."

As he let himself out, Johanna thought he made an unlikely matchmaker, but perhaps that was precisely what she and David Slauson required.

The next afternoon, Sean O'Keefe rode onto the Barclay estate with a six-man patrol. He introduced himself to Byron, and did not mince words as to his purpose. "I'm sure you're aware someone has been distributing seditious propaganda. Lord Dunsmore wants it stopped. Because he is certain you know who's behind it, he suggests you warn them immediately to cease the enterprise. I won't search your home and grounds today, but should I have to return on a similar errand, you may be assured that I will."

Seeing a British officer at the door, Dominique came to her father's side. She was expecting a caller or two that afternoon and was dressed in a coral gown that enhanced her fair coloring superbly. She smiled up at Sean as though he were merely paying a social call.

Distracted by the stunning blonde, Sean repeated himself and then, feeling foolish, waited for Byron to respond. He surveyed the neatly kept gardens and marvelous view of the river, but Dominique's perfume invaded his senses to an alarming degree. There were a great many beautiful women in Williamsburg, but this one was very special indeed.

Byron noted the surreptitious glances passing between Sean and Dominique, and tried not to show his amusement. "You may tell our governor that I said if he's appalled by the pamphlets, he ought to do more to remedy the complaints that prompted them. Now you must excuse me—I have business that requires my attention."

Sean gave a mock bow as Byron turned away, but he was enormously pleased when Dominique did not follow her father off the porch. "I believe we met at the Langs' party," he said with a smile. "Perhaps you don't remember me."

"On the contrary," Dominique replied, "I distinctly recall thinking how handsome you were, and it wasn't merely because of your uniform."

Her voice was pitched lower than Sean had expected, and flavored with a slight French accent. She was the only woman he had ever met who combined a radiant innocence with sultry, flirtatious charm. It was enormously appealing, and for a long moment, he could not think of a compliment to pay in return. He simply stared, as so many of her callers did, while his heart raced far ahead of his brain.

"I'm sorry we've met again under such difficult circumstances," he finally found the presence of mind to say.

Dominique batted her long eyelashes and watched Sean's deep tan darken with an incriminating blush, it was an exhilarating feeling to know she had such power over him. Her glance swept down his sleek frame as she wondered just how easy he would be to arouse. When he shifted his stance awkwardly, she reveled in the knowledge that he already was.

"You must pay us another visit soon, Captain. I do so love to entertain." Her last word was a mere whisper that drew him near. She smiled then, her expression a glorious invitation to delights he could so easily imagine. "Good day."

"Good day, Miss Barclay," Sean responded, and looking back at her over his shoulder, he very nearly fell down the steps. His men snickered at his folly, and he berated them sternly just as soon as the house was out of sight. Their next stop was the Scott plantation, where he told his men to rest while he bid Liana good day.

Liana was surprised to see soldiers with Sean, but he quickly explained their purpose. "I'm hoping to frighten whoever is behind the pamphlets so we won't be bothered with another. The governor believes a show of force will discourage dissent, and I'm hoping he's right. If he isn't, let's just say I've taken precautions to make certain the culprits are caught."

"How very prudent of you," Liana managed to murmur. "Will you have men out searching for them every night?"

Torn between the need for secrecy and the desire to impress her, Sean leaned close to whisper in her ear. "At every crossroads, but I'm trusting you not to tell."

Liana forced a bright laugh. "And whom would I tell,

Captain? My father's a Loyalist, and those opposing the Crown's actions don't confide in us."

"I thought not, but we've no way of knowing how far this conspiracy extends."

"All the way to Boston, surely."

Sean straightened up. "No doubt. Well, I must be on my way, but I'll come back when I have more time."

"Please do." Liana watched him ride away with his troops and fought the impulse to leave a ribbon for Christian. After the way they had parted, he would surely misinterpret her purpose and she did not want to give him that opportunity. Uneasy nevertheless, she decided to wait until the weekend when she felt certain she would see him at a party. If not, she would slip him a note after church, but there would be no more secret meetings by the river.

Liana's carefully considered plan was forgotten the very next day when she and Amanda rode into Williamsburg. They visited the milliner's to purchase ribbon and lace and as they left the sweetly perfumed shop, Amanda called out excitedly.

"Look, there's Beau! Quick, let's cross the street."

Liana searched the people passing by across the way on Duke of Gloucester Street and immediately caught sight of Christian's buckskins. He and Beau were standing in front of Wetherburn's Tavern laughing together, and it did not take much in the way of imagination to guess what they found so humorous. Certain one of them had made a joke at a woman's expense, Liana hung back.

"I don't have a single thing to say to Beau."

"Good. Talk to Christian." Taking her astonished friend's hand, Amanda guided her across the wide boulevard. Never at a loss for words, she greeted Beau with a delighted smile. "How nice to see you, Mr. Barclay. I missed you at the Withrows' party. The dancing wasn't nearly as entertaining without you."

"You're very kind," Beau replied, "but I'm afraid I'm really not much of a dancer."

Her face burning with shame, Liana turned away and tried not to listen as Amanda boldly coaxed Beau into revealing his plans for the weekend. She could feel Christian watching her, which embarrassed her all the more. When he stepped away from Beau's side and came to hers, she had to force herself to look up at him. When she saw him smile, her stomach tightened into a painful knot and her heart skipped a beat.

"Good day, Miss Scott. You're looking well."

"So are you, Mr. Hunter." Liana stole a glance at Amanda and was relieved to see her friend was too absorbed to eavesdrop. They were on a public street, and while this was no place to pass warnings, she feared it might be the best chance she would have.

"I doubt you will be for long, though," she whispered, drawing him close. "Captain O'Keefe plans to post men at each crossroads until he captures the man who's been delivering the pamphlets."

"Is that a fact?" Christian replied casually as though she had confided some bit of inconsequential news. He was elated, however, that she had breached O'Keefe's confidence. He had not insisted that she choose between them, but clearly she had. He winked at her and watched her blush deepen. "Please, Miss Scott, you mustn't take on so or people will suspect we're lovers."

"If you value your eyes, you won't give me yet another reason to claw them out," she hissed.

"I'll be more careful then, for I wouldn't want to miss seeing you."

Beau was chuckling over something Amanda had said, and Liana feared their conversation would drag on forever, leaving her to deflect Christian's amorous jests with growing exasperation. She had at least succeeded in warning him, but she doubted he would heed her words. A carriage rolled by, sending up a cloud of dust that made her choke, and Christian instantly drew her into his arms as he made a great show of patting her back to help her breathe. She didn't know which was worse, the dust or the sweet torture of his embrace.

"It's always been you," he whispered before she pulled away.

Startled, Liana nodded, but she still believed he simply regarded her as a convenient detour on the way to destroy her father. Then why did you warn him? her conscience chided, but she dared not confess the reason even to herself. "Amanda, we really must go," she insisted as she stepped around Christian to approach her friend. "We're expected home for dinner, and we don't dare be late."

Amanda reached out to squeeze Beau's arm. "I'm sorry we won't be attending the same parties this weekend. Perhaps next week we'll have better luck."

"Yes, I hope so," Beau replied.

Amanda looked back over her shoulder to wave, but Liana's only concern was not being struck by a wagon as they crossed the street. When they reached their horses, she hastened to mount and turned her mare toward home. Equally agile, Amanda quickly caught up with her.

"The Barclays have been invited to several parties this weekend, but not the ones we're attending. It's so annoying that we don't have more mutual friends. I do wish you'd give another party, Liana, and ask them."

"My family would not even allow me to invite them to a funeral, so you'll have to wait for someone else."

Amanda turned back to look again for Beau, but he and Christian were nowhere in sight. "What did you and Christian find to whisper about? I swear, if you didn't insist you're forbidden to see him, I'd suspect you're quite taken with him."

Liana pulled her mare to a halt. The seriousness of her expression matched her words. "Don't link our names even in jest, Amanda, or I'll be made to suffer in ways too horrible to imagine."

Amanda's dark eyes widened in dismay. "I do so wish you'd tell me why your parents don't get along with the Barclays. Not that my folks do, but because you're such close neighbors, it's a shame you're not good friends."

"A great many friendships will end if war comes with England."

"Do you really think it will go that far?"

Fear made Amanda's eyes bright. "Yes, the sheer stupidity of the Quebec Act will force a violent response. It can be no other way."

Amanda shuddered despite the pleasant warmth of the day. "I didn't realize until lately what a pessimist you are, Liana. Surely things can't be as desperate as that."

Liana thought of Sean stationing troops at each crossroads and feared they were even worse. "We'll just have to wait and see," she said instead, but she was terrified something awful was going to happen to Christian. Her warning hadn't fazed him, and sick with dread, she listened to Amanda ramble on about the next party, and doubted she could find the strength to attend.

Ten

After supper that night, Christian paced the study as he relayed Liana's warning, but he did not divulge the source. "Captain O'Keefe is posting men at every crossroad to intercept us. We know the countryside better than any British troops ever will so I'll just avoid the roads, but I don't want Beau caught delivering pamphlets in town. What should we do?"

Byron took a sip of brandy as he considered the question. Insulted that Christian apparently believed he could not take care of himself, Beau frowned pensively. Hunter, his arms crossed over his chest, leaned back against the wall. Standing just outside the circle of light thrown by the lamp on the desk, his buckskins faded into the shadows, but he was very much a presence.

Assuming his customary role as the group's leader, Byron sat forward and rested his arms on his desk. "We knew this was going to be dangerous when we began. That the army's trying to stop us comes as no surprise."

"I'll take Beau's place," Hunter announced in a tone that brooked no argument.

"I don't need to be protected," Beau argued. "My life isn't worth more than yours or your son's."

"That's not the issue," Byron interjected, "at least I hope it's not. The concern is for your safety, Beau, and we both know Hunter and Christian have a more extensive knowledge of the wilds. The skills of the Seneca impart a cunning we can't even hope to approach. If they have to flee into the woods, they've a much better chance of getting away than you would."

"What do you mean, 'if'? With soldiers at every crossroads, there's sure to be trouble," Beau predicted darkly.

"Only if they fire at each other," Christian boasted. "They'll have no chance to get me."

"Nor me," Hunter echoed.

"Now that that's decided," Christian continued, "Beau and I will take Johanna and Dominique to the MacGregors' party Saturday night. I'll appear to have too much to drink, and leave early. After partying all evening, everyone will sleep too soundly to hear me ride by, and I'll stay off the roads this time."

Hunter nodded his approval. "I'll leave my horse outside town, go in on foot, pass out the pamphlets, then walk away. The soldiers standing guard won't hear a thing."

"Sounds good to me," Byron said.

"Not to me," Beau argued, but unmoved by his complaints, Byron and Hunter left to rejoin their wives. Alone with Christian, Beau left his chair to face him. "We were together this morning, except for the brief time I was talking with Amanda Tuttle and you were with Liana Scott. Why didn't you tell our fathers she was the one who gave us the warning?"

Anticipating a lengthy interrogation, Christian leaned back against the desk. "Because the source of the information was irrelevant."

"Hardly. First of all, Liana must suspect you have something to do with the pamphlets or she wouldn't have mentioned O'Keefe's plans. Second, it proves she must care about your welfare or she wouldn't have done it. Are you still denying there's anything between you?"

Christian couldn't help but smile. "I haven't denied it,"

he reminded Beau. "I've just said that my interest in her is not prompted by revenge against her father."

Beau saw none of the cocky arrogance in Christian that had infuriated him in their earlier conversation about Liana and his own anger suddenly seemed unreasonable. Trying to make amends, he adopted a conciliatory tone. "If you truly care for Liana, what are you going to do? Ian will never accept you as her husband."

"I know, so the choice will have to be hers rather than his."

"Do you honestly believe she'd defy him on such a crucial matter?"

Christian thought of his last encounter with Liana at the river. While it had ended poorly, there had been some blissful moments. "She's already defying him," he revealed. "Warning me about the soldiers took great courage, and I won't forget it."

Beau could see another problem Christian had yet to anticipate. "Do you honestly believe Ian Scott's daughter would be welcome here? Your father can't be any more fond of Ian than he is of us. Have you ever told Hunter how highly you regard Ian's daughter?"

"If I didn't know you want Liana for yourself, I'd be angered by that comment. My father has the wife he wants, and he wouldn't forbid me the woman I love."

Beau gasped. "You love her, Christian? Has it truly gone that far?"

The words had slipped out so easily, Christian had not realized how much he had revealed. Beau was so earnest in his manner, however, he would not deny his feelings now. "Yes, and she's as wrong for me as Melissa was for my father, but I pray our story won't end as tragically."

Beau swallowed hard, for what Christian had admitted frightened him as much as the danger inherent in producing the pamphlets. He refused to stand by and watch Christian and Liana destroy themselves with a doomed love affair. "Is it too late to warn you that loving her is more dangerous than O'Keefe's soldiers?"

"It was too late the first time I noticed her as a child," Christian replied, and feigning a punch to his cousin's shoulder, he went to work on his next pamphlet.

Liana and her brothers attended a party given by another Loyalist that Saturday night, but claiming they were in no mood for company, her parents remained at home. Unlike the earlier festivities that spring, this gathering was fraught with whispered innuendo, and Liana was relieved when it was over and they climbed into their carriage for the journey home. Even though she'd known Christian wouldn't be there, she had missed him, and was as badly disturbed by that as by the gloom shadowing what should have been a joyful evening.

Morgan and Cameron were seated opposite Liana, and neither looked pleased with how the evening had gone, either. "I heard little but hushed criticism of the Quebec Act," Morgan revealed. "I wish Father and his friends had the nerve to speak out openly against it."

"Father's been getting too drunk to speak out against anything," Cameron grumbled.

"Cameron," Liana cajoled. "That's unkind."

"It's the truth," Morgan exclaimed. "He'd rather drown himself in whiskey than admit he's loyal to a king who despises us."

"Give him time," Liana urged. "He already sees the problems. He'll condemn the king as loudly as the rest of us soon."

"I doubt it," Cameron argued. "If he's too stubborn to admit he lost his first wife, he'll never abandon the king."

"I'm sorry I ever told you about Melissa," Liana admitted. "It's tarnished Father's image in your eyes, and I never meant to do that."

Morgan leaned forward and tapped her knee. "If he's tarnished by the truth, then his character was lacking in the first place. You needn't apologize for anything. It's Father who's at fault."

While she felt very sorry for her father, Liana understood her brothers' sentiments and did not insult them by defending him. They sat staring silently at each other for the rest of the way home, and arrived to find their parents had already gone to bed, so there was no one waiting up to meet them. Relieved they would not have to report on an evening rife with discontent, they parted at the top of the stairs and went to their separate rooms.

Liana undressed, laid her gown over a chair, and heaped her lingerie atop it. Fatigued more by disappointment than the late hour, she climbed into bed and attempted to clear her mind of all troublesome thought. She lay with her arms flung wide, her breathing shallow as she waited for the peace of dreams to overtake her, but all too soon, it was Christian who filled her mind's eye. Rolling over, she buried her face in a pillow and tried to force away his taunting image, but he adamantly refused to go.

Why fate had chosen to torment her with such an impossible young man she did not know, but furious with both fortune and Christian Hunter, it was a long while before she found an easy rest. When an hour later Christian laid his hand on her shoulder, she came awake instantly and cursed him with her next breath. "How dare you intrude on me again!" she challenged in a desperate whisper.

Christian sank down beside her on the edge of her bed. "Please," he begged. "I've been shot, and I can't lead the men following me."

"Shot? Oh, dear God, no." Fearing a fatal wound, Liana hurriedly left her bed and lit the lamp on her nightstand. Christian was holding his left arm, his sleeve soaked with blood. Horrified, she grabbed a towel from the washstand

and, fighting a sickening wave of dizziness, wrapped it tightly around his upper arm.

"I'm afraid I'm going to faint," she moaned.

"Me, too."

Christian had to be in terrible pain, but he was teasing her, and the love she felt for him washed over her with the warmth of a spring rain. She loved him, and always would. Moving close, she pulled his head against her breast and held him tight. "What happened?" she asked.

"I heeded your warning, avoided the crossroads, even reversed my route, but still ran into an ambush. The ball passed cleanly through my arm, so the wound isn't nearly as bad as it looks. I just need to rest a few minutes."

Liana stepped back and smoothed his hair off his forehead. "I knew it was you. Why couldn't you admit it?"

Christian brought her trembling fingers to his lips. "There are others involved, Liana. It's not just me, and I couldn't be sure you wouldn't betray us."

Insulted, Liana tried to draw away, but he held her tight. "Why are you here now if you don't trust me?"

Christian again rested his cheek against her breast. A new burst of agony shot through his arm with every beat of his heart, and he hoped she would understand. "I knew you'd help me hide. I'll go in a few minutes. I swear I will."

After only a slight hesitation, Liana looped her arms around his neck and stroked his hair gently. "My father hasn't been sober since we got your pamphlet condemning the Quebec Act. He'll never awaken and find you here. Come, let me help you out of that bloody shirt, and then you can stretch out on the bed."

Gingerly, Liana unwrapped the towel. The bleeding had slowed, and she attempted to pull the fine linen shirt off over his head. "Why aren't you wearing buckskins?"

"Because I wanted to be mistaken for a white man if I were seen."

Despite his penchant for wearing buckskins, Liana never thought of Christian as Indian, but readily understood the need for what was for him a disguise. After wetting the hem of the discarded shirt, she wiped the gore from his bicep and quickly wrapped a fresh towel around his upper arm. "You were right—there's a clean hole right through the muscle. That will save you the agony of having to dig out the musket ball."

"I've always been lucky," Christian replied, appreciating her show of concern.

Liana stepped back to look at him. His bare chest and arms were the same delicious shade of bronze as his face, but he still looked far from well. "Lie down," she ordered curtly.

"I don't want to get blood all over your bed."

Liana checked the makeshift bandage on his arm. His blood wasn't seeping through it, and she refused to consider that might be because he had no more to lose. "Can you stand up a moment? I'll spread out some towels."

Christian rose slowly, and while unsteady, managed to remain upright while she pulled back the covers and laid out the towels. "I'm afraid my boots are dirty."

"Sit down. I'll get them." Tending Christian came so naturally to Liana, she did not think yanking off his boots was in the least bit demeaning. "There, now lie back and rest. Would you like a drink? My father won't miss a glass or two of whatever you'd like."

Liana's bed was so deliciously soft that Christian doubted he would ever want to leave. "No, thank you. Liquor might dull the pain, but it would also turn my brain to mush and I've got to be able to think. Come lie down with me."

"No, I think I'd better sit over here." Intending to keep a watchful eye on him, Liana pulled a chair up close to the bed. "You need a physician," she worried aloud.

"He'd do no more than wrap my arm the way you have.

Please, lie down with me. Your nearness will do far more for me than any physician could."

His eyes were closed, his skin pale. Desperately afraid he was growing weaker, Liana circled the four-poster bed, climbed up on it, and lay down by his right side. "What did you do with your horse?"

"He's in your barn."

"You hid your horse in our barn?"

She sounded appalled and Christian would have laughed if he had had the strength. "Relax, I didn't lead any soldiers here." He slid his right arm under her shoulders and pulled her close. "If my arm didn't hurt so bad, this would be nice."

"Oh, Christian, please. You could have been killed."

Christian took a deep breath and released it slowly. "It would have been worth it."

"How can you even think that?"

"The pamphlets have already made people more aware of how badly the colonies are being treated, so I would have accomplished a great deal. It wouldn't be tragic to die for a noble ideal."

Tears filled Liana's eyes and spilled over her lashes. "It would be to me."

Christian savored her tender confession. "You see, I've already helped to create an America where a man doesn't need a fine British heritage to be admired."

Liana sat up slightly and Christian opened his eyes to look up at her. It was certainly true that no one would mistake him for a fine British gentleman, but she found his dark good looks deeply stirring. "Surely you must have already known that," she insisted. "After all, the Seneca were here long before the English came."

"Yes, they were, but how many people do you think would have been impressed had they known an Indian was writing the pamphlets?"

"Oh Christian, you weren't just the artist—you wrote the text, too?"

He nodded. "Wait until you see tonight's."

"I don't care what it says. It wasn't worth the cost in blood."

"To me it was." He reached out to pull her head back down on his shoulder. "Hush. My arm hurts too much to argue."

Liana snuggled against him, then laid her right arm over his belly. She had thought his concerns were merely political, but to learn he had a personal stake in ending British rule made him far more human. She listened to his breathing gradually slow and prayed he was falling asleep rather than dying. Still afraid he might bleed to death, she rose up slightly to look at the towel she had wrapped around his arm, and was relieved to find it still unstained.

She again relaxed against him, but didn't close her eyes. She ran her hand over the smooth flatness of his belly and considered the warmth of his skin a good sign. He was resting comfortably, not moaning or crying out, but she still couldn't agree that passing out a pamphlet had been worth such a terrible price.

Imagining Christian riding fast, bent low over his horse, she knew if the man who had fired at him had aimed just a few inches higher he would have struck him in the head. Christian would have been killed instantly, and pitched from his mount, his lifeless body would have fallen to the rutted road in a tangled heap. That ghastly image sickened her thoroughly and she snuggled closer to the sleeping brave. The fact that it would have been considered horribly improper for a young lady of her breeding to share her bed with the injured man did not even cross her mind. She remained awake, silently guarding Christian until, worn out with worry, she also fell asleep.

It was still dark outside when Christian awoke, but he knew he ought to go. He laced his fingers in Liana's, meaning to push her hand aside and leave the bed but as her fingertips brushed across his belly his thoughts swiftly turned erotic. Leaving her then became not simply absurd, but impossible. Unbuttoning his pants with his left hand, he kept hold of her right and slid it beneath the waistband where the sweetness of her touch was instantly stirring.

His breath caught in his throat as the sheer recklessness of what he was doing made the pleasure of her touch all the more intense. God, how he wanted Liana, and not simply with this forbidden haste. He wanted to bury himself in her heat, marking her forever as his own. Thinking only of her, he moved her hand over his hardened shaft, coaxing forth the rapture he wanted so desperately for her to share.

Jarred awake by the vigor of his strokes, Liana tried to pull her hand away, but refusing to release her, Christian's grip tightened around her wrist. "My God! What are you doing?" she gasped, but it was all too obvious he was pleasuring himself. She had been terrified he might die in her bed, but clearly he was far stronger than she had supposed.

Christian reached up to thread his fingers through her hair and pulled her mouth to his. His kiss began as a demanding, bruising command, but gradually melted into a long, slow, deep tribute to the young woman he adored. He drank in the subtle traces of her perfume, then wanting so much more, he let go of her hand so he could rise, and bracing himself on his right arm, kept her trapped in the bed.

"Christian!" Liana begged. "You can't, you mustn't, you—"

His lips muffled her complaints with another leisurely kiss which became half a dozen. His left arm still ached, but the pain existed now on a distant plane; he refused to allow the discomfort to ruin a night he knew he would always remember. Shifting position slightly, he slid his hand beneath her nightgown and ran his fingertips up the silken smoothness of her thigh. She arched against him, but certain he could swiftly end her protests, he ran his hand over her bare hip, and then down between her legs.

Her indignant cries smothered with delicious kisses, Liana tried to push Christian away without further injuring his bandaged arm, but there was no way to escape his magical touch. Encouraged by her own betraying wetness, he traced a light path through the tender valley of her femininity, pausing at the heights to circle the nubbin of exquisitely sensitive flesh. Even as he drew away, she knew he wouldn't leave her suspended on the lip of rapture, and now, sensing her growing need, he began his exotic teasing anew. His touch was feather light, but sure, delving deep and then sweeping wide.

Liana had not even imagined making love would feel so marvelous and ceased to object with word or gesture. Instead, she ran her hands over Christian's muscular back, feeling his strength while she floated on the sensations he coaxed forth with such graceful ease. She raised her hips, pressing against his hand, silently begging for the release she intuitively knew had to come.

When it burst forth in sparkling waves, she bore down, savoring the sweet pain that rushed clear along her legs with a glorious heat. She felt Christian struggling with his pants, and without the slightest embarrassment helped him free himself. She wanted him too badly to consider the consequences of making love and not even the smooth tip of his manhood as it began to press against her still-aching core caused her any sense of alarm.

He moved very slowly at first, gently testing her limits, luring her back down into the radiant joy he had just shown her until he could no longer control his need to possess her fully. He lunged forward then, silencing her startled cry with his palm, and then kissing her to erase the pain as he lay still deep within her. "I remember you," he whispered, "from when you were a little girl."

That his memories of her could be as strong as hers of him filled Liana with still another burst of joy, and she followed his motions, creating an ageless dance. She had no fear of him, or of joining her very soul with his in this, the most intimate of acts. When his climax stole over him suddenly, she held him in her arms and knew to the depth of her heart she had been born to be his just as he had been meant to be hers.

Closing her eyes, she clung to him and wished they could hold on to this blissful glimpse of paradise forever, but all too soon he began to withdraw, and she couldn't stop the tears. "I'm not sorry," she swore.

Filled with a lingering warm laziness, pounding pain, and a desperate desire to reach home before dawn, Christian leaned down to kiss away Liana's tears. "Don't," he begged. "I can't bear to see you cry because of me."

Liana reached up to caress his cheek. "I don't want to lose you."

Christian considered her worry absurd. "That's impossible."

"This will be the last of your pamphlets then?"

Realizing her concern was for his safety rather than his faithfulness, Christian moved off the bed and pulled his pants into place. He bent over to pick up his boots, was nearly overcome by a wave of dizziness, and had to sit back down. "Light the wood in your fireplace. We'll burn my shirt and the bloody towels before I go."

Liana sat up and reached out to touch his shoulder. "You didn't answer me. Does that mean you'll continue delivering pamphlets until you're killed?"

Christian forced a smile as he glanced at her over his shoulder. "No, only until we're free of the king."

Terrified for him and infuriated with him at the same time, Liana rolled off the bed. Her nightgown had been bunched up around her waist and was wrinkled, but still snowy white. One of the towels she had spread across the bed to catch Christian's blood was stained with hers. Eager to get rid of the evidence of their passion, she wadded it up in a tight ball. She fetched his shirt from the floor and, again sickened by the bloodstains, carried it over to the fireplace. She lit the kindling, and when the blaze caught, she ripped the shirt in half and flung it into the flames. When it was engulfed, she added the towels.

Satisfied the fire would continue to burn brightly, she turned toward the bed, where Christian was struggling to pull on his boots. "Wait, I'll help you."

"Thank you." He reached out to catch a strand of her hair and let it fall through his fingers. "Come home with me."

Liana nearly dropped a boot, and with a desperate lunge caught it before it hit the floor with a jarring thud. "What?"

"You heard me. I don't want to leave you here. Come home with me."

Liana waited until she had both boots on his feet before she straightened up to reply. "I'm not some serving wench in a tavern, Christian. You can't just sweep through my room." And my heart, she could have added. "I deserve better than that."

Christian forced himself to his feet. He was dizzy still, but not too weak to ride. "Yes, I agree, you do."

Liana waited for him to offer a gentlemanly alternative, but before he spoke, she heard riders coming into the front yard. "Who can that be at this hour?"

It wasn't until then that she noticed how light the sky had grown. "Oh, dear, it's far later than I thought." She rushed to her window and looked out. "It's Sean and his men. Could they have trailed you here?"

"No, but you'll have to get rid of them or I'll not be able to leave."

Liana grabbed up a mauve woolen shawl and wrapped

it around her shoulders. "To say nothing of what would happen to me should you be found here."

"Do you think I don't care?"

Doubting that he did, Liana shot him a withering glance. "Wait. Put on some perfume. You reek of me."

Startled, Liana doubted she could separate her scent from his after they had been so close, but fearing Sean would notice a difference, she went to her dressing table and dabbed her favorite perfume on her wrists and throat. She then rushed down the stairs before Sean could knock at the door and wake everyone else. "What's happened?" she greeted him in a hoarse whisper.

Her hair was tangled, her cheeks flushed, but Sean thought her disheveled appearance absolutely captivating. He longed to wake her every morning, but with kisses rather than a harsh summons. He bent down to pluck the leaflet from the porch. "The miscreants were out distributing their trash again last night. My men thought they'd shot one and we're out searching for his body but if he got this far, he couldn't have been wounded after all."

Liana reached out to take the pamphlet. The cover featured a knobby toad sporting a heavy crown, and she could easily imagine the adjectives Christian had used to describe King George III this time. The fact that he valued criticizing the monarch more highly than he did her love stung her so badly she had no trouble crumpling the leaflet with a convincing flourish.

"Thank you, but I do believe I'll burn this rather than pass it on to my father."

"I saw the smoke as we approached. Were you cold?"

Sean's grin was an all-too-eager plea for an invitation to share her bed. Revolted, Liana backed away and made ready to close the door. "Is there anything you need? Food or water for your horses, perhaps?"

"How kind of you. Our mounts could do with some water."

"There's a trough out by the barn."

Sean assumed correctly that the pamphlet had upset her, but he could not have imagined the reason why. "I'm sorry if we disturbed you. Surely you can't always be up at this hour."

"Why yes, I am," Liana declared. "There's something quite magical about the dawn."

"I agree. Perhaps one morning we could share it together."

"That's quite impossible, Captain, now good day." Liana closed the front door and leaned back against it while she caught her breath. She had not really expected Sean to search the house, but feeling the weight of Christian's glance, she looked up to find him standing at the top of the stairs. Appalled that he would strut boldly through her home, she tossed the pamphlet on the hall table and hurried up to meet him.

"What if he'd seen you?" she hissed.

Christian followed her back into her room. The fire had died down, and he used a poker to shove the last bit of towel into the embers where it was quickly reduced to ashes. All evidence of their tryst destroyed, he turned to face her. "Meet me this afternoon."

"No, you're too badly hurt. Go home, go to bed, and stay there."

Christian approached her, but took the precaution of stopping out of her reach. "I asked you once if you'd rather call me husband than brother. I'll keep asking until you decide."

His hair spilled loosely down over his bare shoulders, but despite the wildness of his appearance, he was as astonishingly handsome as he had always been. She didn't want to cry again, and bit down on her kiss-swollen lips to contain her sorrow. "As long as the pamphlets mean more to you than I do, you wouldn't make much of a husband."

Not understanding her, Christian shook his head. "You'd rather have a man without ideals?"

"I didn't say that."

"No, you just asked me to exchange mine for yours."

Liana opened her mouth to argue, then decided perhaps he was right. "It's clear you love danger more than you love me. Come on, I'll show you down the back stairs."

"You needn't bother. I know my way in and out of this house."

Liana's cheeks filled with the heat of a deep blush as she realized he could now say the same of her. She wasn't ashamed of what she'd done for love, but she was badly disappointed that it had meant so little to him. "I'll go with you anyway. I want to make certain Sean and his men are gone before you go out to the barn."

Christian followed her to the door with a weary step. "This won't be the last time we're together, Liana."

Certain the anguish in his gaze was due to the wound in his arm rather than any heartache over her, Liana didn't respond. She peeked out her door, made certain no one else was up, and then led the way down the hall to the back stairs. As they started down, Christian tripped once, but caught himself before he careened into her.

"How are you ever going to make it home?" she asked.

"My horse knows the way."

"He'd better." She motioned for him to remain in the stairwell while she opened the back door. The sky, tinged with pink, was growing lighter by the second and she prayed the cook wasn't already in the kitchen. She stepped out into the yard, and reassured by the eerie quiet, went back for Christian.

"The soldiers are gone. Don't let them catch you."

Christian managed a lopsided grin. "Doing what? It's not against the law to go out for a ride at dawn."

"Perhaps not, but how would you explain the wound in your arm?"

After a moment's hesitation, Christian had an answer. "If I'm asked, I'll say I was shot by a fickle young woman who lured me to her bed and then accused me of overstaying my welcome."

That he could laugh at her appalled Liana and she gestured dramatically. "Go."

"Kiss me first."

"No!" Liana meant her forceful refusal, too, but Christian slid his right arm around her waist to pull her close and she didn't turn her head nearly fast enough to avoid his kiss. He barely brushed her lips with his, and then, with a wobbly bow, he backed away. Liana held her breath, waiting for him to offer some obnoxious challenge, but he went straight to the barn. He swiftly reappeared astride a black stallion as handsome as he was, and with no more than a parting nod, rode off toward the river.

Liana watched until he was lost from view, but his image would remain etched on her heart forever.

Eleven

Johanna had never seen Christian even taste a drop of liquor, let alone imbibe freely, and when he left the MacGregors' party early, apparently too inebriated to remain, she was exceedingly suspicious. Dominique did not seem to think his slurred good-bye and hasty departure odd, but when Beau was her partner for the next dance, she immediately asked him why her brother had left.

"Wasn't it obvious?" Beau asked as they moved together in a graceful bow.

"To anyone who doesn't know him, yes, but not to me."

Beau thought of half a dozen plausible excuses, but couldn't lie to Johanna. Instead he changed the subject, which he knew from her perceptive glance didn't fool her, but at least she didn't pester him with questions for the remainder of the evening. It wasn't until they reached home and he saw her heading for Christian's room on the second floor rather than her own on the third that he realized he could no longer postpone giving her a definitive answer.

Johanna knocked on Christian's door, and when there was no reply, she looked in and found the room empty. Turning to Beau, she gestured toward his room across the hall. "I think we'd better have a talk."

Beau nodded, opened his door, and motioned for her to precede him. "You were right at the party. Christian wasn't drunk, but he had an important errand which required him to leave early."

"An errand?" Johanna repeated incredulously. "At such a late hour on a Saturday night? You'll have to do better than that, Beau. Did he go to meet a lady?"

Aghast that he had given her the impression Christian carried on clandestine affairs, Beau quickly denied it. "Good Lord, no."

"Why do you sound so shocked? He's a handsome young man, and no more welcome in Williamsburg's society than I am. Why wouldn't he seek out a lady he might have to meet in secret?"

Not wanting her to suspect Christian's only interest was in Liana Scott, Beau began to pace restlessly. "You're a serious person, Johanna, not given to gossip or carrying tales, but I need your solemn word that you won't reveal what I'm about to tell you."

Intrigued, Johanna's dark eyes widened. "You know you can trust me. Why are you being so mysterious?"

"Because I've no other choice." Beau turned to face her. "You saw the swine pamphlet, and the one condemning the Quebec Act."

Johanna nodded, and then the light of recognition brightened her gaze. "Are you saying Christian has something to do with those?"

Beau came close and rested his hands lightly on her shoulders. "We all do, but he's the author, and he's out delivering the third issue now."

Johanna was so shocked she didn't know what to say. Then she had so many questions she wasn't sure which to ask first. "Does our father know?"

"Yes, he's delivering the pamphlets in town. You know this family has violently disagreed with everything Parliament has done since the end of the war with France. David Slauson was sent down to Charleston to buy printing equipment, and—"

At the mention of David's name, Johanna was so insulted she had to interrupt. "You trusted David Slauson, a complete stranger, more than me?"

"No, of course not."

"Then why was he told when I wasn't?"

Beau sighed regretfully as he dropped his hands and stepped back. "None of the Barclay women know, except you now, but that was to protect you in case any of us were caught."

Furious with him, Johanna went to the door. "None of us either wants or needs to be protected, Beau. Those clever pamphlets were all anyone wanted to discuss tonight and I had no idea they were Christian's. I supposed I should have guessed because he's so vocal in his dissent, but I didn't. I won't tell my mother or anyone else for the time being, but I strongly suggest that the next time you men get together to plot, you confide in us on your own."

"Are you threatening to tell if we don't?"

Johanna regarded him with a disappointed glance. "I always thought you were bright, Beau. It's about time you started to behave like it, and yes, I most certainly will tell the others if you don't. Ask Christian to wake me when he comes in. I want to be certain he's safe."

"All right, I will." Fearing he had handled their conversation poorly, Beau resumed pacing as he tried to think of a better way to reveal the truth should he have to tell his mother or aunt. As for Dominique and Belle, he saw no reason to confide in them, nor Falcon and Jean, for that matter. Still, he knew how badly he felt about being left out that night, and supposed they would feel exactly the same if they discovered they had been excluded from the pamphlet enterprise. Revealing the source of the pamphlets to everyone, no matter how loyal they all were, was so dangerous he was loath to do it.

* * *

Worried about her brother, Johanna slept fitfully and when she awakened at four and he still hadn't come in to tell her he was home, she got up and went downstairs to his room. The lamp was still lit, but the bed hadn't been slept in. She went across the hall to Beau's room and found it empty as well. She hurried downstairs, but the two young men weren't in the study where she had hoped to find them and she grew even more distressed.

After a moment's thought, she decided if Beau were still waiting for Christian he would most likely be out in the stable. Knowing she would never be able to get back to sleep now, she returned to her room and dressed for the day in a muslin dress sprinkled with blue flowers. She twisted her thick, straight hair into a coil she secured atop her head and donned a white cap.

Picking up a fringed blue wool shawl and lantern, she left the house and walked down the path between the silent kitchen and smokehouse, scullery and dairy, past the carriage house, cooper's shed, and smithy to the stable. The glow of a lantern shone through the open doorway, and she heard male voices as she approached. Praying that Christian had returned safely, she entered wearing an expectant smile, but her expression immediately turned to one of alarm when she found Beau talking with David Slauson.

"Christian's not back yet?"

Beau left the barrel where he had been seated and came to meet her. "No, but that doesn't necessarily mean anything's happened to him. He may have chosen to take the long way home. Or he could have been tired and stopped somewhere to rest. I know he'll be here soon."

Beau did not appear nearly as confident as his words sounded, however, and David Slauson looked no better. There were deep shadows beneath his eyes and Johanna doubted he had been to bed at all that night. She hadn't seen him since Christian had urged her to forgive him, and while he looked far from his best, she was impressed by his obvious concern for her brother.

"What time does he usually arrive home?" she asked.

Beau looked toward David, who gestured helplessly. "He's been here by three in the past, but taking an extra hour probably doesn't mean much."

"It's plain by your expression that you don't truly believe that. Did my father return safely?"

"Yes, he did," David assured her. "Check for yourself if you like. His horse is in his stall."

Johanna considered a search of the stable unnecessary. "I believe you, Mr. Slauson. Well, what do you two plan to do, just sit here waiting for Christian, or are you going out to search for him?"

Beau exchanged a worried glance with David before he replied. "He'd been warned soldiers would be at all the crossroads, so he intended to use old trails through the plantations. That's undoubtedly why he's late, Johanna, but I promise you, if he isn't home by dawn, we'll have every available man out looking for him. Now, why don't you go on back up to the house? There's nothing you can do here."

"Nor you either if you're just going to wait for the dawn." Refusing his suggestion, Johanna sat down on the bench near the door and placed the lantern by her side. Fuming, it took her several minutes to realize what Beau had said. "Who warned him about soldiers? Are there men among the king's troops who side with Chris and don't want to see him come to any harm?"

Beau pursed his lips thoughtfully. Fearing he had already said too much, he dared not implicate Liana. "It was merely a friend, and I've no idea how they came by the information."

"Tavern gossip?" Johanna asked.

"Yes, it very well could have been." When she appeared satisfied with that convenient lie, Beau began to pace. Still dressed in the fine clothes he'd worn to the MacGregors' party, he looked completely out of place in the stable. The silver buckles on his shoes caught the lantern's light with each turn and sparkled like the ray of hope he was fast losing. Despite the reassurances he had given Johanna, he was desperately afraid something terrible had happened to his cousin.

Uncertain what he should do, David debated his options until the desire to be with Johanna could no longer be suppressed. He approached the bench. "May I join you?" he asked politely.

They were in the stable rather than a ballroom, and David's request struck Johanna as absurd. "Of course, Mr. Slauson. You might as well be comfortable while you wait."

"Thank you." David took care not to sit too close. "I admire your brother's daring. He's inspired a great many people and I'm certainly among them."

Her glance focused on the mist-shrouded horizon, Johanna was too frantic with worry to take any pride in Christian's accomplishments. "I just want my brother to come home safe," she replied.

"Yes, so do I." Fearing his remark had irritated rather than reassured her, David fell silent. He looked toward Beau, who was also lost in thought, and feeling like an intruder, he gave up the effort to provide more than company. He leaned back against the wall and said a silent prayer for Christian's safe return. He was very worried, but with Johanna seated so near, it was difficult to think of anything but how delicious she smelled and how pretty she was.

He liked the delicate floral print of her gown, but knew this was no time to pay compliments. He let his gaze drift down the gentle curve of her cheek to her half-opened lips, and felt his chest tighten with a painful sense of longing. Believing he had no chance at all to win the love of such an exquisitely beautiful young woman, he chided himself for ever having believed she was just a servant who might notice him. Depressed with the futility of his desires, he was near tears when the rhythmic sound of hoofbeats first echoed in the distance.

"Here he comes!" David shouted, and he rushed to the doorway to greet Christian.

The anxious trio peered through the gray light of dawn, straining to catch a glimpse of Christian, and just when the wait grew excruciating, he burst into view. David ran out to grab his stallion's reins, while Beau went to his side.

With no shirt to cover his bandaged arm, Christian was unable to hide his injury, but he strove to look far stronger than he felt when he swung down from his saddle. "I'm sorry to have worried you by being late," he greeted them.

"You've been hurt!" Johanna cried.

"It isn't much," Christian lied. "I'll be fine with a few hours' sleep."

Beau noted the embroidered "S" on the towel wrapped around Christian's arm, and instantly guessed who had placed it there. "Come on, let's get you up to the house. I'll wake my mother to tend you."

"It's no more than a scratch, Beau. She can look at it later." Christian reached out a hand for Johanna. "If you're here, then you must know what I've been up to."

"Yes, and I don't approve. Now go on with Beau, and don't try and fool Aunt Arielle the way you're trying to fool us."

Johanna knew him too well to be misled, and Christian responded with a faint smile. "Yes, ma'am," he replied, and refusing Beau's offer of support, he started walking toward the house with his cousin. Feeling light-headed and sick to his stomach, every step took a valiant effort.

"You see, I knew your brother would be all right," David told Johanna before leading the stallion into the stable.

Still sick with fright, Johanna didn't feel up to following Christian and Beau back to the house. She returned to the bench in the stable where she had to fight not to dissolve in tears. When David finished tending the horse, he came and sat down with her. She looked up at him and shook her head. "Christian has always taken too many risks. It's truly amazing he's survived to adulthood."

David was so thrilled Johanna was speaking to him, he didn't care that Christian was the subject. "He is daring, but I doubt he's reckless, and there is a difference."

"You don't understand. It's part of being Seneca. He takes everything past the point Beau would. Beau is also bright and athletic, but he has far more common sense. He can weigh the consequences of his actions, but Christian acts as if he always has something to prove."

David shrugged. "What could he possibly need to prove? He's wealthy, handsome, and appears supremely confident to me."

"Yes, he's all that, but don't ever discount his Seneca blood. An Indian is known not by his possessions as a white man is, but by his deeds. The Barclay wealth means no more to Christian than it does to our father."

"Why does Chris stay here? Why doesn't he go up to New York, to the land of the Seneca?"

"He's been there. My father's taken both my brothers home to visit his tribe. They enjoyed themselves, but I don't believe they really felt at home there."

"What about you? Didn't your father want to introduce you to his people?"

Johanna smiled slightly. "I'm embarrassed to admit this, but on one trip he complained that I was too young. On another, that I was so beautiful the unmarried braves would spend our whole visit attempting to convince me to choose one for a husband. I was only fourteen and my parents said the last thing I needed was a spouse at such an early age."

They had never had such a lengthy conversation, and believing it was due to the quiet warmth of the stable,

David hoped to keep her talking for hours. The sky now had a pale rose tint with the approaching dawn, but it was still very early. They would have the stable to themselves for another hour at least, and he encouraged her to continue.

"What about now? Are you still too young to take a husband?"

David was sitting in a relaxed pose, his hands clasped in his lap, and thinking he was merely making conversation, Johanna did not take his question seriously. "I'm eighteen, Mr. Slauson, so my age is no longer the problem."

"What is, then? Don't your parents want a Seneca brave for you?"

Having considered the question quite recently, Johanna had a ready response. "Frankly, they've never discussed it with me, but no, I don't believe they'd be happy to see me living among the Seneca. I've been raised as a white woman, you see, and I'd be very out of place there. Even more than I am here." Thinking she had covered the topic, Johanna rose. "I'm going up to the kitchen to find something to eat. Are you hungry?"

David leapt to his feet. "I must confess I have an enormous appetite. Waiting up all night doesn't sound like hard work, but it certainly feels like it."

As they strolled toward the kitchen, Johanna realized how easy it had been to confide in David. He had impressed her as being genuinely fond of Christian, and she was sorry they had ever had a misunderstanding. "I should have accepted your apology the day you offered it out on the docks, Mr. Slauson. It was most uncharitable of me not to."

"No, not at all," David argued. "I'd been unforgivably rude."

"Nevertheless, you are forgiven."

As they reached the kitchen, David held the door for

her and he rejoiced clear to his toes that she didn't long to visit the land of the Seneca to find a husband.

Arielle tossed aside the towel binding Christian's arm, but meaning to hang on to that bit of evidence, Beau quickly picked it up. When he saw his cousin had been shot through the arm, he cursed under his breath. "It will take more than a few hours sleep for that wound to heal."

Arielle was skilled at tending common illnesses but in a move designed to reassure her patient, she attempted to appear undaunted by Christian's gunshot wound. "Why don't you wait outside, Beau?" she urged.

"No, Mother, Christian and I need to talk."

"It will have to be later—he needs to rest." Arielle cleaned Christian's wound with soap and water, and then sliced the leaf of an aloe plant lengthwise and applied the gel-like sap to the injury. "The aloe will aid in healing, but I'll have to make you some white willow tea for the pain."

The once-excruciating pain had dulled to a persistent ache when he had been with Liana, so Christian doubted he needed the tea. "It doesn't hurt all that much."

Arielle moved closer to look into his eyes. Rather than reflecting his bright inner fire as they usually did, they were opaque and expressionless. She wasn't fooled. "Liar. The agony is plain in your eyes. You needn't act the hero with me."

Christian smiled at her admonishment, but truly he did not feel particularly brave. When she had finished bandaging his arm, he thanked her and then added a request. "Please don't tell my parents I was shot. It would only worry them, and as you can see, I'll recover."

Arielle did not even pause to consider granting the favor. "No, I won't lie to Alanna and Hunter."

"I'm not asking you to lie," Christian stressed. "Just don't tell them."

"That's exactly the same," Arielle argued. "Now, I'll bring you the tea, and I want you to sleep until sundown. By then I hope you'll feel well enough to join us for supper."

As Arielle swept out of the room carrying her basket of herbs and potions, Christian glanced toward Beau. "Well, I thought it was worth a try."

"We're going to have to tell everyone," Beau exclaimed. "It's not fair for Johanna and my mother to bear the burden of knowing while the others are kept ignorant." He held out the discarded towel. "I'm going to have this washed so you can return it to Liana. Unless, of course, the 'S' stands for a family other than the Scotts."

Christian turned to punch his pillow. "Let's have this conversation another time, Beau. I've been up all night."

"So have I!"

In no mood to defend his actions, Christian just wanted to be left alone but he attempted to be more tactful. "I'm sorry. I appreciate your concern, and I hope you know I'd show the same for you. I was shot in an ambush near the Tuttles'. I was bleeding so badly I had little choice about stopping at Liana's, and she was kind enough to bandage my arm and let me hide until Sean O'Keefe's patrol had gone by. I doubt she expects to have the towel returned, so I'll keep it as a souvenir."

"Ian didn't see you?"

"No, I spoke only to Liana. Now please, Beau. We both need some sleep."

Beau knew Christian too well to believe he was telling all that he could, but fearing he was tiring him, he nodded and walked out. He was eager to get to bed himself, but later, he planned to question his cousin until he accounted for every single second of his time.

Though still shaky after spending the day in bed, Christian was able to dress and eat supper with the rest of his family. He tried to join in the conversation, but found Johanna, Beau, and his Aunt Arielle regarding him with so many dark looks, he soon gave up the effort. He had not yet admitted, let alone described, the nature of his injury to his parents, but as soon as he entered the study after supper, he realized he ought not to hide it from his father.

"How did things go in town?" he asked Hunter.

"Far better than they must have gone for you, judging by the late hour you left your bed," Hunter replied. "I waited until after the taverns had closed. The streets were all deserted, and not even a dog barked at my passing. You'll take the town next time."

Christian sank down into a wing chair and rested his head against the high back. In a halting monotone he confessed he had been shot, but omitted any reference to Liana Scott. He glanced toward Beau, silently daring him to say a word, but his cousin merely frowned his disapproval and kept still.

Byron waited for Hunter to speak, but the Indian just shook his head and repeated his intention to take Christian's route in the future. "I'm sorry about this, Christian, I truly am," Byron said. "Does the fact that you've been hurt end your commitment to the pamphlets?"

"No, sir, I intend to keep poking the hornet's nest until the last hornet is gone."

"You were shot," Beau reminded him, "not stung. Don't try and minimize the danger. We've another problem," he added. "Johanna knows we're behind the pamphlets now and so does my mother. It's time we took everyone into our confidence."

Christian's mother had been concerned when she had thought he was merely overtired from the MacGregors' party. He hated to think how upset she would be should she learn the truth. "What do you think?" he asked his father. "Could Mother stand knowing how much danger I'm in?"

Hunter drew in a deep breath and released it slowly. He had been fluent in English all his adult life, but on important issues he would have much preferred to reply in his native tongue. Christian would have understood him, but not Byron and Beau and he did not want to exclude them. "You're a grown man, Christian. You don't need your mother's permission or mine to live your life."

"That's really not the issue, sir," Beau interjected. "It's a matter of secrecy and trust. I'm not concerned Aunt Alanna will betray us. My only worry is that perhaps we're waiting for people to discover the truth on their own, the way Johanna and my mother have, when we should be forthright and confide in them now."

"We agreed that knowledge of our efforts to defy the king wouldn't go beyond this room," Byron advised darkly, "but now it has. Let's take control before the whole town knows we're responsible for supplying the pamphlets." He looked straight at Christian. "You were shot. Did you have to stop and ask for help before reaching home?"

Christian felt his heart rise to his throat, where it lodged so firmly he had great difficulty drawing a breath. He did not dare look at Beau, but he couldn't involve Liana. Unable to deflect his uncle's probing question with humor, he sat staring numbly at the floor.

Hunter knew his son so well he guessed immediately that Christian was shielding a woman. "What's her name?" he asked, "and do you trust her to keep silent?"

His father's insight came as a welcome relief, and Christian found his voice at last. "Her name doesn't matter, and yes, I trust her with my life."

Byron groaned. "We began with the four of us and David Slauson. Now our once-tight circle seems to be spreading faster than butter on warm bread. I'm surprised Captain O'Keefe didn't pay us another visit today."

"I'm afraid I have more bad news," Beau offered. "Johanna insists we tell everyone, or she will do it herself."

"I'll handle Johanna," Hunter responded. "Arielle knows, and I'll tell Alanna. That is as far as this need go."

"No," Byron said and cursed. "It's already further than it ever should have gone. We'll have to be far more cautious. Delay the publication of any more pamphlets, Christian, until we can be certain you'll be safe when you deliver them."

"That might be months," Christian complained. "No, I want to keep right on writing them, but we should move the press. The tobacco plants will have to be transplanted soon, and with more activity in the fields, there's an increased danger someone may discover it in the shed."

"I agree," Byron said. "Do you have another location in mind?"

"Yes, let's put it back on board the schooner David sailed to Charleston. He and I can operate it in the hold, and disguise it as a piece of the ship's equipment when it's not in use."

Byron glanced toward Hunter. "How does that sound to you?"

The Indian nodded. "Good. Soldiers know nothing about ships, and the press will be safe there."

"All right, it's agreed then. You go on up to bed, Christian. Hunter, Beau, and I will move the press and supplies tonight. If we'd only thought of this sooner, we'd have saved ourselves the trouble of hauling them off the ship in the first place."

Christian nodded, and hoped a lack of foresight wouldn't hamper them again. That certainly wasn't the problem with Liana, for he seldom thought of anything but her anymore. As he climbed the stairs, he wished he had the strength to share her bed again that night, but he was so tired, he would have to join her in his dreams.

Liana had floated through the day, untouched by her mother's sweet conversation or her father's increasingly withdrawn ways. Her brothers had found the wrinkled pamphlet she had left on the hall table and gleefully repeated each and every line, but they had prudently not shared it with their father. At supper that evening, Liana watched the pair exchange many a teasing glance, while her mother, showing solicitous concern for their distracted father, had not noticed a thing.

There were few attempts at conversation, and the meal passed quickly. Ian excused himself at the earliest possible moment and retired to his study where they all knew he would have too much to drink. Unable to ignore her mother's tearful gaze, Liana reached out to take her hand. "He can't keep brooding about this much longer," she advised.

After returning her daughter's fond squeeze, Robin brought her napkin to her eyes and blotted away her tears. "Why ever not?" she asked. "There was a time before we were married when I saw him in such despair his friends feared for his life."

Liana glanced toward Morgan, who mouthed the word *Melissa,* and she nodded, knowing he was right. Suddenly the fact that they all knew to what their mother was referring and hadn't said so seemed absurd. "You're talking about Melissa's death, aren't you?"

Shocked that her daughter even knew that name, Robin's eyes again flooded with tears. "How could you possibly know about her?"

"Her tombstone reads Melissa Barclay Scott," Morgan replied, sparing Liana any need for an explanation. "No one's forgotten the scandal, so you shouldn't be surprised we learned of it."

"You must never, ever speak her name to your father!" Robin cried. "Do you understand me, Morgan? I want your promise, and yours, too, Liana and Cameron, that you won't ever torment your dear father with her name."

"Father and I have already discussed her," Liana revealed softly.

"Oh, no," Robin sobbed.

"Mother, really, you needn't take on so." Liana left her chair to give her mother a comforting hug. "The three of us will gladly leave the past where it belongs, won't we, boys?"

"Yes," Morgan and Cameron responded in unison. "Father has enough trouble defending our bumbling king. We don't wish to hurt him," Morgan added. "Now let's go into the parlor and play some music. There's no reason to be as sad as Father."

Liana helped her mother from her chair and gently guided her into the parlor, but in her case, she harbored an excellent reason for sorrow: a secret as deep as her father's tragic first marriage.

Twelve

After the printing press, type, paper, and ink were all safely stowed on board the schooner *Southern Breeze*, Hunter joined his wife in their bedroom. It was the same room Alanna had shared with Melissa while growing up. During their marriage, it had been repainted several times in the creamy mauve the young girls had chosen. Hunter associated the room with his wife, however, and never with the willful blond beauty who had borne his first son.

Alanna, already in her nightgown, was seated atop their wide bed, reading from a small volume of poetry. Hunter stretched out beside her. "I've something important to tell you," he offered in greeting.

"Really?" Alanna closed her book and laid it on the nightstand. She then leaned over to give him a light kiss, but he wound his fingers in her flowing hair and turned it into a passionate exchange that left her breathless. "Perhaps it can wait," she murmured against his fringed shirt.

Hunter hugged her tightly. "No, I've already waited too long." Knowing no matter how he broke the news about Christian she would be alarmed, he rushed through the announcement, and then added that while their elder son had escaped serious injury the previous night, he had in fact been wounded.

Horrified, Alanna pushed Hunter away. "You're absolutely right. You did wait much too long to confide in me.

What did you think I'd do, forbid Christian to write the pamphlets, or interfere in their printing? Or did you simply believe I was far too fragile to be trusted with such a valuable piece of information?"

Hunter reached out for her, but Alanna slapped his hand away and moved off the bed. "I'm going to see Christian. I thought he was awfully quiet at supper, but I never imagined he might have been shot. Dear God, what if he'd been killed?"

"Don't ask for tragedy," Hunter advised. He rolled off the other side of the bed, and with three long strides beat her to the door. "I just looked in on him and he's asleep. Talk to him in the morning."

Infuriated with her husband, Alanna adamantly refused to accept his suggestion. "Get out of my way."

Hunter had had so few arguments with his wife, he had forgotten just how stubborn she could be. When Christian had been an infant, he had made the disastrous mistake of asking her to choose between him and his son. Fortunately, he had learned so much from that grievous error that their marriage had been remarkably smooth. "No, be angry with me, not Christian."

Alanna folded her arms over her bosom. Her hair was very curly and fell to her waist in tight ringlets that shimmied clear to the tips as she shook her head. "I've enough anger for you both," she replied in a guarded whisper. "I've always loved Christian as dearly as my own two children, but perhaps that was because I saw so much of you in him. Now you tell me he's denouncing the king with pamphlets he writes, prints, and distributes in secret. It sickens me to realize how much he might really be like his mother."

Astonished, Hunter dropped his voice lower than hers to assure their privacy. "How can you possibly compare Melissa's desperate secret with Christian's protests against the Crown?"

Believing the similarities obvious, Alanna ticked them off on her fingers. "He's acting in secret, hiding his true purposes, lying about his whereabouts, taking foolish risks, and flaunting the values of truth and honesty this family holds dear. Shall I continue, or have I convinced you he's as much of a smiling liar as his mother was?"

Thinking her list absurd, Hunter would have walked away, but not wanting her to bother Christian, he was forced to remain where he stood. "Melissa was a frightened child who carried the disgrace of being with me to her grave. Christian is an intelligent adult who believes, just as I do, that we've no need of an English king. I won't defend Melissa—all she gave Christian was his life. You've been his true mother. Be proud of him now, as you always have."

"Proud?" Alanna turned away. "You must have read the pamphlets. Didn't the blistering hatred appall you?"

Hunter sorted through the phrases he recalled, and couldn't suppress a small smile. "No, the king deserves every bitter word."

"Yes, he most certainly does, but I can't bear to think Christian's so angry with what life has given him."

Hunter stepped up behind her, enfolded her in his arms, and rubbed his cheek against her tawny curls. "It's a matter of principle, beloved. Nothing more."

Alanna knew in her heart Hunter was wrong, but it was Christian who truly concerned her, and she decided to explore the topic with him rather than his father who was such a fine man he did not even understand the poison of lies. She relaxed against him. "If I didn't love you so dearly, I'd not forgive you so easily for deceiving me."

"I meant only to protect you."

His breath was warm on her throat, and Alanna tilted her head to encourage the nibbling kisses she knew would soon touch her lips. "You are a devil, Hunter."

Hunter smothered his deep laugh against her lace-trimmed collar. "And you are an angel—that's what makes us such a good match."

Fears for Christian forgotten in her husband's embrace, Alanna led him back to the bed where not even nineteen years had dulled their passion. They fed upon it now, and the taste was so sweet neither would ever have need for more. Alanna fell asleep cradled in her husband's arms, but his loving hadn't changed her opinion about his son.

Liana stood at her window, gazing out at the river long past the hour she should have been in bed. Occasionally she would glance toward the four-poster that, depending upon her rapidly changing mood, she and Christian had either shared all too briefly or much too long. She wanted with all her heart to believe his affection had been real; but where did his devotion to his cause end and his regard for her begin? Plagued by the fear that he was using her to shame her father, she was afraid that seducing her had simply been another way to express the hatred that gave his pamphlets such memorable fire.

His delicious kisses had never tasted of propaganda, but she felt betrayed and abandoned now. Bathed in moonlight, she wondered where Christian was. Did he routinely court danger and seek refuge in all-too-willing young women's beds? That she did not know broke her heart. Perhaps she was nothing more to him than a convenience. The humiliation of that possibility brought tears to her eyes and she dried them on her sleeve. Christian had shown her a glimpse of paradise, but alone now, she feared it had turned all too swiftly into a wretched, lonely hell.

"Christian?" Alanna rapped lightly at his door.

He was already up and dressed, and quickly answered his stepmother's knock. One look at the determined set of her jaw and he knew she had come to offer her opinion. "Father told you about the pamphlets, didn't he?"

"Yes, but you should have told me yourself." She walked to the center of the room, and never given to idle chatter, turned and got straight to the point. "Your father believes the anger expressed in your pamphlets is merely political, but I suspect it runs far deeper. You've made the king your target, but he's not really the source of your rage, is he?"

Amazed she saw so much, Christian crossed to the window and sat down on the ledge. He was dressed in comfortably worn buckskins that hid the bandage Arielle had replaced earlier that morning. He felt far better than he had the previous day, but still was not completely well.

"No," he admitted, "but he's a symbol of the prejudice that makes people believe Indians are worth less than white men. If I stood on a corner in Williamsburg and shouted that line, no one would stop to listen, but a pamphlet that ridicules royalty and makes a plea for the nobility of every man is praised to the skies. That's a start."

Alanna moved toward him, her step graceful and sure. "Take care, Christian, not to become lost in the lies that hide your identity. Strive to be honest in all you do, or the consequences may be very high."

"Are you worried I've suddenly become dishonest?"

"No, merely concerned that you may have been captivated by the power of lies."

"But I'm not lying," Christian protested. "We've no more need of a king than a frog needs wings."

Alanna smiled at his joke. "Yes, I believe that's true, too, but when you can justify masking your identity to avoid prosecution, you may soon be tempted to lie in other areas of your life as well."

Liana's face danced in Christian's mind and he feared he understood Alanna's message all too well. Pursuing Liana was as compelling a pastime as defaming the king.

IF YOU LOVE READING MORE OF TODAY'S BESTSELLING HISTORICAL ROMANCES.... WE HAVE AN OFFER FOR YOU!

*L*OOK INSIDE TO SEE HOW YOU CAN GET 4 FREE HISTORICAL ROMANCES BY TODAY'S LEADING ROMANCE AUTHORS!

4 BOOKS WORTH UP TO $24.96, ABSOLUTELY FREE!

4 BESTSELLING HISTORICAL ROMANCES BY YOUR FAVORITE AUTHORS CAN BE YOURS, FREE!

Kensington Choice brings you historical romances by your favorite bestselling authors including Janelle Taylor, Shannon Drake, Rosanne Bittner, Jo Beverley, and Georgina Gentry, just to name a few! Each book is filled with passion, adventure and the excitement of bygone times!

To introduce you to this great club which is part of Zebra Home Subscription Service, we'd like to send you your first 4 bestselling historical romances, absolutely free! And once you get these 4 free books to savor at home, we'll rush you the next 4 brand-new books at the lowest prices available, as soon as they are published.

The way the club works is that after your initial FREE shipment, you will get our 4 newest bestselling historical romances delivered to your doorstep each month at the preferred subscriber's rate of only $4.20 per book, a savings of up to $8.16 per month (since these titles sell in bookstores for $4.99-$6.99)! All books are sent on a 10-day free examination basis and there is no minimum number of books to buy. (And no charge for shipping.) Plus as a regular subscriber, you'll receive our FREE monthly newsletter, *Zebra/Pinnacle Romance News*, which features author profiles, subscriber benefits, book previews and more!

So start today by returning the FREE BOOK CERTIFICATE provided. We'll send you 4 FREE BOOKS with no further obligation: A FREE gift offering you hours of reading pleasure with no obligation...how can you lose?

*We have 4 FREE BOOKS for you
as your introduction to
KENSINGTON CHOICE!
To get your FREE BOOKS, worth
up to $24.96; mail the card below.*

FREE BOOK CERTIFICATE

Yes! Please send me 4 Kensington Choice (the best of Zebra and Pinnacle Books) Historical Romances without cost or obligation (worth up to $24.96). As a Kensington Choice subscriber, I will then receive 4 brand-new romances to preview each month for 10 days FREE. I can return any books I decide not to keep and owe nothing. The publisher's prices for Kensington Choice romances range from $4.99-$6.99, but as a preferred subscriber I will get these books for only $4.20 per book or $16.80 for all four titles. There is no minimum number of books to buy and I may cancel my subscription at any time, plus there is no additional charge for postage and handling. No matter what I decide to do, my first 4 books are mine to keep, absolutely FREE!

Name _____

Address _____ Apt. _____

City _____ State_____ Zip_____

Telephone (____) _____

Signature_____

(If under 18, parent or guardian must sign)

Subscription subject to acceptance. Terms and prices subject to change.

KF0798

4 FREE
Historical Romances
are waiting
for you to
claim them!

(worth up to
$24.96)

*See details
inside....*

KENSINGTON CHOICE
Zebra Home Subscription Service, Inc.
120 Brighton Road
P.O. Box 5214
Clifton, NJ 07015-5214

"Don't worry, Mother. You've raised me well, and I won't disappoint you."

Alanna gave his cheek a light kiss. "I know better than to tell you not to pursue the course you've chosen, but you must be more careful. How's your arm?"

"Better, thank you, but I hope this is the last time I'm ever shot."

"So do I."

Christian rose, and arm in arm they went downstairs for breakfast. Eluding Beau, Christian walked along the river and left a ribbon for Liana, but she failed to meet him. When he returned the next two afternoons and again waited in vain, he was so badly disappointed he considered paying her another midnight visit, but finally decided against it. He longed to see her, to hear her gentle laughter and taste her honey-sweet kisses, but she had been so cool to his offer of marriage he doubted she would welcome him to her bed.

His only source of pride was in the riotous glee with which his third pamphlet had been met. Despite his mother's warning to be more cautious, he went into town and grinned each time he overheard someone quoting his latest work. The phrase "tyrannical toad" sang on so many lips he came home inspired to outdo his earlier efforts on the fourth issue. He strolled around the plantation, giving his imagination free rein. When he sat down in his room that night, he had a great many ideas, but thoughts of Liana proved to be so distracting, he accomplished very little.

Even drinking heavily, Ian Scott was not so completely unaware that he failed to note the sudden change in his daughter's behavior. Liana had been a sunny, cheerful child and had become a high-spirited young woman, but since the weekend he had seldom seen the pretty smile he loved. When Amanda Tuttle came to visit, their laughter had always echoed through the house, but that Thursday, Amanda had had to coax Liana to go out for a ride.

Fearing he had become so lost in his own torments that he had frightened his daughter, Ian confided his worries in his wife. "I owe everyone an apology," he began, "for showing so little in the way of courage. I'm deeply disappointed in the king's treatment of the colonies and can only pray the Quebec Act will be repealed, but I've no doubt once the debts incurred during the war are paid, we'll see a return to more tranquil times. I shouldn't have become so discouraged and burdened you all with my pain."

Robin left her place on the settee to give her husband a delighted hug. She then took his hand and pulled him down beside her on the small sofa. "These are distressing times, Ian, and it's only natural that you'd be distraught."

"Perhaps, but it's wrong of me to darken our children's lives with my despair. I haven't been fair to you, either."

"I'm not always the best of wives," Robin confessed.

"No, that's not true. You are a treasure." Ian's praise was sincere, for she was his ideal: a beautiful, soft-spoken, modest woman. "I wonder if we shouldn't send Liana and the boys to your sister. If the dissent here turns violent, more ports might be closed and it could become impossible to book passage to England then."

Robin could not even imagine her life without the children she adored, and through subtle persuasion had succeeded in convincing Ian not to send their sons abroad for schooling. Now that he wanted to confront the issue head on, and send Liana away as well, she was deeply distressed. Terrified, she gripped his hands tightly even as she strove to present a rational argument.

"I doubt they would want to go, Ian, and they would make very poor guests for Sarah and Graham if they resented being sent away. No, surely the situation isn't so desperate as to justify such a drastic action."

Ian relaxed into the settee and frowned as he mulled over her response. "Liana has been so unhappy of late. Sean O'Keefe comes by so often I know they can't be fighting. Could something else be troubling her?"

While they had once been close friends, Robin absolutely refused to speak Melissa's name and did not remind Ian of his conversation with Liana about her. "It could merely be the current unrest," she proposed instead. "It's affecting us all, or perhaps there's another young man she cares for who's not paying her calls."

Intrigued, Ian leaned forward slightly. "Who?"

"Well, I'm sure I don't know but she never lacks for dance partners at parties."

Ian closed his eyes to force away the terrible image of Christian Hunter's cocky grin. He drew in a labored breath and prayed his daughter had obeyed him and avoided the young man. "Does Liana keep a diary?" he asked.

"No, I don't believe so, but surely you're not suggesting we read it if she does."

Ian shot his wife a dark glance. "What if she's developed an unsuitable attachment? Don't you believe we have the right, nay, the obligation, to end it?"

Thinking only of their friends' sons, Robin couldn't imagine who he might mean. "Well, of course, as her parents we have every right to approve or disapprove of her friends, but—"

Ian rose and pulled Robin to her feet. "Now, while she's away from the house, I want you to search her room for anything, a token, a love letter, any object that would prove she's being courted by someone other than Sean O'Keefe."

Robin considered his demand for a long moment, and then shook her head. "We've no reason even to suspect such a thing, let alone provocation to prompt a search."

Ian drew her close and kissed her lightly. "Do it anyway, Robin, for me."

Uncomfortable with his request, and most especially with the manner in which he had made it, Robin still did not see how she could refuse. "All right," she agreed reluctantly. "I'll glance through her things, but you must keep watch to make certain she and Amanda don't return and discover what I'm doing. Liana would be livid with us for not trusting her."

"Hurry," Ian cajoled. "I'll keep watch." He waited until his wife had gone upstairs, then bolted for the study, where he poured himself a brandy. He carried it with him back to the parlor, and watched the path leading to the house. With every sip he prayed Liana had trusted his judgment where Christian was concerned, but as the minutes lengthened and Robin did not return, his fears continued to mount.

Liana glanced toward Amanda frequently in a futile attempt to force herself to pay closer attention to her friend's words. Amanda was flicking her mount's mane with the ends of her reins as she related her latest scheme to become better acquainted with Beau Barclay. "Speaking with him after church is an excellent idea," Liana agreed, "but won't he become suspicious if your paths cross every week?"

"Not if I'm clever, he won't, and with just a bit of prodding, he should start looking for me after the service."

"Well, yes, that would be the ideal," Liana responded listlessly.

Disappointed by Liana's lack of enthusiasm, Amanda became petulant. "Whatever is the matter with you today? You act as though winning Beau's heart were no more important than catching a butterfly."

An apt comparison, Liana thought to herself. "I'm sorry. I've a great deal on my mind."

Eager to hear more, Amanda's dark eyes took on an engaging twinkle. "Are things becoming more serious between you and Sean?"

Liana pulled her sorrel mare to a halt in the dappled shade of a twisting wisteria vine. "No. In fact, I've been thinking of taking a voyage to England. My father has suggested it more than once, and—"

"England!" Amanda gasped. "How can you possibly want to go there?"

The destination did not strike Liana as odd. "My mother's sister, Sarah, and her family live just outside London. My whole family visited them when I was a child. While I don't recall anything specific about the visit, I'm sure I'd enjoy seeing them again."

While Liana sounded optimistic, all Amanda could foresee was the imminent loss of her closest friend. "I'm so shocked I don't even know what to say, but I know Sean will be furious should he hear of your travel plans. You're far too pretty a young woman to go to London for a visit and not marry there. Is that what you want? Are you hoping to wed one of your cousins and remain in England?"

Liana looked across the fields, which would soon be planted with tobacco, and wished her life had the same orderly progression as the profitable plant. For many years it had, but Christian had ended that. He had taught her what to expect from marriage, and she could not imagine sharing the same depth of intimacy with another man. "I do have male cousins, all younger, but I've no hopes for marriage with them or anyone else. I'd just like to visit London for a change of scene. That's all."

Liana's sad smile failed to convince Amanda. "I thought we were best friends, but you're hiding something from me, Liana, and I'm going to keep asking until you confess. After all, I've told you how much I like Beau Barclay."

"Yes, and I appreciate your confidence."

"But not enough to share your secrets?"

"What a vivid imagination you have," Liana scolded. "We're together so often, when do you suppose I've had time for secrets?"

Amanda followed as Liana turned her mare back toward the road. "I don't know, but you're hiding something. You'd admit it if you wanted Beau, too, wouldn't you?"

Liana couldn't help but laugh at such a ridiculous question, but this time she could at least answer honestly. "Our families don't even speak, Amanda, and I've no interest whatsoever in your Beau."

Amanda studied Liana with a sidelong glance. The stunning beauty's hair was a glorious red, and her creamy smooth skin absolute perfection, but there was a sadness in her expression that was new. "If I didn't know better, I'd believe you were going to England to forget someone."

"You have such romantic notions," Liana replied. "I doubt Beau will be able to resist you for long."

Flattered, Amanda straightened her shoulders proudly. "Let's hope not." Convinced Liana would eventually confide in her, Amanda turned the conversation to the romantic intrigues of their friends, but none of the men's names she mentioned elicited the slightest trace of interest from Liana. Giving up that tack, she fell silent until they neared the Scott home. As they approached the house, she saw Ian standing on the porch, his hands on his hips, his expression one of such fiery rage she was frightened.

"Oh, dear, what could have happened? Your father looks positively livid. Are we late?"

Liana was harboring more than enough guilt to cause her to be alarmed by her father's show of foul temper. "He's been upset lately about politics. Go on home," she urged. "I'll come by to see you tomorrow or the next day."

Dressed in black, Ian was moving toward them with a long, menacing stride but Amanda was far too curious to leave and miss what promised to be an exciting scene. "No, I think I'd better stay."

Liana pulled her mare to a halt, but before she could dismount, her father yanked her from the saddle and slapped her across the face with Christian's beaded pouch. "How dare you go behind my back to meet the one man I've forbidden you to see!"

Stung by the fact that her father had discovered the pouch, read Christian's note, and come to precisely the right conclusion, Liana was jolted back against her mare. Terrified by Ian's hoarse shouts, the agile mare began to move sideways with quick dancing steps, forcing Amanda to turn her horse out of the away. Not recognizing the beaded pouch, Amanda grew even more determined to discover who Liana's unsuitable man might be. She quickly brought her horse under control and stood her ground.

"Get out of here!" Ian shouted at her.

"No—it appears Liana has urgent need of a good friend," Amanda replied.

Undaunted by her refusal, Ian raised his arm and began to flail her mount's rump with the fringed pouch. "Get out of here while you still can!" he shouted.

Believing Ian was either drunk or had gone mad, Amanda called to Liana, "Come with me!"

"No, go!" Liana urged, and with a final fearful glance, Amanda started for home at a gallop.

Leaving her mare for a groom to fetch, Ian grabbed Liana's arm and jerked her toward the house. "I want the truth from you," he demanded, "every damning word of it!"

Robin had come out on the porch, and drawn by their father's angry shouts, Morgan and Cameron came running around the side of the house. When they saw the object of Ian's rage was their sister, they slid to a halt and stared, mouths agape. Liana shook her head, warning them to stay out of it, but at her father's next forceful shove she was caught off balance, tripped, and fell to her knees. Both young men came forward to help her up, but Ian blocked their way, grabbed hold of the back of Liana's riding habit to lift her, and nearly threw her up on the porch.

"Ian, please!" Robin begged, but he prodded Liana on through the open front door without even glancing her way.

"Mother, what's wrong?" Morgan cried.

Choking on tears, Robin just shook her head and followed Ian and Liana down the hall and into the study. She then closed and locked the door to keep her sons out. Exhausted by her husband's wrath, she grabbed the back of a chair for support. "Ian, I beg you. Let her explain."

Ian pushed Liana down into the chair opposite his desk and then leaned close as he dangled the incriminating pouch in her face. "What possible explanation can there be for your having this, Liana? I warned you to stay away from Christian, forbade you even to dance with him at parties, but you've been meeting him in secret, haven't you? Well, haven't you?"

Ian's fair complexion was blotched with fiery rage. His green eyes glowed with a demonic gleam, and his threats stank of brandy. He had become livid the first time Liana had mentioned Melissa, but she had never seen him completely lose control like this. She knew she ought to be frightened, but instead, she felt strangely detached, as though she were watching some terrible argument erupt among strangers. She focused on Christian's beaded pouch, which swung with a pendulum's precision from Ian's fingers as he continued to berate her for defying him.

Her knees were scraped and bloody, her skirt torn, her hat lost somewhere outside, but Liana sat calmly waiting for a chance to respond. When at last Ian paused to draw a breath, she told him the truth, but only a small part of it. "Yes, I have met with Christian. Initially because he swore we were related, and then, because we had a great deal to discuss."

"Whore!" Ian shrieked, and he slapped Liana with the back of his hand so hard he nearly knocked her from her chair.

"Ian!" Robin screamed as she circled Liana's chair and planted herself firmly in front of her to shield her from any further abuse. "This is our darling daughter. How can you call her such vile names?"

For an instant, Ian looked ready to slap Robin out of the way, but then he spit on the floor, and before leaving the room swearing unintelligible curses, tossed the beaded pouch in Liana's lap. Believing she could reason with Ian after he calmed down, Robin knelt at her daughter's feet. "How could you?" she gasped. "Didn't you know how badly a friendship with Christian would outrage your father?"

Ian had hit Liana so hard she was dizzy and sick to her stomach. She clutched Christian's pouch like a talisman, and let the pain her father had inflicted roll right through her. She had often heard love could be agony, but she had never anticipated anything like this.

Ignoring her mother's questions, she asked her own. "Do you think he'll send me to Aunt Sarah's?"

"Perhaps—he mentioned it earlier. I never should have agreed to search your room, Liana, but I didn't dream I'd actually find something there. Give me that wretched little bag. I'll burn it."

As Robin reached for it, Liana snatched it away. "No, Christian gave it to me and I intend to keep it."

Disappointed, Robin pushed herself to her feet. "Melissa didn't simply break your father's heart—she ripped it in shreds. How could you have accepted her son's gifts and attentions?"

Liana gazed up at her mother, her eyesight blurred by

tears. "You assured me that when I met the right young man, I'd know. By some ghastly trick of fate, it's Christian Hunter."

"No, fate couldn't possibly be that cruel."

Before Liana could argue that indeed it was, her father returned, his anger as yet undimmed. "Come on," he ordered as he yanked her from her chair. "We're going to the Barclays'."

Robin trailed after them, pleading all the way to the front door. "You can't want to confront them over this, Ian. You'll only make a wretched situation even worse."

Ian paused only momentarily. "Do you want that Indian bastard's brats for grandchildren?"

Shocked that he would ask such a dreadful thing, Robin grabbed hold of his arm. "Of course not, but surely you can't believe it's gone that far."

Battered, nauseated, dizzy, Liana had no idea what her swollen expression might reveal, but she kept silent and let them imagine whatever they wished. She didn't even have the strength to argue that the Barclay home was the last place she wished to go. A driver had brought their carriage to the door, and with Morgan and Cameron still hovering together on the porch, Liana waved them a feeble good-bye. Pushed rather than helped into the carriage, she sat slumped in the corner. Unable to cry or plead, she looked out the window as they made the short trip to the plantation that lay closest in miles, but farthest from her father's heart.

Thirteen

When their carriage rolled to a stop in front of the Barclay residence, Ian again spoke angrily to Liana. "You stay right where you are—I'll handle this."

Liana stared at her father, her gaze neither accusing nor apologetic, for all she saw in his expression was the malignant hatred he had previously reserved for the Barclays. That he would turn it on her had been a dreadful shock, and she feared anything she might say would drive him to further violence. She risked only a nod, but when he had left the carriage, she moved closer to the window to observe as he announced himself at the front door.

"I'm Ian Scott, and I must see Byron Barclay," he exclaimed to the startled servant. "Send him out here at once." Refusing to enter the house, Ian paced the porch, marking off the distance between the white columns with a measured stride.

Byron soon appeared. In his shirtsleeves, he was relaxed despite his unexpected visitor's agitated mood. "Good afternoon, Ian. Won't you come in?" It had been more than twenty years since the rainy November day when Ian had last visited the Barclay home. He had left Christian with them then, cursed them all soundly as being as guilty of deceiving him as Melissa, and fled in a rage which, from all appearances, had yet to ebb.

"I've no intention of ever setting foot in *your* house,"

Ian replied. "I've come because that evil savage's son has been tormenting my daughter and it's time he answered for it."

Ian had obviously been drinking, and the last thing Byron wanted to do was antagonize him. "Are you referring to Christian?" he asked calmly.

"You know exactly who I mean," Ian shouted. "The savage's bastard!"

"You were my brother-in-law at one time," Byron reminded him, "and I'm still inclined to do all I can to help you, but I won't allow you to call my nephew foul names."

"The cur deserves no better!"

Byron raised his hands. "Please, Ian. Go home, and I'll come to see you first thing in the morning. You're in no condition to discuss anything now."

Drawn by the commotion on the porch, Belle and Falcon appeared at the open door. Swiftly gathering that the irate visitor had some sort of an argument with Christian, Falcon ran to alert his brother while Belle went to tell the rest of the household. With Beau by his side, Christian followed Falcon back downstairs. Even alerted to Ian's mood, he wasn't fearful.

The instant Ian saw Christian, he began to shriek. "Wasn't it enough that your father ruined my life? Did you have to destroy my daughter's?"

Alarmed by that surprising accusation, Byron stepped forward to separate the two men. He had assumed Ian must be referring to what anyone else would call harmless flirting, but now he grew worried. "What's he talking about, Christian? Do you even know his daughter?"

As he tried to find an appropriately noncommittal answer, Christian glanced toward Ian's carriage. He caught only a brief glimpse of Liana before she moved back into the shadows, but he saw enough of her battered face to instantly go to her side. He pushed past Ian, went down the steps, and yanked open the carriage door. Liana shrank away from him, but he reached out for her hands and, finding she was gripping the beaded pouch he had left for her, her dilemma suddenly became clear.

There was a bright red welt where Ian had whipped the pouch across her left cheek, and the whole right side of her face was swollen from his other blow. Not understanding how easily her fair skin bruised, Christian assumed she had been struck repeatedly. Sickened that any man would mistreat a woman so brutally, let alone his own daughter, he did not waste any time inquiring how Ian had discovered the pouch. Instead, he helped her from the carriage and lifted her into his arms. Sharp needles of pain shot all the way down his left arm, but bearing it stoically, he doubted it compared with hers.

"If you weren't Liana's father, I'd kill you for this," he swore convincingly.

Ian started toward Christian, but Byron grabbed his elbow to keep him on the porch. "Stop it, both of you. Threats won't help any of us. If you came here to say something to Christian, then go ahead and say it." Byron was as shocked by Liana's appearance as Christian had been, but the speed with which the young man had come to her defense convinced him he was indeed acquainted with the redhead.

Ian jerked away from Byron's grasp, "I won't allow that conniving bastard to ravage my daughter's reputation the way Hunter did Melissa's. I demand that he marry her before the week is out."

Byron turned to find an astonished Arielle and Alanna standing in the open doorway, while Belle, Falcon, Dominique, Johanna, and Jean had spilled out around them and formed a colorful line against the house. Still inside, several servants were peeking between Arielle and Alanna's shoulders to eagerly observe the embarrassing scene. With his whole family behind him, Byron strove to find an acceptable solution for what was truly a wretched situation. Then he noticed Hunter walking across the yard and prayed the Indian would have sense enough to keep his mouth shut.

"When you despise our whole family, Ian," Byron pointed out, "how can you possibly want your daughter to join us?"

"Your *nephew,*" Ian said, his whole face contorted by bitterness as he pronounced the word as though it were the vilest of insults, "has given me no choice in the matter!"

"There are always choices," Byron argued persuasively, "and surely a forced marriage is an exceptionally poor one."

Christian stepped forward, Liana still tenderly cradled in his arms. She had looped her arms around his neck, and he spoke with convincing pride. "I wouldn't be forced, uncle. I've already proposed to Liana twice. If she'll have me, I'll be honored to be her husband. In fact, I've been looking forward to reuniting the Scott and Barclay families."

Hunter rounded the Scotts' carriage in time to hear his son's remark, and his startled gasp was as loud as those from the rest of the family. He was stunned to think his son would choose Ian's daughter, and in the next instant, she seemed like the perfect choice. When Christian turned toward him and he saw how badly Liana had been beaten, he moved forward to challenge Ian.

"Only cowards strike women. Get out of here, or I'll give you the beating you deserve."

Hunter had been away when Ian had discovered the Indian had fathered his wife's son, but that old wrong stung him as sharply this day as when Ian had first learned Melissa's loving promises had all been lies. Before Byron could stop him, he came flying off the porch and went for Hunter's throat. At the last second, the Indian stepped aside, and as Ian sped by him, he slammed the heel of his hand into the back of Ian's neck, dropping the Englishman in the dirt. He then had to fight the impulse to kick him in the ribs.

"For an English gentleman," Hunter taunted, "you have very poor manners."

Byron hurried to help Ian rise and brushed the dust from his clothes. "Go on home, Ian. Liana will be our guest tonight, and we'll talk again at your place tomorrow morning. I know you and her mother want what's best for her."

Ian shoved Byron aside and staggered toward his carriage. He paused for a long moment to observe how comfortably Liana fit in Christian's arms, and grew so disgusted he could no longer stand the sight of her. "Keep her forever," he snarled. "I disown the slut." He lurched into his carriage, and his driver, who had observed the entire scene in stunned silence, quickly urged his team to a run. He turned too sharply, sending the carriage reeling over on two wheels, but using his own weight for a counterbalance, he was at last able to right it without mishap and rolled on out of the yard with a rumbling clatter.

Knowing his son couldn't possibly carry Liana up the stairs with a wounded arm, Hunter scooped her up and started up the steps. "Where shall I take her?" he asked.

"My room," Christian called, and hurried to follow his father.

Alanna reached out to stop him. "She hasn't said a thing," she whispered. "Take her into the sitting room, Hunter. Arielle and I can see to her comfort there."

Thinking his wife's option the best, Hunter carried Liana down the hall into the bright yellow room opposite the dining room. He placed her on the settee, and then stepped back. "I hope I don't frighten you."

Liana stared up at him, too terrified by everything else which had happened to be alarmed by a courteous Indian. When Christian knelt at her side and took her hand, she managed a lopsided smile for his father. "No, thank you," she replied, but her lips were swollen, and her words slurred. "When did you decide to reunite our families?" she then asked Christian.

Just looking at her distorted features hurt him badly, but the knowing gleam in her eye warned Christian to take care with his response. "The first time I kissed you out in the fields," he confessed before breaking into a wide grin.

Liana hoped she could believe him because the prospect that she was no more than a pawn in a vicious plot against her father was too much to bear. She had tortured herself too often with that possibility, and still doubted she knew the truth. "Are you sure?" she asked, but Christian had no chance to respond.

Byron had shooed everyone else away and shut the door, leaving only Hunter, Alanna, and he and his wife with the young couple. "I don't want to hear the details," he assured them, "but we need to know if Ian is justified in demanding marriage. If he isn't, then I promise you, Liana, I will visit him tomorrow and stay until I convince him this has all been a disastrous mistake. I've known your mother since we were children. She can't want to see you treated so harshly, and with a little urging, she'll take my side and welcome you home."

Christian sent Liana a questioning glance, but she focused her attention on the beaded pouch clutched in her hands rather than providing any hint of the answer she wished him to give. Disappointed, he nevertheless knew what he wanted and leaned over to kiss her unbruised cheek before stretching to his full height. "No, you'd not only be wasting your breath, uncle, you'd be misleading the Scotts. Liana and I ought to wed as soon as possible."

Alanna shot her husband a threatening glance, and he understood precisely why she was upset. Christian had apparently been involved in a romantic intrigue every bit as dangerous as his political venture, so obviously he was adept at lying after all. The disappointed brave wanted to turn and leave, but forced himself to go to his wife's side and take her hand.

"Liana?" Alanna murmured softly. "We've not heard a word from you. This is your life we're discussing. Don't you wish to have a say as well?"

Liana glanced toward Christian's stepmother. Alanna's expression was one of gentle kindness, and she knew the dear woman was sincere. "I was out riding with a friend," she began, "and returned to find my father in the hideous rage you all saw. There's been no time to think what's best for me."

"How much time do you need to consider what you already know?" Christian argued.

When Liana refused to look at his nephew, Byron feared the situation was even more complicated than it appeared. "Come on, Christian, let's give Liana time to rest." He nodded to Hunter, and the Indian left the room with them.

Arielle knelt beside Liana and smoothed her tangled hair away from her face as she introduced herself. "There's little I can do for your bruises, but I can make a soothing cup of tea. After you've rested a bit, you can bathe and we'll find you something pretty to wear. We've so many women here, you're sure to be the same size as one of us."

Arielle's voice had a melodic serenity that made Liana want to believe she was safe there, but she was trembling so badly, she doubted she could hold a cup of tea, let alone bring it to her lips. "I'd like to rest first, please. I'm so sorry to intrude like this. My father has such bitter memories, and I'm so embarrassed that he's abandoned me here. I know I can't go home, but surely I'd be better off with one of my friends than here."

Liana's lashes were spiked with tears, and even with her features swollen and bruised, Alanna could see why her son loved her. "No, you belong here with us now. Please don't feel embarrassed. Ian and I were close once, and I doubt the kind of pain he suffered when Melissa died ever heals. It was her he was yelling at today, not you. Please believe that, and forgive him."

Liana pressed Christian's fringed pouch into her palm. "I know that story," she admitted softly. Tears filled her eyes as she was again assailed by doubts as to Christian's motives. "I don't want the tragedy to widen until it drowns us all."

Arielle rose and again caressed Liana's hair. "Your hair is such a beautiful shade. It has the glory of the sunrise." She imagined Liana and Christian would produce very handsome children, but wisely kept the thought to herself for the time being. "Can you climb the stairs? You'll be far more comfortable in my room than here."

Liana felt too weak to move. "No, thank you. I don't want to be any trouble. I'll be fine right here."

"Is there anything we can bring you?" Alanna inquired thoughtfully. "If not tea, something else to drink, or eat?"

The mere mention of food made Liana's stomach lurch, and she shook her head. "No, thank you. I couldn't eat."

Their reluctant guest looked so miserable, neither Alanna nor Arielle wished to leave her, but fearing they were only tiring the exhausted young woman, they left and quietly closed the door. Once out in the hall, Alanna's manner changed abruptly and she marched into Byron's study, her feelings plain in her hostile frown.

"I thought we had raised you to respect women," she challenged her stepson.

Christian had been dodging his father's and uncle's questions, but he couldn't evade Alanna's. "Yes, and you succeeded. I've never harmed Liana."

Alanna rested her hands on her hips. "Her father just disowned her because of you. What would you call that if not harm? And what about all of us who were caught totally unprepared for Ian's accusations? Did you truly believe you could seduce a well-bred young woman without consequences?"

Christian leaned back against the desk. "I didn't seduce her."

"Christian," Hunter chided, "it's time for the truth."

Christian didn't even know where to begin. Beau wasn't there to contradict him, so he shaded his tale to make his behavior sound far more gentlemanly than it had actually been. "I noticed her in town years ago. The fact that she's a Scott presented a problem, but when I met her down by the river one afternoon not long ago, she was so appealing I didn't care who she was. I convinced her to continue meeting me, but we didn't make love until last Saturday night after I'd been shot."

"My God, I must say I admire your stamina," Byron interjected.

"Byron, that was uncalled for," Alanna snapped.

"Yes, you're right. I'm sorry. Was that when you offered one of the two proposals you mentioned to Ian?" Byron asked.

"Yes, but Liana was too upset that I'd been shot delivering the pamphlets to consider it seriously."

"She knows you're involved with the pamphlets?" Hunter asked.

Christian watched the fearful glances passing about the room. "Yes, but not for certain until then."

Deeply concerned for his son's safety, Hunter moved closer. "Could she have told Ian? If she did, you've no time to waste. You must get away."

"She would have warned me if she had."

Hunter waited for his son to explain, and when he did not, he prodded him. "What makes you think so?"

Christian shook his head. "I trust her."

"How did she come to have your beaded pouch?" Alanna inquired.

Christian decided against mentioning his first visit to

Liana's bedroom. "I gave it to her. Perhaps Ian found it. Something certainly infuriated him today, and it seems likely the pouch was what it was. Liana didn't say."

"No, she didn't say much of anything, did she?" Alanna remarked pointedly. "As much as I hate to think this, it's possible the ghastly scene we all witnessed was no more than an act designed to place a spy in our midst. Maybe Ian wasn't mad at all, but just being extremely clever."

Stunned by that allegation, Christian listened as the possibility Liana was a Loyalist spy was discussed by the others. Hurt and disappointed that anyone might believe Liana was even capable of betraying him in such an underhanded fashion, he still couldn't completely discount how plausible their conjecture sounded. "No, wait," he finally cautioned. "If she had told Ian I wrote the pamphlets, he would either have sent O'Keefe to arrest me, or had her continue our friendship to discover our plans. He'd not have brought her here to demand marriage."

The troubled group mulled over that contention a long moment, and then Alanna spoke. "Ian was such a fine young man. It's horrible to see what a lifetime of harboring resentments against our family has done to him. It's plain Liana isn't eager for marriage, but even if she refuses to wed Christian, we can't ask her to leave. Let's do the best we can to make her feel welcome, and reserve judgment until we know her better. She can have the guest room, and Christian, we will all depend upon you to stay out of it."

Christian nodded, but he doubted he could keep away from Liana for long. He knew she could not possibly be a spy, and with the dreadful way her father had treated her, it was no wonder she didn't feel up to planning a wedding. "I never meant to bring disgrace to anyone," he vowed convincingly.

"Neither did I," Hunter added, but all present knew that he had.

* * *

Robin ran to the front door when she heard the carriage approaching, but when Ian got out alone, she nearly collapsed. "Where's Liana?" she called to him. "Where's my little girl?"

Ian strode toward her, his face a mask of disgust. "We no longer have a daughter."

Robin grabbed his arm to bring him to a halt. "My God, Ian, what have you done?"

Ian peeled her off like a rumpled coat. "Christian intends to make her his wife so I left her with the Barclays." He strode past Robin to the study, where he promptly began to seek solace in brandy.

Standing just out of sight in the parlor, Morgan and Cameron rushed to their mother's side. They helped the nearly hysterical woman into a comfortable chair and hovered close. "What's happened to Father?" Cameron wailed. "He's turned into a madman."

Robin couldn't even speak, let alone explain her husband's brutish behavior. Until recently he had been a kind and loving man and she couldn't believe the change in him was permanent. She knew he would forbid her to visit the Barclays, and she couldn't bear the thought she might never see her only daughter again. Beside herself, she wept huge tears and couldn't be consoled by her sons. When she heard a knock at the door, she sent Morgan a pleading glance and he went to answer it.

Hoping to spend the afternoon with Liana, Sean O'Keefe failed to note Morgan's distress. He commented on the fine spring weather, hoped aloud the Scotts were all in good health, and then asked to speak with Liana.

Morgan struggled to find a way to explain his sister's absence. "I'm sorry, she's, uh, well, unavailable."

Disappointed, Sean began to back away. "I hope she's not feeling poorly."

A nervous smile brought a twitch to the corner of Morgan's mouth. From the last look he had gotten of Liana, he knew she couldn't feel good. Knowing Sean was sweet on her, he hated being so vague, but he couldn't bring himself to report what had happened, either. From the speed with which bad news traveled in Williamsburg, he knew Sean would hear about it soon enough. "It was good of you to stop by," he finally said.

"Will you please tell Liana I asked for her?"

Before Morgan could think of a way to send Sean on his way, he heard his father coming down the hall. He turned in time to see him career into the wall, knock a painting askew, and nearly trip over his own feet. "Captain O'Keefe's here," he called out in warning, but Ian kept right on coming.

Believing Ian to be a gentleman, Sean was shocked by his disheveled appearance, but it wasn't until Ian came within two feet of him that he realized the man was drunk. "I've come at a bad time," he apologized immediately. "Good day, sir."

Ian grabbed hold of the doorjamb for support. "Liana's eloped with an Indian," he announced with a sorry shake of his head. "I forbade her to even speak to the bastard, but she defied me."

Taken aback by what he considered an absurd announcement, Sean didn't know whether to shake the truth from the inebriated man, or just leave him be. "What Indian could that be, sir?"

"The Barclays' bastard who has the audacity to call himself my son."

"Your son, sir?" Sean looked to Morgan for help.

"Christian Barclay," Morgan said. "His mother was Father's wife."

Ian had not known his sons were aware of his first marriage and knowing Liana must have told them, he felt doubly betrayed. He raised his hand as though he meant to slap Morgan, then let it fall, stumbled on out the front door, and started on a weaving path toward the empty fields.

"I don't understand any of this," Sean complained. "Liana never even mentioned Christian's name, and now she's eloped with him?"

Relieved he no longer had to lie, Morgan nodded. "You could say that."

"I don't believe it. Liana is a lady, and she'd no more wed a savage than she would attempt to swim to England."

Cameron came up to his brother's side. "Why don't you visit the Barclays and ask her yourself?" he suggested.

Sean had spent very little time with Liana's brothers, but they had impressed him as likeable and courteous lads. "Perhaps I ought to speak with your mother before I go."

Cameron and Morgan shook their heads. "She's not accepting callers this afternoon," Morgan said. Sean offered no argument, and they watched him ride away. "I feel sick," Morgan murmured. "What we saw didn't look like any elopement I've ever heard about. What do you think? Are you up for riding over to the Barclays' and talking with Liana?"

"Father would kill us if he found out."

"Well, he damn near killed Liana today, and for what? He never tells us anything, so I say we ought to go see for ourselves what's happening. Stay here if you like, but I'm going."

When Morgan started off toward the stable, Cameron ran after him. Thinking of his dream of being a soldier, he saw pursuing Liana as a mission. "Wait for me!" he yelled, but he sure hoped Morgan would know what to say when they got there.

Beau was waiting far Christian when he left the study. "Come on outside," he ordered. "I want to talk to you."

"I've heard enough lectures for one day," Christian replied, but Beau grabbed his good arm and gave him such a forceful shove he decided just to follow Beau out to the garden without arguing. He wished there were one person in his family who understood how he felt, but it was plain from Beau's angry frown it wasn't going to be him.

"Did you rape Liana?" Beau asked accusingly.

"What? No, of course not." Disgusted with his cousin, Christian had a difficult time keeping his voice down. "You're as bad as Ian. Does the fact that a girl as pretty as Liana could love me, an Indian's bastard, seem impossible to you, too?"

Shocked that Christian would repeat that insult, Beau nevertheless stood his ground. "I know you go after whatever you want, and I've never seen you let anything stop you. Even being shot didn't make you want to give up the pamphlets so if you wanted Liana, for whatever reason, then forcing yourself on her might have seemed like the fastest way to make her your wife."

Christian glanced toward the windows of the sitting room and wondered if Liana were observing them. Hoping she was, he shoved his cousin in the chest. "I don't feel up to fighting you, or I'd tear off your head for saying that. I want Liana for all the right reasons, and Ian would have refused me for all the wrong ones. So I went behind his back. So what? I'm the man Liana wants and that's all that matters."

"If she wants you so badly, then why didn't she say so when her father was here?"

"The man was drunk," Christian replied. "I don't fault her for ignoring him."

"It wasn't him she was ignoring," Beau countered. "It was you."

Christian clenched his fists at his sides. His left arm felt as though it were on fire, but he could barely contain the urge to shove Beau's words back down his throat. "You're just jealous," he finally said, "because I had the courage to go after Liana when all you did was dream about her."

The truth of that charge stung, but exercising remarkable self-control, Beau kept his hands off Christian. "In a few days, when Liana feels better, she'll be the one to decide what she wants to do. I'm willing to let her choose. Are you?"

Christian's dark eyes narrowed. "She's already made her choice, Beau."

Beau smiled knowingly. "Wait and see."

Christian watched his cousin walk away, but he wasn't worried by his threats. He followed the path to the sitting room windows and peeked in. Liana was curled up on the settee asleep, and he waited there, simply enjoying watching her until Falcon came to his side.

"This family is like a lady's fan," Falcon complained. "At the dinner table, it's spread wide and everyone shares equally, but when anything exciting happens, it folds to shut most of us out. What did they say to you about her?"

Falcon was almost as tall as Christian, but still possessed an adolescent's spare leanness rather than the hardened muscles of a man. His buckskins fit snugly, while the deep fringe swayed with a fluid grace as he gestured toward Liana. He was as handsome as Christian, but had a wildness all his own.

"You know what we are," Christian confided. "There's not a man in Williamsburg who'll give his daughter to either of us willingly, regardless of what she wants. I'd hoped Liana would come to me on her own, but now that she's here, what difference does it make how she arrived?"

From Falcon's point of view, it mattered a great deal, but he did not feel like arguing with his brother. "There's one man who'd have to give us a daughter," he advised instead. "Our dear Uncle Byron."

Christian studied Falcon's teasing smile and wondered aloud, "Which one do you want, Dominique or Belle?"

Falcon shrugged. "I haven't decided."

"Good, but—"

Before Christian could offer any more advice, they heard a rider approaching and were too curious not to walk to the front of the house. When they found Captain O'Keefe dismounting, they drew to an abrupt halt, but he had already seen them, and it was too late to get away. Christian walked toward him. "Good afternoon, Captain."

Ignoring his greeting, Sean nodded toward the house. "I was told Liana Scott is here. Please tell her I've come to see her."

"I'm sorry, she's taking a nap and asked not to be disturbed."

To take every advantage of his impressive uniform, Sean squared his shoulders proudly. "If I have to return with soldiers, I will, but I intend to see Miss Scott this afternoon."

Christian shook his head. "If you care for her, you'd not even consider embarrassing her so badly. You have my word she's not a prisoner here. Now go."

Christian's usual arrogance was missing that afternoon, and that fact alone made Sean suspicious. "I was told a preposterous tale about an elopement and quite naturally I was concerned. I want to hear the truth from Liana's lips."

Again Christian refused his request. "That's impossible, but let me assure you there's been no elopement. When Liana and I marry it will be in the Bruton Parish Church in front of the whole town. I'll see that you're sent a special invitation."

Hearing Christian make such a boast sickened Sean. "You won't have to because I'm not leaving until I see Liana."

Thinking the two men were so stubborn neither would

ever give in, Falcon offered his brother a solution. "Liana's asleep, and she won't know if you let the captain look in on her. If you do, I'm sure he'll leave quietly."

Understanding the sense of Falcon's suggestion, Christian gestured toward the front door. "If I let you look in on her, will you give me your word as an officer that you'll leave then?"

"Yes, but only for the time being. I'll come back tomorrow and every day after that until I'm finally able to speak with her."

Christian hesitated a long moment, then decided offering O'Keefe a glimpse of Liana would be worth it to be rid of him for one day at least. He moved toward the door. "Take care to walk softly so that you don't disturb her," he cautioned.

"I know better than to tramp through your house," Sean said and followed Christian inside and down the hall to the sitting room. Christian opened the door slowly, then pointed to the settee where Liana was snuggled among the embroidered pillows. Even from the doorway, Sean noted her torn skirt, tangled hair, and swollen features.

"My God," he gasped.

Christian quickly pulled the door closed. "Her father's disowned her, but I intend to do what's right and marry her."

Shocked that the young woman he had esteemed so highly had behaved in a fashion scandalous enough to prompt Ian to banish her from the family, Sean reached out for the wall to steady himself. In the next instant, he focused his anguished rage on Christian. "You bastard," he snarled.

Christian raised his hands. "Captain, you gave me your word you'd leave after seeing Liana. I intend to hold you to it."

Sean looked ready to spit venom, but he turned and, forgetting his earlier attempt to walk softly, he strode from the house without making the slightest effort to be quiet. He mounted his horse, and with one last angry scowl toward the house, rode away.

Remaining in the hall, Christian listened at the sitting room door, and when there was no sound, he was relieved the foul-tempered captain hadn't awakened Liana. He longed to go in and talk with her himself, but not wanting to disturb her dreams, he went down to the river. He practiced what he wished to say, but the whole while he feared his words would sound as empty as the swiftly rushing current.

Fourteen

Morgan was truly concerned about his sister's welfare, but the fact that she had been exiled to the Barclays' home also presented him with a plausible excuse to see Dominique again. Then he hated himself for thinking of the pretty blonde at such a difficult time. What kind of a brother was he to dream of other girls when his sister was suffering so terribly?

He cursed his own weakness all the way to the Barclays', then, concentrating on being a loyal brother, he led Cameron up to the front door with a proud swagger, but it was opened even before he had raised his hand to knock. He recognized Beau, although they had never been formally introduced.

"Good afternoon," Morgan greeted him. "We've come to see our sister."

As he stepped out onto the porch, Beau pulled the door closed behind him. "Do you have any idea why she's here?"

Morgan refused to repeat their father's ludicrous tale of an elopement, but was too curious not to refer to marriage. "We heard she's going to marry Christian."

"And you'd like to ask her if it's true," Beau added.

"Well, yes, of course," Cameron exclaimed. "If one of your sisters suddenly took up residence in our house, wouldn't you question why?"

The brothers had their sister's vivid coloring, but thoroughly masculine features. Despite their aggressive attitudes, Beau doubted they knew how to fight as well as Christian and he did, but considering the wretched history between the two families, he hoped he would never have to find out. He smiled and attempted to be more friendly.

"Liana's asleep, and I don't believe we ought to disturb her. You'll always be welcome here, though, so why don't you come back tomorrow, or whenever you wish? You needn't worry about Liana. We're taking very good care of her."

"We'd like to see for ourselves," Morgan insisted.

"I appreciate your loyalty to your sister, but you must have seen what your father did to her." When Morgan and Cameron exchanged a disgusted glance, Beau was certain that they had. "No one has made any wedding plans as yet, so please allow Liana a few days to recover and again look her best. I know she'll be eager to see you. I'll tell her you were here."

Uncertain what he should do, Morgan hesitated to agree. "Is she really all right?" he asked fretfully.

Touched by the young man's concern, Beau attempted to speak the truth without insulting Ian. "Your father has an old grudge against our family, and mistreated your sister as a result. How would you feel if he had beaten and disowned you?"

Morgan's expression hardened and it was plain from the defiant light in his eyes that should Ian ever raise a hand to him, he would hit back. "We aren't the ones in question," he reminded Beau. "We'll go now because we don't want to upset Liana if she's embarrassed about her looks, but we'll visit her again soon."

Beau again relied on a smile to convey his sincerity, "Your father's argument with the Barclays is one-sided," he assured the brothers. "Please feel free to visit your sister whenever you wish."

"Thank you." Somewhat relieved, but still disappointed they hadn't seen Liana, Morgan and Cameron didn't stop to confer until they reached the main road. Then Cameron began to talk excitedly. "That was Beau, wasn't it? He seemed real nice, or did you think he was just pretending to be helpful so we'd be on our way?"

"With all that's happened today, I don't know what to think. Maybe the Barclays are nice, and maybe they're as evil as Father has always said they were. Let's wait until we have a chance to speak with Liana. Then we'll know what to do."

"I hope so," Cameron replied. "Do you think Father might disown us for visiting her?"

"Do you care?"

"Well, yes," Cameron insisted. "Don't you? Where would we go?"

Morgan urged his horse on down the road. "Anywhere might be better than home if things get any worse."

"How could they get any worse?" Cameron asked, but when Morgan sent him a threatening glance, his imagination supplied more than enough dire possibilities.

Christian's lips brushed Liana's brow lightly and she opened her eyes. For a desperate instant she didn't recognize the sunny yellow room, but then her memory became painfully clear. She sat up and tried to repair the damage to her hairstyle, but quickly realized it was impossible and removed her combs. Her hair tumbled over her shoulders, and she let it dip over her badly swollen eye.

"I've brought you some chamomile tea," Christian said as he placed the cup and saucer on the cherrywood table at her left. "Our cook makes delicious little spice cakes, so I brought a couple for you."

"Thank you." Liana reached for the teacup, then drew

back when her hand began to shake. "I'm sorry to show such little courage."

Christian pulled a chair up close and sat down. "Here, I'll hold the cup for you." He was surprised he wasn't shaking himself, but held the delicate teacup steady so she could take a sip. "You needn't apologize. You've already proven your bravery to me. Can you tell me what happened?"

Liana blinked away a fresh threat of tears as she told him what little she knew. "I've no idea what my mother was looking for when she found your beaded bag." She picked it up from where it lay in her lap. "My having anything of yours was enough to enrage my father. Until today, he's always been so kind."

When she paused, Christian fed her a bite of freshly baked cake. It was moist and sweet, but reminded her of home—and the fact that she no longer had one. The thought increased her anguish tenfold. "I've always known he had a temper, but he's never directed it at me. I never even dreamed he could treat any of us so cruelly."

Christian continued to hold Liana's teacup. She had taken care of him when he had been shot, and he was more than willing to return the favor. He remembered the times when they had been together and her fiery defiance had excited him as much as her beauty. Instead of that lively spirit, all he saw now was an immense sorrow that pained him as deeply as her bruises. He encouraged her to eat every last bite of the cake and finish the tea before he asked his next question.

"What did you expect would happen when your parents found out about me?"

His gaze was sympathetic rather than challenging, but Liana didn't know how to respond. Every second of the time she had spent with him had held a magical appeal she had not even attempted to describe to her closest friend. Now as she tried to imagine how their affair might have evolved had it not been discovered, she felt the same bittersweet pain as when he had left her Sunday morning. She couldn't lie and say she hadn't considered the future, but she knew he wouldn't like the decision she had reached.

It was difficult meeting his gaze and not losing herself in the wonder of him, but she fought to make herself understood. "I thought it would be best for both of us if I went to England, but before I could discuss a trip with my parents, well, you know what happened."

Christian's expression changed instantly from one of hopeful expectancy to bitter disappointment. Devastated that she had intended to leave him, he rose and set the chair back in its place. "I didn't realize until now how like my mother you really are. You're ashamed of me, aren't you?"

Liana reached out for him but he stepped back to avoid her touch. "Christian, wait. It isn't like that at all."

Christian laughed derisively. "Oh, yes, it is. You had the choice of coming with me on Sunday, but you refused. I should have known then that the pamphlets weren't the problem. You just didn't want to take your Indian lover for a husband. I should ride over to your house and thank your father for bringing you here because I would never have won you on my own."

Knowing how deeply he actually loved Liana tore at Christian's soul and he ran from the room before he began calling her the vile names he could never take back.

"Christian!" Liana left the settee, then found she was too dizzy to follow him. She sank back down on the comfortable little sofa and wondered what she had done to deserve the abuse she had suffered that day. She cared deeply for Christian, but he had turned against her as swiftly as her father and she doubted anything she could ever say or do would save her from further scorn.

Arielle saw Christian run from the house and immediately went into the sitting room to check on Liana. One look at the young woman's distraught expression was enough to convince her it was time to intervene. "Come, let me help you upstairs," she called as she came through the door.

She eased Liana to her feet, then wrapped her right arm around her waist. "Your brothers came to see you, as did Captain O'Keefe, but they were asked to return another time. I know this has to be the worst day of your life, but regardless of how you came to be with us, I hope you'll never want to leave." Hoping to distract the young woman, Arielle confided her own experience.

"I remember when I first arrived in Williamsburg as though it were yesterday. Byron brought me here when the Acadians were expelled from our homeland. His father was very ill, and his mother was appalled that he had taken up with a French widow. When his father died soon after my arrival, his mother blamed me for his death."

Despite her pain, Liana became so absorbed in Arielle's softly voiced tale that she reached the third floor without difficulty. "How awful," she exclaimed. "What did you do?"

"There was nothing I could do except be who I am," Arielle explained. "Alanna was a true friend to me, and when Beau was born, my mother-in-law grew more accepting. She remarried a few years later, and moved to her second husband's plantation near Charleston. She's been dead several years now, but I'm grateful we became friends long before she passed away."

Liana held a bedpost while Arielle helped her out of her riding habit. She had known about Melissa, but now hearing Arielle's story, she couldn't help but wonder aloud, "Is life always so dramatic for the Barclays? Doesn't anything ever run smoothly for your family?"

Arielle laughed as she laid the rust-colored garment aside. "It's only our romantic involvements that provide an element of turmoil—the rest of our lives seem remarkably uneventful.''

As Arielle peeled away Liana's petticoats, she was shocked by her torn stockings and bloody knees. "Oh, my dear girl, why didn't you tell me you'd scraped your knees? I'll get my medicines at once."

Surprised by Arielle's concern, Liana looked down. "I seem to have ruined my only pair of stockings," she murmured distractedly, "but I really don't care about my knees."

"Well, I do. Sit down on the bed and I'll be right back." Arielle paused at the doorway. "I'll have the girls bring a tub and hot water."

"Thank you." As Liana waited, she couldn't help but wonder if everything her father had ever told her about the Barclays hadn't been a lie. From what she had seen that day, their home was as beautifully furnished and neatly kept as her own, and despite the wretched circumstance that had brought her there, everyone had been attentive and kind. Except for Christian, and despite her best efforts to be considerate she had alienated him.

Arielle soon returned and brought clean clothes as well as her basket of herbs and salves. "You're closest to Johanna's size, but we'll provide you with new clothes of your own as soon as you feel up to going into town for fittings."

"You're very kind, but I can't accept new clothing or anything else. I won't be staying here. I can't."

Servants arrived with the tub and hot water and Arielle had to wait to continue their conversation until they were again alone. "Let's talk while I wash your hair," she encouraged gently.

Liana cast off the last of her lace-trimmed lingerie and stepped into the tub. The hot water stung her knees, and then began to feel good. She sat still as Arielle shampooed her hair. "There's really nothing to talk about. My father may have turned me out, but I needn't stay here and become a pawn in an endless feud between our families."

"A pawn? Is that all you think you are?"

"I'm afraid so."

"Hmm." Arielle considered Liana's view most unfortunate. "There is only one question you need ask yourself," she finally advised. "Do you love Christian?"

Liana bowed her head, for the love she felt for him was indistinguishable from the pain it had caused.

Surprised by her silence, Arielle refused to accept it as proof of Liana's feelings. "You needn't tell me, but please don't lie to yourself, or to Christian. Lies bring far too terrible a consequence, while speaking the truth brings either joy, or only momentary pain."

Liana nodded, but while she understood the wisdom of Arielle's words, she doubted they applied in a case as tragic as hers.

Despite Arielle's expert attentions, Liana did not feel up to joining the family for supper and when Christian heard she would not be coming downstairs, he lost his appetite and left the house. Byron smiled as his wife took her place at the opposite end of the table, but it had been an extremely difficult day for them all. While none of the adults wished to discuss Liana's arrival, the children all did.

"Just what is it Christian did to make Liana's father disown her?" Jean asked as soon as his father had said grace.

Jean was a bright, inquisitive lad and Byron knew he should have anticipated such a question, but there was no way to give a truthful answer at the dinner table. "Let's talk about it later, son."

"Father, really," Dominique complained. "Jean is old enough to know."

Byron's eldest daughter was seated at his right so he

could reply without raising his voice. "I agree, but that doesn't mean I have to tell him now."

Falcon's place was beside Dominique, and he looked across the table to Jean. "Christian didn't have to do anything, Jean. He's part Seneca and that's enough to set a girl's father against us."

Alanna placed her hand on her son's arm. "That will be enough," she commanded firmly.

"You know he's right," Hunter exclaimed. "We can speak the truth here."

Alanna kicked the brave's shin under the table. "I absolutely refuse to call such biased thinking the truth."

Hunter leaned out to look past Johanna at Jean. "A great many men share Ian Scott's bias," he told the boy, then sitting back, he winked at his wife.

"You are incorrigible," she murmured under her breath.

"I am merely Indian," Hunter replied.

"This is a most distressing situation for us all," Arielle said. "What Christian and Liana need is our love and support, not more questions."

"We're not the only ones with questions, Mother," Beau protested. "Liana's brothers will be back."

"Captain O'Keefe won't," Falcon interjected, still proud of his part in sending him away.

Beau nodded, for he had heard about the captain's visit. "Lord knows who else will appear tomorrow. It wouldn't surprise me if the whole town came trooping up to the front door."

Arielle caught her husband's eye, and as confused as she, he just shook his head. Appreciating his dismay, she speared a bite of sweet potato with her fork. "Please. Let's enjoy this fine supper and talk of other things. Can you catch us some fish for breakfast, Belle?"

Belle shared Beau's distress, but didn't voice it. "Yes, easily. Do you want to help me, Falcon?"

"Yes, but I'll catch more than you."

"No, you can only try," Belle vowed, eager to accept the challenge.

After supper, Johanna walked through the garden to the well. Since Sunday, when she and David had resumed speaking, they had begun meeting each evening—quite by accident, it seemed to them both. He had gotten there first tonight and greeted her warmly. "Good evening," she replied. It was a lovely night, with a slight breeze that bathed them in the garden's sweet fragrance.

She sighed wearily and leaned back against the well to rest. "This has been a very trying day, but I'm sure the gossip must have already reached the hands' quarters."

David would never have asked had she not mentioned the subject, but now that she had, he prompted her to explain. "I didn't pay any attention to what the men said after I heard Christian's name and their sly snickers. I knew if anything important had happened, you'd tell me whatever I ought to know."

Johanna had enjoyed their evening conversations immensely, and while they never began with personal topics, David was so pleasant and sympathetic she usually found herself confiding in him before they said good night. Now she saw no reason for rambling pleasantries when such a dire problem had presented itself.

"A neighbor is demanding that Christian marry his daughter, but neither Christian nor Liana seems eager to wed. As you can imagine, that complicates an already difficult situation considerably."

"Yes, indeed." In the twilight, David had difficulty making out Johanna's expression, but he knew her to be devoted to her elder brother and assumed she was most distressed. While she had described the problem in dispassionate terms, from what he had overheard, there was a terrible scandal brewing. Unwilling to point it out if she didn't know, he veered away from such a provocative topic.

"Marriage is a serious step," he said, "and not to be taken lightly."

David had mentioned that he had studied briefly for the ministry, and that struck Johanna as a phrase he must have learned then. "I agree, but in this case, it's much too late to consider the wisdom of the match."

Knowing that Johanna did indeed understand why Christian had become the butt of the hands' jokes embarrassed David badly. He had never discussed such a sensitive issue with a young woman, and didn't know how to proceed. "I'm so sorry to hear it, I truly am."

"David," Johanna cajoled, "you needn't be so apologetic. After all, it's Christian who's caused all the trouble, not you."

"Well, yes, but still, I'm sorry for your family. What's Christian going to do?"

"I don't believe he has any choice. Do you mind if we walk a bit tonight?"

Relieved beyond measure by her change of subject, David answered too quickly. "No, not at all. Where shall we go?"

Johanna laughed. "We don't have to go anywhere, David, we can just stroll down to the river and back."

"It's a fine night for a stroll—I should have thought of it myself." He had never called on a young woman, which he feared was becoming dreadfully obvious. As they started along the path, he wondered if he ought to take Johanna's hand, but fearing she would consider him forward, he jammed his hands into his pants pockets.

"We're going to start transplanting the tobacco plants on Monday," he said, then regretted it the moment the words left his mouth. "How stupid of me. You must already know that."

"No, I don't pay much attention to the crops. I probably

should, though, so thank you for keeping me informed. I hope you won't find the work too demanding."

Realizing she thought he was as weak as when he had arrived upset David badly. "It shouldn't be," he argued. "I'm much stronger than I look."

"Forgive me—I didn't mean to sound as though I didn't think so." Johanna didn't know what had happened, but neither of them seemed able to converse easily. Fearing she had insulted him, she waited for him to say something, but he didn't speak until they reached the water.

"I've walked alone here at night several times," David revealed. "The river sounds more musical at night, even with all the crickets chirping. I like the way the water scatters the moonlight into bright bits. Not that I just stand around watching the river most nights. I usually try to read awhile."

Enjoying his poetic comments, Johanna instantly thought of a way to help him. "If you run out of things to read, come up to the house some afternoon and I'll lend you some books from our library."

"Oh, no, I couldn't take them. The other men like to grab whatever I'm reading and toss it around to tease me. I wouldn't want to subject any of your books to their carelessness."

Shocked that he had been treated badly, Johanna took a step closer. "Have they ruined any of yours?"

"No, not really. One lost a few pages, but I found them all and slipped them back into place. I just don't read that book when there's a breeze."

David was such a shy young man, Johanna could easily imagine him being tormented with an endless succession of ridiculous pranks. "Tell me which men are bothering you, and I'll have my father put an end to it," she offered immediately.

Embarrassed that she believed he was unable to take care of himself, David knelt down by the riverbank, found a stone, and tossed it into the water. "No, they'll have no respect for me if they think I complained about them." He was already badly worried he had sounded so pathetically inept that Johanna might also lose respect for him. "I just go my own way, and ignore them. Most have tired of making fun of me."

"Well, that's good, but aren't you awfully lonely?"

David rose and turned toward her. He knew he ought to tell her the truth, but try as he might, it never seemed to come out right. "Yes, but I didn't come here to make friends. I came to learn about farming. I hope to have a place of my own someday soon."

Rather than impressing Johanna with his ambition as he had hoped, David had only succeeded in reminding her that his stay there would be temporary. She rubbed her arms and took a step toward the house. "It's gotten chilly all of a sudden. We'd better go back."

Again wishing he could hold her hand but too timid to reach for it, David walked alongside her to the well where they said good night, but as he watched Johanna enter the house he felt none of the sweet elation he had enjoyed on their previous visits. Certain he had bored her, or worse, evoked pity, he went on an extended walk before going to bed, but he didn't come up with a single amusing story to enliven their next conversation.

Supper had not even been served at the Scott residence. When Robin had refused to leave her bed and Ian had locked himself in his study, Morgan and Cameron scavenged the kitchen for bread and ham and ate outside on the lawn. Their home had once rung with music and laughter, but when they finished eating, neither felt like going inside.

"I'm beginning to suspect we were born into the wrong family," Morgan mused darkly. "Do you realize if Melissa hadn't died, she'd be our mother and we'd be part of the Barclay clan?"

"No, I don't think so," Cameron argued. "Father would have left her after Christian was born and we would be sitting here tonight, just as we are."

After a moment's reflection, Morgan decided Cameron was right. "Yes. If he was so angry with Liana, he would have been furious with Melissa. He may even have killed her." That ghastly thought made him shiver. "Let's go back to the Barclays' tomorrow."

At thirteen, Cameron was content to let his elder brother plan their strategy, but he was still worried. "Fine. I miss Liana already."

Morgan nodded. "I miss everything." He wished he knew what to do, but like Cameron, his life was flying apart too fast for him to think very clearly.

When Christian finally went up to his room that night, he found Hunter stretched out on his bed. He closed his door and waited for the angry tirade he had successfully avoided all day. "If you're going to hit me, we ought to go outside."

Hunter sat up with a lazy stretch, rolled off the side of the bed, and walked toward his son with a soundless step. "When have I ever hit you?"

With the door at his back, Christian had no way to escape whatever his father intended to do, but he had been well-trained to accept punishment bravely and didn't flinch. "Never, but you certainly have justification today."

Highly amused by his son's comment, Hunter laughed and pulled him into a hearty hug. "I'm proud of you for owning up to your responsibilities. I'd never punish you for it." He stepped back and grew more serious. "I was surprised to find Ian here, but after I'd seen Liana, I knew you'd made a wise choice."

"I'm not sure she would agree."

Hunter responded with a sly grin. "She must have agreed Saturday night. You can charm her again."

Christian didn't see how. "It's one thing to spend the night with an amusing savage, quite another to take him for a husband."

All trace of humor left Hunter's face, and feeling sick, he found it difficult to speak. "That's what your mother thought, but I didn't know. If it's what Liana believes, then you'll have to change her mind quickly or you'll find yourself with a very beautiful but disagreeable wife."

Christian had realized that sorry fact hours ago. "Yes, I know. The only trick is how to go about it."

Hunter stared at his son a long moment, and then nodded. "That won't be nearly as difficult as you might think. Just listen a moment, and I'll teach you how."

Christian didn't even want to admit that he cared, but he listened with growing attention, and he was so intrigued by what Hunter described that he was very glad he had.

Fifteen

Liana awoke crying, so miserably unhappy that not even sleep had erased her despair. She lay snuggled among the pillows, sobbing silently, and relived her last conversation with Christian in a succession of imaginative dialog which all ended in the same tragic way. She had been jarred from her pleasantly predictable life the day they had met. "Met," she mused darkly, was not the correct word. He had captured her in what to him had been an amusing game, but she had been the one to bear the horrible consequences when his brand of fun had changed her life irrevocably.

Sick with dread, she remained in bed, distractedly listening to the rest of the household come awake. Doors opened and closed, children called to each other, and adults spoke in hushed voices. The familiar sounds were the only reassurance she had that life was continuing, for the Barclays, at least, in a comfortably predictable pattern.

Her room was painted a soft green that called spring to mind, but she was untouched by the season's naturally uplifting sense of wonder. When Arielle came to encourage her to join the family for breakfast, Liana was ashamed not to be up and dressed. She left the bed then, and gathering her courage, looked in the mirror above the dresser. Startled when she did not recognize the badly bruised face that greeted her, she leaned close to make certain she really was gazing at herself.

Her right eye was swollen shut now, and her left lid so puffy from tears it had narrowed to a mere slit. Her right cheek was a ghastly deep purple that would take weeks to fade. On the left side of her face, the thin mark created by the swipe of the beaded pouch was mercifully faint. She tried to smile, but her injuries turned her usual expression into a grotesque grimace.

"No one will have any appetite with me at the table," she remarked as she turned away from the mirror. "Please tell them to go ahead without me."

"You needn't hide," Arielle encouraged sympathetically. "We all feel badly about what happened yesterday, but no one blames you."

Feeling dizzy, Liana leaned back against the dresser for support. "I hope no one blames Christian, either."

"No, of course not," Arielle caught herself in that lie. "Well, perhaps some. Come, let me help you dress. Even if you don't feel up to coming downstairs this morning, you'll feel ever so much better in pretty clothes."

Liana sincerely doubted it, but lacking the strength to object, she donned the garments Arielle had brought. The chemise was the finest linen, the corset of flowered silk, and the petticoats decorated with ribbon. The cream-colored bodice of the gown was embroidered with forget-me-nots while the skirt was the lovely blue obtained from making dye of the paper used to wrap sugar, but rather than appreciating the distinctive shade, Liana thought only of how closely it matched her mood. She sat dejectedly staring at her hands while Arielle brushed and styled her hair, then pulled the lace-trimmed cap she had been loaned down low, but was unable to hide her battered face sufficiently to feel presentable.

Sorry her attentions hadn't brightened Liana's mood, Arielle laid the silver handled brush aside. "I'll send you

some breakfast as soon as I get downstairs. I imagine there
will be quite an argument as to who brings it up to you,
but I hope our curiosity doesn't offend you. Please believe
me when I say it's tinged with affection."

After the despicable way her father had abandoned her
there, Liana was grateful not to have been thrown into the
root cellar. "After yesterday, I doubt anything that could
happen will ever strike me as offensive. A curious glance
won't bother me in the slightest, although I do wish I
weren't so ugly."

Arielle touched Liana's sleeve tenderly. "Please, a few
bruises scarcely mar your beauty."

Arielle turned and left the room before Liana could dis-
agree. She made up the bed, then went to one of the pair
of windows facing the James River. It was a different view
of the river than the one she had enjoyed at home, but
still achingly familiar. The day promised to be warm and
bright, but she stared unseeing until there was a knock at
the door. As she went to answer it, a shiver of fear shot
down her spine, and a sudden flash of intuition warned
her who it would be.

Christian was holding a silver tray with a bowl of blackberries in cream, a plate of muffins still warm from the
oven, and a cup of hot cocoa. "I want to apologize for
yesterday," he said, as the door swung open, but his first
glimpse of Liana made him wince. He had hoped she
would look better, if not completely herself again, and to
find her bruises had deepened and spread pained him
badly. When she quickly turned away, he entered the room
and carried the heavy tray to the table between the windows with the river view.

"If you'd rather have something else, I'm sure our cook
can prepare it."

The seductive mixture of delicious smells emanating
from the tray wasn't enough to lure Liana to the table.
"I'm really not hungry. Maybe later." She wrapped her

arms around a bedpost. Afraid Christian would twist anything she said into an insult, she didn't add more.

Christian walked up behind her. He longed to slip his
arms around her waist and hug her tight, but she was being
so maddeningly distant he didn't dare even touch her.
"Please don't feel you have to hide away up here," he said.
"Everyone is anxious to get to know you."

"I wouldn't impress anyone today."

"They're my family. You needn't strive to impress them.
They'll accept you as you are."

When she failed to reply to his encouragement, Christian was at a loss. She had not even acknowledged his apology, let alone accepted it; discouraged he would not be
able to implement his father's advice, he walked to the
door. "I don't want you to be lonely, so I'll have someone
look in on you every hour or so."

"You needn't trouble anyone about me," Liana assured
him. "I'll be fine."

Christian doubted she felt any better than he did, but
left without describing the hollowness that pained him so
badly. He made a quick pass through the dining room,
grabbed a muffin, and went on outside to eat it where he
could avoid his family's well-intentioned but totally unwanted concern and advice.

One glance at Christian's disgusted expression when he
had come down the stairs told Beau things hadn't gone
well with Liana. Torn by a sense of loyalty to his cousin
and his fondness for Liana, he debated with himself half
the morning before going upstairs to see her. He carried
a bouquet of white camellias and several novels to provide
a believable, if inaccurate, reason for his visit.

"It's a beautiful day," he greeted her. "Would you like
to see our garden?"

Liana placed the vase of flowers on the dresser, then,
knowing she would be unlikely to glance toward the mirror, moved the pretty bouquet to the table between the

windows. "It's very thoughtful of you to want to entertain me, but I'd rather not go outside today. Another time, perhaps."

Beau had intended to pick up her breakfast tray and ask what she would like for dinner, but she had not touched the food Christian had brought earlier. "Please come and sit down," he invited. "I'll sit with you while you eat." He drew up another chair but waited for her to be seated before taking his.

Liana turned toward the window. The fact that the James River could not leave its banks without causing the worst sort of damage to the countryside wasn't lost on her, but the uncomfortable comparison to her own life didn't dampen her appreciation of the view. "You needn't stay. I'm not hungry."

"If you don't eat, you'll fall ill," Beau warned.

"I doubt I'd notice." Liana actually found the idea strangely appealing. "How long do you suppose it takes to die of a broken heart?"

Circling the table, Beau moved to her side and took her hand. "Please, don't even think such awful thoughts."

Liana had to turn her head to look at him, but he had sounded so painfully sincere she didn't doubt him. She scarcely knew him, though, and was surprised by the sorrowful catch in his voice. He tried to smile, but she could readily see he was as horrified by her looks as she.

"Amanda Tuttle is enormously fond of you," she confided. "I hope you like her, too."

"Amanda?" Finding it impossible to think of the lively girl with Liana so near, Beau frowned slightly. "No, I'm sorry. I know she's a close friend of yours, but I've no special feelings for her."

Liana knew Amanda would be badly disappointed, but merely shrugged. "I shouldn't have mentioned her. Please don't reveal what I said about her to anyone as I don't want her to be embarrassed."

"You have my word on it. Now, please, come sit down with me and have a few berries at least." Before she could protest, Beau coaxed her into the closest chair, and then took the other. "The blackberries are especially good this year. Polly—she's our cook—will make gallons of preserves, but I like the berries fresh. Don't you?" When Liana made no move to sample them, he picked up the spoon and scooped up one, "Here, try this," he urged.

Beau was trying so hard to please her, Liana reluctantly obeyed. The blackberry was as delicious as promised, and taking the spoon from him, she ate one more. Believing two berries might already be enough to keep her alive, she ceased to fast and finished the whole bowl. Though cool now, the muffins had the same spicy sweetness as the cakes Christian had given her yesterday afternoon. The thought of him brought tears to her eyes, and she laid the muffin aside after only one bite.

"I'm sorry. I can't eat anything more."

A bowl of berries in cream and a bite of muffin didn't seem like nearly enough sustenance to Beau, but he was grateful he had convinced her to eat something. Liana still looked so dreadfully unhappy, however, he couldn't bear to leave her without offering more. He leaned forward slightly.

"What I'm about to say may come as a surprise, but please believe me when I say I'm sincere."

Beau had never impressed her as anything else. "I'm sure you mean well, Beau, but there's nothing you, or anyone else here, can do to help me."

"Just let me finish," Beau begged. "Christian so often acts without thinking, but he has a good heart. I know he didn't mean to cause you such grievous harm, but now that he has, there's still a way out."

Liana glanced toward the window, and wondered if he was about to suggest she jump. The soil was soft in the spring and she doubted a fall from the third floor would kill her. It would definitely leave her badly injured, though, and an even greater burden to the Barclays than she already was.

"I don't see how," she finally replied.

Beau reached out to take her hand and gave it a gentle squeeze. "I was furious with Christian for catching you down by the river, and not simply because it was mean, but because I'd always wanted to meet you and doubted I'd ever have the chance."

Barely able to see through her swollen eyes, Liana listened with growing alarm. "Beau, really, I—"

Beau waved off her objection. "What I'm trying to say is that if you don't want to marry Christian, please don't feel that you must. I'd be proud to have you as my wife, and I can promise you I'll never give you any reason for sorrow, as he surely would."

Beau was such an earnest young man, and Liana did not understand how he could have become so terribly misguided. "You can't possibly be serious," she replied.

"Oh, but I am. We haven't had the opportunity to become well acquainted as yet, it's true, but now that you're living here—"

Liana yanked her hand from his. She was so insulted she could barely spit out her question. "Is Christian behind this?"

"Good Lord, no!" Beau assured her. "This is entirely my idea. I think we're much better suited to each other than you and Christian could ever hope to be. Rather than allow you to compound what has already been a tragic mistake by marrying him, I wanted to speak now, so you'd know you still have a choice." Beau broke into a warm smile. "Amanda must think I'm a good catch. I hope you do, too."

A wave of dizziness curled through Liana and despite Beau's protests, she thought it likely that Christian had tired of her and simply passed her along to his cousin.

More of a gentleman than Christian could ever hope to be, Beau was trying his best to salvage both his family's honor and hers. Sick that such a sacrifice was necessary, she had to refuse.

"You're forgetting Melissa married my father rather than admit she loved Hunter. That mistake has haunted my father ever since, and I'll never follow the same disastrous course. How can you even imagine that I would? It really doesn't matter whether this was your idea or Christian's. It's the worst possible choice for all three of us and I won't even consider it. Now will you please go? I don't feel well and I want to lie down and rest."

Devastated that his proposal had met with such a poor response, Beau reluctantly rose to his feet. "Melissa was living a lie when she was married to your father. Our circumstances are entirely different because we all know the truth," he reminded her. "That changes everything."

Liana couldn't bear to look up at him. "Not if our first child were a black-haired, brown-eyed boy, it wouldn't."

Beau had not even considered that possibility, but it didn't change his mind. "I'm not like Ian," he swore. "I'd love our firstborn because he's yours, regardless of who his father might be. I'd be as proud to raise him as I would be to have you as my wife." With a sudden burst of inspiration, Beau chose to act as he knew Christian would. He bent down and kissed Liana as though he had no more than an instant to sear his name on her heart, and then left the startled young woman alone with his proposal.

True to their word, Morgan and Cameron returned to the Barclay estate Friday afternoon and again asked to see their sister. Prepared to remain on the porch until their request was granted, they were relieved when they were immediately shown up to her room. Morgan rapped lightly on the door.

"Liana, Cameron and I have come to call."

Liana hurried to open the door and quickly pulled them inside. They appeared to be pained by how ghastly she looked, but that no longer concerned her. "How are things at home?" she asked. "Has Father calmed down, or Mother stopped weeping?"

Morgan shook his head. "If anything, their moods are growing worse by the hour. I don't think Father even left his study last night, and Mother is carrying on as though we're all dead. I suppose we should send for a physician to tend her, as Father surely won't."

Liana slumped into a chair by the table. Johanna had brought her a bowl of vegetable soup, several slices of bread, and a bowl of apples at noon, but she had not touched any of it. Following her, Cameron picked up a slice of bread and took a bite. Seeing his brother's disapproving frown, he shrugged.

"I'm hungry, and we haven't had a good meal since Liana left."

"I didn't leave," Liana argued. "I was thrown out."

"I was just trying to be polite," Cameron insisted. "Amanda came by this morning, and we didn't know what to say."

"Oh, poor Amanda. What did you tell her?"

Morgan walked past Liana and went to the window, where he found the view of the river far easier to observe than his badly bruised sister. "That you'd come to live here, but we didn't tell her why. She was flabbergasted, as you might well expect."

Liana could easily imagine Amanda riding through Williamsburg alerting their friends to her plight. She had certainly seen enough yesterday to supply an element of truth, and embellished by her lively imagination, it would be a spellbinding tale. Liana had been too lost in her own troubles to consider how painful the gossip would be, but now only one course of action seemed appropriate.

"I've got to get out of here," she announced suddenly. "How much money have you two saved?"

"Not nearly enough," Morgan replied. "Where would you go?"

Liana sighed sadly. "To Charleston, I suppose. I should be able to find work as a governess or in one of the shops, so even if this scandal follows me there it won't matter. It won't be the life I had expected, but that doesn't necessarily mean it can't be good."

Morgan and Cameron needed no more than an instant to reach similar decisions. "We'll go with you," Morgan offered. "Nothing's the same at home, and there's no reason for us to stay. We can all work and make a home for ourselves."

"Oh no," Liana cried. "I won't allow you to give up everything, too. There's no need for you to run away. I'm the only one who's made a mess of things."

Morgan rested his hand on her shoulder. "The way Father's been drinking, he'll be dead in a year. Don't ask us to stay and watch him commit suicide with brandy. We'll all go home together when he's gone. Mother won't turn us away. You know that."

Liana glanced up at Cameron, who was eating an apple. At thirteen, nothing affected his appetite, but he looked as determined as Morgan to run away. "I never thought it would come to this."

"What did you expect?" Morgan asked.

"That's exactly what Christian asked," Liana replied, "and I didn't have a satisfactory answer for him, either. It wasn't that I didn't think, but once I'd met him, nothing went as it should. It's almost as though we've been cursed."

Cameron laid the apple core on the plate. "By whom? Father?"

Liana shuddered. She had felt the force of her father's temper and knew his hatred went deep enough to curse Christian for being born. The fact that his curse might

destroy his own family was a bitter irony she had no wish
to contemplate.

"We'll need a plan," she said instead, and her brothers
drew close to listen.

Johanna brought Liana's supper, and hoping she would
like company, lingered a while, but when Liana appeared
to be too distracted to follow her attempts at conversation,
she excused herself. Enormously relieved the woman
hadn't spent the whole supper hour with her, Liana quickly
stuffed her pockets with apples, grabbed the pale blue
shawl Arielle had given her, and after a final quick glance
around the room, was ready to go.

Seeking to delay any pursuit, she went to the bed and
used the pillows to create what she hoped would look like
a sleeping figure. She turned the lamp down low, and then,
with no other reason to delay her departure, tiptoed down
the back stairs. She had to wait in the shadows as the Barclays were served their evening meal; listening to their
laughter, she grew convinced that none harbored a single
thought of her.

How could they joke amongst themselves when she had
been banished from her home? Convinced she was better
off running away, she darted out the back door, and circling the opposite side of the house, ran down to the river.
Morgan and Cameron were already there, and helped her
into the *bateau* they frequently used for fishing. The row-
boat wasn't large nor comfortable, but the desperate trio
wanted to get moving too badly to care. Gliding into the
current, they floated down the river, and gathering
strength from each other, no one looked back.

Christian tasted little of his supper and didn't contribute
anything to the conversation. He kept thinking of Liana,

alone upstairs, and felt guilty that he was still surrounded
by his family's love when she had been treated so badly.
Dominique was teasing Falcon, as she often did, but Christian kept glancing toward the empty place opposite him
where Liana should have been. Missing her terribly, he
feared it wasn't simply her bruises which had kept her secluded, but he wanted to respect her feelings if it were.

Hurt and confused, he was the first to leave the table,
but Beau hurried after him. Christian waved him off as he
started out the front door. "I'm going for a walk, and I'd
rather be alone."

"I can appreciate that, but there's something you ought
to know."

"Not now, Beau."

Beau let Christian get a few steps ahead of him and then
unable to let him go, ran to catch up. "I talked with Liana
this morning."

Resigned to having his cousin's unwanted company,
Christian jammed his hands deep in his pockets. Scowling,
he muttered his response. "I doubt she said much."

"No, she didn't, but I had plenty to say."

Christian shot him a sidelong glance. "Which you can't
wait to tell me."

Now that he had Christian's full attention, Beau chose
his words with care. He offered only a brief summary of
their conversation, and omitted any reference to his parting kiss, but proudly announced he had asked Liana to
become his wife.

Halting in mid-stride, Christian didn't believe what he
had just heard. "You did *what?*" When Beau repeated that
he had proposed to Liana, Christian grabbed the front of
his coat and yanked him close. "How dare you interfere
in this? Doesn't Liana have enough anguish without you
creating more?"

Beau broke free of Christian's grasp and backed away.
"I'm not adding to her troubles," he declared as he

smoothed out his clothes. "I'm simplifying them. If she doesn't want you, why would you want her?"

That insulting question ignited Christian's temper. Consumed by a blind rage, he went after his cousin with all the strength he possessed. He tore into him with his fists, aiming more often for his body than his face, and while Beau defended himself bravely, he was no match for the infuriated young man. It was all he could do to stay on his feet, but fortunately they were still close enough to the house for Christian's angry shouts to be heard.

Hunter reached them first, but it took a combined effort with Byron to separate the embattled cousins. "My God," Byron cried. "What's gotten into you two?"

Pulling free of his father's grasp, Christian backed away. Refusing to offer any explanation, he continued to regard Beau with a look of utter loathing. Dominique ran to her brother's side, as did Belle, while Jean hung back, observing them all with wide-open eyes. Johanna and Falcon stood with Alanna, and Arielle, hands on her hips, appeared to be disgusted with them all.

"Isn't it obvious?" Arielle asked. "Only a woman could prompt such a vicious confrontation. It's a pity Liana missed it, although I doubt she would be flattered."

Christian looked up toward her windows, but she wasn't silhouetted against the dim light and he doubted she had seen the fight. He had accused Beau of being jealous when Byron had selected his version of the first pamphlet, and again chided him for wanting Liana, but he was stunned by the depth of his own anger now. There was no way he would ever let Liana marry Beau, or any other man, and that threat lit his eyes with a demonic glow.

Because his son had clearly gotten the worst of it, Byron dismissed him. "Go on inside and clean up, Beau. I'll speak with you later. As for the rest of you, I'm sure you can find something more productive to do than stand out here and gawk. I'd like to speak to Christian in private."

While the others followed Beau into the house, Hunter didn't move. Byron was the head of the family, but he never insulted the Seneca brave by giving him orders and wouldn't break that tradition now. "That's the last time I ever want to see you trade blows with your cousin. I hope you would have come to your senses before you'd killed him, but I'm certainly glad Hunter and I were here to stop you tonight.

"I don't care whether you were fighting about Liana. The subject of the dispute is unimportant. All that matters is the loyalty we owe each other. Now I want your solemn vow you won't fight Beau again. Ever."

When Christian didn't reply, Hunter slapped his shoulder to encourage him to speak. His knuckles were scraped and bloody, his hands sore, but he still clenched his fists at his sides. "Tell Beau to stay away from Liana, and we'll get along fine," he finally murmured.

Byron shook his head. "That's not what I want to hear." For a fleeting instant he was tempted to ask Hunter to hold Christian's arms while he made his point with his fists, but knowing that was no way to insure peace in the family, he discarded the idea. "I haven't had the opportunity to speak with Liana, but after the abuse she suffered at her father's hands, you'll never impress her with violence. Why don't you take Falcon and go hunting or fishing for a few days? It would give everyone a chance to calm down."

Having his uncle suggest he leave, when that would only provide Beau with the unlimited opportunity to see Liana, struck Christian as a particularly poor alternative. "I'm not going away unless I take Liana with me," he stated firmly.

Byron glanced toward the house this time, and he was relieved they weren't being observed from a third floor window. "This is your home, Christian. It's not my intention to drive you and your intended bride out, but I won't tolerate another fight like the one we stopped tonight."

Christian stared at his uncle, silently daring him to banish him in the same uncaring way Ian had disowned Liana, but Byron wisely chose not to carry his threat any further. Instead, he turned toward the house, leaving Hunter to talk some sense into his son. Several minutes passed before the Indian spoke.

"Beau is no threat to you," Hunter insisted. "Treat him as a younger brother, as you always have. Liana needs friends here. Let Beau be one."

"It isn't friendship he's after," Christian pointed out sharply.

"That doesn't matter. In many ways he's still a boy, and you're a man. Liana is wise enough to know the difference."

Christian found it difficult to take any comfort in that fact, however. "I don't know what she wants," he swore bitterly.

Hunter chuckled softly. "I told you how to convince her. This might be a good night to begin."

"She'll probably lock her door."

Hunter began to back away, his moccasins sinking into the soft soil. "Don't let that stop you. You know where Byron keeps all the keys."

Christian watched his father walk away, and envied him his confidence with women. He would have to wait until everyone had gone to sleep, and he definitely couldn't go to Liana with Beau's blood on his hands, but he wanted to be with her too badly to wait another day. There was still plenty of time for a walk, and moving down toward the river, he concentrated solely upon what his father had advised him to do, rather than what he thought he ought to say.

Sixteen

His hair still damp from a late-night swim, Christian climbed the stairs to the third floor with the same graceful stealth he had shown moving through Liana's home. He paused at the top to make certain no one was awake to observe him entering Liana's room. Dominique and Belle shared the spacious bedroom across the hall from their reluctant guest, but due to the hour there were no girlish giggles to be heard. Johanna occupied the bedroom next door and, while she sometimes stayed up reading, there was no light showing beneath her door. The remaining bedroom belonged to Falcon and Jean, and it was dark and silent as well. Relieved they were all sleeping as soundly as their parents on the floor below, Christian still took care not to wake them as he approached Liana's door.

He rapped lightly, then counted to ten before tapping a bit more insistently. Quickly convinced she was sleeping too soundly to hear him, he tried the knob. When it turned easily, he was grateful he would not need the key he had taken from his uncle's desk. He would have used it without a qualm, but was glad he would not have to answer for it.

Remaining cautious, he opened the door slowly and when there was still no response from Liana, he stepped inside her room. She had not slept with a light at home, but he wasn't surprised she had left a lamp burning low here. He closed the door, then to make certain they would not be disturbed before dawn, he turned the key that had been in the lock and slipped it into his pocket with its twin.

It wasn't until then that he realized the room was too quiet. Holding his breath, he strained to hear the soft sound of Liana's breathing, but the bedroom was as still as the hallway. Nestled under the covers, she looked to be sleeping comfortably, but Christian still sensed something was amiss. His moccasins muffled the sound of his steps as he crossed to the bed, but he couldn't stifle the oath that sprang from his lips as he discovered it was filled with no more than a heap of artfully arranged pillows.

He had been well aware Liana wasn't happy there, but he had never imagined she might run away the day after she had arrived. Her supper tray was still on the table, the meal untouched. He had thought it odd someone as curious as she had not come to the window when he had fought Beau, but now it seemed likely she had already gone. That meant she had fled hours ago; the fact that no one had even noticed her absence tore at his heart.

Intending to follow her, Christian went out to the stable. Liana was an excellent rider and he had expected her to have taken a horse, but none of the stalls was empty. She wouldn't have gone home, but he had seen her in town with Amanda. Could she have walked all the way to her friend's house? Hoping there was still time to overtake her if she had, he quickly saddled his stallion and took off at a gallop. Consumed with thoughts of Liana, he forgot soldiers would be stationed at each crossroads, but having nothing to hide that night, he halted at their command.

"What's wrong?" he asked the red-coated men who approached him. His left arm still ached from his bout with Beau, but he had rebandaged it after his swim, and doubted they would strip him to search for wounds.

"Dismount," the sergeant shouted.

Christian swung down from his saddle. "I'm looking for

Liana Scott," he announced before the sergeant could begin questioning him. "She disappeared from my home, and I've no idea were she's gone. She shouldn't be traveling the roads alone at night and I'm anxious to find her. Did she pass by here?"

The sergeant recognized the Scott name as that of a family living nearby, but didn't know who Liana was. "We haven't seen anyone but you all night. Now step away from your horse. Search his saddlebags," he ordered one of his men.

"He's not carrying any."

"Then search him!" the sergeant cried. He was tall and thin, and his uniform hung from his shoulders in awkward folds. His pale blue eyes regarded Christian with an accusing frown.

Christian raised his hands, and while the man who came forward shoved and prodded rudely, he didn't notice the thick bandage on the brave's left arm. "He has a knife," the man called out, "nothing more."

Disappointed not to find evidence of wrongdoing, the sergeant slowly circled Christian. Meeting a man who spoke like a gentleman but dressed as a savage confused him. Reminded of the buckskin-clad culprits in Boston who had thrown the tea into the harbor, he was positive his captive must be guilty of some equally nefarious deed.

"You may not be carrying any treasonous leaflets tonight, but that doesn't mean you haven't before. I think Captain O'Keefe will want to speak with you."

Impatient to be on his way, Christian had a ready argument. "Captain O'Keefe will be as upset as I am should he learn Liana Scott is wandering the countryside alone. If you want to impress him, help me find her."

"Cocky lad, aren't you?"

The sergeant was no more than a year or two older than Christian, but the brave pretended not to be insulted by his condescending tone. "I'm Christian Hunter, one of the Barclays, and I have every right to be out on the public roads any time I wish. Now stand aside and let me pass."

The sergeant shook his head. "My orders are to stop all riders. This is as far as you're going tonight." He gestured to a couple of his troops. "Take him into town. O'Keefe can question him in the morning."

Christian stared at the sergeant. The man who'd searched him hadn't taken his knife, and he knew he could draw it fast enough to take the sergeant hostage. He could then force one of the men to tie up the others, and then, leaving him bound to the sergeant, take their horses and flee. It was a bold, effective plan, but because it would help neither Liana nor him, he didn't attempt it.

"If you absolutely insist, I'll go into town," he replied, "but then O'Keefe is going to send me right back out here with orders for you and your men to help me find Miss Scott. He won't be pleased by the time you've wasted, either. In fact, I doubt you'll still have your sergeant's stripes at sunrise."

Perplexed by Christian's confident boast, the sergeant gathered his patrol for a brief conference. He wanted to arrest the obnoxious Indian, but having no evidence the brave had done anything illegal, he feared O'Keefe really might demote him and he could not abide the fact that it would be over a woman. Although he had not been in Williamsburg long, he had heard the Barclay name, and because they were such a prominent family, he reluctantly decided to let Christian go with a stern warning.

"We know who he is and where he lives," he told his men. "O'Keefe can question him whenever he likes." He turned back toward Christian. "I've chosen to be generous tonight," he declared as though he truly thought he had a choice, "but if you're stopped again at this hour, things won't go as easy for you."

"Well, if Liana runs away again, I'll have Captain

O'Keefe help me search for her. I doubt you'd attempt to prevent him from traveling the public roads."

The sergeant struggled to think of a suitably caustic reply, but none occurred to him before Christian had mounted his stallion. He gestured for his men to move out of the way, but as Christian rode off, the sergeant felt sadly disappointed with the whole exchange. Maybe Captain O'Keefe knew Miss Scott, and maybe he didn't, but the sergeant sincerely doubted any man would be out at such a late hour searching for a woman who wasn't a beauty. Amused that she had run from the Indian, he hoped she still might appear to brighten an otherwise long and boring night.

It was after two a.m. when Christian reached Joshua Tuttle's impressive residence. He remained astride his horse while he gazed up at the second story windows. An only child, Amanda would surely have one of the front bedrooms; the only question was, which one? Then he realized if Liana were there, she and Amanda would undoubtedly still be up talking. He rode all the way around the house, searching for a light, but every room was dark.

Not encouraged, he dismounted and strode up to the front door. He gave the brass knocker half a dozen hearty raps, then stood back to await a response. When Joshua Tuttle appeared in his nightshirt, he greeted him politely.

"Good evening," Christian began in a considerate whisper. Although he had attended the Tuttles' recent party, he reminded Joshua who he was and then explained his purpose. "Liana Scott was our guest, but left suddenly and I'm trying to locate her. Is she here?"

Like everyone else Amanda knew, Joshua had heard about the appalling manner in which Liana had suddenly changed her residence. He was astonished that the young man responsible for the girl's disgrace would brazenly admit she had run off, and responded in an angry shout. "No, she is not, and even if she were, I'd not tell you." With that stinging announcement, he slammed the door in Christian's face and went back upstairs to bed.

Backing away from the house, Christian stood out front, watching for the pale light of a candle as Joshua returned to his room. When he saw a brief glow in the windows to his left, he assumed Amanda's bedroom was on the right. He walked around to the side of the house, and, scooping up a handful of pebbles, hurled them up at her windows, In an instant, Amanda opened one and peered out.

Shocked to discover Christian Hunter standing in the flower bed, she called down to him. "Have you already tired of Liana?"

"No, I'll never tire of her, but she's disappeared. Have you seen her?"

Greatly intrigued, Amanda leaned out almost dangerously far. "You mean she's vanished?"

"Yes. If she's not here with you, do you know where she might have gone?"

Amanda wished now that she had trusted her instincts because although Liana had refused to admit it, Amanda had suspected her friend liked Christian all along. She had been positive there was a man behind her friend's sudden desire to visit London, and thought it a terrible shame Liana had not left weeks ago so that she could have avoided what was easily the most tantalizing scandal Amanda had ever enjoyed.

Toying with Christian, she offered a possibility. "She mentioned a trip to London. Would you follow her there?"

"Yes," Christian assured her without needing any time to consider his reply. "But where would she go tonight?"

Amanda caught sight of a falling star, but was too pre-occupied with Christian's predicament to make a wish. "She could be anywhere. Ask her brothers—they might know." Afraid her father would overhear their conversation and punish her severely, she brought it to a close with a wave and shut the window.

Sorry he had learned so little from Amanda, Christian debated what to do next. Certain he would have seen a note by the supper tray had Liana left one, he knew there was no point in going home to search for clues. If she hadn't come to Amanda's, she might have gone home to enlist her brothers' aid, but he did not dare knock on Ian's door to ask. Fortunately, he knew his way around the Scotts' home, and again leaving his stallion in their barn, he let himself in the back door and went upstairs.

Reaching Liana's room, he slipped inside. The fragrance of sweet lavender still clung to the air, and recalling the last time he had been there with bittersweet memories, he approached the bed. He ran his hand over the spread and found it taut and cool. Clearly Liana hadn't slept there that night. The doors of the wardrobe were closed and the dresser drawers shut, leaving no sign of the careless disarray Liana would surely have caused had she been there to gather her belongings.

He crossed the hall to Morgan's room and peered in. Dark and still, he soon realized it was empty. He went next door to Cameron's and discovered it stood vacant as well. He had not realized Liana and her brothers were so close, but if the boys were gone, too, he was convinced they were with her.

He had just pulled Cameron's door closed when he heard the sound of shattering glass downstairs, followed by a slurred curse. Christian was amazed that Ian wasn't already in bed asleep, but not caring what treasure the man might have knocked to the floor and broken, he slipped back into Cameron's room to avoid meeting him in the darkened hallway. Only then did the possibility that Ian might make a practice of looking in on his sons each night occur to him. Pressing himself against the wall behind the door, Christian grew increasingly uncomfortable.

He then had to endure an extended wait as Ian made his way up the stairs with a sluggish stride. When he reached the top, he paused, providing Christian with a fresh scare, but he finally entered his own room. The instant Christian heard Ian close his bedroom door, he left his hiding place, raced down the hall, took the back stairs, and hurried out to the barn.

A quick search of the stalls revealed none was empty, so clearly, Liana and her brothers had not escaped on horseback. He led his stallion from the barn and walked him out of the yard before mounting. He had no idea where else to look, but he was by no means ending his search. He chose the path alongside the river as he rode home, and with growing dread began to believe that Liana had taken to the water to escape him.

Morgan had forgotten to bring a lantern and while the moonglow provided some illumination, he had to strain to keep the boat centered in the river. The temperature was much colder out on the water than on the shore, and he and his brother and sister were soon shivering. Hoping to reach one of the settlements downriver by dawn, none wished to stop, but cold and frightened, it was a miserable trip unbroken by any attempt at conversation.

Rowing through the shimmering blackness, Morgan had no warning of impending danger before the *bateau* struck a submerged log with a force that tore a gaping hole in the bow. Jarred from their seats, all three passengers were flung into the river where, weighed down by their clothes, they fought the swiftly flowing current to remain afloat. Filling with water, the *bateau* pitched wildly, battering Cameron, but Morgan was close enough to reach out and grab his brother's collar and keep his head above water.

"Where's Liana?" Cameron cried, but in the darkness, neither young man saw his sister. They screamed her name, but their voices failed to carry over the sound of the rushing river. Clinging to each other, they swam with short, frantic strokes toward the shore, all the while searching for a glimpse of Liana's white cap. When at last they reached the muddy riverbank, they huddled together, and now hoarse, continued to scream her name, but still there was no reply.

Liana could swim as well as her brothers, but she had never gone in the water wearing half a dozen petticoats and her shoes. She got tangled in her shawl, but just as she wrenched free of the thickly woven wool, the now-empty *bateau* struck her a glancing blow. Too terrified to feel the pain, she watched it career on by while her efforts to reach shore failed to wrench her from the powerful current.

Sucked underwater, she clawed her way to the surface, only to be dragged down again when her skirt caught on a jagged piece of debris. She tore it loose, but tumbled head over heels, she had only a quick breath before, wound in the river's frigid grasp, she was tossed and bounced downstream. The water's numbing chill seeped through her limbs, making the constant struggle to lift her head to breathe exhausting, but Liana stubbornly fought to swim rather than merely being swept along like the empty *bateau*.

With every graceless stroke she reached out for the shore, but drew no closer to that safe haven. Even dazed with fear, she saw Christian's face clearly in her mind; encouraged by his dazzling smile, she continued to swim as long as she could move her arms. The fact that he filled her thoughts now, as he had for so long, was strangely comforting, but damning as well.

Her energy nearly spent, she didn't see the bend in the river, nor the gnarled tree whose branches dipped low into the water, until they raked across her scalp and caught her hair. She had just enough strength to catch hold of the closest limb, clinging to it fiercely as she waited for the dawn. Knowing she had to be within a few feet of shore, she finally gave in to the tears she had been too frightened to shed. Hauling herself along the low branches, she inched toward the riverbank, but her progress was pitifully slow.

After seeing to his stallion's comfort, Christian left the stable and walked up to the house with a weary stride. He doubted Beau would feel well enough to leave his bed for several days, and even if he were fit, Christian did not want his help in searching for Liana and went instead to Falcon's room.

He shook his brother's shoulder and brought his hand to his lips to warn him to be still, then waited outside his door while he dressed. Falcon joined him in a moment. "I didn't want to wake Jean," Christian cautioned, "nor anyone else." He waited until they had reached the bottom of the stairs to explain that Liana's mysterious absence had brought the need for secrecy.

"I want to take the *Southern Breeze* and search for her and her brothers. Will you come with me?"

Elated that Christian wished to have his company, Falcon broke into a wide grin. "Of course. How many men do you need? I'll go and wake them."

While he didn't want to waste any time gathering a crew, Christian doubted they would be able to conduct an effective search before dawn. Still, he wanted to get underway as quickly as possible. "Six ought to do it, and bring the new man, David Slauson, along. He's aching for adventure."

Falcon had never claimed to have any skill as a sailor, but admiring Christian's daring, he nodded as though they sailed the schooner every day. He woke the hands, then followed his brother down to the docks. "Did you tell Father or Uncle Byron that we're taking the *Breeze*?" he asked.

"There's no reason to disturb their sleep," Christian replied. "If this all works out as I hope it will, we'll be back before breakfast and they'll never know we were gone."

Falcon leaned back against the rail as they waited for the crew to arrive. "If we do find Liana—"

"When we find her," Christian corrected firmly.

"All right, when we find her, how will you stop her from running away again?"

That wasn't a question Christian wanted to contemplate, let alone answer, and he just shook his head. Running away in the dead of night had been a desperate act, and he did not want Liana to ever again feel as lost and alone as she must have. Then again, if she did not want to be with him, nothing he could ever do, despite his father's well-meaning advice, would be enough to convince her to stay. Fearing her disappearance was merely another defiant rejection of his proposal, his mood turned from dismay to despair.

"I'll find a way," he murmured, but he didn't convince Falcon, or himself, that he would.

Told to hurry, the hands they'd awakened to crew the *Breeze* soon reported to the ship. As the dawn broke, Christian gave the order to cast off the lines securing the two-masted vessel to the docks, and the search for his reluctant bride began. David had been the only man with questions, and Christian had stubbornly refused to answer them. He stationed the young man on the starboard side and took up his own vigil in the bow.

It was Falcon who spotted the Scott brothers first, but Christian's joy was shortlived when he saw that Liana wasn't with them. "Where's your sister?" he called to the unkempt pair walking along the riverbank. It was obvious from the sorry state of their clothes that they had taken an unexpected swim, but he did not even want to imagine what might have happened to Liana. Signaling the man at the tiller, he brought the *Breeze* as close to shore as he dared and waited for their reply.

"This is your fault!" Morgan yelled.

Christian was in no mood to argue. "Where's Liana?" he shouted again.

His hands on his hips, Morgan stared at him a long moment, and then shrugged. "We don't know. We're looking for her body."

"Liars!" Falcon cried, and then to Christian, "shall we bring them on board?"

"She can't be dead," Christian answered numbly. The beautifully carved angel on his mother's gravestone flashed across his mind and, horrified that he might have lost Liana, too, he refused to waste another second on her brothers. "No, we needn't stop. Let's get on with the search."

Christian's hands began to sweat, making his grasp on the rail slippery, but his voice was confident as he ordered the *Breeze's* crew to continue its steady course down the river. Refusing to accept even the possibility that Liana might be dead, he scanned the riverbank for the young woman rather than the shallow water along the shore. They had sailed nearly a quarter-hour past where they had sighted Morgan and Cameron when, rounding a wide bend, he saw her huddled beside an ancient tree. She looked so bedraggled that had it not been for her bright red hair, he would not have recognized her.

At his shout, the men quickly lowered the anchor; leaving his brother and skeleton crew on board, Christian rowed the lifeboat to shore. "Morgan and Cameron are walking along the opposite bank," he called to Liana as he pulled the boat up into the marsh grass. "How did you get separated?"

Liana had been certain her brothers had drowned, and Christian's report to the contrary rocked her to her soul. She began to sob with relief and couldn't stop even after he reached her and knelt down to draw her into his arms. "I thought I'd killed them," she murmured against his chest.

Her hair was still wet and filled with twigs and leaves she had picked up in the river. Her bruises were just as garish a deep purple, her eyes as badly swollen, and her once-attractive gown ruined. She'd lost her slippers, and her stockings hung around her ankles in shreds. Christian sat back slightly. and while he doubted Liana would ever look worse, he had never been happier to see her. "They feared you had drowned, too. What happened?"

Liana just shook her head. "It doesn't matter now."

Christian was about to argue that it most certainly did when he felt her shiver and knew this was not the place to discuss her perilous effort to flee his home. "Come on. Let's go on board where there are plenty of blankets to keep you warm. I'll stop for Morgan and Cameron and take them home, too."

Whatever his plan, Liana was too tired to object. She clung to the sides of the lifeboat with a frantic grasp as Christian rowed them out to the *Southern Breeze,* and then was grateful for his help in climbing the rope ladder. Knowing how dreadful she must look, she hung her head and didn't begin to relax until she entered the captain's cabin. Small, but warm and dry, she eyed the bunk with a longing glance.

"I've been up all night, too," Christian said. "Let me help you out of those wet clothes and then you can sleep all day if you like."

Liana didn't feel well enough to refuse his attentions, and stood silently shivering as he pulled off her sodden garments. It wasn't until he reached her chemise that some sense of modesty returned. "That's far enough," she warned.

Christian stepped back. "You can't sleep in that wet chemise or you'll get sick for sure." He turned back the blankets on the bunk, then bent down to pull another gray wool blanket from one of the drawers beneath the bunk. "Here, I'll close my eyes. Take off the chemise, wrap yourself in this, and climb into the bunk. That way you'll be warm." When Liana didn't immediately reach for the blanket, he turned his back. "There, does this make you feel safe?"

Liana was far from pleased, but let the chemise fall to her feet, stepped out of it, and hurriedly wrapped herself in the blanket. She sat down on the side of the bunk and peeled off her torn stockings. Tossing them atop the chemise, she lay down on her side and closed her eyes.

"Move over," Christian urged.

Alarmed, Liana rose up on her elbow. "What do you think you're doing?"

Christian kicked off his moccasins. "I told you I've been up all night looking for you. I deserve a few inches of the bunk at least, since you didn't bother to thank me for rescuing you."

There was a sharpness to his voice that Liana hadn't heard in a while; lacking the strength to argue, she moved over, but seeking what privacy she could manage, faced away from him. Gripping the blanket tightly over her breasts, the rigidity of her pose made it plain she did not want his company.

Foiling her plan, Christian stretched out behind her and slipped his arm around her waist to snuggle close. She smelled of the rotting bark that floated in the river rather than perfume, but considering her ordeal, he didn't complain. He plucked the leaves from her hair and tossed them over his shoulder. He hoped she would be in a more reasonable mood when she awoke, and, exhausted with worry, he closed his eyes and went to sleep.

Liana had thought it would be impossible to relax with Christian wrapped so tightly around her, but when she realized he had fallen asleep, the tension left her body.

Worn out, she found his warmth more comforting than the blankets. She didn't understand why he had come after her. Perhaps a sense of duty had driven him to search, but she refused to be a burden to him, and when she again felt up to the task, she would definitely tell him so. After all, it was only her father's outrage that had brought them together, and that was no reason to stay.

Seventeen

Liana was sleeping too soundly to hear Ian's blustering tirade, but it jarred Christian from his dreams. When he rolled off the bunk, she felt him draw away and then heard her father's angry voice. Sitting up, she turned to Christian, who was pulling on his moccasins. "What can he possibly want now?" she asked.

Christian hoped Liana's face would return to its normal prettiness before he got used to the swollen and bruised mask she had been forced to wear. "It sounds as though he's looking for Morgan and Cameron, but if they're still on board, I want to hear what they have to say."

Liana eyed the damp heap of filthy garments she had discarded. "I've nothing to wear or I'd come up on deck with you. I won't allow my father to blame my brothers for last night's disaster when it was entirely my fault."

"I don't even know what actually happened last night," Christian reminded her. "But I'm your husband, and I'll handle your father."

Liana's swollen eyes opened as wide as they could. "I've not agreed to marry you. How dare you call yourself my husband!"

Ian was still yelling, but Christian let him wait. He leaned down to kiss Liana's unblemished cheek, and then broke into a deep, rumbling chuckle. "I've chosen to observe the traditions of the Seneca side of my heritage. According to Seneca custom, you became my wife when I shared your bed last week. I'll still be happy to marry you in a church ceremony, but it really isn't necessary."

Dumbfounded, Liana couldn't find her voice before he left the cabin, but she wasn't about to accept whatever peculiar traditions the Seneca might treasure. Taking a firm grip on the blanket wrapped around her, she followed Christian up the steps to the deck, but remained hidden in the companionway where she could listen without being seen in such a disheveled state. Her father was standing on the dock, his hands on his hips, demanding that Christian produce his sons without further delay.

Distancing themselves from the irate Englishman, Byron and Hunter were waiting on the path and gestured helplessly when Christian glanced toward them. "I've no idea where your sons are if they aren't in the house enjoying breakfast." He glanced up to gauge the sun's position and saw it was close to midday. "Or dinner. Did you look for them there?"

"Yes, I did." Disgusted by the fact he had had to again tread on the Barclays' porch, Ian spit on the dock.

With no more work for a Saturday, David Slauson and a couple of the other men were fishing off the stern, and he called to them. "Have you seen Liana's brothers since we docked?"

"No, sir!" they replied.

Christian vaulted over the side of the *Breeze* and landed lightly on the dock. Considering how late Ian had gone to bed, Christian thought he looked remarkably rested, but he appeared to be no more content than he had when he had abandoned Liana. "I do know where your daughter is." he offered graciously. "You're always welcome to visit with her."

"I have no daughter," Ian replied in a bitter snarl. "Now what have you done with Morgan and Cameron?"

Christian was Ian's equal in height and stared him

straight in the eye. "You needn't shout. Because your sons are my wife's brothers, I'll help you find them. If they aren't at home or up at our house, they must be around here someplace. Let's ask everyone to look for them." Determined to be agreeable no matter now obnoxious Ian remained, Christian started up the path toward the house, but just as he reached his father and uncle, Captain O'Keefe rode into the yard with a patrol.

Refusing to look guilty for being out on the roads past midnight, Christian walked forward and greeted him with a smile. "If you've come to call on my wife, I'm afraid you'll have a bit of a wait."

"Your wife?" Sean repeated incredulously. "I've not heard of any wedding."

Christian attempted a sorrowful expression, but doubted he was convincing and relaxed into a smile. "I promised to invite you, didn't I?" He glanced toward Ian, who was still scowling angrily. "I'm sorry to disappoint you, Captain, but we've decided to follow Seneca custom and all it requires is an act, which I'm certain I needn't describe in detail, for us to become husband and wife."

Revolted by the intimacy Christian's comment and wide grin implied, Sean swung down from his saddle. "Is Liana even here?" he asked. "From what I was told, you were out searching for her late last night. Or at least that was the excuse you gave Sergeant Reynolds."

Puzzled by the captain's comment, Ian looked as though he might actually inquire about his daughter, but when he abruptly looked away, Christian realized he was far too proud to show such concern. "It was no mere excuse," Christian insisted. His father and uncle moved behind him to present a solid family unit, but he was confident he could handle the arrogant officer on his own.

"I was looking for Liana, and I found her. Regrettably, she's not had the time to bathe and dress or I'm sure she would be happy to tell you so herself."

"Have you seen your daughter this morning, sir?" Sean asked Ian.

"I came to find Morgan and Cameron," Ian informed him tersely. "They're missing."

"The whole family appears to have suddenly taken to wandering," Christian remarked.

Infuriated by that sly comment, Ian lunged for Christian, but Sean quickly shoved the younger man back against his father and uncle and stepped between them. "That's enough, Ian," the captain ordered. "I can handle only one problem at a time. Christian was stopped by one of my patrols last night at an hour which suggests he may well have been hiding his true purpose. While he wasn't carrying any leaflets, he'll be watched closely from now on. If he's found to be part of the conspiracy distributing the pamphlets disparaging the king, you can rest assured he'll be promptly tried and severely punished."

Sean regarded Christian with a challenging stare, but the brave merely laughed. "I'm flattered you believe me to be that clever." Ian was studying him with an astonished gaze, and for an instant, Christian wondered if he might guess the truth as easily as his daughter had. But then Ian's glance darkened and he turned away without voicing any opinion.

Christian yawned and stretched lazily. "Forgive me, I don't mean to be rude, but Liana kept me up most of the night."

Again disgusted by the young man's indiscreet references, Sean adopted an even stronger tone. "I want to speak with her to confirm your tale. Then we'll look for Mr. Scott's missing sons."

Sean started toward the house, but Christian stopped him. "She's on board the *Southern Breeze*, but as I said, she's not had time to dress and isn't able to accept callers."

"She wasn't accepting callers the last time I was here," Sean exclaimed, "but I finally managed to see her even if she was asleep. I don't care whether she's properly clothed or not. I'm going to speak with her without delay."

"That's a mistake," Christian warned, but the officer started off toward the dock with a long stride, his shiny black boots kicking up little dust clouds with each step. Unwilling to allow him to interview Liana alone, Christian followed. Left with Byron and Hunter, Ian promptly turned his back on them and pretended he was alone.

The men had been standing too far away for Liana to overhear their conversation, but she had ventured up on the deck to observe and had seen enough to know her father was still furious with Christian. From Sean's defiant stance and threatening gestures. it was plain he was no friend of Christian's, either. When Sean started toward the ship, she cringed at the thought that anyone else would see her at her worst and ducked out of sight.

"There's no reason to embarrass my wife," Christian argued as they reached the dock. "Why don't you help Ian find his sons while I fetch some clothes for her?"

Amazed her so-called husband would be so considerate, Liana remained on the steps, hoping Christian would prevail. But when Sean stubbornly refused to give in and demanded to see her immediately, she was as provoked with him as Christian was. Clad only in the gray blanket, she stepped out on the deck.

"If the matter is so dreadfully urgent, Captain," she called out, "then here I am."

Proud of her spirit, Christian forced himself not to laugh. Even after having had a glimpse of her on Thursday, Sean was appalled by Liana's battered appearance. As for her unusual attire and tangled hair, they astonished him completely. "My God," he gasped, "what's happened to you?"

Liana shrugged. "I scarcely know where to begin. Is that all you wished to ask?"

When Sean sent him a threatening glance, Christian

readily answered his question. "Ian's to blame for her face, and a regrettable incident on the river accounts for her, shall we say, bedraggled state, which I assure you is only temporary."

Sean turned back to Liana. Aghast at her scandalous liaison with the insolent savage who now claimed her as his wife, the bitterness rose in his throat and he decided that as her father, Ian had been well within his rights to punish her so brutally. He had believed her to be a virtuous young woman. He had hoped she had some tender feelings for him, as he had cared deeply for her, but feeling betrayed, he gave no further thought to her ugly bruises. In his opinion, she deserved them.

"I have a question about last night," he finally asked. "Can you account for your whereabouts?"

"Tell him the truth," Christian urged.

"Stay out of this," Sean ordered brusquely.

Believing her father must have summoned Sean to search for her brothers, Liana reluctantly admitted how the three of them had taken a *bateau* and left for Charleston. "We didn't get far before it capsized," she reported without providing any of the harrowing details. "Christian brought us all home this morning." Or at least she thought he had, but she had not been awake when Morgan and Cameron had come aboard the *Breeze*, and could not actually swear that they had.

"Did you inform Christian of your plan before you left?" Sean asked.

Sean had never impressed her as stupid, and she answered crossly. "No, of course not. What would have been the point when he would have stopped me?"

Sensing a rift between the unlikely pair, Sean began to enjoy himself. "You came here to live on Thursday, and by Friday night you had had enough wedded bliss to run away from your new husband?"

"Christian is not my husband," Liana replied with a defiant toss of her tousled curls.

Despite her denial, Sean caught the edge of despair in her voice. She had made her choice, however, and while he condemned it, he wasn't even tempted to step in and make an effort to undo it. He turned to Christian. "The story you gave Sergeant Reynolds last night appears to have been the truth, but heed my warning. If you're stopped another night with even one leaflet, you'll be lucky to go to prison."

Christian didn't dare glance toward Liana, but he managed a noncommittal nod for the captain. "Save your threats for guilty men," he advised. "Now let's go find Morgan and Cameron so Ian can go home and leave us in peace."

As Christian and Sean started back toward the house, Falcon came around the corner with Morgan and Cameron. All were carrying bows and arrows and totally unaware of the disturbance Ian had caused. When they saw their father, the Scott brothers came to an abrupt halt, but they didn't argue with his sternly voiced command to get into his carriage. They handed Falcon the hunting implements he had just taught them how to use, and without noticing Liana standing on the deck of the *Southern Breeze*, rode away.

While Liana was indeed relieved to know her brothers were safe, she was too frightened by what Sean had revealed to go below. She had had no idea Christian had been stopped by soldiers and did not understand why he hadn't told her something so important. Having lost her to Christian, Sean had every reason to hate him and she knew if he could find even the smallest shred of evidence to prove Christian was behind the pamphlets, he would arrest him. Sick with apprehension, she began to tremble and this time not with cold, but fear.

Believing she needed attention, David Slauson rushed

to Liana's side. When she didn't immediately turn to him, he cleared his throat to alert her to his presence. "Miss Scott, would you like me to fetch you some clothes?"

Too troubled to be aware of such an insignificant problem as her shocking lack of appropriate apparel, Liana shook her head. "No, thank you. Christian said he would take care of it." She kept watch until Sean O'Keefe rode out of the yard, leading his men. Then, turning toward the companionway, she raised the edge of the blanket so she would not trip on the stairs.

Christian entered the captain's cabin a few minutes later with more of Johanna's clothes, a copper bathtub, and a steaming bucket of water. He filled the tub, and then, meaning to give Liana the privacy to bathe, gathered up her soiled garments and carried them to the door. "I'm sorry O'Keefe wasn't more reasonable, but after the way you stood up to him, he won't bother us again."

"How can you even think that? Why didn't you tell me you'd been stopped last night? I warned you there would be patrols out. How could you have run right into one?"

Christian hoped her indignation was prompted by genuine concern rather than mere annoyance at his stupidity. "We haven't had a chance to discuss last night, but you have far more explaining to do than I."

Liana got up from the bunk, not realizing her carelessly draped blanket showed off more of her creamy smooth shoulders than her lowest-cut gowns. "I don't have to explain anything to you after the insulting way you passed me along to Beau. You treated me as though I meant no more to you than a pair of breeches you'd outgrown."

Shocked by the absurdity of her assumption, Christian let out a hoarse moan. "Was that why you ran off? You thought I'd told Beau he could have you?"

"Well, didn't you?"

"No, I most certainly did not," Christian quickly countered, "and I gave him a beating when he told me he'd proposed. Now go on and bathe before the water cools. We'll talk again later." Even with his arms full of dirty clothes, he managed to slam the door on his way out.

Christian hadn't thought to bring soap or towels, but anxious to complete their conversation, Liana searched the cabin until she found the items she needed. Kneeling beside the tub, she washed her hair, then scrubbed herself clean in the soapy water. Once dry, she appreciated Johanna's generosity with her wardrobe, but wondered how many more garments Christian's sister could spare. This new chemise was another of fine linen, the embroidered corset every bit as pretty as the first. The gown was a deep forest green, with a delicate lace fichu she quickly tucked inside the neckline.

Only then did she realize Christian had forgotten to bring stockings and shoes, but doubting he would return any time soon, she wound her damp hair atop her head, covered it with a cap, and went up on deck barefoot. Christian was standing in the bow, and David and the other men who had been fishing were gone. He turned when he heard the hem of her gown brush the deck, then noticed her pretty pink toes.

"I'm sorry. I'm not used to dressing women, but I'm sure we can find you another pair of stockings and slippers when we go up to the house."

His apology caught Liana off guard, but she hadn't forgotten what she wanted to say. "Tell me what happened last night," she insisted.

Because she had been so insulted by Beau's proposal, Christian began by describing their fight, but took care not to brag. "Beau's liked you all along," he confided, "but he shouldn't have taken advantage of your unhappiness as he did. Our being cousins made it doubly wrong."

"You don't own me," Liana warned. Christian cocked a brow, as though he considered her boast absurd, and not daring to explore that opinion, she quickly prompted him to continue. "Go on, what happened next?"

Christian didn't describe how he had gone to her room hoping to spend the night making love to her so thoroughly she would never want to leave him. "I discovered you were gone, and thought you might have walked to Amanda's. With no reason to be wary, I didn't even think of the patrols, and rode right into one."

"I can't believe you were that preoccupied."

Christian focused his attention on the left side of her face, which was still lovely even if her eye was swollen. "Believe me, I was." He provided only a brief hint of his conversations with Joshua and Amanda Tuttle, and paused as he tried to find a way to describe how he had found her brothers were missing by visiting their bedrooms. Finally deciding there wasn't a delicate way to put it, he admitted the truth.

"You were in my house again?" Liana gasped.

"No more than five minutes."

Liana's anger colored each of her words. "Which was five minutes more than you should have been."

Christian left the rail and moved close. "Would you rather have sat by the riverbank until your father went looking for your brothers?"

"I would rather never have met you," Liana blurted out.

Christian refused to allow the hurt he felt show in his expression. Instead, he ran his hands lightly up her arms. "I refuse to believe you mean that."

Liana had known it was a lie the instant she had spoken, but she couldn't take it back. After all, she had not simply met him. He had stalked her like a delicious bit of prey and swiftly proceeded to turn her comfortable world inside out. "What are you going to do now that Sean has sworn to watch you? Are his threats finally reason enough to stop printing the pamphlets?"

Again, Christian grabbed at a flicker of hope that she

was truly concerned about his safety. "Is that still your price?"

Liana tried to pull away from him, but Christian tightened his hold. "I don't have any price. I'd just rather not marry if I'm going to be widowed within a few weeks."

Disappointed that she was more worried about herself than him, Christian rested his forehead against hers. He was positive he was right not to give up writing the pamphlets, but being close to her filled him with such desperate longing he knew he could never give her up, either. He straightened up. "You're right," he agreed, and the beauty of her smile urged him on.

"O'Keefe despises me with good reason, and he's going to be so suspicious I probably won't be able to ride into town without one of his men following me. But if I'm gone, and the pamphlets still appear, he'll have to look elsewhere for the author."

That wasn't the promise Liana wanted, but it was at least a start. "Where would you go?"

Taking heart from her anxious glance, Christian began to smile. "Into the Ohio Valley, but I won't go alone, Liana. I want you to come with me. It won't be an elegant honeymoon, but no one will think it odd that I want to take you away from Williamsburg." When she appeared hesitant, Christian brushed her lips with a light kiss. "I don't want you to be widowed, either. Come with me where we'll both be safe."

After a terrifying night and only a few hours sleep, Christian's embrace held a comforting sweetness Liana ached for. She had tried to leave him, and the attempt had very nearly cost her and her dear brothers their lives. And Christian risking being shot again chasing after her only added to her burden of guilt. When leaving him had nearly caused four deaths, could staying with him possibly be as dangerous?

"Was Beau's proposal really his idea?" she asked.

That she could even think otherwise was heartbreaking. "Yes. Come, let's go up to the house for dinner, and you can ask him if his bruises don't prove it."

"They can't be any worse than mine."

"I haven't seen him today, but they undoubtedly are. Now come on, I'm hungry. Aren't you?"

"I'm afraid I swallowed too much of the river, maybe even a couple of fish." But she took his hand, and refusing his offer to carry her, walked barefoot up to the house.

Christian did not give her the option of eating in her room, and after Johanna brought stockings and slippers, he showed her to the place opposite his at the table. The rest of the family was just gathering for the meal; they were as confused as Christian had been about Liana's disappearance, and sat forward in their places hoping for an explanation. When, after Byron gave the blessing, neither Christian nor Liana provided one, an uneasy rumble passed among them.

Beau had taken his place on Liana's left, but seeing the scowl Christian gave his cousin, she was almost afraid to look up at him. When at last she did, she found his right eye was as black as hers. Christian broke into a triumphant smirk, but she wasn't at all pleased Beau's face provided the proof he had promised she would find. "I think we've been cursed," she said suddenly.

Startled by that depressing opinion, none of the Barclays knew how to respond, but Christian quickly used the stunned silence to announce his plans. "Liana and I have decided to visit the Ohio Valley. It's very beautiful in the spring, and neither of us has any reason to remain in Williamsburg."

"Aren't you getting married?" Belle asked with her usual innocent charm.

The first course was a delicate cream soup, but Liana couldn't seem to raise her spoon from the bowl to her mouth. Amanda and her other friends had occasionally shared their dreams for beautiful weddings, but Liana had never had any such romantic ideas. Now, as she gazed into Christian's dark eyes, she was glad she had no illusions to shatter.

"Indians don't need fancy ceremonies to be married," Christian finally answered.

Dominique had to lean out past Falcon and Alanna to see Christian. "Liana's no Indian, which I'm sure you know. You mustn't deprive her of the joy of a lavish wedding."

Arielle noted Liana's stricken expression, and quickly silenced her eldest daughter. "Liana's only been with us two days, my darling. Let's not presume to know her feelings, or make plans for her without consulting her. Tell me what you think of the soup. It's a vegetable puree with a cream base and I'm wondering if the flavor is too subtle."

Liana was relieved when, following Arielle's lead, her companions gave their attention to the soup. She finally managed to take a sip and thought it superb, but tasted very little of the rest of the meal. No longer able to hide her yawns by the time it was over, she begged to be excused.

Christian still had both keys to her room in his pocket, and not wanting her to discover that the one usually in her door was missing, he left the table, too. "I'll walk you to your room," he offered, and putting his hand on her waist, guided her to the stairs before she could object. "Please don't worry," he whispered. "I won't force myself on you—today, or ever."

As they entered her room, Christian quickly replaced the key he had taken. He then remained at the door and waited for Liana to turn toward him. When instead she went to the windows overlooking the river, he followed but stopped several paces back. "I know you won't feel up to traveling for several days, but I hope we can leave soon. Would you mind wearing buckskins? They'd be far more comfortable for riding than a fancy habit."

He wasn't touching her, but Liana could feel his presence as strongly as a caress. "You mean to dress me like an Indian, too?"

"Only for this trip. When we come home, I want you to order as many new gowns as you please. You had such pretty clothes, and I don't want you to have to settle for anything less here."

He was being very kind, but it was difficult for Liana to think past the moment. His family had been equally considerate, but she feared after the ghastly way she had joined them she would always feel like a stranger in their midst. She could not spend the rest of her life hiding in her bedroom, and believing it might be very nice to get away where no one would ask even polite questions, she glanced over her shoulder.

"Let's leave on Monday," she suggested. "If I don't feel completely rested, then we needn't go far the first day, but I'd like to get away quickly, too."

"At least you'll be taking me with you this time," Christian teased.

"I very nearly drowned. How can you joke about it?"

"How can you not? Nap all afternoon if you like. I'll wake you for supper."

Liana was surprised when Christian left her room without kissing her good-bye, and sadly disappointed.

Byron was waiting for Christian at the bottom of the stairs. "Come with me," he directed.

Christian knew what was coming but dutifully followed his uncle into the study and closed the door. "We're leaving on Monday," he told him.

Byron sat down at his desk and immediately provided his nephew with definite terms. "Fine. Go off and live like the Seneca for as long as you please, but when you come home, you will marry Liana in a proper ceremony."

"Don't lecture me. I'm not the one delaying the wedding."

"Perhaps not, but you're certainly the one who's made it necessary and I'll not allow you and Liana to live together under my roof unless you're legally wed."

"Your roof?" Christian rested his hands on the desk. "I thought this house belonged to all of us."

"Not in this case, it doesn't. I refuse to allow you to set a dangerous precedent your brother might then follow. Think of your sister and cousins. As the eldest, you set an example for them. Disgrace yourself, and you disgrace us all."

"As I have since the day I was born?" Christian challenged in a darkly threatening tone.

"I've never said that!"

Christian straightened up. "No, you don't have to when the whole town whispers it behind my back. I'm not ashamed of loving Liana, and she's done nothing to deserve anyone's scorn, either. I'll leave the cartoons and text for the next two pamphlets with you. David Slauson can carve the woodblocks and handle the printing. My father had already planned to take my route, and perhaps David can take the town. Having the next pamphlets appear while I'm out of town should confuse O'Keefe sufficiently to keep us all in the clear. Can I count on you to help my father and David?"

Byron rose from his chair. "You may, but then I'm going to count on you to respect my rules when you return."

Christian nodded, but he feared he might be away a very long time before Liana agreed to marry him in a legal ceremony in front of a churchful of witnesses.

Eighteen

On Monday, in the silent mist of dawn, Christian saddled a matched pair of bay geldings. He loaded an ample supply of provisions on the back of a pack mule, and wished his hopes could be as easily contained. When he went back to the house, he found Liana waiting for him at the bottom of the stairs. He had knocked lightly at her door to wake her before going out to the stable, and thought it a good sign she had gotten ready so quickly.

She was dressed in buckskins carefully stitched for Falcon rather than him, but they had had such little wear before being outgrown they still looked very good on her slim figure. She was wearing a pair of Johanna's beaded moccasins and carrying a wide-brimmed straw hat Arielle had insisted she take. It was a ridiculous costume, but with her proud posture, she looked no less attractive than in satin and silk.

"Ready?" Christian asked in a hushed whisper, taking care not to wake the rest of the house. Liana's bruises were fading into soft mauves tinged with green; relieved, he found it easy to smile at her. "I thought we could ride along the river a while, then stop and catch some bass for breakfast."

As determined as he to make this trip a success, Liana paused by the mirror in the entryway to don the hat. She tied the bright blue ribbon in a bow beneath her chin, then stepped back for a last glimpse of the borrowed garb which was comfortable if not at all ladylike. It was practical, at least. and not burdened by her usual heavy petticoats, she picked up the satchel holding a few personal items and was ready to go.

"I haven't fished in a while," she told him as they slipped out the back door. "If I have no luck, will you share your catch with me?"

Christian assured her he would and took her hand as they walked to the stable. It was a lovely hand, but very small compared to his, and he hoped she wouldn't prove to be too delicate for the rigors of an extended overland journey.

"I'm not taking my usual mount, but the geldings are sturdy beasts better suited to travel. Jean named them Lion and Tiger, which makes little sense, but they haven't complained."

"Which will be mine?"

"Tiger, I think. He's the more placid while Lion is a bit of a clown."

Having seen his impressive black stallion, Liana understood that the magnificent horse was valued for his speed, and on their lengthy journey such an attribute wasn't required. Christian had drawn a map for her yesterday, and while striking out for the Ohio Valley was a great adventure, she was glad numerous hunting trips with his father had taught him the way. She tied her satchel behind Tiger's saddle and patted him on the rump.

She hadn't ridden astride since she was a little girl, but, putting her foot in the stirrup, easily swung herself up on Tiger's back and instantly recalled a pony she had shared with her brothers. "We owned a little ginger-colored pony called Tommy when I was small," she remarked as they got underway. "He was a stubborn fellow, but he had a passion for apples. He would give us rides all day long if we kept feeding him, so we cut the apples into thin slices so we wouldn't run out."

They rode side by side as they left the yard, and Christian thought it a shame he would soon have to lead the way and miss the pleasure of looking at her. The cool gray morning was perfect for travel, but covering a great distance wasn't really his goal. Easily picturing Liana and her brothers riding a fat little pony in endless circles, he could almost hear their laughter.

"You were an adorable little girl," he replied.

"Thank you." Liana was about to tell him she had noticed him, too, but then began to wonder. "When did you come to regard me as your sister?" she asked instead.

Christian frowned slightly, for there had been a time when he had not seen that imagined relationship as an advantage. "I don't know the year," he hedged, "but it was a long time ago. The path narrows here, so we'll have to talk later."

As he urged his mount ahead of hers, Liana got the distinct impression that she had touched upon a subject he would rather not discuss. It was an unsettling sensation since she would have no one else to talk with for several weeks. Growing fearful, she glanced over her shoulder at the house. She had understood why Christian had wanted to leave early, but now, with no one to bid them farewell, she felt like an outcast again and it hurt. Of course, he and Beau weren't speaking, and because she was the reason it was probably just as well that they had left early. She leaned forward to pat Tiger's neck and comb his thick black mane, but at the same time wished she were riding her own gentle mare.

Without Christian by her side to distract her, she had to take a deep breath in an effort to overcome her lingering fear as they neared the river, for last Friday night's horror was still fresh in her mind. Even glancing away, she was surrounded by the James' churning roar and knowing it

could so easily have been the last sound she ever heard
was terrifying. Blocking out that ugly memory, she watched
a bluebird swoop low in an azure streak. Nearby, mocking-
birds greeted the day with exuberant cries, and overhead
a marsh hawk circled beneath the clouds. The countryside
was alive with creatures anxious to embrace the promise
of the morning, and putting her disturbing memories
aside, she strove to share their enthusiasm.

As the sun rose higher, the early morning chill was replaced by a comforting warmth Liana welcomed. Up
ahead, Christian's hair glowed with a raven's iridescent
sheen and she could not help but wonder how their story
might have differed had he not been such a handsome
young man. Ashamed of herself then, she knew it wasn't
merely his striking good looks she had found so attractive.
After all, Sean O'Keefe was handsome, but that hadn't
been nearly enough to inspire love for him.

"Love," she whispered softly to herself. She had never
spoken the word to Christian, but she had felt the elusive
emotion's strength in his arms. He had treated her so
sweetly the last two days that she had few reservations
about traveling with him. No, she thought sadly, her misgivings were all for herself and as soon as they stopped to
catch their breakfast, she was very nearly overwhelmed by
them.

Christian had to bait her hook, but she managed to toss
her line into the river without catching it on the marsh
grass. In an instant she had a bite, but the fish was too
small and Christian promptly removed the hook from its
mouth and tossed it back. He got a bite next and caught
a beautiful bass she thought would feed them both. "Isn't
that enough?" she asked.

"Not if you're as hungry as I am, it isn't."

Unconsciously, Liana had kept inching away from the
river. "Well, perhaps one more then," she agreed.

She looked so cute dressed in Falcon's clothes and his

aunt's floppy hat that Christian had a difficult time not paying more attention to her than to fishing. He wanted her to catch the next fish, but again, there was a tug on his line. This second bass was as fine a catch as the first, and satisfied he had supplied them with plenty to eat, Christian called a halt to their first joint effort. He bent down to clean the bass in the water.

"Why don't you build the fire," he suggested.

Delighted she could move further up on the riverbank, Liana tossed the bait into the water and wound up the fishing line. "Build a fire? Well, I suppose I could. There must be some dry wood nearby."

Christian hid his smile as she traipsed up and down collecting sticks and twigs and an occasional branch large enough to burn. He had not realized until then that while his father had carefully tutored Falcon and him in the skills they would need to thrive in the wilds, Liana had been raised for a far more genteel way of life. Even in buckskins she had a lady's elegance and grace and while she took much longer than he had anticipated to gather enough wood for a fire, he enjoyed watching her every move.

He lit the fire, then pulled an iron skillet from the mule's pack. "If I'd come alone, I wouldn't have bothered to bring so much, but because we have a pan, let's use it. There's some cornbread, too."

Liana watched closely as Christian fried the fish. He placed thick squares of cornbread near the flames so they would be warm when the fish was done, then produced a couple of pewter plates and handed her a fork. "Thank you. I'm glad you know how to cook as I certainly don't." Following his example, she sat cross-legged and balanced her plate on her lap.

"Don't worry. You'll soon learn."

Liana tried to look forward to it, but lacked his confidence. "My brothers would love this," she said, then instantly regretted it. "I'm sorry, that didn't sound right. I didn't mean that I can't appreciate the taste of freshly caught bass because I do. It's just that they would be far more help to you on this trip than I'll ever be."

Christian waited for her to look up at him. No longer swollen, her pretty green eyes held a questioning innocence. "Liana, it isn't help that I need, but a wife. That's why we've come away together."

Liana felt a bright blush creep up her cheeks. "Yes, I understand." Dreadfully embarrassed that she had forced him to say so, she ate the rest of her fish in silence. They had always had so much to discuss, and now, she couldn't think of a single thing to say to him. She broke off bits of cornbread and swallowed them without tasting their sweetness.

Christian had been eager to accept the responsibility for this dear young woman, but it was suddenly painfully obvious that warm meals and a dry place to sleep weren't going to be nearly enough to make Liana happy. She had not made a single demand, but he doubted she had ever eaten a meal on the riverbank before that morning. He did not want her to fear that this was all he would ever provide.

"I want to show you the Ohio Valley, because my father and uncle fought the French there. It's also where the Seneca hunt, so it's long been a part of me, but when we come home I want you to help me design a house. We've plenty of land, and my uncle's home is getting much too crowded. We can't squeeze another generation into it, and you deserve a beautiful house of your own."

Amazed by his suggestion, Liana again met his gaze. His enthusiastic smile was endearing, but she saw a problem. "It would be *our* house," she corrected. It was an enchanting idea, and yet she didn't want to expect too much. "Can you afford it, Christian? Even if there is land, it costs a great deal to build a house, and then it has to be furnished and maintained. That's also an expensive proposition."

Her worry about the cost amused Christian. He reached for her empty plate and stacked it on his own. "The Barclays are a wealthy family. My mother was Byron's sister, and I'm her sole heir." Liana frowned slightly, and he paused. "What's the matter?"

"Nothing, but until this instant I hadn't thought of my father as her heir, too. I've never heard him express a positive thought about your family, so clearly he has no desire to claim part of your mother's estate, but what if he suddenly changed his mind?"

Christian did not even want to consider what a catastrophe that would be. "Oh Lord, just to make things even more difficult for you? Is he truly that evil?"

"No, he's not evil at all, just furiously angry. Your mother betrayed him, and he believes I did as well."

Hoping she would continue, Christian waited until it was clear she would not. Then, feeling foolish for having hoped for even a hint that she considered him worth the disgrace, he directed his anger at Ian. "I really don't care what he believes. You're the only one who's important to me. Do you feel as though you've betrayed yourself?"

Confused, Liana shrugged slightly. "In what way?"

Christian tried not to sound as impatient as he felt. "In becoming my wife in the manner you did."

"Oh, well—" Liana looked out at the river and was instantly sorry as a shiver of watery dread coursed down her spine. "I'm sure you'll agree it would have been much easier for us and our families had we followed tradition and become engaged and wed in church."

"You're forgetting that your father wouldn't have allowed me to call on you, let alone ask for your hand in marriage."

He was getting angry, and Liana understood it was with good cause. She reached out to touch his knee. "Please forgive me. I shouldn't have mentioned my father. He's forsaken me, so there's no reason for me ever to mention him again. Besides, when your mother died, her parents were still living, so she hadn't inherited anything to leave my father anyway, other than her jewelry."

"No, I suppose not." Relieved that their discussion had not deteriorated into an argument, Christian forced a smile. "Now where was I? Anyway, with my mother and Uncle Elliott dead, Byron owns the Barclay estate, but quite naturally as his nephew, I have a share in its profits. Alanna is a cousin, but Byron considers her a younger sister, and calls Johanna and Falcon his niece and nephew, too.

"I suppose our family ties are a bit more complicated than most, but the love is just as strong. If I want to build a house, or a dozen of them, I can well afford it. We sell a great deal of tobacco to England. That may cease if the colonies seize their independence, but without the king to tell us where we can do business, there's France, Spain, and the rest of Europe to consider.

"Our Aunt Arielle taught us all to speak French, and I'd love to take you to Paris. Would you consider that a more proper honeymoon?"

The word implied an idyllic interlude after marriage and despite his claims, Liana needed a good deal more than Seneca custom to consider herself his wife. Because she had refused his offers of marriage, she did not want to force the issue. Instead, she rose, picked up their plates, and nodded toward the river. "I'll wash these. We'll not get far today if we spend any more time just sitting here talking."

Christian put out the fire, then stomped the ashes with more than the necessary vigor. He had just offered to build Liana a fine home and take her to Paris. What more could she possibly want? Spending several weeks meandering through the woods and not finding out was a discouraging prospect, but he tried not to let it depress him as they continued their journey. After all, his father had convinced him that deeds meant more than words to women as well as men, and he would have Liana all to himself that night.

Late in the afternoon, they took a ferry across the river and began the trek west toward the Shenandoah Mountains. Fearing he had already tired Liana, Christian stopped at the first good place to make camp. On high ground, they were close to a stream which provided cool water to drink, cook, and bathe. Sheltered by an ancient oak, their comfort would be assured. He unsaddled the horses, freed the mule from his burden, and after watering them all at the stream, tied the animals where they had plenty to graze. He had planned to hunt along the way, but that night chose to offer the ham he had brought.

"Yes, that's fine with me," Liana replied.

She had an easier time gathering wood here, and Christian soon had a fire burning brightly and a pot of beans bubbling. He unrolled a couple of blankets, and while Liana did not even want to think about sleeping on the ground, she sat down on the end of one while they ate. They had skirted the plantations near the river and followed hunting trails all day. Other than the few people gathered at the ferry, where she had drawn justifiably curious stares, they had seen no one. She hoped that same pattern would continue.

They drank water from the stream, had more cornbread with the ham and beans, but ate supper without either of them offering much in the way of conversation. Liana felt as though she ought to be charming and witty, but unlike a festive party where gaiety came naturally, absolutely nothing occurred to her here. She was accustomed to responding to men's comments as much as offering her own, and when Christian didn't speak, she grew increasingly uncomfortable. "Be yourself," her mother had advised, but Liana wasn't at all sure who she was anymore. She had always been inquisitive, perhaps too high-spirited, but now, dressed in buckskins and dining on the edge of a forest, she simply felt lost.

"I'm glad you know the way," she said almost to herself.

"If we follow the setting sun, we can't miss the Ohio River," Christian replied. "No one could get lost."

"Well, I certainly could," Liana argued.

She had taken off her hat when they had stopped for the day, and shaded by the oak, her bruises were faint. She looked very lovely, but there was a sadness about her that pained Christian. "Women are very important to the Seneca," he announced suddenly. "They own the houses and fields where they grow corn, beans, and squash. They choose the chiefs rather than the men.

"When a man marries he goes to live with his wife's family, in their longhouse." He gestured as he spoke. "The Seneca build huge houses. They're more than sixty feet long and eighteen feet wide. They're made of logs and poles curved into an arch and covered with elm bark. There are fire pits in the center, and a hole above to let out the smoke. That's not the type of house I want to build for you, though. I want you to have a home you'll be proud to own."

Entertained by his knowledge as well as his enthusiasm, Liana drew a quick comparison. "That's definitely a good thing since neither of us would be welcome in my parents' home."

Astonished she could joke about it, Christian continued before she changed her mind. "At one time, my father was going to build a longhouse for Alanna, but she insisted it have a wooden floor so I wouldn't have to crawl in the dirt. He asked her what else she would like, and she asked for glass windows, too. The Seneca build platforms for seats and sleeping along the walls, with racks above to store belongings, but Alanna said a real bed would be nice, and she would need a wardrobe for her clothes."

Liana laughed along with him. "She wanted the kind of house she was used to living in, didn't she?"

"Yes, and my father never bothered to build a longhouse when it would not have been what he had hoped when she had finished with it. You and I don't have any such differences, Liana. We're used to the same things, very beautiful things."

It had sounded strange to hear him refer to his stepmother by her name, but Liana had no doubt that he loved Alanna. He could not have missed a mother he had never known, but ever since she had learned of Melissa's existence, she had been fascinated by her. "What do you suppose really happened between your mother and father?"

"I just told you. They decided against building a longhouse."

"No, I was thinking of Melissa."

An owl called out in the gathering dusk, and looking up, Christian was surprised to see the sun was so close to setting. "I told you that, too. She lacked the courage to wed an Indian, and married your father instead. It was a tragic mistake, but she was young."

"So are we."

Positive their being together was no mistake, Christian reached out to caress her cheek. "I think she must have been like Dominique, all pretty blond curls and carefree smiles. You look deeper, and understand more, than my mother ever did. I'm not my father, either. We're nothing like them, and we haven't been cursed, Liana. You'll see."

Christian leaned forward to kiss her, but she dipped her head to present her cheek. Badly disappointed by her rebuff, he got to his feet. "I'm going to gather more wood while it's still light enough to see."

Meaning to call him back, Liana raised her hand but the words stuck in her throat and he walked away. The day had passed so quickly, and while it had not gone as well as she believed it might, it had not gone too badly, either. Worn out as much by worry as travel, she washed their dishes in the stream and stacked them by the fire to dry. Christian had placed the blankets close together, and not wanting to hurt him, she didn't move hers away. She stretched out on it, and before she finished a silent prayer for her mother and brothers, she was fast asleep.

Christian made no effort to fetch wood, and instead walked along the stream until he found a good place to sit a while and rest. He could not help but recall how excited he had been the times he and Liana had left ribbon signals and met by the river. Now, rather than a few stolen moments, they could spend the entire day together, but while he still felt the same thrill, apparently Liana did not. Maybe she never had, he thought sadly.

He reminded himself that her father had turned her out, and she had nearly drowned, so perhaps it was merely too soon to expect the affection he craved. It certainly wasn't too soon for him, though, and he longed to make love to her again. In the forest he wouldn't have to speak in hushed tones for fear of being overheard, and he wanted to shout her name. The owl called again, an endlessly inquisitive hoot, but Christian knew exactly who he was.

He wanted Liana to acknowledge him, though, and her maddening reluctance was getting increasingly difficult to endure. This was only the first full day they had spent together, but that didn't matter. He wanted her now. Getting up, he dusted off his buckskins and headed back toward camp. Their mounts and the mule were content, but he approached Liana without any hope for more than a polite "Good night."

When he found her sleeping soundly, he could barely contain his disappointment. He had not been gone all that long, and he really thought she should have stayed awake until he returned.

He unfolded his blanket, then lay down so close to Liana he could cover them both with the top half. He slipped his left arm around her waist and cuddled up behind her. She stirred slightly, but didn't wake and, telling himself this was as close as he was likely to get for a while, he savored the softness of her curls and looked forward to a great deal more.

The first time Liana awoke, it was still dark. Disoriented, she was frightened until she recognized the man beside her as Christian. Her fears quickly subsided then. He had handled their first day with a relaxed self-assurance she was confident would continue. He was at ease on horseback and at home in the forest. Throughout the day he had smiled and laughed as though they really were taking a trip for pleasure rather than merely getting away from the poisonous gossip which might follow them all their lives.

She laced her fingers in his and tried to imagine the house he had offered to build, but it refused to come clear in her mind. Driven from the once-sweet security of her family home, she longed to find a place where she would feel safe again, but doubted a house, even a fine one, would be enough on its own. Easing against Christian's embrace, she wanted very badly to believe they could be happy, but painful doubts brought tears to her eyes. She had cried too long and hard to weep again, but even as she fell asleep, sorrow clouded her dreams.

The noisy sparrows nesting in the oak roused Christian, but despite their eagerness for the dawn he had no real reason for an early start that day and lay still, waiting for Liana to open her eyes. He thought about building a fire with the wood he would still have to collect, but staying with her was far more appealing. A doe and her fawn wandered by on their way to the stream, but he and Liana were so still the deer passed within inches of their feet without taking note of them.

Listening closely, Christian identified half a dozen birds by their calls. The catbird's shrill cry was as annoying as always, but the whippoorwill's chirped lament made him smile. Lost in daydreams as colorful as the dawn, when he finally noticed Liana was watching him, she had been awake for some time.

"Good morning," he greeted her. "Are you hungry?"

Liana had simply been trying to adjust to the fact that she had again awakened in Christian's arms. There had been a reassuring peacefulness in his embrace, but now that he had spoken, the mood was lost. She felt stiff and sore from sleeping on the ground, but not a bit hungry. "No, but maybe we can find some wild berries once we get on our way."

Christian propped himself on his right elbow, then swept her hair from her eyes and curled it around her ear. Her bruises had again changed shade, the colors blending in hideous splendor, but to him she was still a beauty. "You're already too thin, so we better eat before we leave. I don't want people to think I can't take care of you."

His hair had come loose from the tie at his nape and spilled over his shoulders in careless profusion. He looked as wild as she truly believed him to be and her first thought was only natural. "I can't believe you've ever cared what people think."

It would have been a simple matter to trap her where she lay, kiss her until she was too breathless to complain, and then take the love she refused to give, but Christian again chose restraint. "I wouldn't have written the pamphlets if I didn't wish to influence public opinion. They've been very effective, too."

The cursed pamphlets were the last thing Liana wanted to discuss. "How's your arm?" she asked pointedly.

"Nearly healed, thank you." Christian was tempted to

ask if she cared, but was afraid he already knew the answer. The challenging look in her eyes was exciting, and before she could avoid him again, he leaned down and kissed her. He was not gentle, either, but every bit as demanding as when he had kissed her the very first time. She had been outraged, but he had known what he was starting, and he did not ever intend to let it end.

"Don't push me," he warned as he drew away. "It's harmony I want, but if you're determined to wage war you'll find me a savage enemy."

Liana didn't move as he rose and yanked his buckskins into place. He had slept with his knife in a beaded sheath on his belt and while that hadn't bothered her during the night, it now struck her as menacing. Yesterday he had been kind, but his expression was anything but tender now.

"Don't look at me like that," she protested. "You're frightening me."

Christian responded with a mirthless laugh. "Good. At least I have some effect on you. I'm going to see to the animals. Gather wood for a fire."

Insulted by his demanding tone, Liana didn't move until he was gone, but when she tried to stand, she found just getting up wasn't all that easy. Once on her feet, she reached out for the oak's massive trunk and stretched to work the soreness out of her spine. Not having ridden astride in years, as she took a step toward the stream her thighs responded with an additional agonizing burst of pain.

"Some honeymoon this is," she muttered under her breath, but she was much too proud to complain to Christian about how sore she was, and because they again rode in single file, he failed to see her tears.

Nineteen

Sean O'Keefe came to the Barclays' alone on Tuesday afternoon. Johanna and Dominique were in the garden, and Beau had just closed the front door when the captain rode a high-stepping gray gelding into the yard. All three watched him dismount, their features displaying thinly veiled contempt, and none offered a word of greeting.

"I've come to see Christian," he called out.

Unable to slip back into the house unseen, Beau could only hope the Englishman wouldn't ask about his black eye. He walked toward him, but stopped part way. "He left for the Ohio Valley yesterday. Can I be of some service?"

Dominique handed the basket in which they had been gathering flowers to Johanna and started toward the two men. Sean recalled speaking with the attractive young woman on a previous visit, and gave her a warm smile before answering her brother. "Thank you, but no. It's Christian I must see. When is he expected to return?"

Hoping to send O'Keefe on his way, Beau shook his head emphatically. "We've absolutely no idea. He could be away for weeks."

As Dominique reached Beau's side, Sean thought her even more lovely than the last time they had met. She was dressed in a muslin gown sprinkled with rosebuds and looked sweeter than the flowers in her well-tended garden. "Good day, Miss Barclay," he said.

"Good day, Captain." Too curious to miss out on what promised to be an interesting conversation, Dominique linked her arm through her brother's.

"We were just talking about Christian," Sean informed her. "Isn't this a peculiar time for him to have gone hunting? Or has the responsibility of a wife already proved too taxing?"

Dominique had a sparkling laugh, and she used it to every advantage before gazing up at Sean through a dense sweep of long lashes. "Christian hasn't gone hunting. He's taken Liana away on their honeymoon. The Ohio Valley may seem an unusual choice, but not to an Indian brave."

Johanna had continued to work in the garden, and Sean watched her moving down a row of bright pink azaleas while he fought to control the jealousy driving up his temper. "That may be true, but what made him imagine Liana would enjoy tramping through the woods?"

Forced to defend his cousin, Beau found the words almost too easily. "Like any new husband, Christian was more concerned with what he intended to do than where he and Liana would be doing it."

Revolted that Beau had no better manners than Christian when it came to alluding to activities better left to the imagination, Sean's eyes narrowed slightly. "Well, when he does come home, tell him I asked for him. I intend to keep an eye on him personally, and in the future, he'll need to inform me should he wish to leave town."

Dominique cocked her head to assume a coquettish pose, but her words were meant to sting. "For a number of weeks, Christian's only interest has been Liana, so I can't imagine why you'd need to concern yourself with him. Unless, of course, it's simply to vent the anger you dare not show her. I should hate to discover you're the vindictive sort, Captain, as it's such an unattractive trait. Liana may have chosen Christian, but there are so many other pretty

young women in Williamsburg, I can't believe you'll be
lonely for long."

Her voice was pitched low, and she spoke in such a soft
tone Sean had to strain to catch every word. At first insulted, but then intrigued, he was fascinated by her clear
blue eyes and sultry charm. She looked very young and
sweet, and yet spoke with a sophistication that promised a
full knowledge of womanly charms.

"You must have so many callers, Miss Barclay, that you'd
have scant time for me."

"I will make the time, Captain," Dominique promised
in a throaty whisper. "We've all been invited to the Algrens'
on Saturday. Perhaps we'll see you there."

Dominique had a luscious mouth, and following her
words closely, Sean grew even more eager to taste her kiss.
"Yes, I believe I did receive an invitation. I'll be sure to
send an acceptance immediately."

"Oh yes, please do," Dominique encouraged.

Beau had feared he would be embarrassed by questions
about his black eye, but Dominique had Sean so enrap-
tured, he doubted the officer remembered he was standing at his sister's side. At last the Englishman excused
himself and mounted his horse, but Beau didn't wait for
him to leave the yard before he began to complain. "You
flirt as gracefully as a hawk soars on the wind, but couldn't
you have found more appropriate prey?"

Dominique gave his arm a malicious squeeze before re-
leasing her hold. "Did you actually imagine that I liked
the man? I despise him and all he stands for as much as
you. I simply wanted to confuse him so he won't come
back to question Christian again about the pamphlets."

She had spoken with Sean when he had made an earlier
visit searching for the pamphlets' author, but Beau wasn't
certain how much Dominique knew. "What have you been
told?" he asked.

"I didn't have to be told," Dominique scoffed. "I've

read the pamphlets, and they echo Christian's remarks at the dinner table so closely it's plain he wrote them. You needn't look so stricken. I'll not tell. Is that your fear, that I'll take a British officer as a lover and betray you all?"

Beau swallowed hard. In truth, he had never been able to successfully predict what Dominique might do. "In your own way, you're as wild as Christian," he said, "so it's no wonder I'm worried. Just avoid Sean—then none of us will have to worry about what you might inadvertently reveal."

Dominique tapped her finger on his chest. "I'll speak to whomever I please, Beau. Now, weren't you going in to the college this morning?"

"Yes, I've neglected my studies. I can see I'm wasting my time with you so I'll be on my way."

Rather than tell him good-bye, Dominique turned on her heel and flounced back to the garden. "My darling brother fears I'm about to run off with Captain O'Keefe. Can you even imagine such a ridiculous notion, Johanna?"

Positive that wasn't a serious question, Johanna nevertheless gave a thoughtful reply. "No, but I wouldn't have guessed Christian would wed Liana Scott, either."

"He hasn't married her yet," Dominique insisted.

"He will."

Not bothering to use the shears in the basket, Dominique snapped off a white camellia with her fingers. "Yes, Christian always gets what he wants, doesn't he?"

Johanna watched a fiercely determined light fill Dominique's eyes and wondered just what she was plotting. "So do you."

"Only because I know how to go after it. What is it you want, Johanna? Is there anyone going to the Algrens' party that you're anxious to see?"

"We better hurry," Johanna cautioned. "The flowers we cut earlier are wilting. Let's go inside and put them in water."

"Minx! I've seen you talking with one of the hands more

evenings than not. Are you merely flirting with him, or is it something more serious?"

For a brief, painful instant, Johanna feared Dominique might show an interest in David just to see if he would react with the same pitifully adoring gaze as Captain O'Keefe. Then she was ashamed of herself for thinking so little of her cousin. Still, she couldn't bear the thought of losing David to Dominique, who would treat him as an amusing diversion, but surely wouldn't love him.

"I like him very much," she announced proudly, "and I'd appreciate it if you stayed away from him."

Shocked by the sharpness of Johanna's tone, Dominique began to laugh. "Oh, Johanna, I wouldn't try to seduce your beau. Don't you know me any better than that?"

"I know you only too well," Johanna replied.

Dominique hesitated a moment, but then hurried to follow her cousin into the house. "You're right," she admitted reluctantly. "I do love to flirt, but family ties are sacred, and I wouldn't betray you for any reason, and most especially not for a man."

Relieved, Johanna didn't criticize her cousin further. They busied themselves arranging the flowers for the dining room table and made another bouquet for the parlor, but Johanna kept thinking of David, and was embarrassed by how quickly she had claimed him when he had never offered her more than a smile and a pleasant evening of conversation.

It wasn't until Christian helped Liana from her mount that afternoon that he noticed how pale she was. "Are you feeling ill?" he asked anxiously. The day had gotten off to such a poor start that neither of them had felt like talking when they had stopped to eat, but now that he really looked at her, he was frightened. He had again led her to a familiar campground, but realized suddenly that having water and a thick meadow for the horses and mule did not make it an ideal place for her.

"I'm just tired," Liana assured him, for indeed she was exhausted as well as sore. She tried to move away without limping, but failed to produce her usual graceful gait.

She looked so pathetic, Christian didn't waste his breath arguing but swept her up into his arms and carried her to the rise where he had planned to sleep. There was a hickory tree at the crest, and still holding her, he sat down with the tree at his back and cuddled her on his lap. He untied her hat and tossed it away, then pressed her cheek against his shoulder and hugged her.

"I'm sorry. I shouldn't have been so cross with you this morning. Nothing that's happened has been your fault. If you miss your family so much you find it difficult to be with me, I'll try and be more understanding. I was trying," he swore, "perhaps just not hard enough."

Relaxed in his embrace, Liana didn't miss her family at all. "No," she assured him. "I don't long for home. It's just that I'm not a very good Indian, it seems. I can't ride all day and still have the energy to dance at night."

"I don't expect you to become Seneca," Christian explained. "You're fine just as you are. Besides, Seneca women tend their fields all day. They don't ride as far as we've come." He was tempted to ask if she wanted to go back home, but then they would have to confront Byron's demand for a proper wedding. He wasn't about to risk that when she was bound to refuse him again.

"I don't know what to do," he finally admitted.

Believing he was referring to her fatigue, Liana was ashamed for not having more stamina. "Maybe if I take a short nap while you tend to the animals, I'll feel more like helping you prepare supper."

When she used both hands to cover a wide yawn, Christian readily agreed. He eased her off his lap, then stood. "I'll bring you a blanket." But when he returned with it, she was asleep right where she sat. He spread it out beside her anyway, and then lifted her gently to place her on it. She curled up more tightly, but didn't open her eyes, and he bent down to kiss her cheek. Sitting back on his heels, he watched her until he was certain she was resting as easily as she could on the ground.

As he rose, he made a mental list of ways to make their camp more comfortable for her, and having little time before nightfall, he hurried away to begin.

Teased awake by the succulent aroma of the roasting turkey, Liana lay still and watched Christian adjust the spit he had constructed over the fire. Again, it was clear in his relaxed motions that this was nothing new for the talented brave. "How did you trap the bird?" she asked as she sat up.

"I didn't trap him. I used my bow. I'm sorry you weren't awake to pluck the feathers."

Her hands were the only part of her that didn't ache, and Liana was confident she could have managed it. "Yes, so am I. It smells delicious."

"Thank you, but it will take a while longer to cook."

"Then I'll have time to wash up." Liana was eager to rinse away the dust of the trail, but slow to rise. "Does this creek have a name?" she asked.

"It's a branch of the Nottoway River," Christian called over his shoulder. "Tomorrow night, we'll camp by the Otter River. Then we'll follow the course of the New River through the Alleghenys to the Kanawha. Or, we can stay right here if you don't feel up to going on."

Liana had gotten to her feet now, but swayed slightly and had to grab a low branch of the hickory. Going on meant more of the same agony that had made her whole body rebel, but staying here might well bring pain of another sort. "I want to go on," she assured him, but there was no enthusiasm in her voice. She walked down to the creek, shuffling slowly, and knelt down to wash her hands and face. The water was very cold, and didn't invite a prolonged stay, but she took her time getting back to camp.

When she reappeared, Christian nodded toward a plate he had heaped with blackberries. "Have a few of these if you're hungry."

Liana took only one. "Let's save them for dessert."

"I wish I had some cream for you." Christian used a stick to poke the coals, then sat back and propped his arms on his knees. "It won't be much longer now."

Liana glanced around the small clearing, searching for anything which might inspire conversation. "Tell me more about the Seneca."

Christian rubbed his chin with the back of his hand as he tried to think of something worth sharing. After sifting through his memories, he recalled a tale he thought she would enjoy. "My father used to tell us stories when he brought Falcon and me out to the woods. One of my favorites was about the first woman. She had lived with her people in the sky, but fell. The earth was covered with water then, and when the birds who lived on the water saw her plummeting toward them, they soared up to meet her. She floated down on their wings, and when they reached the water, they dove deep and brought up the earth. The Great Turtle then supported the new land on his back."

Intrigued, Liana reached for another berry. "Where did the Great Turtle come from?"

Christian looked puzzled. "Well, I haven't heard this tale in a while, but I believe he was simply here, like the waterfowl."

"That makes sense."

Christian laughed. "Wait until you hear the rest of the story. The woman was pregnant and had a daughter, who later had a son." Anticipating Liana's next question, he raised his hand to beg her patience. "Apparently there is

some argument as to whether his father was the Great Turtle or the North Wind, but he is thought to be half of
earth and half of the sky."

"A celestial warrior?"

"I've never heard him described in such poetic terms,
but it's a fine name. He had a twin brother, who was not
simply naughty, but evil. The good twin became the Crea-
tor who endowed the earth with its many blessings, while
his brother could have tutored the devil. To the Seneca,
it's a sacred story, but it's no more fantastic than that of
God creating Adam and Eve out of clay."

"No, I suppose not, but if there are people living in the
sky, why do you suppose only one woman ever fell to
earth?"

"Perhaps she was pushed," Christian offered with a low
chuckle, "or maybe she dove, like a person diving off a
cliff into a lake. Who knows? It's an ancient tale, and I like
it."

"Oh, I didn't mean that I didn't," Liana hastened to
explain. "Thank you for telling it."

"I don't follow the Seneca religion," he explained.
"They're just stories to me. You called me a heathen once,
but we share the same faith."

Mortified that he recalled her ugly remark, Liana
quickly apologized. "I should never have called you all
those awful names. I'm so sorry."

"I deserved every insult, Liana, and you know it. The
turkey looks ready. Shall we try a slice?"

He drew his knife as he rose, but the sight of the gleam-
ing weapon no longer disturbed her. He cut a hunk from
the breast and handed it to her. She waved it in the air a
few seconds to cool it, then had a bite. Tender and flavorful, it was easily the best turkey she had ever tasted. "It's
wonderful!" she exclaimed, then held out the rest for him.

Christian grasped her wrist and bent down to take the
sliver of meat from her fingers. His lips brushed her skin,

and she yanked her hand away. Amused rather than insulted, he removed the bird from the spit, laid it across two plates, and began to carve it. "I'm glad you like it. What we don't eat tonight, we'll save for breakfast, and I'll shoot one again tomorrow if you like."

"Can you be certain of finding another wild turkey?"

"No, but I can always try."

He smiled as he made the promise, and Liana was touched. "You are a good man, Christian. Please don't think I don't appreciate that."

Astonished by her compliment, Christian shook his head. "You must have been hungrier than I thought."

Liana took the plate he handed her. He had sliced the meat into strips she could easily pick up in her fingers. She was hungry, but not so dizzy and weak she had not been sincere. Thinking it a pity he did not realize that, she began eating rather than argue. The roast turkey truly was delicious, and she did not look up for several minutes. When she did, Christian was observing her with an amused smile.

"What's so funny?" she asked. "Do I look ridiculous for some reason?"

Christian swallowed the bite in his mouth before he replied. "No, you look wonderfully content. Your hair catches the fire's light, and you're eating with the same dainty bites you'd use at home. You make a very pretty picture. If I can find an artist with sufficient talent, I'd like him to paint you just as you look tonight."

"Sitting in the dirt, eating with my fingers?"

"Yes—believe me, it would be a masterpiece."

"And I suppose you'd hang it above the mantel in the parlor of the house you wish to build?"

Christian considered her suggestion a moment. "No, I'd want to keep it for my own enjoyment, not for company. So I'd hang it in our bedroom."

The thought of sharing a bedroom with him very nearly

made Liana choke. She looked around for a cup of water, and didn't find one. "I forgot to fetch the water. I'll go and get some now."

"No, it's here." Christian leaned over to scoop a cup from the bucket he had filled in the creek and handed it to her. He had taken note of precisely where she had gotten flustered and while he had thought he had pleased her the night they had made love, now he began to wonder. He wanted her to eat, though, and didn't mention sharing a bedroom again. The turkey was good, but even after eating his fill, he still had an unsatisfied appetite—for her.

He scooped up a handful of berries and longed to taste the juice that stained her lips. "I should have gone to your father," he said. "Even if he had kicked me off your porch, I should have done the right thing and asked his permission to call on you."

Liana ate several berries before commenting. "Have you forgotten that I begged you not to? He would have sent me to England and you would have accomplished nothing."

"Other than not being born, how could I have courted you more politely?"

"What an odd thing to say." The fire was dying down, but still provided enough light for her to see his expression clearly. He looked very serious, and rather sad.

"What's done is done, Christian, and despite my father's ugly show of temper, I don't feel as though I've done anything wrong. Does that sound absurd? I was raised in strict observance of society's rules, but despite the fact that I've broken a major one—or several, I suppose—I don't feel in the least bit guilty. You asked me yesterday if I'd betrayed myself, and I said no. Perhaps that's why I don't feel any sense of shame. I feel as though my parents have betrayed me, and that's what hurts so much."

"Ian has always been a fool," Christian murmured, "except for the night he saved my life. He was a true hero then."

"Yes, we should always be grateful to him for that."

"We?" Christian repeated softly.

Liana had spoken without considering what the pronoun implied. As she met Christian's mocking gaze, she saw the handsome young man she loved, but she had not forgotten that his thirst for danger meant more to him than she ever would. "Do all the Seneca love adventure more than their wives?" she asked.

Christian shook his head sadly. "Now you are the one asking odd things. I asked my father once if he didn't miss the Seneca. He told me that he did, but that he would miss Alanna more. It isn't adventure I love, either, Liana, but you."

At twilight, the forest was hushed. The birds, snug in their nests, were still, and the animals which loved the night had not yet begun to prowl. Crickets chirped in an ambitious rhythm, but Liana didn't hear them over the wild pounding of her heart. "I hope you're not just being gallant," she whispered.

"Why would I lie?"

"Because you have no choice, and you're trying to do what's right."

Frustrated that she understood so little, Christian was sorely tempted to wring her neck, but got up and excused himself instead. "I've kept you up so long you're not making any sense. Go to sleep. I'm going to check on the animals a last time."

Liana watched him fade into the shadows, but remained where she sat. Despite the fine meal, she felt slightly sick to her stomach and lacked the energy to move. Not wanting the fire to go out, she leaned over to grab several branches from the pile Christian had gathered earlier, but that was the extent of her initiative. She heard a rustling sound in the underbrush as what she distractedly assumed

was a raccoon or opossum circled the clearing. There were
a few berries left, and she considered tossing them into
the shadows for whatever was scavenging nearby, but fearing Christian would scold her for encouraging the pest,
she simply ate another and left the rest for him.

Coasting the edge of despair, she was unaware the noises
she had heard signaled danger until a fierce growl echoed
all around her. On her feet in an instant, she turned slowly,
but the circle of light thrown by the fire didn't extend far
enough for her to identify the beast who had made the
awful howl. "Christian!" she called in a trembling voice
that barely reached the surrounding trees.

Then came another, much louder growl, and she swallowed hard to clear the fear from her throat. This time
she screamed for Christian but before she heard an answering cry, a huge black bear lumbered into view. Rising
up on his hind legs, he swung his head from side to side
displaying wickedly sharp teeth Liana was certain he intended to sink deep into the most flavorful part of her.
She moved back to keep the fire between them, but the
beast continued to study her with a menacing gaze.

Responding to Liana's scream, Christian came running
into the clearing, but stopped the instant he saw the bear.
"Come to me," he urged Liana, who stood a dozen paces
to his left.

The bear's tiny eyes reflected the red glow of the fire,
and while Liana willed her feet to move, she took such
small steps she scarcely seemed to budge. The bear
dropped back down to all fours, but he did not take his
eyes off her. She took a step back, and he responded with
another challenging snarl.

Certain the bear was about to charge Liana, Christian
ran forward. He grabbed the last branch she had added
to the fire and swung it in a wide arc, flinging a sparkling
shower of cinders into the air. He shouted at the bear, his
call as deep and threatening as the shaggy beast's. When

the bear again rose up on his hind legs, he towered above Christian but the brave kept coming toward him, waving the burning branch. Then, with a daring leap, he smacked the beast on the nose with a mighty blow.

His tender flesh burned, the bear howled in pain and swung his paws at Christian but his razor-sharp claws caught only the fringe on his sleeve. Moving with sly cunning, Christian dodged yet another swipe, and then struck the belligerent bear a second time on the nose. Before the bear could react, he jabbed him hard in the stomach, scorching his thick, black fur.

Brandishing the flaming torch, Christian shouted again, "Run, or I'll roast you alive!"

The bear made another attempt to catch the wily brave with his claws, failed, and with a last outraged howl, dropped down into a clumsy run and fled. The whole encounter had taken less than a minute. Christian was not even breathing heavily as he tossed the branch back into the fire, but Liana couldn't stop shaking. Awed by Christian's remarkable display of courage, she didn't know what to say.

"A simple thank you doesn't seem nearly enough for saving my life," she mumbled.

Christian laughed until he slipped his arms around her waist and felt her trembling all over. He pulled her close and hugged her tight. "I would be a very poor husband if I let a bear eat my bride on our honeymoon."

Not seeing a bit of humor in their situation, Liana tried to pull away, but he refused to release her. "Is that why you were so quick to come to my rescue," she asked. "You didn't want your reputation sullied?"

The realization that nothing he did touched Liana's heart had finally become too much for Christian. He grabbed a handful of her hair to force her to look up at him. "I didn't take the time to consider anything. Did you stop to think the night I came to you for help after being shot?"

His dark eyes burned into hers with an accusing glow and Liana wondered if she might not have been better off with the bear. "No," she finally replied. "I didn't need to think, either."

His father had urged him to be gentle, and while such a sweet approach might have charmed Alanna, Christian doubted the defiant beauty in his arms would ever respond to anything other than strength. He lowered his head. "I would gladly kill any beast or man who dared to try and harm you," he breathed against the gentle curve of her throat.

His promise seared her skin, and believing his vow, Liana clung to him. She had been frightened of the bear, but even more terrified that it would kill him. He was wild, but the bravest man she had ever known. He may have sworn that he loved her out of duty, but he had just proven that he valued her life more highly than his own.

"Kiss me the way you used to," she begged.

Startled by her anguished plea, Christian drew back to search her face and found a confusing mixture of fear and love. It tore at him. "I don't want you to be afraid of me."

"Oh, Christian, my only fear is that I might lose you."

Relieved, his answering kiss was deliberately light, but her response was so eager he lost all sense of restraint. If she wanted him as badly as her kiss proclaimed, then he would not disappoint her. Not wanting her to change her mind, he kissed her until she was dizzy with desire, then carried her to the blanket where she had napped. He stretched out with her, savoring every berry-flavored kiss until their soft buckskin garments became far too confining.

She helped him pull his shirt off over his head, and he removed hers with a tug. When he discovered a short be-ribboned camisole underneath, he fumbled with the ties, but it soon landed on her shirt. Cradling her in his arms, he leaned down to kiss the sweet fullness of her breasts. She was all warm and soft, her skin as smooth as thick cream. Her pale pink nipples puckered beneath his tongue, and he sucked first one, and then the other into his mouth in grateful admiration of her beauty. She freed his hair from its tie, spilling it over his shoulders, and having no fear that she would stop him now, he paused again to help her out of the last of her clothes.

He then stood briefly to kick off his moccasins and cast off his breeches. As he rejoined Liana on the blanket, her skin felt cool against the heat of his, but holding her again thrilled him clear to his soul. The glowing fire contoured their flesh with flickering light and shadow, and captivated by her, he saw them as complete opposites who were, by some miracle, perfectly matched.

He kissed her again, his tongue swirling deep in a seductive invasion. Shifting his weight to free his hand, he traced the luscious curves of her slender figure, caressing her with a feather-light stroke before delving into her inner heat. She was already slippery with wanting him, but he teased her with his fingertips, and then with the tip of his hardened shaft. Such exquisite torture soon had her arching up against him. His lingering kisses silenced whatever plea she might have made, but he understood her need for release and, no longer able to deny his own, entered her with a slow, deep thrust.

Forcing himself to lie still, he savored her body's fiery welcome. Her hands were at his shoulders, in his hair, urging him toward a frantic coupling but he moved very slowly, his strokes tantalizing, shallow then deep as he traced her inner path. He wanted to bring her to rapture before finding his own glimpse of paradise, and when she tensed beneath him, her tremors of joy triggered his. He thrust to her depths, and lost in the wonder of her love, again surrendered his heart.

Liana held him locked in her embrace and, convinced they had done nothing wrong, she savored the blissful sweetness that filled her whole body and warmed her heart. However Christian had been born, she knew he had been destined to love her, and she would never again deny that she loved him. The only challenge would be to keep him safe from the danger he courted with every breath.

Twenty

"What if the bear comes back?" Liana whispered anxiously.

Christian combed his fingers through the thick folds of her hair and continued to gaze up at the stars. With the woman he adored in his arms, their sparkling brightness filled him with a joyous optimism. "Bears don't think the way men do," he explained, "and have no honor to avenge. I caused him pain, and he'll avoid me. If I had thought he would follow us and wait for another opportunity to menace you, I'd have killed him."

Focusing on the forest's mysterious darkness rather than the stars above, Liana was still afraid and spoke in a strained hush. "How can you be so confident? He was a very large bear."

"It isn't a matter of confidence, Liana. I would have done what had to be done."

Snuggled against him, Liana felt the steady beat of his heart. Knowing he was driven by the same remorseless rhythm to constantly prove himself wasn't at all reassuring. It was much too easy to foresee the day when he would finally be overmatched, and no matter how heroic his efforts, he would fail. She could not even imagine a greater tragedy.

"There are a great many things you feel compelled to do, aren't there?"

Christian gave her a fierce hug. "You ask too many questions. Am I going to have to lure a bear to our camp every night to frighten you into my arms?"

Liana rose to kiss him. "It wasn't the bear, but your willingness to risk your life to save mine that made me want you."

While he was enormously glad that she had, Christian thought her reasoning flawed. He fought to keep the annoyance out of his voice. "I wouldn't be much of a man if I hadn't. Why did you call for me if you doubted I'd come?"

As Liana settled down into his embrace, her answer was suddenly clear. "I didn't doubt you for an instant, Christian. You have a courageous tenacity no one could ever mistake."

Cheered, Christian began to smile. "Is that all?" he asked in a sly whisper.

"No, but without it, nothing else would matter."

Christian wanted her again, but when she sighed softly and yawned, he held her in a relaxed grasp as she fell asleep. She was an amazing woman, but he understood her. What she admired were courage and strength, but he knew those very same qualities were what she feared. He had not realized love was so complicated, but he hoped he would have a lifetime to learn all the secrets hidden in Liana's heart.

Taking care not to tire her again, Christian didn't insist they move ahead on Wednesday, nor on Thursday either. Instead, they fished in the creek, gathered berries, picked wildflowers, roasted another wild turkey, shared stories of their childhoods, and made love until Liana felt strong enough to enjoy travel. This time Christian slowed their pace so their days were as pleasantly relaxed as their nights. The journey became what he had meant it to be, a joining of their hearts and lives in the most magnificent of settings.

The splendor of the heavily wooded mountain range

filled each day's journey with a sense of discovery and wonder, but Christian and Liana lost none of their initial appreciation of each other. Surrounded by spectacular vistas
as they reached the crest of the Allegheny Mountains and
began the descent into the Ohio Valley, they shared a sense
that their travels were leading not merely over great dis-
tances, but inward as well. Christian's sly smiles carried
new meaning, and Liana believed his tender promises were
real.

The Kanawha River was wide and deep, the water tumbling down from the mountain heights in such thundering
torrents that Liana wasn't even tempted to wade out into
it as she bathed. She hugged the rocks along the shore
and splashed hurriedly after washing her hair. The sun
warmed her body as she patted herself dry with the camisole she intended to wash, but before she had donned a
stitch of clean clothes, Christian stepped from behind a
maple and pulled her into his arms.

Melting into his buckskins, Liana tried to affect the outrage she didn't actually feel. "Were you spying on me the
whole time I bathed?"

Christian nibbled her lower lip. "No, of course not. I
merely kept watch to make certain you were safe. Can you
think of a nice way to thank me?"

Liana's lazy laugh conveyed her doubt, but because her
own desire was as natural as his, she did not lack for ways
to satisfy his request. She loved teasing him, too. She
rubbed against him and rejoiced in her own power as she
felt him grow hard. "If you shoot another wild turkey, I'll
pluck the feathers."

Christian nodded. "Yes, that's a good start. Then what?"

"I might sing for you while you roast it."

"Yes, that would be very nice. Then what?"

Liana slipped her hands under the fringed tail of his
shirt to caress his back. His skin was smooth and the muscles rippled beneath her touch. She reached up to give

his earlobe a teasing bite. "Then I'd be wonderful company while we ate supper."

"Good. Then what?"

"Then I'll make you very happy that you brought me along, but must we wait until then?" she asked with a seductive purr.

It was Christian who laughed now, and he took Liana's hand and led her up the riverbank to the blanket he had already spread on the ground. He pulled her down beside him and without bothering to remove his clothes, he kissed her deeply and brushed his palm over her breast, lightly tickling the sensitive crest. She trembled beneath his touch as he nuzzled the hollow of her throat, then licked her nipples into rosy buds.

The softness of her flesh provided a sharp contrast to his muscular leanness and he loved the gentle, feminine sweetness of her. He spread lazy kisses down her ribs, then thrust his tongue into her navel and chuckled through her giggles. His hands were on her hips now, holding her fast while he continued to explore her graceful curves with playful nibbles. Moving lower, he combed the triangle of bright red curls and slid his hand along her inner thigh to separate her legs. She was used to his intimate caresses now and welcomed his touch with relaxed anticipation, but today he wanted more.

Moving down beside her with an easy stretch, he rubbed his cheek against her knee, and licked a last droplet of water from her river-cooled skin. He wanted to warm her clear through, and tightening his hold, traced a teasing trail of whispered kisses along the tender flesh of her thigh. He felt her hands in his hair loosing the tie, but she was guiding him, not pushing him away.

He pressed his mouth against her crease, then parted the folds. He licked the length of her, and paused at the top to flick the delicate bud with the tip of his tongue to bestow the most delicious excitement. Then, using the whole length and breadth of his tongue, he caressed her again. With a languid joy, he savored her salty taste with broad strokes and light tracings until she thrust her hips to press against his mouth in grateful surrender. He rolled his tongue and plunged deep with quick jabs, making her writhe with longing. He then sucked gently at the tender nubbin crowning her being and felt the ecstasy shoot through her with a sudden jolt that lingered in joyous spasms.

Before her rapture had blurred into a mellow bliss, he shed his clothes and entered her with shallow thrusts he timed to her gasps. Coaxing another burst of exquisite joy from her depths, he smothered her moans with deep kisses that pierced her heart. The most ardent of lovers, Christian enticed Liana's passion to a wild crest that flooded through him like rolling thunder and had he died in that instant, his life would have been more glorious than he had ever dreamed.

Lost in that magnificent moment, a long while passed before he found the strength to prop himself on his elbows and look down at Liana. "You turn my blood to flame, but having you a thousand times won't quench the fire."

Delighted he would use his gift for words to please her rather than incite rebellion, Liana reached up to caress his cheek. He did not have a heavy beard, but shaved every morning. By late afternoon, he had only a hint of stubble, but she liked the rough, masculine feel of him. "Shall we keep count?"

Christian kissed her palm very gently. "It's too late. I'm so bewitched by you I've already lost track."

Raising her arms, Liana laced her fingers at his nape and with a gentle tug drew him into a lingering kiss. "I don't want to count something as precious as this, as though it might some day come to an end."

"I can't even think with you in my arms," Christian confessed against her lips. He kissed her lashes, her brows, and the delicate crescent of her ears. Her bruises had faded to faint shadows, but he still remembered, and hated Ian Scott for causing them even as he loved her.

Having traveled the Ohio Valley, Christian knew which outposts were worth visiting. It wasn't a matter of which had the better supply of goods or the best prices, but which had an owner who had treated his father with the respect he deserved. Those were the places he intended to patronize to replenish their supplies, but at the first, they found only a burned-out ruin rather than the prosperous trading post he had recalled. Stunned, he drew Lion to a halt and raised his hand.

"Wait here," he told Liana. He dismounted and slung his bow and quiver over his shoulder, then drew his knife. "I don't like the way this looks."

Keeping a careful watch on her, Christian prowled all that remained of the small fortress. Lying in silent ruin, a single wall of logs and three stone chimneys were the deserted remnants of the once-bustling outpost. Encased in stone fireplaces, cooking fires did not usually spread up and over the walls of a dwelling, much less to the exterior stockade. Lanterns could always be dropped, but burning oil was easily stamped out on dirt floors.

Suspicious the fire had not been accidental, he took his time searching for its source, but the destruction was so complete, he had little luck until he felt the snap of a charred arrow beneath his foot. Pulling it out of the ashes, he studied the angle of the feathers and the faint trace of a painted design. Convinced he knew what had happened, he hurried back to Liana.

"The fire was no accident. The Ohio Valley was once the hunting grounds of many tribes—Seneca, Mingo, Shawnee, and Cherokee, among others. The king made promises to respect Indian lands, but that hasn't stopped settlers from pouring into the Ohio Valley." He raised the blackened arrow. "Each tribe marks its arrows differently. This belonged to a Shawnee brave. They may have attacked this outpost to push out the white men, but they'll never succeed."

Envisioning further senseless destruction, Christian stared past the ruins, but Liana was completely unnerved. "Will they come back?" she asked in a breathless rush. "Are we in grave danger here?"

Christian rested his hand on her knee. "The ashes are cold, and whoever made the raid was probably gone before the flames consumed the roof. Besides, you're in no danger as long as you're with me. I'm not a white man, remember?"

Looking into his dark brown eyes, Liana saw something else entirely. "You're as much white as Seneca," she insisted.

"True, but only when it suits me." He tossed the broken arrow aside and remounted his horse. "I've been preoccupied with other things," he confided with a wink, "and not following news from the valley the last few months. Let's go on and see what we can learn at the next outpost."

Liana's mouth had suddenly gone paper dry. "Do we dare?"

She was so obviously terrified, Christian had a difficult time not being insulted. "Haven't I already proven that I can take care of you?"

Liana tugged on the brim of her hat to shade her face before she responded with a hesitant nod. "Yes, and exceedingly well, but you didn't anticipate marauding savages."

Christian nudged Lion with his heels. "What's your real worry? That we'll be attacked, or that I'll run off with them?"

Liana urged Tiger into place beside him. "That isn't the least bit funny, Christian."

Christian was far more worried than he would allow her to see, but at the same time, he was disappointed by how quickly she had reduced men who might be his kin to savages. "We'll see what news we can gather in the next few days, and if it's all bad, I promise to start for home. Will that make you happy?"

There were sycamores growing nearby, along with sugar maples, and willows. As she searched the surrounding woods with a troubled glance, she imagined an Indian, his bow already drawn, his arrow aimed at her heart, hiding behind every single tree. "Will we reach another settlement before nightfall?" she asked fretfully.

"We might. I haven't been through here in over a year and there could be many new settlements." Christian did not confide the opinion that any neighboring settlers' cabins would have been attacked along with the outpost, but he was positive if any had existed they would also be deserted. "We'll stay off the well-worn trails for the rest of the day and that should keep us from suddenly happening upon anyone you'd rather not meet."

Liana nodded, but was scarcely reassured. "Did you find any graves at the outpost?"

"Not a one. An elderly man and his son ran the place. They must have gotten out safely, along with whatever travelers there might have been visiting. The raid was obviously a success, though. Just look how frightened you are, and the valley's other settlers would surely have been equally scared when they heard about it."

"How can you be so flippant," Liana complained, "when Alanna lost her whole family in an Indian raid?"

Christian gave a sharp tug on Lion's reins to bring him to a halt and Liana stopped Tiger at his side. "I haven't forgotten Alanna's anguish, but the Abenaki were bloodthirsty demons the French priests easily whipped into a wild frenzy of hatred for the English. That any man, savage or otherwise, would slaughter helpless children is thoroughly reprehensible. But until we know exactly what's happened here, let's not start conjuring up hellish visions of murdering renegades. Maybe only an outpost or two were burned to protest the presence of settlers on Indian land. If that's the case, then I'll gladly light the next torch."

Liana rolled her eyes toward heaven. The last few days had been so tranquil she had forgotten how dearly Christian loved to rebel. "Just how many causes will you have time to fight in a single lifetime?" she asked. "Isn't battling the king enough for you?"

Rather than pale with fright, a furious blush filled Liana's cheeks and, reminded of the afternoon he had first swept her into his arms, Christian could not help but laugh. "I will admit to possessing a passion for justice, but you need never fear it will ever lessen my passion for you." He nodded slightly and continued their trek through the woods. He did not have to look back to know Liana was following, when she had not bothered to whisper her curses.

Still following the Kanawha River, Christian continued as long as there was sunlight to guide their way. When they made camp for the night, he caught half a dozen trout while Liana gathered enough wood to light an inferno rather than a small cooking fire. Noting her preoccupied frown, he appreciated her burning off her anger in productive work, but she did not appear to have used up nearly enough to make it a pleasant evening.

"Do you love me?" he asked in a challenging tone.

Caught completely off guard, Liana did not know what to say. He was staring at her, his mouth set in a determined line, and she knew better than to try and avoid such a sensitive question. Despite their earlier argument, she found it easy to smile. "I can't remember when I didn't love you," she admitted softly. "Perhaps it was as early as the first time I saw you in town with your father. I thought you were so handsome, but Mother scolded me and told me not to stare. I kept looking for you, though, in town, or church, or during the entertainments at Publick Times when the square was full."

Christian had expected a simple yes, or, God forbid, a no; overwhelmed by the sweetness of her response he was slow in moving forward. "I wish I had known. I would have stalked you years ago if I had."

Liana waited for him to come close. He ran his hands down her arms and his touch gave her chills. "No, we're in so much trouble now, that had I met you any earlier, I would have been banished to England for sure. You would have forgotten me and it would be another woman entirely standing here with you now."

The fire sent dancing streamers of light through her hair, turning the deep red to gold, and Christian could not even imagine taking another woman as his wife. "I would have followed you," he swore. "An ocean wouldn't have stopped me from loving you."

Liana was already well aware of how seriously he pursued his aims, but she longed to be enough all by herself to make him feel complete. Sadly, she doubted that would ever happen. "You might have been too young to follow me."

"I was never that young." Christian wrapped her in his arms and hugged her tight. "You must trust me, Liana. I'll never fail you."

Liana rubbed her cheek against his shoulder. His buckskins provided as sensuous a delight as his bare skin, and she thought it remarkable such a strong young man was so comfortable in these incredibly soft clothes. She slid her arms around his waist to return his fond hug. "I know you'd never intentionally let me down," she said.

"Nor unintentionally, either," Christian argued.

In Liana's view, every time he chose the more dangerous

path, he already had. She kept that opinion to herself, but a sudden loud, rasping cough from the edge of their clearing made her gasp. Certain they had been surrounded by a fierce band of hostile Shawnee, she clung to Christian even as she twisted around to see them, but there was only one heavy-set trapper looking their way. Embarrassed, she wondered how long he had been observing them.

The trapper removed his raccoon skin cap with a graceful flourish and arched into a low bow. "Forgive me, ma'am, I didn't mean to startle you."

Liana scanned the path behind him, but saw only a mule. The trapper's buckskins were ragged, and his thinning gray hair was matted against his scalp. His scraggly beard was stained with tobacco juice, and while he was regarding them with a gap-toothed smile, she couldn't bring herself to welcome him to their camp. Christian, however, left her to take a step toward their unexpected visitor.

"We came upon a burned outpost today, and the fire was no accident. What news do you have of the valley?" he asked the older man.

"Oh, I could tell you stories all night, but I could do with a good meal first."

Christian was no more anxious to have the slovenly man's company than Liana, but gestured toward the fire. "Come and sit down with us. We were about to have some trout and biscuits. Will that suit you?"

"Whatever you're having will be fine. Just give me a minute to see to my mule."

"Take your time," Liana called to him. "I haven't started the biscuits yet." She waited until the trapper had led his mule around to the far side of the clearing where their animals were tethered before speaking to Christian. "Must we entertain him?" she whispered.

"It's never wise to make an enemy of a man by turning him away when he's already seen there's food," Christian replied softly. "You needn't worry. I'll keep a close eye on him, and he might know something valuable."

"And he might not," Liana answered through clenched teeth.

Christian thought her anger charming. "Little old men sleep very soundly. You needn't fear he'll spoil the night."

Liana refused to believe he was being serious. She placed her hands on her hips to show him she most certainly was. "If you think I'll make love to you with him near, sleeping or not, you're very wrong."

Christian nodded to concede the point, but as she bent down to remove the sack of flour from their supplies, her darkly determined frown did not lighten. He had taught her how to bake passable biscuits, but he doubted she would give much effort to making them light and flavorful that night. "Why are you angry," he leaned down to ask, "because he's here, or because we can't make love?"

Liana glared up at him through a thick sweep of long lashes and hissed, "I'm not angry—I'm scared to death!"

Christian squatted down beside her. "Had he wished us any harm, he would have taken a shot at me rather than interrupting us with a polite cough. Trappers often share a meal with whatever company they can find. We're not in any danger. Let's just see what he knows."

"Do I have any choice?"

"No, not tonight, but when you're mistress of the fine house I'm going to build, you need never entertain anyone you don't like."

Liana pretended a rapt interest in measuring the flour, but she did not understand how he could possibly believe there would be anyone to entertain. All her parents' friends would surely shun them. Add to that the divisiveness of politics, and a great many more people would have a reason to avoid them. Tears filled her eyes, but she kept her head down so Christian wouldn't see. After all, they wouldn't be completely alone. His family was large, and they would stand by them.

"I'll look forward to that day," she assured him.

"So will I, because we'll have all the privacy we'll need to make every night as special as tonight should have been."

He rose and set the skillet on the fire to fry the trout. When he got them cooking, he turned to the trapper, and Liana quickly wiped her eyes on her sleeve. Christian made such sweet promises at times and she hoped every one came true. She scolded herself then, because she could not seem to find the same faith in the future to make equally endearing promises to him.

When she at last placed the pan of biscuits over the fire to bake and glanced the trapper's way, he again removed his cap. "Name's Josiah Peabody, ma'am, and I'm mighty grateful for your invitation to stay for supper. Ladies are getting right scarce in the valley and it's sure nice to meet such a pretty one."

Now that Liana had a better look at him, she was even more repelled than she had been at first. Even with the fire sending up hickory-scented smoke, she could smell the odor of stale sweat. They were camped near the Kanawha, but clearly he had not bothered to bathe in weeks.

"Thank you, Mr. Peabody. We're anxious to hear your news." Liana sat down and gestured for him to take his place opposite her, while Christian sat down by her side. "I'm surprised you didn't mistake us for Indians."

Josiah thought Liana was making a joke and laughed so hard he again broke into a rasping cough. "Forgive me, but I saw your red hair and recognized you for white despite your buckskin clothes. A white woman wouldn't ever be cuddling up to an Indian. I will admit your husband gave me a bit of a start when he first turned my way, but he spoke like a gentleman and that put my mind at ease."

"Did it, now?"

"Why, yes, of course," the trapper vowed. "That sure smells good. Nothing like hot biscuits and fresh trout on a cool night."

Liana glanced toward Christian, who just shook his head. It was plain to him that Josiah Peabody wasn't going to provide a particle of information until he had been fed, but she was badly disappointed. "Excuse me, I don't want the biscuits to burn."

"No, ma'am, that would be a terrible waste seeing as how you went to all the trouble to make them."

Liana wanted to toss one at him, but composed herself. The biscuits were almost done and the trout were sizzling in the skillet. She turned the fish, then got out three plates and utensils. Preferring to remain by the fire rather than coax conversation out of their taciturn guest, she tapped her foot impatiently until she was certain the trout were thoroughly cooked. She gave both Christian and Josiah two trout and three biscuits, while she took only one trout and two biscuits for herself.

"If you don't mind my saying so, ma'am, you ought to eat a bit more," Josiah said. "A woman needs a little padding, if you know what I mean."

Afraid she knew precisely what he meant, Liana just nodded and peeled the flaky white fish away from the bony spine. "I always eat my fill, Mr. Peabody. Now why don't you tell us what you know."

"Wouldn't make fit dinner conversation, ma'am." Peabody ate the simple meal with gusto, and when Christian encouraged him, he took the last trout and the remaining biscuits. He savored every morsel and then licked his fingers when he finally set his empty plate aside. "I don't suppose you have any rum with you?"

"No, we don't," Christian replied. Moving closer to Liana, he took her hand. "You've been fed as promised, sir. Now give us your report."

Josiah responded with a restless snort, and then in one disgusting gesture wiped his nose on the back of his hand and dried his hand on his breeches. "Well now, I can't just jump into it because like strong tea, the troubles have been brewing for a mighty long time. Trappers always have plenty of Indian friends, and I have my share, so I hear everything from both sides. I even had myself a Shawnee squaw for a year or two."

When both Liana and Christian raised their brows in disbelief, Joseph paused. "Yes, ma'am, and a fine woman she was. I was gone too much to suit her so she took up with a Shawnee brave and I didn't blame her. I respect the Indians' ways, you see, but settlers are a different breed.

"They've been trickling into the valley these last few years, hungry for land they don't see the Indians using. None of the trappers is happy about it, me included. Settlers start clearing land and damming up the rivers to water crops, and before you know it, they've driven away the otter and beaver. The fox gets scarce and the mink disappear. The Indian can't find deer to hunt."

"Please, Mr. Peabody, we're aware of those problems. They've happened elsewhere," Christian commented, "but if outposts are being attacked, something more is going on here."

"Oh, there have been attacks," Josiah readily admitted. "Are you sure you don't have just a drop or two of rum?"

"Positive," Liana assured him.

Josiah sighed sadly with disappointment. He noticed a cluster of crumbs clinging to the shirt stretched over his rounded stomach and brushed them away. "You're right. Everywhere the white man goes, the story's the same. It's a sad story, too, ain't it?"

"Mr. Peabody," Christian complained, "it's getting late. If you've no more to tell us, we'll say good night."

Peabody raised his hand. "Now don't rush me or I might get the facts confused." He paused and studied the fire a long moment before clearing his throat and continuing. "There's a Mingo chief by the name of *Tahgahjute*. His English name is Logan. Lives up at Yellow Creek."

"Yes, I know the man," Christian said.

"Good, then you can understand this story," Peabody replied. "Now, I readily admit to liking a sip of rum now and then, but there's other men who like a good deal more. There's one by the name of Greathouse. He and his friends got real drunk one day and killed off Logan's family. Murdered every last one. No man can take that, and when Logan called for vengeance, other tribes joined in. They've been tearing up the whole valley. Murdering settlers, running off livestock, burning houses. I don't blame them, either. The whites may have started it, but the Indians mean to finish it."

Liana listened in absolute horror as Peabody began to describe atrocities in such brutal detail it was plain he was relishing every shocking revelation. "That is enough," Christian cautioned. "I'll not allow you to frighten my wife any further. Sleep near the edge of the clearing and be gone at first light."

"Well now," Peabody said. "Didn't you invite me to stay and give you the news?"

Christian got to his feet and gave Liana a hand up. "Yes, and that was obviously a mistake. Good night."

Peabody let out a frustrated growl as he hauled himself to his feet. "Nice couple like you ought not to be out here in the woods. The Shawnee will kill you quick, son, but they'll make your pretty little wife long to be dead."

"Not another word." Christian took a step toward the trapper. "I'm Seneca but I speak the Shawnee tongue and I've no fear of them."

"Seneca, but—" Peabody sent a hasty glance toward Liana and then, eyes widening, stared at Christian. "I saw it,

I swear I did, but she was what threw me off. I'm leaving now. Thanks for the supper, ma'am, but I think I'm better off on my own tonight."

Grateful he was leaving, for whatever cause, Liana watched him fetch his mule. He reloaded his pack and led the animal away with such haste his revolting stench had yet to leave the air before he was gone. She grabbed a branch and tossed it on the fire. "Do you want to bury the bones, or shall I?"

"I'll do it." Christian scooped all that was left of their dinner onto one plate and carried it away. When he returned, he took all the pans and plates down to the river to wash, but even that chore didn't cool him off. "We'll start for home in the morning. It's bad enough that we stumbled into this, but I won't drag you through a war in hopes both sides will see me as an ally. I am not that great a fool."

Liana didn't understand his anger. "You're not any kind of a fool," she argued. "Why are you letting Peabody upset you so? He isn't worth it."

Christian just looked at her, his glance as forbidding as the deepening night. "Aren't you angry, too? He insulted us both."

Liana grasped his arm. "I'm sorry. I should have stopped him when he made that ignorant remark about white women cuddling up to Indians. It was just that I was so apprehensive about what he might tell us, I couldn't wait to hear it. That was a mistake. If anyone else ever dares make such a rude comment, I'll interrupt before he's finished. I'm not ashamed to be your wife, Christian. Please don't think I am."

A slow smile spread across Christian's face. Liana had said the words herself, and with such fervor he could not mistake her sincerity. While he was disappointed he had been able to show her such a small sample of the Ohio Valley, he had accomplished all he had intended. Besides, it was time to write another pamphlet. He pulled his lovely bride into a fond embrace, but he was already imagining new ways to insult the king.

Twenty-one

Sean O'Keefe reached for Dominique's hand as soon as they were settled on the wooden bench. With a charming view of the Barclays' garden and the James River, it was an idyllic spot and he wished to make the most of his opportunity to be alone with her. "There's been no word from Christian?" he asked, then silently cursed his stupidity for mentioning the man.

Dominique immediately withdrew her hand from his and began to toy with her fan. Fashioned of the same lavender silk as her dress, it was a superb implement for flirtatious gestures, but also served as a wonderful distraction when she was distressed. "No, but then we didn't expect to hear from him. What we have learned of the situation in the Ohio Valley isn't good, though, and quite naturally, we're all terribly worried. Is it true Lord Dunmore might lead the Virginia Militia into the valley to put an end to the unrest?"

"Unrest is scarcely a strong enough word to describe what the murdering savages have been up to there," Sean responded. Dominique glanced away, and he knew he had made another careless error when the Barclays had chosen to include savages in their family. Trying to make up for it, he reached out to caress her cheek with his fingertips. Her skin was incredibly soft, and he longed to lean over and kiss her.

"You're so lovely, Dominique, let's not waste what little time we have together this afternoon discussing anything other than ourselves."

Dominique turned toward his touch, but then swatted his hand away with a gentle swipe of her fan. "We have only just become acquainted, Captain. Personal topics would be most inappropriate."

Ignoring her rebuke, Sean focused on her lips' seductive pout. He had heard other men praise the fair beauty's creamy skin, azure eyes, and pale yellow curls, but he found her mouth her most enchanting feature. He longed to trace the outline of her lips with the tip of his tongue, and then kiss her so deeply he would never forget her taste. With an easy motion he hoped she would not notice, he raised his left arm and rested it along the back of the bench, gently encircling her although they weren't touching.

"That's where you're wrong," he argued persuasively. "It's the only way we'll ever become friends."

Dominique was used to manipulating the emotions of ardent boys. At thirty, Sean was a full-grown man who presented an intriguing challenge, but she felt equal to it. "Just how close a friend do you wish to become, sir?"

Her question was asked with a charming insouciance, and yet her gaze danced with teasing mischief. Amused, Sean slid his hand along the back of the bench and wound his fingers in the curls that had escaped her lace-edged cap. "I want to become the best male friend you could ever hope to have, Dominique. I want to know you better than any man ever has or ever will and I can promise that you'll enjoy every single minute of our friendship."

Dominique watched Sean's gaze stray to the fullness of her bosom, and refrained from taking a deep breath. "Are all the king's officers as forward as you, Captain?"

"I don't believe I'm being forward. I admire you enormously, and there's no reason to hide my feelings. I'm sure you already know without my having to speak them aloud, anyway. You're such a popular dancing partner that I have little chance to be with you at parties. If I seem too eager now, it's entirely your fault. No man could resist you."

Dominique rose and folded her fan. "You're beginning to sound like all the others, Captain, and I had so hoped for something original from you."

Astonished by her coolly voiced rejection, Sean was on his feet in an instant. "Perhaps I was too forward. Why don't we stroll down by the river, and I'll do my best to make more acceptable conversation."

Dominique fanned herself with an impatient rhythm. "Christian is your real interest, isn't he? Or perhaps you're still smarting from Liana's elopement with him. Whatever your reason for coming to call, I doubt it has anything to do with me and I would like you to leave."

"You couldn't be more mistaken," Sean protested. "I'll admit I admired Liana for a time, but not anymore, and it was never as deeply as I admire you. As for Christian, I still believe he's involved in those heinous pamphlets and it's my duty to investigate their source."

Glancing away, Dominique found the river provided a more entertaining view than the handsome officer. "And you believe flattering me will somehow facilitate that goal?"

"No!" Dominique was easily the most vexing young woman Sean had ever met and were she not such a fascinating creature, he would have left at once. Instead, he began to peel off his red coat. "If my uniform confuses you, then I'll remove it so you'll see only me."

"Mon Dieu," Dominique gasped. "Just how much of yourself do you intend to expose?"

Sean flung his coat on the bench and began to unbutton his waistcoat. "How much will it take to distract you from my occupation?"

"That is more than enough." Tall and lean, even in his shirtsleeves, white breeches, and black boots, Sean was still extremely attractive, but Dominique doubted his sincerity and his declarations of affection rang false. She eyed him coldly. "I mistrust your motives, sir, and it is not solely because of your uniform. You cannot accuse my cousin of sedition in one breath and attempt to seduce me in the next. Do not call on me again."

Sean grabbed his coat and caught up with her before she had taken three steps toward the house. "Please, Dominique. This has all been a ridiculous misunderstanding. Allow me to call on you again, and I assure you my behavior will be above reproach."

Again toying with her fan, Dominique refused to meet his gaze. "You are an exasperating man, Captain, and I doubt you'll ever change."

Sean moved close before she could step away. "I'm also your devoted servant. Please don't send me away."

Dominique glanced up, her blue eyes filled with a suspicious glint. "Did you say the same pretty things to Liana?"

Sean's expression darkened instantly. As he saw it, Liana had never cared for him. She had been seeing Christian behind his back, and he felt badly abused. "I can't recall a single conversation I had with her," he exclaimed, "but she was the one who was insincere, not I." Dominique looked merely puzzled rather than disgusted with him now, and seizing the initiative, he pulled her into his arms and kissed her with all the passion she continually aroused within him.

Rather than a cool sweetness he had expected to have to warm, Dominique's lips burned his with a taste of fire. Consumed by desire, he clung to her all the more tightly. The scent of her perfume washed through him, and the soft silk of her skirts whispered against his thighs. He wanted her so badly, he would not have let go, but Byron Barclay demanded otherwise.

"Captain, you disappoint me," Byron shouted as he strode toward them.

Sean released Dominique and stepped back, but not before noticing her befuddled gaze and the way her short gasps caused her delectable bosom to swell. It was plain his kiss had an effect on her, but before he could fathom how much, her expression resumed its usual innocent sweetness. He hurriedly pulled on his coat and yanked on the cuffs to adjust the fit.

"Forgive me, sir. I meant no disrespect."

Byron took Dominique's hand and drew her close to his side. "Just what was it you did mean then?"

Sean shook his head sheepishly. "Just to make Dominique like me as much as I like her."

Surprised by the officer's candor, Byron softened his tone slightly. "You would do better to court her in a more respectful fashion, Captain. In fact, if you can't promise to behave as a gentleman must, I will forbid you to return."

Dominique looked from her father to Sean, amazed to hear them argue a decision she felt should be entirely hers. She had been kissed a time or two, but never with Sean's desperate wildness. It had been a dizzying experience, and not at all unpleasant. It was also frightening, for he was a man, after all, and could be expected to have increasingly demanding appetites.

Striking the proper docile pose was difficult, but she waited until her father had gotten Sean's word that he would be better behaved in the future before she allowed a small smile to cross her lips. Leaving Sean in the garden, she walked with her father back toward the house, but she turned once, and sent the officer a fleeting smile calculated to insure his return. It wasn't until they had entered the house that she realized her father was as angry with her as he had been with Sean.

"Just tell me what you thought you were doing, Dominique, because it is a complete mystery to me why you would allow a British officer to kiss you."

Dominique licked her lips nervously. "You needn't be outraged. I didn't give him any indication that I'd welcome his kiss. In fact, I'd already asked him to leave when he grabbed me. I'm merely trying to confuse the man, which I believe I did. I don't want him to be so suspicious of Christian. If he becomes fascinated with me, then he'll take scant note of anyone else here."

Byron clasped his hands behind his back and rocked back on his heels. "Did it occur to you that he might be attentive to you merely as an excuse to visit us and spy?"

"Yes, of course it did," Dominique admitted. "But after that kiss, I don't believe he's interested in anything but me."

"Well, I saw something quite different," Byron replied. "I think each of you is using the other as a means to an end, and I forbid you to take it any further."

Dominique's sultry smile was the same one she used so effectively on other men. "You didn't forbid him to call on me," she reminded him.

"No, because it wouldn't have been wise to insult an officer, and I have another excellent reason I'll not discuss."

They were standing in the back hall, whispering so as not to be overheard by the rest of the family. Dominique took the precaution of glancing toward the stairs to make certain their privacy was assured before she revealed more. "Didn't Beau tell you I know Christian's writing the pamphlets? You needn't keep secrets from me."

Shocked and disappointed that their once-tight inner circle had grown another bulge, Byron sagged against the wall. "Did you tell your sister and little brother?"

"No, they're too young to be trusted with such incriminating knowledge."

Byron took Dominique's arm and started for the stairs.

"And so are you, young lady. I want you to discuss your involvement with Captain O'Keefe with your mother. She'll tell you just how dangerous it is to manipulate men's feelings, no matter how noble your motives."

Dominique laughed. "She's always gotten away with manipulating yours."

"She does not!" Byron protested adamantly, but in his heart, he knew Dominique had learned more from her delightfully feminine French mother than he had ever stopped to consider.

Rain marred Christian and Liana's journey home, forcing them to take shelter among a grove of sugar maples. Christian constructed a hasty tent of fallen branches angled against a lower limb growing at a convenient height. Liana helped him thatch it with clumps of leaves and they crawled inside. Cozy if not water-tight, it at least kept them from being drenched.

Christian hugged Liana close. "I'm sorry this trip hasn't been better."

Liana leaned into a kiss. "You're not responsible for the violence in the valley or this weather. Just think of it as an adventure."

"Yes, it's been that," Christian agreed. Liana had grown increasingly confident the farther behind they had left the Ohio Valley. Now camped beside the New River, they both felt safe. He peered out at the gray afternoon. "If it stops raining soon, we'll travel a few more miles."

Liana felt no sense of urgency to move on when she doubted they could maintain the peace they had found together here surrounded by others. "I don't care if we ever leave," she mused quietly.

"Then I won't exhaust myself building you a fine house, if this crude hut satisfies you."

Stretched out on her stomach, Liana rested her cheek

on her crossed arms. "I'd rather not think past this minute. It may be cold and damp, but at least it's tranquil."

Christian reached out to brush aside a wet strand of hair that had fallen across her eyes. "We haven't had many of those moments, have we?"

Liana sighed softly. "No, and I fear we never will."

The wistfulness of her tone saddened Christian and he ran his hand down her back and over the gentle swell of her buttocks. "You've gotten too thin. I haven't fed you nearly enough."

Liana smiled to reassure him. "I've always been slender. You just never saw me out of my clothes. Wrapped in so many yards of brocade, it was impossible to tell how I really looked."

"No, you always looked good." Christian watched Liana's soft smile widen and loved her so dearly he feared his heart might burst. Unable to give voice to the emotions tightening his throat, he watched her fall asleep while the rain's gentle patter on the leaves above played a lullaby. Even sound asleep, he felt her presence so strongly that she was with him still. Her lashes made shadows on her cheeks, the deep red contrasting sharply with the pale cream of her skin. Arielle's hat had done its job and shaded her face so perfectly she hadn't freckled, although he was certain she must have as a child.

They had missed so much not being friends as children. They had lived so close, and yet Ian had erected a barrier of hatred between their plantations that only a man could surmount. "I love you," he whispered, as content as she to spend a rainy afternoon in a leafy tent without a single piece of the magnificent silver or delicate crystal that would surround them when they returned home. He knew home was here with Liana, and, closing his eyes, he hoped to dream of her.

* * *

The afternoon Christian and Liana finally reached home was dry and clear. The tobacco plants were nearly two feet tall. Their light green leaves were reaching toward the sky and men with hoes were moving along the rows, lopping off the weeds. After the first had sighted them, others stood and waved. David Slauson yelled a welcome home, and it soon became a chorus of good wishes.

"It sounds as though you've been missed," Liana said.

"No, they're all happy to see you."

Liana laughed at his flattery. "They don't even know me."

"I know, but they would like to. Look, here comes Falcon. Doesn't he look several inches taller?"

Liana did not recall how tall Falcon had been, but looking at him, she saw a younger version of Christian and found it easy to smile. "He's as handsome as you."

"Impossible," Christian swore with a rumbling chuckle. He stopped in the yard rather than at the stable and helped Liana down from Tiger. Not that she needed any assistance, but he enjoyed giving it too much to stand back. "I want to hear only good news," he called to Falcon.

"It's very good," Falcon assured him. "Welcome home, Liana," he added shyly. "Everyone has missed you."

"But not me?" Christian asked.

"Have you been away, too?" Falcon teased, certain he was fast enough to dodge Christian's playful blow.

Liana laughed as the brothers fell into a hearty hug, then quickly drew away. Arielle called to them from the porch, and as Liana turned toward Christian's aunt, she felt a sudden, painful stab of regret that they wouldn't receive an equally warm welcome at her parents' home. Hiding her sorrow, she took her husband's hand and walked with him to the door.

Hearing a burst of greetings, Byron left the study, Alanna came downstairs, Johanna and Dominique appeared, Jean and Belle came running from the docks, and Hunter came in from the fields. Along with Falcon and Arielle, they all crowded into the parlor, and Christian immediately missed Beau. He waited while everyone found a seat, but then could no longer contain his curiosity.

"Where's Beau?" he had to ask. "Is he still too angry with me to say hello?"

"He's in town or he'd be here," Byron quickly replied. "Dunmore is organizing troops to quell the disturbance in the Ohio Valley and he went to get the latest reports. Did you see any of the fighting?"

As everyone leaned forward, their inquisitive expressions eager, Christian shook his head. He described their journey as uneventful, which it definitely had been if he did not consider the passion he had shared with Liana. Not about to confide the details of those glorious interludes, he related only the more mundane aspects. "Oh, yes, I did have a brief skirmish with a bear, but he ran off without giving us much trouble. We learned of the problems in the valley from a trapper, and turned right around and came home. Are you going with Dunmore?"

Byron shook his head. "No, the House of Burgesses has called for a Continental Congress in Philadelphia in September, and I have to be there. We're sending supplies to Boston, and have suspended commerce with England in retaliation for the closing of Boston Harbor. A lot has happened while you've been away."

Christian glanced toward his father. "Will you go with Dunmore?"

Hunter felt his wife's fluttering anxiety as she slipped her hand into his. "No, I've seen enough of war."

"Good." Christian was relieved. "Liana and I would like to be married in church as soon as it can be arranged. I realize it will take a while to have new clothes made, plan the menu for the reception, and send invitations, but I hope it won't take too long. Can we set a date before Uncle Byron leaves for Philadelphia?"

The excitement drained from his relatives' faces and was instantly replaced with flashes of alarm. When the adults began an exchange of embarrassed sidelong glances, Christian thought their reactions damn odd. He knew they all wanted him to marry Liana in a proper church ceremony, and demanded an explanation. "What's wrong? You all know I consider Liana my wife, and I'd like the rest of Williamsburg to celebrate our marriage."

Unlike Christian, Liana wasn't at all confused by the distressed reaction his announcement had received. She laced her fingers in his. "Your family and mine share a great many friends, Christian. If we invite everyone to the wedding, my parents' friends will surely send their regrets. I imagine a large percentage of your family's friends will feel attending the wedding will mean condoning behavior they can't accept. They won't come, either. Let's save everyone the embarrassment of having to deal with the matter and marry right here, with just your family."

"But we haven't done anything wrong," Christian insisted. "It's Ian who ought to be the outcast for the way he treated you."

Before Liana could reply, Byron did. "Liana's right, Christian. You've been away and haven't had to listen to the gossip, but we've all been subjected to it and some has been absolutely vicious. I won't give anyone the satisfaction of seeing you wed in an empty church. As soon as Liana has a dress made, we'll hold the ceremony here as she suggested."

"Since when have we bowed to gossip?" Christian asked.

"Christian," Hunter warned, "your uncle is right. People can be mean. You and I are strong enough to walk through Williamsburg with pride, but I don't want Liana insulted. Do you?"

Christian hadn't considered such a possibility, and it sickened him thoroughly. "No, of course not." He turned to Liana. "Is it an insult to marry me?"

His anguished expression made it plain any show of doubt would devastate him, but Liana had none. "It will be the proudest day of my life," she answered confidently, and the love shining in her eyes warmed him clear through.

Christian drew her into a fervent embrace, then stood and pulled her to her feet. "We need to change our clothes before supper. Will you excuse us, please?"

"Certainly," Byron replied. He waited until the affectionate pair had gone upstairs before rising. "I'll leave the wedding plans to Alanna and Arielle. Dominique, perhaps you and Johanna can take Liana into the dressmaker's and help her select something appropriately spectacular for the occasion. The rest of us will do what we're told or stay out of the way."

"The first of our weddings," Arielle enthused. "You needn't worry, my darling. We'll have a beautiful ceremony, but I do think we ought to invite Ian and his family. They'll undoubtedly refuse, but if we don't send them an invitation, they'll tell the whole town we snubbed them. I don't wish to provide them with that opportunity."

"Thank you," Alanna murmured. "Because we expect to be snubbed, we won't be hurt by it but poor Liana surely will. Isn't there some way we can make peace with her family so they'll attend the wedding?"

"Short of killing Ian, I don't see how," Hunter offered darkly. He caught Falcon's eye, and winked. "I'm only joking, not threatening Ian's life."

"I know." Having no interest in hearing about weddings, Falcon got up and led Belle and Jean back outdoors.

"Planning a wedding will be such fun," Dominique exclaimed, "but what if I were about to wed Captain O'Keefe? Would any of you attend the ceremony?"

Arielle scoffed. "Is that even a remote possibility?"

Dominique had seen Sean several times since the afternoon he had kissed her and while he had not tried to kiss her again, she was rather sorry that he hadn't. "No, I suppose not, but I can't help but wonder."

Alone now with those who knew about the pamphlets, Byron could state his opinion openly. "Independence will surely be the main topic at the meeting in Philadelphia. Our latest pamphlets have met with such overwhelming support I'll have no qualms about voting for it. If we're forced into war, it would be difficult to have to fire at my son-in-law, but in that splendid red coat, he makes a very good target."

Dominique rose and went to the doorway. "It was only a question, Father. I'd not wed a man whose politics oppose yours. Come out to the garden with me, Johanna. Let's see which flowers will be blooming for the wedding."

After the two young women had departed, Arielle went to her husband's side. "We were married here ourselves, but I don't want Christian and Liana's ceremony to be as sad as ours was."

"It isn't the ceremony that matters," Hunter remarked. "Alanna and I were married by the only person we could find to say the words to make an Indian and a white woman man and wife, but we have been happy together all these years."

"Yes, so have we," Arielle agreed, "and that's what we want for your son and Liana."

Byron caught Alanna's eye and knew precisely what she was thinking. They might have to invite Ian, but neither of them wanted him to attend and spoil what ought to be a festive and sacred occasion.

Rushing with the wedding preparations, Liana and Johanna left Dominique at the dressmaker's completing her fittings while they made a quick trip to the millinery shop for ribbon. They hadn't taken more than a dozen steps when they saw Sean O'Keefe coming their way. He had also seen them, making it too late to avoid him by slipping into a shop, and steeling herself for what would surely be a ghastly confrontation, Liana produced a triumphant smile.

"Good morning, Captain," she greeted him. She was dressed in Johanna's attractive green gown and felt not merely confident, but attractive.

Sean nodded slightly to acknowledge Johanna's presence, then focused his full attention on Liana. His mocking gaze was as biting as his words. "Good morning. I'd expected to see you in buckskins and feathers rather than a lady's clothes. Tell me, what do you call yourself now, Mrs. Chief Something-or-other, or do you simply answer to 'squaw'?"

Christian wasn't there to hear her response, but Liana felt him in her heart. Ignoring the officer's rudeness, she answered politely. "My husband's name is Christian Scott Hunter, so I'm Mrs. Hunter."

Sean was amazed Liana could look him in the eye while she spoke the name. "I congratulate you, madam. You haven't sacrificed any of your spirit along with your virtue."

Liana's palm connected with Sean's cheek before he saw her lift her hand. Not only did the vicious slap sting like scalding water, but the resounding blow was heard all up and down Duke of Gloucester Street. Passersby stopped in their tracks to stare. Struggling to maintain his dignity, Sean spoke through clenched teeth.

"Were it not for my regard for your family, I would arrest you for assault. Do not presume upon my affection ever again." He walked around Johanna and, lengthening his stride, hurried away.

"Did you really do that?" Johanna gasped. "Not that he didn't deserve it for what he said, but dear God, he already despises Christian, and—"

"Yes, I know. Let's not tell anyone what happened. Sean

surely won't repeat the tale, and if we don't, either, Christian will never hear it."

Johanna pulled Liana into the next doorway to escape the steady stream of foot traffic on the cobblestone walk. "He's been calling on Dominique while you two were away. He's been such a gentleman I never expected to hear him abuse you so badly. We have to tell Dominique. If he's capable of that type of hatred, then she has to be warned."

"If we tell Dominique, then we might as well tell everyone. Christian will feel compelled to defend my honor, and call him out. Do you want to be responsible for that?"

"A duel?" Johanna's golden complexion paled. "No, I'd never put Christian's life at risk."

Liana looked out, and was relieved that the town had resumed its usual bustling pace and they weren't being observed. "I don't care if everyone we meet spits on me. I don't want Christian to know. Now promise me you won't breathe a word of this."

Johanna understood that Liana's reasoning was based on love, but still she hesitated. "I promise, but I'm frightened, Liana."

"So am I but that's not going to stop me from visiting the milliner's." She took Johanna's arm and they continued down the walk, two lovely young women who appeared to have nothing more troubling on their minds than a choice of ribbon, but each was sick at heart.

Twenty-two

Liana's satin wedding gown was adorned with a delectable abundance of ruffles and lace. Sentiment had prompted her to choose the same luscious pale peach color she had been wearing the afternoon she and Christian had met and it flattered her beautifully. The petal-soft shade gave her skin a vibrant glow, and her hair, piled atop her head in curls, shone with golden highlights reflected off the satin.

A picture of feminine perfection, Liana felt none of a bride's usual breathless anticipation, and paced her room waiting to be called for the ceremony. She had remained in the guest bedroom, but Christian had shared her bed in what continued to be the most passionate of nights. That evening she would move into his room on the second floor, but the change in scene mattered very little to her when they had already been together so many times.

She walked to the window and looked out over the lawn, but there were no carriages parked out front. She had not really expected her parents to come, but still, she had held out the slender hope that they might and it hurt very badly that they hadn't. Beau had taken an invitation to Amanda Tuttle, too, but there was no sign of her, either. Liana had hoped her best friend would stand by her and it was another bitter blow that she had not.

Johanna rapped lightly at the door and peered in. "The priest is here. Are you ready?"

"Yes," Liana called, but she lingered at the window.

Troubled by Liana's hesitation, Johanna came in and closed the door. Dressed in pale blue, she had also styled her hair for a party and had achieved an elegance she did not recognize in the mirror. "Shall I tell everyone you need a few more minutes?"

Liana sent a last glance down the long drive, but there was still no sign of guests and she turned away. "No, there's no reason to wait. I'll just have to accept the fact that my family didn't want to be with me. I no longer have a family, actually, and I'll have to get used to being alone on all the important days of my life."

Saddened by Liana's pessimism, Johanna came forward to take her hands. "Please don't even think such depressing thoughts. We all love you already and you'll never be alone here. You may have traded one family for another, but you're not an orphan."

Johanna was so earnest in her tender words of comfort, Liana was nearly moved to tears. She squeezed her hands and quickly moved away. "Thank you for being so sweet to me. Now let's go on downstairs. My husband's waiting."

Delighted her encouragement had had an effect, Johanna broke into a beatific smile. "You really do love Christian, don't you?"

Amazed by her question, Liana paused at the doorway. "Who wouldn't?" she asked. "He's bright, attractive, affectionate, courageous. What more could any woman want?"

A man without Indian blood, Johanna did not dare add. "Forgive me. I didn't mean to sound as though I suspected your motives."

"Oh Johanna, you're such a dear person no one could ever be insulted by your questions. Now let's go." Lifting her skirt, Liana left the room and started down the stairs.

Byron was waiting at the bottom to escort her into the parlor, where the rest of the family was assembled. He had grown increasingly fond of Liana and greeted her with a charming grin. "You're always beautiful, but today, you look positively angelic."

Liana took his arm. "I doubt anyone would imagine me with wings, but thank you, and not just for today, but for everything you've done to make me feel welcome here."

Rushing ahead of them, Johanna gave Dominique a wave, and she struck the first notes of a romantic melody on the harpsichord. For the simple wedding, the lilting tune was far more appropriate than the celestial harmonies a pipe organ produced in church. Huge bouquets of camellias, gardenias, and roses scented the air with the garden's lush perfume, and the whole room was filled with a delicious atmosphere of excitement.

Christian was dressed in the elegantly tailored gray suit he wore to formal parties and looked very much the proper gentleman, as did Byron and Beau. Hunter and Falcon were in their customary buckskins, but equally handsome. Arielle and Alanna had chosen to wear their prettiest gowns, and Belle and Jean were in their best clothes, too. Like Johanna, Dominique had had a new gown made for the occasion.

Liana and Byron paused at the doorway, but despite the beauty of the room and her splendidly attired new family, she knew this simple ceremony wasn't the one she and Christian should have had. Feeling more like an actress playing a role in a tragedy than a bride, she refused to give in to regret. She was warmed by the smiles sent her way and walked toward her husband with a pride she felt clear through.

Christian had lived his whole life without regard to what the good people of Williamsburg thought of him, but he could not help but wish the day could have been different for Liana's sake. He smiled as he took her hand and drew her to his side, for she was already his wife in his heart. He loved her so dearly he would have been happy to repeat his vows in a dozen ceremonies, but he knew it would take only this one to satisfy the demands of Williamsburg's finest families.

They had waited past the hour they had invited the Scotts to join them, and while Christian had known the delay was completely unnecessary, he had so hoped Liana's family would appear that he had not argued. Now, as he folded her hand over his arm, she squeezed his fingers and while cheered by the gesture, he still felt sad. She did not deserve to be abandoned any more than he had. Even without being present, he still felt Ian Scott's disapproving frown and heard his angry voice condemning them all to the fires of hell.

Shoving the man they both called father from his thoughts, Christian listened attentively as the priest began to read the marriage ceremony. He repeated his vows in a steady tone, and rejoiced when Liana's promises were spoken just as calmly. This was no mistake, but the way things were meant to be, and he had every intention of giving his bride the very best of lives. When he at last leaned down to kiss her, he brushed her lips lightly.

"I do love you," he swore so softly only the priest overheard.

Liana responded with an affectionate hug, and they were swiftly surrounded by his family, who all wished to hug and kiss them, too. It was a bit overwhelming, but caught up in their laughter and good wishes, Liana found it easy to smile. The Barclays were a diverse but handsome lot. Some were fair, others dark, but whether their eyes were blue, green, or brown, the love that shone in their faces touched Liana's heart with the same remarkable sweetness. Knowing her own dear family wasn't among them caused an anguish she carefully hid.

There was champagne, and toasts both sincere and

amusing before they entered the dining room for a superb supper. Christian wanted Liana seated at his side now, and Belle traded places with her so they could be together. That put Liana on Arielle's left and across from Beau. His earlier conflict with Christian forgotten, the young man smiled at her with sincere affection.

The priest intoned an appropriately gracious blessing and the meal began. Roast duck, ham, and veal had all been prepared, along with delicately seasoned vegetables. There were hot rolls, and cool wines and cider. The main course was followed by rich custards with heaps of beaten egg whites, known as floating islands, and fruit tarts filled with fresh berries. There was a cake, too, flavored with almonds and iced with honey. After the sumptuous meal, the family drifted back into the parlor. Anything more strenuous than pleasant conversation was difficult, but enveloped in a lazy euphoria, it was enough for a while.

"I want to build Liana a house," Christian announced for the first time. "We're getting crowded here, and—"

Byron raised his hand. "You needn't justify your request. I agree with you. I won't even argue that times are too troubled for such a project as this may be the most placid autumn we'll have in a great many years."

While her father's warning of dark days ahead wasn't lost on Dominique, she was touched by Christian's desire to build Liana a home. As they had so often that evening, her thoughts strayed to Sean O'Keefe. He spoke of his home in England with great fondness, but this was the first time she had ever considered where continuing to see him might lead. Despite her protests to the contrary, she did find him appealing. There was a toughness to him that so many of the boys she knew lacked. Perhaps it was merely his age, or his military training, but she was drawn to his strength.

The question that troubled her that evening was how far did she wish to pursue the attraction when it could so easily lead her to a distant land and away from everyone she loved? She had grown up surrounded by her family's love, and while she had learned as a small child she would one day marry and leave, she could not bear to think she might never be able to return. Every face was dear to her, and she could not even imagine loving a man more. She studied Liana's expression as she glanced at Christian and saw no trace of sorrow, but did not understand how she could have chosen him over her family.

Since his return, Beau had not spoken with Christian about anything other than the pamphlets or the possible deployment of the Virginia Militia. As he watched his cousin holding Liana' s hand and planning for the future, his doubts about his suitability as a husband began to fade. Clearly Christian was devoted to Liana, and Beau was glad of it, but he still found it difficult to look at Liana without experiencing a painful sense of regret.

Christian had been right to criticize him. He had admired Liana and not done anything about it. Losing her to Christian was his own fault. Still, he could not help but wish things had worked out differently so that he might have had the opportunity to court her that his cousin had simply seized. He knew there was a lesson to be learned here far more valuable than anything he would ever master at the College of William and Mary, and he hoped the next time he met a woman he truly wanted, he would have the courage to pursue her and claim her for his own.

The discussion of the new house filled Johanna with a sad, sweet longing for she doubted she would ever inspire the depth of love such a grand gesture required. Considering envy a sin, she was ashamed of herself, and growing restless, she slipped away from the parlor for a breath of fresh air. She had not really expected David Slauson to be waiting for her by the well that evening, but was delighted when she found him there.

It was still light enough for David to see her clearly, and

struck by the elegance she affected for parties, if not for him, he found it difficult to do more than stare. The Johanna he adored was a young woman of simple tastes, and the beauty who joined him that night was a sophisticated stranger. Horribly self-conscious of his own plain clothes, he nevertheless attempted to pay the compliments he knew she deserved.

"You look, well, very beautiful. Not that you aren't always beautiful, you are, but what I mean is, you look especially beautiful tonight. It's not just your hair or gown, either, but all of you." Flustered into silence, he took a step backward and shrugged.

"Thank you. Do you have to leave so soon?"

"No, I've nowhere to go." David caught himself quickly. "Nowhere I'd rather be, I should have said. Tell me about the wedding. Did everything go as planned?"

"Yes, and no. We decorated the house, wore our best clothes, provided a priest to conduct the ceremony, enjoyed a delicious meal, but we couldn't convince Liana's family to attend, and I know that must have hurt her terribly. Perhaps if she had married Beau, they would have come."

Afraid he understood the source of her sorrow, David exhaled slowly. Because he had made such inappropriate references to Indians when they had met, he did not dare mention them now. "Christian is a fine man, too."

Johanna responded with a wistful smile. "Thank you, but to a great many people that really doesn't matter. Liana is much stronger than she looks, though, and she'll survive whatever lingering gossip there is. She's very protective of Christian, and I didn't expect that."

"Protective in what way?" As far as David was concerned, the last thing Christian required was a delicate young woman as a champion.

"Of his feelings. Captain O'Keefe said something very cruel to her recently, and she wouldn't repeat it to Christian because he would have been hurt, too. I admire her for wanting to shield him, and yet—"

Fascinated by the shy brunette, David hung on her every word. "And yet what?"

In a melancholy mood, Johanna confessed her fears without thinking. "Our Indian blood has always made us different. Christian and Falcon would argue it's made us better. Stronger, wiser, I don't know exactly. I just wish there were someone who could love me as fearlessly as Liana loves Christian."

David owned nothing of any value, and while he enjoyed working for the Barclays, his prospects for the future weren't particularly bright. All he felt he could offer Johanna was hope. "There must be a great many fine young men who would love you. Maybe one will please you real soon. It's getting late. You'd better go on back inside."

Too late, Johanna realized she had as good as begged for David's love and she was mortified that he had urged her to wait for someone else. She had hoped the evenings they shared had meant something to him, too. Obviously he had just been bored and found her better company than the other hired hands. Fighting back tears, she nodded and turned away, but she was more convinced than ever that she was doomed to spend her whole life alone.

It was quite late by the time Christian and Liana reached his room. Dominique had put a vase of yellow roses on the dresser, and while he had been annoyed by that feminine touch when he had first noticed it, now he appreciated her thoughtful welcome for Liana. This was to be their room, not merely his, he realized silently, and he wanted it to be perfect for his bride.

"I'm sorry about today," he said.

Liana sat down on the side of his bed and kicked off her slippers. A beautifully carved four-poster, it was covered in a cream-colored spread. The room was painted in terra-cotta and the woodwork a rich cream. An Aubusson rug, as magnificent as the others in the house, in shades of rust, olive, and cream covered the highly polished pine floor. It was a thoroughly masculine room, and yet she felt completely at home.

"You needn't apologize. Everything went as smoothly as we'd planned."

Christian began to peel off his clothes. Then, fearing this might be a lengthy conversation, removed only his coat and hung it in the wardrobe. "I'm not talking about the ceremony, but the guests. I knew Ian wouldn't cross the street to attend my wedding, but I had hoped he would come to yours."

After a day of silent heartache, Liana felt drained, and moved slowly as she began to remove the combs from her hair. "I've decided I have two choices. One is to mourn the loss of my parents as though they were dead, the other is to simply forget they ever existed. I'd prefer to do the latter. I know my brothers still love me, and as they get older, it will become easier for them to visit us."

Christian couldn't agree. "I lack your patience. I've always hated Ian. He was devoted to my mother, so how could he have despised her child? Now he's turned on you in the same despicable fashion and it makes me sick. He doesn't deserve to have sons. We should ask your brothers to come here and live with us."

Liana had just begun to shake out her hair, but dropped her hands to her lap. "This is our wedding night, Christian. Can we please talk about something else?"

Christian understood her request, but he couldn't help himself. "I mean it. When we have our own home, I intend to invite your brothers to come and live with us."

Liana just shook her head. "Have you taken another cause? Are you transferring your rage to tearing my family apart?"

"I have more than enough rage to go around," Christian swore darkly. He unbuttoned his waistcoat, then looked up to find Liana observing him with a troubled gaze. "I'm sorry. You're right, this is no time to stir up old hatreds. I just want you to know that I blame your father, not your mother or brothers, for what's happened, and the three of them will always be welcome in our home."

Liana rose and went to him. She raised her hands to frame his face; he grasped her wrists, then kissed her palms. "You were my choice, Christian, and once I'd met you, I could never have loved anyone else. Put your anger aside for tonight, at least, and make love to me."

Not merely willing, but eager, Christian kissed her soundly, then wrapped her in an exuberant hug and lifted her clear off her feet. "I want such wonderful things for you," he whispered between fervent kisses.

"When I have you, what else could I possibly need?"

Rather than offer suggestions and put ideas in her head, Christian helped her out of the stunning peach gown. "I love this color. Have a dozen more dresses made in the same shade."

"You'd soon grow tired of looking at me if I wore the same thing every day."

"What a preposterous thought. No, I'll never tire of you." Christian took care not to tear the delicate lace trimming her lingerie, but it was difficult to remove it layer by layer without giving in to the urge to grab a handful of the linen and silk and yank it away in a single swirl.

"I've changed my mind," he told her. "I like you better in buckskins."

Liana had never felt the slightest bit of shyness with him, and waited until she had stepped out of her last bit of apparel to respond. "Somehow, I thought you liked me better like this."

Her hair tumbled over her shoulders in luxuriant disarray, the deep red curls licking her creamy breasts like tongues of flame, and he had to agree. "Yes, nature is the best dressmaker after all. Now help me out of my clothes."

Liana ran her hands up his waistcoat. "Have you forgotten how to remove them yourself?"

"I can't remember anything with you cavorting about the room naked."

Liana laughed at that ridiculous image, and rubbed against him. "I'm not cavorting. I'm barely moving at all."

Christian slid his fingers through her curls to keep her face pressed to his and kissed her long and hard. He knew a groom was expected to treat his bride gently on their wedding night, but they had been together so many times he felt no need to display the restraint he didn't feel. He released Liana only long enough to yank off his waistcoat and pull his shirt over his head, then he kissed her again.

He loved the feel of the warm fullness of her breasts pressed against his chest, and wrapped his arms around her narrow waist to bring her close. Her seductive perfume inspired more creative ways to show the devotion brimming over in his heart and he broke away again to remove the last of his clothes. "You are such sweet perfection," he whispered.

Liana responded with a grateful kiss, then took his hand and led him to the bed. She flung back the spread, but before she could climb in, Christian moved behind her and stopped her. "Put your hands on the bed," he urged.

Liana glanced over her shoulder, but Christian gave her only a quick kiss before running his hands up her back and across her shoulders to curl her over the bed. She caught herself on outstretched arms, and understood in an instant what Christian wanted. He slid one arm around her waist to pull her bottom back against his swollen shaft, and rubbed against the base of her spine. He bent over her and rested his cheek on her left shoulder. He cupped her breasts, then moved his hands down over the soft flatness of her stomach. Straying lower, he teased apart her tender folds.

He knew just where to spread her slippery wetness to

create a longing as intense as his own. Then, drawing back for an instant, he slid his manhood between her legs to entice even more delicious sensations with the smooth tip. He moved with deliberate care, biting her earlobe and thrusting with short, fluttering strokes until she was as eager as he to join more deeply. He entered her then, wrapped his arms around her waist, and plunged to her core.

He remained still, braced against her, poised on the brink of rapture as her fiery inner heat seeped through him, taunting him, torturing him with desire. Rapidly drained of restraint, he began with gentle thrusts, then quickened his pace to create a more forceful rhythm, and raced toward the ecstasy he had always found in Liana's arms. Their bodies molded together, he felt quivers of pleasure tighten around him, and then surge through her in spasms of delight that carried them both away.

He smothered a jubilant cry in her thick curls, and when he could, at last drew away and pulled her up on the bed. Filled with a blissful exhaustion, they lay in each other's arms, sated for the moment, but so desperately in love they would each want the other again soon. "This would have been worth a trip to England," Christian whispered in a lazy drawl.

Tickled by that comment, Liana ran her hand over the hollow of his belly and hugged him tight. "There simply was no escaping you, was there?"

"Absolutely none."

Liana closed her eyes and relaxed against him. "I do so want us to have a happy life together, Christian."

Surprised by her wistful tone, Christian rose up slightly. "I thought I was all you needed to be happy."

"Yes," Liana replied, "you are."

A sheen of tears brightened her gaze, and stunned to discover she feared losing him, Christian offered promises with his strong, lean body rather than words, but he knew as well as she did that no man could promise more than he already had.

They had not even been married a week the night Christian walked Liana up to their room for bed, then turned back to the door. "I'm going out. I'll see you in the morning."

Liana stared at her new husband in shocked disbelief. Yesterday Byron had left for Philadelphia and she had assumed the men's hushed meetings in the study after supper each night had been focused on the coming congress. Now she realized they had been planning another pamphlet and she felt sick clear through.

"Don't lie to me," she chided. "You're going to pass out another of your tracts ridiculing the king, and I'll be lucky if I'm not a widow before dawn. Can you at least keep your wits about you this time and avoid whatever patrols are on the roads?"

Christian had known she would be furious with him, but he had not thought of a way to soften her anger. He had considered making love to her and leaving after she had fallen asleep, but that had struck him as cowardly. Committed to leaving, he remained by the door. "While we were away, my father and Falcon delivered two more leaflets from the words and drawings I'd left. They didn't have any trouble, but I can't let Falcon take my place again."

"Your concern for your brother is touching. Why haven't you the same regard for me?" Liana walked toward him, her expression etched with fury. "What about the meeting in Philadelphia? Isn't it enough that the representatives will be discussing independence? Must you keep prodding the people of Williamsburg toward rebellion on your own?"

"Yes," Christian replied. "It isn't an idea that can simply be planted and expected to grow on its own."

"Like tobacco, it has to be cultivated," Liana scoffed. "Is that your claim?"

The walls of the house were thick, but Christian still took care to keep his voice down. "It isn't an idle claim, it's the truth. Inciting rebellion is easy when the king provides such a lengthy list of complaints, but for it to be accomplished, for the colonies to truly be free, will take far more than clever pamphlets, Liana. There's sure to be war, and I intend to fight. I'm fighting now."

War meant only one thing to Liana and that was the bloody specter of death. The very thought of him risking his life, and she knew it would be recklessly, made her sick with fear. "And what am I to you?" she asked in a caustic whisper.

Drawn to the wildness that matched his own, Christian reached out for her and drew her close. "You are my heart and soul, but don't ask me to give up the quest for independence."

Although he had not finished the threat, Liana understood he had already made his choice and she had lost. She saw it all so clearly—it wasn't a war with Great Britain he wanted, but a far more personal battle. "This isn't about independence," she argued. "It's about you. It's about demanding respect from my father and every other man who refuses to accept you as his equal. You can disguise your motives and fool others, but I know you too well."

Christian had always found Liana exciting, especially when her eyes were ablaze with anger. Rather than argue, he silenced her insults with a bruising kiss. "It's the same fight," he insisted when he had caught his breath, "whether it's between the king and the colonies or Ian and me, and I intend to win them both."

Crushed against him, Liana did not struggle against his strength. "Or die trying!"

At that moment, Christian felt very much alive. He glanced toward the bed, but the look of revulsion that filled Liana's eyes warned him. "I want only what's right," he argued. "If I were to settle for anything less, I wouldn't be worthy of you."

Liana was so shocked that he could hold such a low opinion of himself that she couldn't find the words to convince him he was wrong before his mouth covered hers in a deeply stirring kiss that seared his name on her heart. Left too breathless to speak when he finally released her, she watched in awestruck silence as he slipped out the door and ran down the stairs. There was no time to call him back, but she was terrified this last angry exchange would be their final farewell. She wanted him to choose life, to choose her, but he had chosen the path of destruction and doomed them both to the loneliness of hell.

Twenty-three

Christian came barreling into the stable, breathing hard. Hunter had already saddled their horses, and Christian grabbed the bunch of pamphlets David Slauson held out and stuffed them inside the white shirt he had again worn as a disguise. "I'll take the plantations," he told his father before mounting his stallion. "You take the town."

Hunter reached out to grab the stallion's reins. "Wait. Have you a route planned?"

"Yes, I'll ride along the river and through the fields. Don't worry, I won't go near the roads and I won't be shot again."

"Don't get caught, either," Hunter warned.

Christian nodded, turned the spirited horse in a tight circle, and left at a gallop.

"You take care too, sir," David urged.

Hunter wasn't called "sir" more than a couple of times a year and this struck him as a completely inappropriate moment for that. "Hunter," he corrected. He took the rest of the pamphlets from the serious young man and slipped them into the leather pouch slung over his shoulder.

"You needn't fear me," Hunter continued. "I haven't killed a man in years." When David gawked, he knew his joke had not been understood. "I was trying to make you laugh. If there's something you wish to say to me, just say it. Don't go sneaking around bedrooms at midnight the way Christian did."

David was so embarrassed he did not know how to respond. That Hunter could even imagine he might pay Johanna secret midnight visits made his heart pound with fright. "No, sir, I wouldn't even think of it, sir."

"Hunter," the Indian reminded him. Hunter laughed as he swung himself into the saddle. He nudged his mount with his heels and left the stable as quickly as his son.

"Oh, my God," David moaned. Badly rattled, he had to sit down on a barrel to collect his wits. Several minutes passed before he realized Hunter had just invited him to speak for Johanna, rather than forbidden him to do so. Amazed the proud Indian would consider a hired hand for his daughter, David doubted he could gather the courage to even talk with him, let alone ask his permission to propose to Johanna.

His hands were stained with ink, and he wiped them on his leather apron. When he had absolutely nothing to offer Johanna, how could Hunter possibly allow him to propose? "I should have stayed with the ministry," he cried. He had not the slightest doubt that he loved Johanna, but love was scarcely enough. A woman needed a husband who could provide a home, and income. All he could furnish was pleasant company.

Deeply discouraged, he began to pace the stable. It would be hours before Hunter and Christian returned, but he would wait. Waiting was something he could do, but he couldn't expect Johanna to wait the years it might take for him to earn enough to support her.

Christian rode with the speed and cunning which marked all his actions and delivered all but the last of his share of pamphlets without mishap. Approaching the Scotts' residence, he did not merely slow to toss the leaflet on the porch, he stopped and dismounted. Rather than using his own knife, he had brought one which could not be identified and pinned his latest tract to the front door. Slamming the blade into the wood gave him a surprising surge of satisfaction, but he still wished it could have been Ian's heart.

He leaped astride his horse and was gone before anyone in the Scott residence stirred, but the anonymous deed thrilled him clear through. He arrived home elated, and was grateful to learn his father had encountered no problems, either. Leaving his horse for David Slauson to tend, he started toward the house. He had already known Liana wasn't happy with him, but he had not expected her to still be up. Hoping the fact he had returned safely would reassure her, he walked to the chair where she had curled up and bent down to kiss her cheek.

"You see," he boasted proudly, "your fears were unfounded. Other than being tired, I'm fine. You have to be tired, too. Let's go to bed."

Each of the hours he had been away had seemed so terribly long, Liana felt as though she had been awake for centuries. Her limbs cramped and cold, she doubted she could move, but she made her intentions clear. "I'm leaving you," she stated calmly. "You'll never change. You'll chase after danger until it catches you, and I don't want to be there to watch—and grieve."

Hurt that she still had such little faith in his judgment, Christian fought to remain calm. "It's late. This is not the time to discuss this."

"No time would ever be good."

"That's certainly true, but tomorrow morning would surely be better than this. Where are you going? Have you really thought this through?"

He had given her too much time to think that night, but Liana still didn't have an answer. "I don't know, just away. Perhaps I'll visit my aunt and uncle in England. It would be much too awkward for me to leave you and remain in this house, but I thought I could stay aboard the *Southern Breeze* until I've made plans."

Christian stared down at her, certain she could not possibly be the same delightfully affectionate woman he had so recently wed. She was every bit as beautiful, perhaps even more lovely in the soft candlelight, but the sadness she had displayed upon coming there had become a cold indifference he didn't recognize. "Why didn't you tell me you'd leave me if I delivered the pamphlets tonight? Don't you think I deserved a warning if the consequences were going to be this dire?"

Liana had a ready answer. "Would you have let another man take your place if I had?"

Christian let out a weary sigh. "No."

"Then you already know why I didn't waste my breath with threats. You made your choice and I'm making mine. I'm leaving you and that's all there is to it. I won't subject myself to another night as wretched as this, and with your lust for danger, there will be no end of them."

"What did you expect?" Although he had tried to remain calm, Christian was rapidly losing his temper. "You knew what I am."

Liana could not argue with that. "Yes, God help me, I did." She rose, her legs stiff after her long wait. She stretched and tried to hide her pain. "I'm going out to the ship."

Christian moved to block her way. "Not alone, you're not."

Liana was sorry Byron was away, because he would have been able to control the situation even if he would not have taken her side. As for Hunter, she feared he was as unpredictable as his son and she did not want him drawn into their dispute. "Keep your voice down, please. There's no reason to shout at me. I'm going, and that's the end of it."

Christian spoke through clenched teeth. "Fine, go, but I'll not have you walking out to the docks in the dark. You're liable to fall in the river again and I won't have anyone accuse me of pushing you when they find your body washed up downstream."

That grisly thought didn't faze Liana. "I'd rather be dead than spend the rest of my life waiting to hear you've been killed." She had already packed the satchel she had taken on their trek to the Ohio Valley, and reached down to pick it up from beside the chair. "Escort me to the ship if you need to be sure I'm safe. God forbid you should ever have to worry about me as I did about you tonight."

She moved past him with a determined stride, and fearing he deserved at least part of her scorn, Christian picked up the candlestick from the nightstand and followed her down the stairs. He caught up to her when she reached the front door. "I know you love me," he said, as they left the house.

"Yes, if I didn't, I'd have no reason to leave."

Christian opened his mouth to tell her how ridiculous that sounded, but kept still when her meaning finally struck him. She was angry and so fearful of losing him she couldn't bear to stay. The fact that he had done that to her made him very sad. Confident they could straighten things out when they weren't so tired, he escorted her out to the *Breeze* and made certain she was comfortable in the cabin they had shared.

"I want to stay with you," he said with real regret, "but I'll go, and we can talk tomorrow. Good night."

He hesitated at the door. Liana felt his sorrow as deeply as her own, but she couldn't ask him to remain with her now when it had been his stubborn refusal to consider her feelings earlier that had caused her to leave. "Good night," she repeated numbly, but she couldn't stop her tears the moment he was gone.

* * *

Sean O'Keefe held his head in his hands. He had been given a copy of the latest pamphlet as soon as he had awakened that morning, and he knew Lord Dunmore would have one, too. The whole town would be reading them at breakfast and a great many of the residents would be laughing at the king. With their next breath, they would be laughing at him for being unable to catch the culprits who kept showering their outrageous views on the populace with the ease of a spring rain.

When Christian Hunter had been away, he had fully expected the pamphlets to cease, proving the brash young man was behind them, but they had continued to appear, filled with the same insolent rhetoric. Soldiers were still patrolling the roads after dark, but they had not caught Christian, nor anyone else, last night. Thoroughly disgusted, Sean sat back and eyed the pamphlet on his desk.

The cover cartoon was a rattlesnake coiled around the colonial map and the text, as always displaying a razor-sharp wit, claimed the king's promises rolled off his forked tongue as venomous lies. Sean had been reluctant to conduct a house-to-house search, but by God, he now had no other choice. As soon as he found the printing press, which had to be a cumbersome piece of machinery to hide, he would have the traitors who kept writing the libelous trash about King George III.

Leaving his desk, he assembled his men and started combing the town. With methodical precision, he prowled through each shop and tavern, and with cold glances and sarcastic commands he made it known that he would not stop until he had arrested the men responsible for the disgraceful diatribes. When a complete search of the commercial enterprises yielded nothing, he sent his men out through the homes where they searched well-kept parlors, dusty attics, and dank root cellars, but found not so much as a line of type, let alone a printing press.

Sean slapped his gloves against his thigh and swore under his breath. He had known the only printing press in town was in the print shop and the printer had been cleared of any involvement in the scheme right after the first pamphlet had appeared. That meant the culprits were operating from a plantation. Because each and every one covered a considerable amount of acreage and had so many outbuildings, searching them might take all week.

He returned to the barracks and consulted a map. After crossing off the homes of men like Ian Scott, whose loyalty to the Crown was unquestioned, his task was not nearly so formidable. He traced a path with his fingertips, calculating the easiest route, but quickly decided what he really wanted to do was search the Barclays' holdings first. He would explain to Dominique that it was merely a formality and that all plantations were being searched, but he was certain if he started with the Barclays, he would finish promptly.

Christian slept late, and when he came downstairs the servants were setting the table for the noon meal. Not really hungry, he decided to go without breakfast, but he could not go without seeing Liana. Before he could leave the house, however, his mother called to him. Fearing she knew what had happened, he entered the parlor and made no attempt to fool her.

"Sit down," Alanna invited in a tone that brooked no argument.

Christian dropped into the chair across from the settee where she had been sitting while working on a piece of floral embroidery. He had seldom seen the dear woman look so disgusted, and was certain he didn't deserve it. "Before you accuse me of doing a poor job as Liana's husband, please consider the fact that she's not showing me a wife's loyalty. I've done nothing but be who I am."

Expecting that remark, Alanna set her needlework aside. When Christian refused to look at her, she knew his heart as well as his pride was aching. "You were born to be the firebrand you are, Christian, and I won't criticize you for it. You are your father's son, schooled in the Seneca ways which value courage and daring above all. Liana had a far more genteel upbringing, and what she prizes, and with good reason after the way she's been treated by her family, are loyalty and devotion."

"I haven't betrayed her trust."

"No, of course you haven't, but you've made it plain you'd rather incite rebellion than be with her—and that's unforgivable."

"Is that what Liana told you?"

"No, I haven't spoken with her, but when she went to the kitchen to fetch her own breakfast this morning and returned to the *Breeze* to eat it, I understood why she'd left the house, and you. A Seneca woman would never question her husband's actions, but I can't imagine you being happy with such a complacent wife. Liana is the perfect match for you, Christian. Don't lose her."

"I don't intend to, but I'll be damned if I know what to do. I can't be something I'm not just to please her."

Alanna left the settee and came to his side. She stroked his hair lightly. "No, of course not. All you need do is convince her there are some things a man *must* do. It's not a question of choice at all, but a moral imperative. When a man encounters injustice, he must act. As your father so often says, 'Words aren't deeds.' You are a man of action, Christian, and you need never apologize for it, but you must never allow Liana to doubt that your first choice is always to be with her. You see, regardless of what a man wants to do, there are always things he must do. Choose wisely."

Before Christian could respond, they heard several men ride into the yard. Alanna turned to glance out the window. "It's Captain O'Keefe and he's brought a patrol with him so I doubt he's come to call on Dominique."

"I'll handle him." Christian rose and started toward the door, but then paused and turned back. "Thank you for being the best mother any man could ever have."

Alanna regarded him with a loving smile. "That's very easy where you're concerned."

Christian laughed. "Tell Liana that, will you?"

He opened the front door just as Sean raised his hand to knock. "Good afternoon, Captain. If you've come to join us for dinner, I'll have extra places set."

Sean glanced past him, hoping for a glimpse of Dominique, but was disappointed. "I'm sure I needn't tell you another pamphlet was distributed last night. I've come to search the premises. If a printing press is found, you'll be arrested and charged with sedition."

Hearing that, Alanna left the parlor to greet the captain. "Did you say a printing press, Captain? I'm sure I would have noticed one had it been here, but do come in. We're very proud of our home, and miss no opportunity to show it off."

Alanna's sweet smile was so sincerely warm that Sean was quite startled by it. Obviously she had no fear he would find any incriminating equipment, but he still intended to look. "Thank you, Mrs. Hunter." He turned to give his men the order to search the other buildings on the plantation, then entered the house himself.

Having seen Sean arrive from an upstairs window, Dominique hurried down the stairs to meet him. His guarded expression warned her this was no social call, and she remained on the bottom step. "Is something wrong?" she asked.

"Yes, there most certainly is," Sean replied. He explained the reason for his visit, then, without offering an apology for disturbing the household, he strode into the parlor. He had often spent time with Dominique there and did not really expect to find a printing press standing in the middle of the room, but still gave it a cursory glance before crossing the hallway into Byron's study.

Arielle had been in the sitting room and, hearing voices, came out into the hall. "Good afternoon, Captain."

Sean again repeated the reason for his visit, and having found nothing other than the usual contents of a man's study, he followed her back into the sitting room. Painted a sunny yellow, it was an attractive room, and again, held nothing out of the ordinary. The dining room also provided no clues to the identity of the pamphlet's author.

When he approached the bottom of the stairs, Dominique moved aside. "I think you'd better escort him upstairs, Christian, and please don't tell him which bedroom is mine."

"Certainly not," Christian agreed. He winked at his cousin, and followed the captain up the stairs.

Servants moved through the house each morning, making beds, dusting furniture, opening windows to let in the fresh new day, and Christian was positive all the inquisitive officer would find was a beautifully tended home. He moved ahead of him to open the door of the master bedroom. "This is Byron and Arielle's room. It has one of the best views of the river."

"A commentary won't be necessary," Sean insisted curtly. He walked around the immaculately kept room, glanced at the beautiful clothes hanging in the wardrobe, then strode out. Alanna and Hunter shared the room across the hall. It also had a splendid river view, and absolutely nothing of any interest to the authorities. Moving on down the hall, Sean opened the door to Christian's room. Although he had been up less than half an hour, the bed had already been made.

Sean walked around, observing Christian's belongings

with a desultory glance, then walked across the hall to Beau's bedroom. Growing bored, he spent less time there, then led Christian up to the third floor. The instant he entered the pink bedroom, Sean caught the scent of Dominique's perfume and knew it was hers. Doubting her father would allow anyone to hide a printing press there, he quickly left.

The guest room offered no clues, either, but as Sean glanced out the window to observe his men's progress, he saw Liana on the deck of the *Southern Breeze*. "What's Liana doing aboard the ship?" he asked. "Are you planning a voyage?"

With the press hidden in the hold, Christian was sorry Sean's attention had been drawn to the vessel, but kept his anxiety out of his voice. "No, Liana is merely peeved with me and living aboard the *Breeze* for a day or two."

Sean laughed with real pleasure. While he was still hurt that Liana had married Christian, it did soothe the ache to know she wasn't happy with him. "Forgive me, but I can't help but feel you both have the trouble you deserve."

"I'm sure you'll get what you deserve, too," Christian swore softly.

The evil glint in Christian's eye made the insult in his words clear, but Sean chose to ignore it and pushed past him. Johanna's pale blue room was next, and he searched it swiftly before entering the bedroom Falcon and Jean shared. Filled with the boys' clutter, he was soon assured it was as innocent as all the rest.

Christian waited by the stairs. "Are you satisfied now?"

"No, and I won't be until I find the press and the men who've been running it."

"So many people have grievances against the king, it's surprising you haven't found a press in every parlor."

Sean did not dignify that remark with a response and went on down the stairs and out the front door. His men were still away from their horses, so Sean made his way alone to the docks. "Good afternoon," he called to Liana.

Dressed in one of Johanna's simple gowns, Liana looked frail and drawn and Sean was overcome by a sudden swell of tenderness. He walked up the gangplank and joined her on deck. He lowered his voice to a conspiratorial whisper. "Your husband is watching from the porch so try and look as though we're discussing the weather."

Having slept very little, Liana had to raise her hand to cover a yawn before she replied. "I can't imagine anything else we have to discuss."

"Christian admitted you'd left him. Come with me now, and I'll do what I can to have your marriage annulled."

Liana was positive it was too late for that. "No, that's completely out of the question."

Frustrated by her obstinate refusal to see what was so obvious to him, Sean tried once more to entice her. "You shouldn't have married that damn Indian in the first place, but you were smart enough to leave him, so why not make a clean break? Come with me now, and in a few months, when this ridiculous interlude has been forgotten, we can marry. I can give you a much better life than any savage ever could."

He was speaking with an intensity that made it impossible for her to doubt his sincerity, but Liana had never loved him and despite her problems with Christian, she wasn't even tempted to go with him. "I'm sorry, but what you suggest is impossible."

Disgusted that she would leave Christian but refuse to come to him, Sean ceased to argue. As he turned to go, he noticed a scrap of paper caught in a coil of rope. He bent down to pick it up and turned it over, expecting to see the corner of a sarcastic cartoon or a few sentences insulting the king, but both sides were blank. Frowning slightly, he carried it back to Liana.

"Where did you get this?"

Not understanding his question, Liana's expression was puzzled but innocent. "Get what?"

"This bit of paper!" he cried, shaking it in her face, "It's the stock used for the pamphlets. I knew they were printed here." He reached out, grabbed her upper arms, and began to shake her. "You've no reason to protect your husband now. Tell me where they hide the press!"

The instant Sean reached for Liana, Christian leaped off the porch and raced to the ship. His moccasins made only soft thuds on the dirt and before the captain heard him coming, he took hold of his shoulder and yanked him around. "Take your hands off my wife!" he yelled, and in the next second, he slammed his fist into Sean's face. Staggered, Sean dropped the telltale scrap, and after regaining his balance, went after Christian, but he was no match for the wily brave and soon found himself punched, pummeled, and shoved off the ship.

As the fight continued on the docks, Liana picked up the tattered piece of paper, ripped it into tiny bits, and hurled them over the side into the river where the tide carried them away. Shaken, she clung to the rail as Christian continued to give the conceited officer the beating he deserved without receiving more than a scrape in return. It wasn't until the patrol gathered around them menacingly that Christian dropped his hands and backed away.

Hunter and Beau were supervising the workers in the fields and were unaware of the officer's visit, but Falcon came running to join his brother, quickly followed by Belle and Jean. Raising her skirt, Dominique ran ahead of Alanna and Arielle, and Johanna joined them as the captain was still wiping the blood from his nose on his handkerchief. "We saw it all from the porch," Dominique cried. "You were abusing Liana, and Christian had every right to punish you for it."

His eyes still ablaze with anger, Sean returned Dominique's accusing stare. Then, realizing she had seen far too much ever to believe he cared more for her than for Liana, he knew their flirtation was over and offered no excuses. Instead, he carried out the task which had brought him there in the first place and questioned his men. "Did you find anything?"

"No, sir," a husky corporal replied. "There's nothing but meat in the smokehouse and washtubs in the laundry. The tobacco sheds are empty this time of year. The blacksmith is shoeing a horse, and in the kitchen, they're preparing to serve what looks like a delicious dinner."

"Search the ship," Sean ordered, "and be quick about it."

Startled, the men hesitated a moment, then circled the Barclay family and clattered up the gangplank with a running step. Two men remained on deck while the rest went below. Sean observed Christian's reaction with a challenging stare. "Perhaps you'd like to say good-bye to your family now. It might be a very long time before you see any of them again."

"I'm not going anywhere," Christian replied. Counting on the fact that the soldiers wouldn't spend more than a minute in the hold where they would not know the difference between the bilge pump and the canvas-wrapped press, he did not even flinch. Of course, if David Slauson had not bothered to conceal the press again after printing the last pamphlet yesterday, then he was in serious trouble, but knowing David, he doubted he would make such a disastrous mistake. He looked up at Liana and smiled. "None of us are."

Sean wasn't surprised by that defiant boast, but he waited with growing impatience as his men searched the *Breeze*. When they finally reappeared and reported another fruitless search, he spat out a bitter curse and pointed to Christian as he began to back away. "It *is* you, and I'm going to prove it."

Christian broke into a cocky grin and just shook his

head. Several truly ingenious insults immediately sprang to mind, but deciding to save them for the next pamphlet, he chose not to waste them here. "Good day, Captain."

Sean did not even nod to the ladies before stomping off to his horse. As he rode away with his men, their red coats were quickly obscured by the dust kicked up from the road, but the tension of their visit remained. With a gracious gesture, Arielle began to nudge her children toward the house. "What a disagreeable episode. Come on, everyone, let's go inside and have something to eat."

Eluding her mother's grasp, Dominique looked up at Liana. "What was he saying to you?"

Liana hadn't told Dominique when Sean had insulted her in town, but she knew she ought not to keep his latest remarks a secret. "He offered to have my marriage annulled so he and I could marry. When I refused, he started yelling about the pamphlets."

Dominique responded with a coarse word in French, but her meaning was clear. "Thank you. I shan't speak to him ever again." Looping her arm through Johanna's, she joined the others walking toward the house.

Christian walked up the gangplank. "Will you come inside with us for dinner?"

Liana shook her head. "I've lost my appetite." Now that the others couldn't overhear, she told him about the scrap Sean had found. "I tossed it into the river, and who's to say it was the same paper used in the pamphlets anyway. I'm afraid he'll come back over and over again until he finds the press. Where have you hidden it?"

Christian moved close, hoping she would think the subject required whispers and wouldn't back away. He was relieved when she didn't. "It's in the hold."

Liana's eyelashes swept her brows. "You don't mean it!"

"It's wrapped in canvas, along with the type and supplies. We doubted soldiers would know enough about a ship to identify the things that didn't belong, and obviously we were right."

Appalled, Liana began to back away. "When you knew your involvement with the pamphlets terrified me, how could you have let me take up residence aboard the ship where you've hidden the press? Was that just some sort of evil joke?"

Christian took a step toward her, but when she took two away, he stopped and leaned against the rail. "I didn't even think of the press last night. All I cared about was you."

Liana looked away. She felt sick clear through as she did too often lately. "You may have hidden the truth, but you never lied to me, Christian. Don't start now."

"I'm not!"

"I'm afraid I'm going to be sick. Go away and leave me alone."

Christian watched Liana hurry below, and positive this was no time to persuade her to his point of view with the stirring speech on the merits of duty versus choice his mother had suggested, he felt sick, too, only it was disappointment that plagued him. He left the *Breeze* and started for the house at a slow shuffle. He would have to wash Sean O'Keefe's blood off his hands before joining his family for dinner, but he knew he would never want to wash his hands of Liana. Even when she was dead wrong he still loved her, and somehow he would convince her a love that strong was too precious to lose.

Twenty-four

Christian took his place at the table and instantly became the focus of his family's attention. Hunter and Beau
had just come up to the house to eat, and learning of
Captain O'Keefe's visit, were full of questions. Christian
satisfied their curiosity as best he could without admitting
any guilt by revealing the location of the printing press.
As he glanced around the table, he realized now only Belle
and Jean were unaware that their family was producing
the pamphlets, but wanting to prolong their innocence,
he dismissed O'Keefe for the fool he was and changed the
subject to the tobacco crop.

Understanding his cousin's intent, Beau went along with
him. "We'll have a good harvest," he replied, and Hunter
agreed.

Christian listened as Beau and his father discussed the
work accomplished that morning, but Beau kept glancing
toward Liana's empty chair, and his real interest was plain.
Christian just shook his head, warning him to keep still,
but at the close of the meal, he drew Beau out on the front
porch before he could return to the fields. "I'm sure this
isn't the only argument Liana and I will have, but I hope
you'll have the good sense to stay out of it."

"I know enough not to meddle," Beau swore. "If Liana's
just angry about the pamphlets, then I'll deliver the next
one—if I'm here."

"Where are you going?" Christian braced himself against a column, and as he listened to his cousin's reply, he kept an eye on the deck of the *Breeze*, hoping to see Liana.

They were alone on the porch, but Beau still glanced over his shoulder before he spoke. "I want to go into the Ohio Valley with Lord Dunmore. If Father's home, he may try and stop me, but it looks as though the militia will be leaving before he returns from Philadelphia."

"You're the student," Christian admonished. "I'm the warrior of the family."

"You've also got a wife, and I don't." Beau lowered his voice. "If the delegates to the Continental Congress vote for independence, it will surely mean war with England. There won't be a student left at William and Mary or any other college then, and you know it. If I'm going to be a soldier, I might as well begin now."

Christian sucked in a deep breath. No one wanted to throw off the tyranny of the king more than he, but Liana's dark vision of war invaded his thoughts and brought a numbing chill. A great many good men would die if the colonies had to fight for their independence and he did not want Beau to be one of them. "All the militia knows how to do is march," he chided. "They can't fight."

Insulted, Beau began to argue. "They fought in the French and Indian War, my father and Uncle Elliott among them. Your father served as a scout. He knows."

"That was twenty years ago, and those same men either can't, like Elliott, or won't, like our fathers, be following Lord Dunmore into the Ohio Valley." Christian punched Beau's shoulder lightly. "The Shawnee won't be easy to defeat. I'm not saying killing settlers is right, but they'll be fighting on land their hunters have roamed for centuries, and it's doubtful any Virginia schoolboys can chase them off."

Having taken more than enough of Christian's ridicule,

Beau's mood turned surly. "I'm eighteen years old," he reminded him. "I'm a man, not a schoolboy."

Christian straightened up and backed away. "Wait for the real war, Beau. Don't risk your life in a frontier skirmish."

"Just whose side are you on? Would you go if you could fight with the Shawnee?"

That question made Christian wince. "You're worse than O'Keefe," he shot back. He turned around and went down the steps. He wanted to check on Liana, and having no desire to remain with Beau when he was voicing such absurd opinions, he loped on out to the *Breeze*. He called Liana's name as he started below, but heard no reply. He had not expected her to welcome him to her cabin, but when he glanced in and saw her curled atop the bunk asleep, he couldn't bring himself to leave.

Weary in both heart and body, he decided he could also use a nap and came in and closed the door. He stretched out on the edge of the narrow bunk and with a gentle nudge, coaxed Liana into moving over to allow him more room. She sighed softly, but didn't wake as he eased his arm under her neck to encourage her to use his shoulder as a pillow. Content just to hold the stubborn beauty he adored, he stroked her hair lightly, and when he could no longer keep his eyes open, fell asleep with her nestled snugly in his arms.

Liana felt so warm and safe she didn't wake for hours. Then, slowly becoming aware of the softness of Christian's buckskins beneath her cheek, she sat up with a start. He laughed at her dismay, and infuriated anew, she drew her hand back to slap him but he caught her wrist before she could.

"You're beginning to try my patience," he warned. "A wife belongs with her husband, but I've never been able to stay away from you."

Christian flashed a rakish grin that made looking at him

hurt, but when he pulled her back down into his arms, Liana lacked the spirit to resist and relaxed against him. "I don't want to leave you, but you've made it impossible for me to stay."

After searching his mind for a convincing argument, Christian replied with a story. "When Seneca braves go hunting, each takes along a little doll made of cornhusks. They don't put any faces on the dolls, though, because they want to be able to look at them in the evening and see the faces of the women they love. If I made you a faceless doll, could you look at it when we're apart, remember me, and know I'm always with you?"

Liana had had no idea Indian braves could be so sentimental and the idea of them cherishing faceless cornhusk dolls brought tears to her eyes. She had not fully understood until that moment that no matter how she saw Christian, he saw himself as Seneca. Proud Seneca braves roamed the forest as freely as the deer, but as long as they were able, they came home to the women they loved. She knew she could as easily reverse the direction of the James River as tame Christian Hunter, but she couldn't stand being sick with fear all the time, either.

"Whatever am I going to do with you?" she asked with an exasperated sigh.

"Just love me as I am, and know that no matter what I feel I must do, in my heart I'm always with you." He hugged her tight. "You are my heart, Liana. Truly you are."

Convinced she would never love another man as desperately as she loved Christian, Liana rose slightly to kiss him. Her lips trembled as they brushed his, but she had never been more certain of his love. He shifted his position to look down at her, but his expression was as sincere as his vow. There wasn't a hint of the teasing light that so often brightened his dark eyes. For a terrifying instant, she held her breath and prayed he would not expect her to respond with words when she could not have forced a whisper past the tears clogging her throat.

What Christian saw in Liana's eyes was a fear-laced sorrow so deep he doubted his words had even touched her, let alone convinced her to accept his point of view. She had kissed him, though, and, more than willing to complete the bridge of affection she had so hesitantly begun, he slid his arm around her waist and leaned down to kiss her very slowly and deeply. She was trembling still, and he did not want to rush her and risk losing her to fears about things that he prayed would never come to pass.

Gradually he felt her dread subside, but remaining cautious, he kept his own need for her under firm control. He led her at a leisurely pace, waiting until she had slid her hand up under his fringed shirt to caress his back before he traced the soft swell of her bosom through the bodice of her gown. Her fiery temperament hid a delicate soul, and he dared not bruise her feelings again when she wounded so easily.

Reveling in Christian's newfound tenderness, Liana poured her love into him with an adoring touch. She loosened the tie from his hair and, closing her eyes through another delicious kiss, imagined him running, his glossy black mane streaming in the wind like a knight's satin banner. Truly he was a man who ran to embrace his destiny, and she would have to find the courage to step out of his way.

He had warned her once that he had been conceived in sin and born of death, but what she had always felt at his touch was a surge of life that thrilled her clear to her soul. She would never have enough of him, and wanted him so badly now, she did not care how many arguments they might have. "Our clothes are in the way," she whispered with an unmistakable urgency.

Christian bit his lip to stifle a triumphant shout, and rolled off the bunk only long enough to yank off his buckskins and help her remove the gown he had just wrinkled quite badly. He pulled her combs from her hair and placed them on the captain's desk where she could find them later. Then, leaving their clothing scattered about the cabin, he returned to the bunk and slid down over her. He kissed her throat, her breasts, the silken hollow of her stomach, and then licked her to the brink of ecstasy before entering her with a forceful thrust.

She clung to him, pulling him down into her bliss, and he timed his thrusts to her gasps, making them slow and sweet. She coiled her legs around him, and drawing him deep, held him prisoner. She ground her hips against his in a demand for surrender that he was all too eager to give. Hers in every way, he offered all of his youth and strength in a passionate blaze that seared her heart with the heat of his love. Still lost in that glorious haze, he rolled away to spare her his weight, but kept her locked in his arms as they again drifted off to sleep.

It was the rain that woke them later. It splattered on the deck with a light, dancing rhythm that brightened rather than dampened their spirits. Christian hugged Liana, then left the bunk and began to pull on his clothes. "Let's stay here tonight. I'll run to the kitchen and fetch supper for us. You missed dinner, so you must be even hungrier than I am."

Liana opened her mouth to say she had not been hungry at all, what with either being sick to her stomach or sick at heart, but she caught herself before revealing more than she wished. Looking back, she thought she had probably conceived the night he had shared her bed at home. That had been almost two months ago but she did not want to complicate their tenuous hold on marriage with hopes for a child just yet. Instead, she smiled easily. "Yes, I would like something to eat."

Quickly dressed, Christian leaned down to kiss her goodbye. "Don't move. I want you to stay right where you are."

The sheet covered her breasts with a modest drape, but Liana couldn't agree. "Toss me my chemise, please. It would be most improper for me to dine in the nude."

Christian scooped the linen shift from the floor and handed it to her with another hasty kiss. "I'll never consider anything you do improper, but I don't want you to be cold." As he turned to go, he almost added a teasing word about missing him while he was gone, but realized at the last instant how cruel it would be and hurried away without risking the bond it had taken him so long to forge anew.

"There's something different about you," Christian remarked. He had brought a roast chicken from the kitchen, and though he was finished with their picnic supper, Liana was still nibbling a wing. She looked up at him with such an astonished expression he could not help but laugh.

"If I didn't know better," he teased, "I'd swear you looked guilty, but because that can't possibly be the case, I'll have to assume you're simply surprised."

Liana was positive guilt didn't apply to the secret she had chosen to keep for the time being, and nodded. "I can imagine how I look. 'Disheveled' is probably the best word, and it's unfair of you to criticize my looks after insisting I not dress for supper. The chicken was very good, don't you think?"

"Almost as good as you," Christian replied with a wink that made Liana blush. "No, it's not your appearance that I noticed, but something else. Maybe I'm just relieved to see you smile at me again."

Liana tossed the wing on the plate of bones and wiped her mouth and hands on her napkin. "It would be easy to smile if there were only you and me to consider. I wish we could go back into the woods and leave the rest of the world behind."

Christian got up to carry their dishes to the door. When he came back, he still had difficulty responding to her wistful remark. "We can be happy anywhere, Liana. Besides, the woods might not be all that peaceful much longer with Lord Dunmore threatening to lead the militia into the Ohio Valley. Of course, one of his responsibilities as Royal Governor of Virginia was to prevent settlers from moving onto Indian lands in the first place, but everyone knows he's bought land in the valley himself."

It was Liana's turn to study her companion's face closely now, and she was every bit as perceptive as Christian. "Are you going to write a pamphlet about that? It would certainly be easy to make Dunmore look a fool for allowing settlers into the valley, then having to go and defend them."

Christian couldn't help but smile. "That's a fine idea—why don't you write it?"

"I don't want anything to do with your blasted pamphlets and you know it."

"Yes, but when you have such good ideas, it would be a shame not to use them."

It was still raining, or Liana would have suggested they go up on deck to clear their heads. As it was, they were trapped in the cozy cabin. Christian had brought a jug of cider, and she took a sip from her tankard. "I do wish we could agree on the important things."

Because the pamphlets were most definitely important, her comment struck Christian as odd until he realized they weren't like most other couples. "Had I been able to court you as a gentleman should, we would have discussed all manner of important topics to discover each other's views. We might have found many similarities, and I hope not too many differences. As it was, we spent most of our time chasing each other through the marsh grass and had no opportunity to settle anything before you became my wife. That means we'll have to be tolerant now. Nothing about you disturbs me, so that's easy for me. Perhaps it will be very difficult for you."

Christian had presented their problem in such reasonable terms that Liana wished she could find an equally compelling argument. "I'm proud to be your wife, Christian, and I'd be content if all you ever did was raise tobacco, but I know that's not nearly enough for you. You have to be right in the thick of things, and if there were no trouble, I'll bet you'd stir up some. It will take me a while to get used to the way you live—and I hope I'll have a lifetime to learn how—but I can't promise not to be frightened for you."

Christian would have assured her there was no need, but then he thought of Beau. He did not want to see his cousin go with Lord Dunmore when there was a chance he might not come back, and Liana would always have the same fears for him. He kept that thought to himself, though. "I understand," he assured her, "but life is dangerous for women, too. I could be the one to lose you."

Taken aback by that possibility, Liana hastened to reassure him. "I've always been healthy, and I doubt I'll fall in the river again. You needn't worry about me. I don't seek danger, and what harm could come to me here?"

Christian caught her eye. "Do you suppose your father worried about my mother, or was she dead before he even had the chance?"

Chilled to the marrow by that grim comment, Liana could only shake her head. Melissa had died in the Barclay house, and she had never wondered in which room. Now she did not want to know. "He must have. Surely every man must worry his wife might not survive childbirth."

"Yes, he'd be a poor excuse for a husband if he didn't," Christian agreed. Despite having made love to Liana at every opportunity, he had given absolutely no thought to fathering children. The sudden realization that he had put Liana at risk of suffering the same excruciating death as his mother caused him a painful burst of guilt. The thought of losing Liana twisted his stomach in an agonizing knot, and for a moment he did not even recognize the sensation. Then the truth struck him with a sharp blow: he was afraid.

Completely unwilling to voice his terror, he crawled up over the end of the bunk and forced Liana back against the pillow. "I don't want to waste a second of tonight worrying about what might happen to either of us. There's only tonight, and I want to fill it with love."

Liana reached up to pull him down into her arms but she sensed the change in him and intuitively felt that he had secrets, too. Knowing him, she was certain they were dangerous. Praying she had gained the wisdom not to inquire, she joined with him in the glory of being together.

The next morning the skies were clear and Liana moved back into the house. She rejoined the other Barclay women and followed the same graceful patterns she had shared with her mother, and Christian, wanting to stay close, helped supervise the work in the fields. The hands were now topping the plants, cutting off the pink flowers so the leaves would grow large and heavy.

With Christian to take his place, Beau made frequent trips into town. The fall term was about to begin at the College of William and Mary, but like him, many young men were more interested in politics than studying the classics. He followed the discussions at the Rawleigh Tavern closely until the day he learned Lord Dunmore was ready to make his move. He then came home not to seek permission to join the militia, but to announce that he fully intended to do so.

Because this was not their first conversation on the subject, Arielle was not surprised, but with Byron away in Philadelphia at the Continental Congress, she turned to Hunter and Christian for help in dealing with her son. Closeted in the study with the three men, she stated her case plainly. "I feel as though you're taking advantage of the situation, Beau. Please don't make any decisions until we can write to your father and ask his opinion."

Anxious to be on his way, Beau paced in front of her. "I'd value his opinion, but I don't need his permission to enlist. There's really no time to pursue a lengthy conversation through the mails. Dunmore is taking half the militia up to Pittsburgh to sign a treaty with the Delaware and Six Nations of the Iroquois. Then he'll travel down the Ohio River to meet with the troops General Andrew Lewis will march overland. The combined forces should defeat the Shawnee in a matter of days. I'm not volunteering to go off to war, Mother. I just want to fight in one battle."

"There is no guarantee there will be only one," Hunter chided. "I know you know how to hunt, but shooting a man is different. It's not a sport I recommend."

Beau knew once Hunter made up his mind he was as immovable as the Alleghenys, and he did not waste his breath trying to influence him. "I'm eighteen," he reminded everyone. "I don't need your permission. I hope you'll wish me well, but I'm going with or without your blessings."

Arielle turned a beseeching glance on Christian. "Maybe he'll listen to you."

Christian was leaning back against the massive mahogany desk, his arms folded across his chest. He sincerely doubted he could stop Beau, but for his aunt's sake, he had to try. "This is merely a diversion," he argued. "The British allowed settlers into the valley and provoked the Indians just to distract everyone from the real problems, which are the grievances against the king that Uncle Byron has gone to discuss. He would say the same thing. You

ought to enroll in school and learn all you can before the
real war begins."

His conviction clear, Beau went to the door. "I won't
listen to them, Mother. They're Indians. They'd never send
me off to shoot the Shawnee and you know it. That's what
you were counting on, wasn't it? Well, it won't work. I'm
going. I believe what you write in your pamphlets, Chris.
We ought to rebel, and this will be good experience for
the fight for independence."

Beau was half out the door before he remembered
something. "I almost forgot. I heard Ian Scott will be one
of Lewis's officers, but you needn't worry. I'll stay away
from him."

Beau slammed the door on his way out, and Arielle began to weep. She dabbed her eyes with her handkerchief,
but couldn't stem the tears. "Thank you both for trying.
I know Beau thinks of himself as a man, but he's very
young and I hate to see him volunteer for something he
could so easily avoid. I'm afraid his father will be furious
with me for letting him go."

Christian glanced toward his father and the same
thought leapt between them. His aunt had not asked him
to go with Beau, but should anything happen to her eldest
son, he would be blamed forever for not having been there
to prevent it. That scorn would be a slight burden compared to what he would do to himself, however. Torn by
the loyalty he owed his family and the devotion he owed
Liana, he felt sick clear through.

"I'll have to discuss this with Liana," he told them, "before I make plans to go along."

Grasping that hope, Arielle choked on a sob. "Oh, Christian, would you please go with Beau? It would mean so much
to me if you would. You're as close as brothers and I know
you'd look out for him as no one else could. It's an enormous favor to ask, but Byron and I would be ever so grateful
if you would go."

Christian tried to recall Josiah Peabody's gruesome tales to justify a war on the Shawnee, but it was still difficult to feel even a flicker of indignation. Maybe Beau was right and he couldn't fight Indians, but he could at least keep Beau alive, and that would be worth risking his own life to accomplish. He paused to rest his hand on his aunt's shoulder. The Algonquin had murdered her first husband, and while she had tactfully not mentioned being terrified of Indians, he knew that she had to be.

"I will do what I can," he promised. As he climbed the stairs, he hoped he would be able to describe his torment convincingly to Liana, but he feared she would push him into making another agonizing choice that would have disastrous consequences for them all.

Liana was in their bedroom trying on the first of the new gowns she had had made. It was apricot rather than peach, but she hoped Christian would like it, too. She turned when he came in, and expecting compliments, was alarmed by the darkness of his frown. "What's happened?" she asked. She rushed toward him and took his arm to draw him into the room. She had sworn she no longer had a family, but she had a terrifying premonition someone dear to her had died.

"Tell me this instant," she cried.

Not having meant to frighten her needlessly, Christian forced a smile. "I don't know where to begin." He took her hand and coaxed her down beside him on the bed. "There's a verse in the Bible about reaping what you sow, and I've just begun to appreciate it. Beau's eager to fight, and I know my pamphlets have encouraged his spirit of rebellion so it's partly my fault. He's going with Lord Dunmore, or rather with General Lewis, and Aunt Arielle is quite naturally terrified that he won't come back. I don't know what my uncle would do, but my father and I were unable to stop him."

Liana had seldom seen Christian so subdued, or she

would have voiced her first thought which was that he was
the one who wished to fight, and Beau had merely provided a convenient excuse. The enthusiasm he showed for
the pamphlets was completely lacking now; all she saw was
despair. Still, she knew him to be a man who loved risk
dearly. She squeezed his hand. "And you want to go with
him?"

"No, it's the last thing I want to do, but it's what I *should*
do. My aunt asked me to go and look after Beau—no, *begged*
is the better term. I could refuse. There are plausible excuses: we've just gotten married, Uncle Byron is away, I
don't believe in the cause. It really wouldn't matter which
I chose, any would be accepted, but if something happened
to Beau—" Christian couldn't complete the thought but
he was certain she understood.

Liana laid her head on his shoulder. She almost wished
that he had simply announced he was going so that she
would have been justified in flying into a rage, but to know
he did not want to fight, but felt he must, made it much
worse. There was the baby whose existence she sensed
more plainly with each new day, but if she told him, it
would only make his choice all the more agonizing. What
if he were to stay with her and Beau was killed? Would he
always blame her and their sweet baby for Beau's death?
She did not even want to risk it, although sending him
away would be the hardest thing she had ever done.

Tears welled up in her eyes. "Hasn't Arielle considered
the risk to you?"

"No, I don't think so. She believes I know a great deal
more about warfare than her son, and I do. I don't believe
it even crossed her mind that I might be the one who
doesn't come back."

A tear rolled down Liana's cheek and splashed on her
new gown, "Oh damn, I don't want to ruin my new dress."

Christian could not help but laugh and he pulled her
into a rambunctious embrace. "I meant to stay with you

for as long as I could. I never dreamed it would only be a few days."

Liana clung to him. "Nothing has ever been easy for us, has it?"

Christian kissed away her tears. "One thing always has," he whispered against her lips, and knowing he could catch up with Beau, he gave her a very loving farewell.

Too sad to bid him good-bye in front of the others, Liana remained in their room when he left. She slipped on Johanna's green gown and thought she might go for a stroll to have time by herself, but met Arielle on the stairs.

"May I speak with you a moment?" Arielle asked.

"Yes, of course." Expecting apologies for forcing Christian to leave, Liana reluctantly followed her into the master bedroom.

Arielle shut the door and gestured toward the pair of wing chairs by the windows. "Sit with me a moment. Christian doesn't know about the baby, does he?"

Liana nearly fell into the comfortable chair. "No, but how could you know?"

Arielle had a lovely smile. It was sweet and yet knowing. "I'm a midwife, and I recognized the radiant glow of your complexion for what it was when you came home from your honeymoon trip. I didn't want to ask and embarrass you, but I thought a question was appropriate now. Christian told me you'd agreed he should go with Beau, and I'll always be grateful. A lesser woman would have demanded that he stay home, and Byron and I appreciate your unselfishness."

"I don't believe that word applies here, but thank you. I'll pray that both Christian and Beau return home safely."

"Oh, my dear, I hope you don't believe I'm not worried for Christian as well. It's just that he was born to be a warrior, and Hunter's taught him more than most generals know. Now please, let's talk of less stressful things. With your father away, perhaps you'll be able to call on your mother. Please invite her and your brothers to visit you here. I'd love to entertain them."

Startled by Arielle's last comment, Liana leaned forward slightly. "Where has my father gone?"

"Didn't Christian mention he's going with General Lewis, too? I imagine there's a need for seasoned officers, and your father knows the Ohio Valley well."

"Oh, yes, indeed he does." Liana glanced out the window toward the river, knowing it was a deceptively peaceful scene. Why hadn't Christian mentioned her father's plans? Did he fear she would ask him to watch out for him, too, or, God forbid, did he intend to do just the opposite?

"Yes, I would like to visit my mother. I just hope she'll receive me," Liana confided softly, but she knew that would be the very least of her problems while Christian was away.

Twenty-five

Christian and Beau had only been gone two days when Morgan and Cameron Scott came to the Barclays' to see their sister. Delighted to find Liana looking well, they followed her into the parlor. "The trouble in the Ohio Valley is the best thing that's happened since you left home," Morgan offered excitedly. "It caught Father's attention, and when he realized General Lewis needed officers, he quit drinking and volunteered. As soon as he left we started making plans to come see you. At first Mother advised against it, but we kept arguing that we had every right to visit you, and I think she would have liked to come with us today. She's just afraid you blame her for turning you out."

"No, I don't blame her at all." Liana took the chair opposite the settee and motioned for them to make themselves comfortable. "I should have gone to see her before this. Please tell her I'll come by tomorrow."

"She'd like that," Cameron assured her. "She's been real lonely without you."

Liana had worked so diligently to force thoughts of her family from her mind, it was difficult to admit she still cared. "I'm sorry to hear that. Mother has so many good friends, I thought she'd simply spend more time with them."

Reluctant to admit the truth, Cameron looked down at

the rug. "Well, I think she's kind of embarrassed about what happened. People were curious and asked such tactless questions that she's just kept to herself to avoid them. She wanted to be here for your wedding. We did, too, but you know how Father is. He won't even speak your name. Mother still cries a lot."

Distressed by the dismal scene her brothers painted, Liana nevertheless felt helpless to change the situation at home when her father was so intractable. She cleared her throat and redirected the conversation. "Christian and Beau have gone with General Lewis, and I certainly hope they won't spend their time fighting with Father rather than the Shawnee."

"Oh, Lord," Morgan moaned. "I don't even want to think about that, but Father will probably just ignore them and they can't fight with a man who refuses to acknowledge their existence."

"I hope you're right." Liana looked up to find Dominique at the doorway and invited her to join them. "I believe you've met my brothers," she remarked, but because it had been a while, she introduced them again.

"Yes, of course, I remember you both," Dominique assured them. Hoping for callers, she was dressed in her pretty coral gown. She did consider the Scott boys handsome lads and sat down between them on the settee. "You must come and visit us more often. We keep Liana very busy, but she must miss you terribly."

"We'd come to see her every day if we could," Cameron said.

Liana watched with an amused smile as Dominique flattered her brothers with dazzling smiles and occasional soft caresses to a sleeve or knee. They had not seen Sean O'Keefe since the day he and Christian had fought. She was very glad of it, and from the way Dominique was eyeing Morgan, she did not miss the haughty captain, either.

"Do either of you know if Captain O'Keefe went with General Lewis?" Liana asked.

Morgan found it difficult to tear his eyes away from Dominique's enchanting smile and answered without looking Liana's way. "No, he's in town. I saw him only yesterday. He's still trying to arrest the men responsible for the pamphlets, but they're much too clever to be caught."

"Do you know who they are?" Dominique asked.

Morgan shook his head. "Not for sure, but I wish them well. I suppose if they've gone with Lord Dunmore or General Lewis, there won't be any pamphlets for a while and I'll miss reading them. Father was furious when he found the last one pinned to our door, but Cameron and I laughed about it for days."

Liana doubted she had heard him correctly. "The pamphlet was pinned to the front door?"

"Whoever brought it used a knife," Cameron exclaimed, "and nailed it on the blade."

"My goodness," Liana mused. "What could have inspired such a hostile act?"

Morgan had a ready opinion. "I'm sure it was because Father is so staunch in his support of the king. If you were pushing independence, wouldn't you want men with Father's views to understand why?"

Certain her father's political views weren't the issue, Liana had to force a smile. "Yes, of course, that must have been the reason." She added a word or two as the discussion continued, but she knew Christian had been exceedingly foolish to insult her father in such a personal fashion. Obviously Ian had not taken it personally, but Christian could not have known that he wouldn't. If he left her father alone on the march to the Ohio Valley, it would be a miracle. Preoccupied with that concern, she enjoyed her brothers' visit, but was relieved when they left for home.

After supper, when the rest of the family left the dining room and started toward the parlor, she drew Hunter aside. "Christian told me he'd left notes for a couple of pamphlets when he and I went into the valley. He didn't mention doing so again and I wonder if he had anything prepared."

Shocked that Liana would wish to discuss such a sensitive subject, Hunter took her hand, led her into the study, and closed the door. "You must be careful not to mention the pamphlets in front of the others."

Not understanding his rebuke, Liana was quick to defend herself. "I didn't. I waited to speak privately with you. Apparently O'Keefe's still searching for the author, and I think we ought to publish another pamphlet while Christian's away to confuse him even more than he already is."

Hunter frowned pensively. "I did not think you approved of the pamphlets."

He had her there, and Liana didn't dispute him. She had never been alone with Hunter, but his manner, despite his obvious strength, wasn't threatening. Christian had inherited his father's thick black hair and dark eyes, but his complexion was lighter and his features favored the Barclay side of the family. They were both handsome men, however.

"I don't. I think they're much too dangerous, but it might be even more perilous for Christian if none appeared while he's away."

"Half the town has left," Hunter reminded her. "It could be any of the men who are gone."

Remembering, the comfortable warmth of her father's study, Liana moved about the room admiring the rich walnut paneling and shelves filled with well-loved leatherbound volumes. Her brothers' visit had prompted poignant thoughts of home; that night she missed both her parents with a child's natural longing. "Yes, it most certainly could, but we both know it isn't. I think we should produce at least one pamphlet just to keep everyone who's still in town interested."

"Do you intend to write it?" Hunter asked.

Liana hadn't thought that far, but now that he had asked, she thought it a very good idea. "Yes, Christian encouraged me to write one, in fact."

Hunter glanced toward the empty chair behind the desk and wished Byron were there to talk some sense into Liana. The pamphlets had begun in that room, and with the rest of the original conspirators away, he felt responsible for what was decided now. "I don't know. If the writing didn't have the same fire, O'Keefe would know someone was trying to fool him. So would everyone else. No, I don't think you can do it."

Disheartened by his poor opinion of her abilities, Liana still wouldn't give up on the idea. "I'll write something and show it to you. If it's a convincing duplicate of Christian's work, will you agree to distribute it for me?"

Hunter moved to the door, but just rested his hand lightly on the knob. "Each time we do this, the odds are greater that we'll be caught. You'll have to persuade me that it's worth the risk."

"I'm only trying to protect your son," Liana pointed out, "and Lord knows there's plenty more to be said about the pathetic creature who calls himself King George III."

Amused by that show of spirit, Hunter nodded. "Write your piece and show it to me. Then I'll decide."

When he opened the door, Liana preceded him from the room, but she still did not join the others in the parlor. Instead, she slipped out the back door and went out to the well, where she found Johanna talking with David Slauson. "I'm sorry to interrupt, but I've something important to ask."

Thinking Liana wished to speak with Johanna, David mumbled a hurried good night, but Liana quickly reached out to catch his sleeve. "Please wait. I need to speak with you both. Christian told me that you know about the pamphlets, Johanna, and that David has printed them, so I'm certain it's all right if we discuss them together." She quickly outlined her plan and requested their help, but the pair was no more enthusiastic than Hunter had been.

"Forgive me, Mrs. Hunter, but I doubt you could write like Christian any more than you could sign his name with the same flourish, and what about the cartoons? I may have carved the last two, but he drew those, too."

Liana sighed impatiently. "All I'm asking you to do is try. If we aren't successful, believe me, I'll know it before you, and I won't insist you print anything that isn't as good as what Christian wrote. I just want to convince the authorities the author is still in Williamsburg." She sent Johanna a pleading glance, and when the shy girl appeared to be wavering, she gave her an additional nudge.

"You know Christian better than I do. If I choose a topic, could you please help me to express it in your brother's words?"

"I'd like to help," Johanna insisted, "but I'm just no good with words. Why don't you ask Dominique? She's the one with the real flair for the dramatic."

"Well, that's certainly true, but does she know about the pamphlets?"

Johanna nodded. "Yes, no one can keep a secret around her. I'll bet Falcon would help, too. He knows how Christian talks better than anyone."

As Liana listened, she was at first overwhelmed by the number of people who might have to participate to present a convincing copy of her husband's work, but it made her appreciate his lively intelligence even more. "Can Falcon draw?"

"Yes," Johanna assured her. "As well, if not better than, Christian."

"Good, then we ought to be able to manage this. I'll write the first draft tonight. Thank you, good night."

David had never spoken with Christian's wife, and was completely captivated by her beauty and charm. He waited until Liana had returned to the house, then leaned close to murmur, "I can see why your brother loves her."

Although impressed by Liana's commitment to her brother's work, Johanna still doubted she would be of any help to the project, and David's compliment struck her as evidence of her own failings. "Yes, she's not only attractive, but very bright. Everyone believes them to be an excellent match. Please excuse me—I want to go inside, too."

It had been a long while since Johanna had been curt with him, and David was caught by surprise. "Have I insulted you somehow?"

"No, of course not. Good night."

Disappointed they had chatted so briefly, David watched her walk toward the house and reluctantly turned toward the hands' quarters. He glanced back over his shoulder for a last glimpse, and caught her standing at the edge of the garden watching him. Even in the gathering dusk, he could see her tears, and hurriedly returned to her side.

"I knew something was wrong." He searched through his pockets for a handkerchief, did not find one, and used his fingertips to brush away her tears. "Tell me why you're crying, and I'll do what I can to help."

Embarrassed that he had caught her in such a melancholy mood, Johanna could scarcely reveal that he was the cause. She looked up at him, her lashes spiked with tears, and wished she had Liana's vibrant personality, or Dominique's charming grace. She was grateful to have her mother's gentle sweetness, but sadly, David wasn't anything like her father, so the attribute was of little value.

Johanna's sadness touched something deep within David, and for once ignoring the gulf society had created between them, he slipped his arms around her waist and pulled her close. He meant to offer only a bit of tender comfort, but she felt so good and smelled so sweet that he forgot everything but how much he had grown to love her.

He tightened his embrace, and near tears himself, couldn't let her go.

"I can't bear to see you cry," he whispered. "You deserve to be happy, Johanna. I just wish that I could be the one to make your dreams come true."

At first shocked, and then elated that he would say such sweet things, Johanna slid her arms around his waist and rested her cheek against his shoulder. After working in the fields several months, his body was hard and lean and she felt the warmth of security in his arms. She didn't know what Dominique would say, but she had to speak what was in her heart.

"I don't want anyone else, David. I want you."

David took a step back to force her to look up at him. The beauty of her smile convinced him she was telling the truth, but he didn't dare dream they could have more than this one precious moment. He leaned down to kiss her, and the softness of her lips drew him back again and again. Breathless with desire, Hunter's warning echoed in his mind and he broke away.

"I didn't really believe it at the time, but your father urged me to come to him if I had something to say. I want to do what's right, Johanna, but if he turns me down, I'll have no choice but to go away."

Elated that he cared for her, Johanna was certain she could persuade her father to give his consent. She clutched David's hands and pulled him toward the house with a lively dancing step. "If he suggested you speak up, then he's already said yes!"

"Wait a minute, how do I look?" David pulled one hand from hers to smooth down his hair.

"You're even better looking than the first time I saw you. Byron warned me that you wouldn't stay, but I couldn't help having feelings for you."

David pulled her back into his arms, lifted her off her feet, and swung her around. When he put her down, he caught a glimpse of his future with a clarity that had always escaped him. "I've never really felt I belonged anywhere until I met you. Then I was so afraid—"

Johanna touched his lips. "Please, don't say it. There's no reason for either of us to be afraid anymore. I want this to be your home always."

"Just as long as you're here," David promised, "it will be."

Hunter had started keeping an eye on his attractive daughter soon after she had begun meeting David Slauson after supper. He stood at the back door now, hoping he could look appropriately stern when she and David finally made it up to the house. He liked David, but the fact that Johanna obviously cared for him was all that truly mattered, and he was so happy for her, he felt like dancing himself.

"Keep out of sight!" Christian shouted to Beau. It was early October, and they were among the 1200 men camped at Point Pleasant at the mouth of the Great Kanawha River with General Andrew Lewis. They were waiting for Lord Dunmore to arrive with the other 1300 men gathered to battle the Shawnee, but Christian doubted the Shawnee would show an equal amount of patience.

They had marched over much of the same ground Liana and he had covered but this trek had been long and hard rather than leisurely and enjoyable. He had seldom crossed paths with Ian Scott, but even those infrequent sightings had been unsettling because Ian had looked right through him rather than at him, and Christian had stubbornly refused to speak first. For Liana's sake, he did not want Ian to come to any harm, but it was plain Ian was hoping he would meet with disaster.

Christian turned to whisper to Beau. "Chief Cornstalk's village was deserted. That has to mean he and his warriors are stalking us even as we're tracking him. Choose your cover wisely today, and don't give them a target for their bows and arrows."

Like so many of his companions, Beau had come to rely on Christian's wealth of practical knowledge, but with the fight near, he was determined to prove he was his own man. "I don't need you to tell me—"

Beau's response was interrupted by a frantic shout. The camp was just coming awake, and the cry pierced the crisp morning air. Christian saw one of the men who had left early to go hunting running through the camp, and easily understood the message in his hysterical cries and gestures. "This looks as though it may be what we've been waiting for. My advice goes double now. Get behind that stump and keep out of sight."

Beau grabbed his musket. "I came to fight, not hide!"

Those were the last words the cousins traded for several hours as Chief Cornstalk led a fierce surprise attack on the camp. As the battle began in earnest, shrill war whoops and screams of pain echoed through the forest. Smoke from hastily abandoned cooking fires as well as muskets brought tears to the Virginians' eyes, but Christian maintained a steady hand and fired only when he had a sure target. More often than not, he shielded Beau, but to his credit, Beau also got his share of the enemy.

Heeding a call for help, Christian edged over to fill a gap in the line of soldiers and found himself kneeling next to Ian. "Fine morning for a battle," Christian greeted him, but as usual, the Englishman failed to respond. The officer had been continually moving, encouraging his men, but thick fire from the Shawnee had forced him to seek the safety of a stand of sycamore. He had been about to push on when the mass of savages swelled forward and trapped him in place.

Christian fired his musket, then, not having any time to waste in reloading, he removed the bow from his shoulder, an arrow from his quiver, and took careful aim at the brave lunging for Ian. He saw him in exquisite detail. He was missing a front tooth and his small eyes were mean. While Beau might have doubted his cousin's ability to fight an Indian foe, Christian had no difficulty whatsoever. He waited until the howling savage swung his tomahawk within inches of Ian's head before shooting an arrow straight through his heart.

Hit in mid-stride, the brave shrieked and pitched forward as he died, splattering Ian with his blood. Ian scrambled out from under the grisly burden; his voice hoarse with fright, he continued to exhort his men to repel the attack. The incident had taken only a few seconds, and not pausing to ask for thanks from the ungrateful officer, Christian drew another arrow.

Cornstalk had sent his braves around behind the camp, and with the river at their backs, General Lewis's forces could not retreat. Having no wish to, Christian fought on with a calm bravery that inspired all those around him. It was his example, rather than Ian's leadership, that enabled the beleaguered soldiers to stand their ground. Gradually the Virginians gained the upper hand and kept the Shawnee from breaching their line.

That was merely one skirmish in a bloody battle that lasted all day, but when the final shot had been fired, the Virginians were in control and Chief Cornstalk's surviving braves had been chased across the Ohio River. Although their faces were blackened with gunpowder and dust, Beau and Christian were unharmed and joined the other able-bodied men in sending up a rumbling victory cry before helping to tend the wounded.

It was nearly dusk before Christian saw Ian again. His blue officer's coat was tattered and dirty, but he had also survived the day uninjured. With obvious difficulty, Ian approached Christian. Unwilling to look him in the eye, he glanced down at the ground.

"I want to thank you for saving my life," Ian began hesitantly. "I realize some would say it was no more than your duty as part of the militia, but we both know that wasn't the case."

Christian had hoped Ian would come to him, and was ready. "I could say that now we're even," he offered, "but I won't. I saved your life because I know you're an honorable man, and you'll give me what I ask in return."

Alarmed by that comment, Ian's posture stiffened and his gaze locked with Christian's. "And what is that?"

Christian was surprised by how little joy he took from making his request. "I want you to treat your daughter with the respect she deserves and welcome me into your family."

Appalled by that calmly voiced demand, Ian's expression filled with resentment. There had been too many witnesses to Christian's heroism for him to deny it had happened, but he was still loath to grant his request. As he studied the young man he had always despised he was shocked to discover so much of Melissa in him. He had his father's dark coloring, but that was all. While masculine in form, the oval shape of his face and the gentle curve of his features were all hers.

Absolutely sickened by the sight of him, Ian had to look away. He had loved Melissa with all his heart and soul and she had betrayed him too cruelly ever to forgive. Telling himself Christian did not deserve his scorn failed to dissolve even one drop of twenty years of torment and he shook his head. "You took Liana. That's all you'll ever get from me."

As Ian walked away, Beau came to Christian's side. "You saved the man's life and he acted as though it were nothing!"

Christian continued to stare after his father-in-law. "Forget it. He must have buried his heart with Melissa. Liana and I are better off without him."

Beau did not understand how Christian could take Ian Scott's rebuff so calmly, but then he remembered that he would have Liana to greet him when he returned home and understood why her father's insults meant so little.

The family gathered around Arielle as she read excerpts from Byron's latest letter. "It's as he feared—rather than demanding independence, the Congress has ended in a compromise. They'll publish a Declaration of Rights and Grievances requesting the repeal of Parliament's acts since 1763, declare the 'Intolerable Acts' void, and form an association which forbids trade with Great Britain, but they'll also send an expression of the colonies' loyalty to the king."

Intending to savor the more personal portions of the letter in private, she returned it to its envelope. "As you can imagine," she added, "he's not at all pleased."

"Independence will come," Liana announced confidently. "There are too many brave men and women committed to the idea for it to fail."

Having heard enough about politics, Jean wandered to the window, then began to call excitedly. "Here's Beau! Beau's home!"

Liana leaped to her feet. "Only Beau?" she cried, desperately afraid he was alone. She rushed to the window, Dominique and Johanna crowding around her. For one terrible instant she saw only Beau; then Christian, who had dismounted first, stepped out from behind their horses. Seeing the faces at the window, he waved, but Liana wanted so much more. She pushed her way past Dominique and ran out the front door, straight into her husband's arms.

Delighted to be greeted so warmly, Christian wrapped her in an enthusiastic hug. "I don't have to ask if you've missed me. I can see that you have."

"Looks like no one noticed I was gone," Beau grumbled.

"I'm sorry, Beau," Liana called to him. "Welcome home."

"Thank you." Beau started toward the house, but before he reached the steps, he was engulfed by his family and greeted with hugs and kisses.

Taking Liana's hand, Christian leaned down to whisper. "I'll let them welcome me home later. You're the only one I want to see now. Let's go down by the river and talk."

Liana sent Alanna a wave. "I think they'll understand. Was it awful?"

"Being away from you?" Christian asked. "Yes, it was."

"I meant the fighting," Liana responded with a throaty laugh.

Christian paused again to pull her into his arms, but then swiftly led her down to the trail he had once followed so often to see her. "There was only one battle and yes, it was every bit as awful as you must have imagined, but there'll be no more senseless slaughters in the valley, so it was worth it." He waited until they found a secluded spot, and then stepping behind Liana, he pulled her against him so they could both enjoy a view of the river.

"Your father came home safely, too. Beau will tell you I saved Ian's life, which is true, but that's not the whole story. I'd always thought I despised the man, but when he was in danger, I didn't hesitate to save him. Perhaps I finally saw him for what he is—simply a bitter man who deserves my pity. I don't need recognition from him any longer to know my own worth."

Christian paused to nibble Liana's earlobe, then rubbed his cheek against hers. "I know each of us has doubted the other, but what I remembered most while I was away were the times we were together, not the bitter words spoken in anger. I'll readily admit to wanting to hurt your father, but I never wanted you to be caught in the middle.

I wish we could start all over. There's so much I'd like to undo, beginning with the way I grabbed you off this trail."

Liana slid her hands over his and then turned to face him. She longed to speak with equal seriousness, but she was too happy to do anything but smile. "It's much too late to begin anew," she told him. "For one thing, we managed to publish a pamphlet while you were gone so I'm now part of your conspiracy against the Crown."

"You didn't!"

He looked not merely startled, but aghast at the idea, which Liana found terribly amusing. "Yes, but it took a combined effort to come up to your standard. Johanna and Dominique helped me with the text and Falcon drew and carved the cartoon. Your father said he wouldn't deliver it if it couldn't pass for your work, but it did. I likened the king to the black bear you swatted on the nose, and everyone liked comparing King George III to an ill-tempered bear that gets chased away by brave colonists. I saved a copy for you."

Christian couldn't believe his ears. "But you've been so opposed to my writing the pamphlets! Why did you do it?"

Liana could appreciate his dismay. "To make O'Keefe believe the author was still here, for one thing, and to keep the spirit of independence alive, for another. I still despise the risk, but I do believe in your cause. You tried to coax those words from me once, and I wouldn't say them, but I do believe in independence, my darling, and in you."

A kiss seemed the only appropriate response, but when Christian could at last bear to draw away, he saw the bright sparkle in Liana's eyes and knew there was more. "Do you have another secret? Tell me."

"Johanna and David Slauson are planning to wed, but, they wanted to wait until both you and Uncle Byron were home before they set the date."

"You mean he finally found the courage to propose?"

"Apparently." Too happy he was home to stand still,

Liana reached up to kiss him again, and then couldn't stifle a revealing giggle.

He had recognized a difference in her the last night they had spent aboard the *Southern Breeze*. He saw it again, but its nature still eluded him. "I know you too well, Liana. There's something more, isn't there?"

Liana raised her hands to his nape to loosen his hair. "What would you think about creating a tribe of red-haired Indians?"

In an afternoon already filled with surprises, Christian was still shocked. He doubted any man could be criticized for behaving like a fool at such a time. "Wait a minute—are you merely suggesting we hope for a child, or are you saying we're going to have one?"

Liana caressed his cheek. "You're definitely going to become a father in the spring. I think it must have happened the first time we were together. I've never been sorry for that night, only for the wretched scene my father created at your home afterward."

Christian kissed her palms, then yanked her close. "You must have known about the baby before I left. Why didn't you tell me?"

Liana looked out over the river. "You already felt torn. I understood you had to go and didn't want to make the trip any more difficult for you. Beau looks fine, so everything worked out as it should."

Christian brushed her lips with a tender kiss. "I will never stop loving you."

Liana slipped her arms around his waist as she returned his next kiss. "We all hoped you'd be home for the harvest," she murmured, "and I hope you'll never want to leave."

Christian reached into his pocket and withdrew the little doll he had made out of cornhusks on the way to the Ohio Valley. He pressed it into her palm. "There was no time to make a doll for you, but here's the one I made to keep me company. Save it, and we can tell the baby how Seneca braves make dolls of the women they love."

Liana looked up at her husband and loved him so desperately she did not know how she had survived so many long, lonely days without him. "I'll keep the doll, but right now, all I want is you."

Christian let out an ecstatic whoop, then scooped her up in his arms and carried her through the marsh grass to the secret place where he had once stolen so many kisses. The river rushed to the sea, and the golden tips of the grass danced in the breeze—but the lovers saw only each other. No longer handsome savage and defiant captive but loving husband and devoted wife, the sweet promises they shared that day would linger in their memories and warm their hearts for all eternity.

Epilogue

April, 1775

Christian sat down at the top of the stairs and rested his head in his hands. "Something's wrong. It's taking too long."

Trying to be good company, Hunter sat down beside him and rested his back against the wall. "Don't lose heart. Arielle would have told us if the birth weren't going smoothly."

It was past midnight, and Christian was both anxious and tired. "The wait has to be as difficult as giving birth. How did you stand this agony three times?" he asked without thinking.

"I've only done it twice. I wasn't here when you were born, but I remember feeling just as frightened when Alanna gave birth to Johanna and Falcon. I could not get Melissa out of my mind."

Surprised by that admission, Christian nodded. "Neither can I. There are times I think she haunts this house, and surely she is with us tonight."

Feeling her presence just as strongly, Hunter was quiet a long while. "Liana has an angel watching over her then, and she'll be safe."

"My mother an angel?" Christian laughed under his breath. "You're the only one who's ever said that."

"I loved her," Hunter whispered.

Christian had never talked with his father about Melissa and this struck him as a strange time to invoke her name. "I wish Ian had such fond memories. Then perhaps he would welcome his grandchild."

"He is at war with himself," Hunter replied, "and your child won't miss him."

"If he's ever born." Christian turned to look over his shoulder. "Do you think it's too quiet?"

"Would you rather hear Liana scream?"

"No, but I've heard no more than a whimper or two and that doesn't seem right, either."

Hunter searched for another way to reassure his son. "Arielle is a very good midwife."

"Yes, I know, but—" Christian leaped to his feet at the sound of a tiny cry. Followed by a brief pause, it came again, this time louder and unmistakably an infant's high-pitched wail. Christian ran down the hall to his room, then, nearly paralyzed with fright, tapped lightly.

Alanna opened the door a crack. "Just give us a moment, Chris, and we'll have your baby ready for Liana to show off."

Christian sagged back against the wall to catch his breath, then straightening up, he began to pace the hall as he had hours earlier. He didn't have long to wait before Alanna and Arielle appeared.

"Don't tire her," they cautioned, moving aside to allow him to enter the room he shared with his wife.

Christian moved silently across the floor. When he reached the bed, Liana greeted him with a wan smile and he leaned down to kiss her. She was holding a tiny bundle and parted the folds so he could see their child. The babe looked up at him and yawned.

"It's a girl," Liana whispered. She drew the baby's wispy hair through her fingers. "I do believe she has red hair, too, and her eyes look green. I really thought she'd look like you."

"She'll be a beauty like her mother." Christian stroked his daughter's hand and she gripped his finger tightly. "We must have had a dozen names. Do any of them seem to fit?"

"I'd like to call her Melissa, but that seems too sad. What do you think of Liberty?"

"With talk of rebellion growing louder every day, I think it's perfect. May I hold her?"

"Of course." Liana handed him the little bundle. "We have so much to teach her, Christian, but with a name like Liberty, I think she'll understand."

Christian sat down on the edge of the bed, and delighted with his daughter, leaned down to give his wife another kiss. "I was so afraid for you."

"There was no reason."

"Love is enough."

Liana reached up to caress his cheek. "I hope by the time the house is finished, I'll feel well enough to run up and down the stairs."

"If you don't, I'll carry you both."

Christian cuddled his daughter and teased his wife until Arielle returned to send him away so they could sleep. As he gave Liana a last kiss and wished her a good night, he knew that no matter what fate had in store for the colonies that spring, he would remain wonderfully content.

Note to Readers

The members of the Barclay and Scott families are purely imaginative characters rather than actual Virginians, but I have endeavored to bring the historical events of the times to life through them. They have a variety of backgrounds to reflect the diversity which has always been our country's strength. The colonies were plagued by many years of unrest before the First Continental Congress met to discuss independence in Carpenter's Hall in Philadelphia in September, 1774. The Virginia delegation included George Washington, Patrick Henry, and Richard Henry Lee, father of Robert E. Lee.

In 1908, the United States Senate recognized the battle of Point Pleasant on October 10, 1774, as the first Colonial victory of the Revolution, rather than the shot fired at Lexington on April 19, 1775. Because the British agents were responsible for inciting trouble between the Indians and settlers in the Ohio Valley as a diversion from the many grievances against King George III, the designation seems entirely proper.

I do hope you've enjoyed this tale of love in turbulent times and will send me your comments. Please write to me in care of Zebra Books, 850 Third Avenue, New York, NY 10022, and include a legal size SASE for a bookmark and reply.

TALES OF LOVE FROM MEAGAN MCKINNEY

GENTLE FROM THE NIGHT*   (0-8217-5803-$5.99/$7.50)
In late nineteenth century England, destitute after her father's death, Alexandra Benjamin takes John Damien Newell up on his offer and becomes governess of his castle. She soon discovers she has entered a haunted house. Alexandra struggles to dispel the dark secrets of the castle and of the heart of her master.
    *Also available in hardcover (1-577566-136-5, $21.95/$27.95)

A MAN TO SLAY DRAGONS   (0-8217-5345-2, $5.99/$6.99)
Manhattan attorney Claire Green goes to New Orleans bent on avenging her twin sister's death and to clear her name. FBI agent Liam Jameson enters Claire's world by duty, but is soon bound by desire. In the midst of the Mardi Gras festivities, they unravel dark and deadly secrets surrounding the horrifying truth.

MY WICKED ENCHANTRESS   (0-8217-5661-3, $5.99/$7.50)
Kayleigh Mhor lived happily with her sister at their Scottish estate, Mhor Castle, until her sister was murdered and Kayleigh had to run for her life. It is 1746, a year later, and she is re-established in New Orleans as Kestrel. When her path crosses the mysterious St. Bride Ferringer, she finds her salvation. Or is he really the enemy haunting her?

AND IN HARDCOVER . . .
THE FORTUNE HUNTER   (1-57566-262-0, $23.00/$29.00)
In 1881 New York spiritual séances were commonplace. The mysterious Countess Lovaenya was the favored spiritualist in Manhattan. When she agrees to enter the world of Edward Stuyvesant-French, she is lead into an obscure realm, where wicked spirits interfere with his life. Reminiscent of the painful past when she was an orphan named Lavinia Murphy, she sees a life filled with animosity that longs for acceptance and love. The bond that they share finally leads them to a life filled with happiness.

Available wherever paperbacks are sold, or order direct from the Publisher. Send cover price plus 50¢ per copy for mailing and handling to Kensington Publishing Corp., Consumer Orders, or call (toll free) 888-345-BOOK, to place your order using Mastercard or Visa. Residents of New York and Tennessee must include sales tax. DO NOT SEND CASH.

ROMANCE FROM FERN MICHAELS

DEAR EMILY   (0-8217-4952-8, $5.99)

WISH LIST   (0-8217-5228-6, $6.99)

AND IN HARDCOVER:

VEGAS RICH   (1-57566-057-1, $25.00)